THE
CAVEMAN
CONSPIRACY

PROLOGUE

Frank tucked the victory cigar into his shirt pocket as he drove the old pickup along the highway. He should be able to smoke this one early tonight. No questions or problems remained on his mental list. They had more than enough men. No one lived out there but the old man, so no close neighbors or likely witnesses to worry about. They'd checked and rechecked everything.

The only concern Frank had was with his passenger. He glanced over at Jonathan "Mack" Macintosh sitting ramrod straight, holding an MP5 machine gun in his fists like a staff. The kid unsettled Frank. He was a capable soldier with tremendous skills, but he had some issues. He liked the blood a little too much.

The skin tightened around Frank's eyes. In this kind of work, you achieved success with discipline, predictability, and as much information as possible. Order was the goal—on a mission, and in life. Throughout human history, the strong dominated the weak. Logical and natural, it was better for everyone, even if it sometimes required violence.

Actually liking the blood and the pain, however, was—well, crazy. And this kid liked it a lot. It wasn't normal. Worse, it was often erratic, and Frank was leery of such things. Especially on a mission.

He sighed. The problem was, he really liked Mack. The boy was as close to a son as Frank was ever likely to have. No, he finally decided, Mack wouldn't be a problem. As usual, the kid's benefits would outweigh his liabilities.

Frank turned off the main highway onto a dirt road and doused the lights. Stars littered the western Kansas sky over miles of wheat, gently waving in the breeze like an ocean.

Parking behind a screen of bushes, he killed the engine and waited. In the distance, the squat, wooden house sat nestled in a cluster of trees. The shadowy forms of Frank's men moving through the darkness emerged from hiding places on either side and silently settled into position.

He stepped out of the truck and cocked his head. Leaves rustled in the gentle breeze. A dog barked off in the distance. He inhaled the chilly air and sighed it out. Nothing nagged at him.

Mack slid out of the truck and adjusted his body armor. He pulled the magazine from his rifle, checked it, and slammed it back home. Touching his throat mic, he asked under his breath, "Turk, anything on the police scanner?"

The response came through Frank's earpiece: "Nothing. All's quiet."

Mack cracked his neck, his short, white mohawk bobbing from one side to the other, and grinned. He was half Frank's age and taller, but not nearly as broad in the chest and shoulders. "Showtime?"

Too eager. Why did he like this kid so much? "Remember, Mack, he's just some pencil neck. He probably won't even put up a fight. We need him alive, at least until we get what we came for. Got it?"

Mack nodded. "Roger." His whole body was tight as a bowstring.

Frank turned back to the team surrounding the house. Probably overkill, but that was how he'd made it to forty-seven in this business. Surviving wars, covert ops, cover-ups, and various other felonious acts didn't happen if you were always the underdog. He turned back to Mack and shook his head. "Go get him."

The younger man silently disappeared into the darkness.

Frank carefully closed the truck door, looked back down the dirt road one final time before sliding a pistol into his fatigue pants and heading toward the house. His black tee shirt was tight over his broad shoulders, and he flexed thick fingers, getting them loose and ready.

They needed to get out of here as soon as possible. A small town like this always noticed strangers, especially those dressed in black tactical gear. He'd grown up in southeastern Missouri, in a town very similar to this one, and it gave him the creeps. He checked his watch. Less than an hour to stay on schedule. He still had one more stop tonight. As he strolled up the driveway, he heard a faint crack and then a second as his men breached the house. Quiet. Nicely done.

Frank mounted the front stairs and Mack opened the door, ushering him inside. An elderly man sat tied to a chair in the middle of the living room. His white hair stood up disheveled, and his watery, light brown eyes were wide but curious.

Men in tactical gear filled the house, some at windows peeking past curtains, and others standing tense and ready around the room.

Frank eased his bulk down onto the edge of a plush chair opposite the prisoner. "Mr. Houk, my name's Frank, and I need to ask you a few questions."

The man licked his lips. "What about?"

Pulling a paper from his pocket, Frank read: "Project JBC12623037, more commonly known as After Image."

Houk raised bushy white eyebrows. "I think you've made some sort of mistake. That was a complete failure." His gaze darted from Frank to Mack and back again, the whites of his eyes prominent. "We closed it up after a couple of years with no progress. It crashed and burned. We didn't even share the results with related projects, just reassigned the equipment."

Frank nodded. "And what did you do with the paperwork?"

"They took it all. It just disappeared one night. I only kept the stuff that got left behind, by accident or whatever."

"Where?"

Houk hesitated.

Frank waited. A clock ticked somewhere in the house.

The old man darted a quick look to his left.

Frank raised one dark, bushy eyebrow and turned. "What's over there?"

Houk licked his lips again. "I'm telling you. Nothing came from it."

"Then why'd you keep some of the paperwork here?" Frank stood and walked over. Pulling out his Glock, he nodded at Mack.

A wild look came into Houk's eyes. "I didn't keep them because they were important or anything. I kept all the boxes that—well, all the boxes I didn't know what else to do with."

Mack stepped up beside Frank, who kicked, placing his boot next to the handle. The door flung inward, splintering as it gave way, exposing a bedroom scarcely larger than a closet. Against the far wall, banker's boxes stood stacked floor to ceiling. Frank checked the number on each.

Houk yelled from the other room, "I really don't know why anyone would care about them. There's nothing of value. I promise you."

The top left one matched. Frank pulled it down and checked inside. It seemed right. He looked back up at Hauk. "Is this it?"

The older man swallowed and nodded. "For After Image? Yes, just the one."

Frank carried it back to the living room and turned to the two men standing ready. "Take the rest of the boxes to my truck and stay frosty." The men leaped into action. He nodded at the prisoner. "Thanks again."

Houk shook his head. "Why would you want those papers? What could you possibly use them for?"

"I don't know, Mr. Houk. The people I work for seem to think they're worth something, though. Have a good night."

Mack followed him to the door. Frank leaned in and said under his breath, "Knock him out easy and then burn the house with the body inside. Make it look like an accident. I don't want anyone to know we were here. Then get the crew back to your plane and head to the rendezvous point. I've got to take this to Gemini, and I'll catch up with you tomorrow. Got it?"

Mack nodded, his eyes bright. The slight curve of a smile lifted the corner of his lip.

Frank grimaced and walked into the night.

• • •

Later, he stood at the edge of the parking garage and slowly tracked from the skyline in the distance to the dark street below. Holding a cigar in thick, strong fingers, he studied each rooftop, corner, and alley. He had good line-of-sight of all the places where *he'd* position a sniper, hack into communications, or try to prevent an escape. Taking a deep drag, he blew the smoke out in a slow stream.

He didn't doubt that the building, here on the outskirts of Richmond, was secure for the organization. The question was, was it safe for him as well? There always was the possibility that he'd become a liability. He'd thrown his lot in with this group because they gave him money and power, but he always covered his own ass.

He ran a hand through dark hair that was short, simple, and neat—the approach he tried to take with everything. Grinding the cigar butt under his boot, he picked up the box. It was time. As he descended the stairs to the street, he relaxed. There were better places to kill him than here. Odds were, he wasn't walking into trouble. He moved the Glock closer to his hip and crossed the dim, orange-tinted street with one last look at the rooflines.

The two-story structure was simple and blocky, the building number stenciled in black above a flat gray industrial door, and an intercom on the wall beside it.

Frank pressed the button and the steel door clicked and popped open half an inch.

Inside was the same short, unremarkable hallway, with linoleum tile and cheap fluorescent lighting he'd seen on his few previous visits.

A tall, young man in a suit stood behind a folding table with a square, black bin. "Your gun, please, Mr. Carson."

Frank noted the keycard hanging from his pocket, the bulge under the left side of his jacket, and his overall posture. Everything seemed normal, so Frank placed his Glock in the box.

The man nodded and stepped aside, gesturing to a door.

Keeping one eye on him, Frank entered and closed it behind him. The stairs only went down. Bent tubing handrails and concrete steps with a hard rubber no-slip covering—all a neutral brown, like some middle school.

His boots echoed in the stairwell as he descended. Why hadn't the man frisked him? Was there a metal detector he didn't see? There had to be many security measures he was unaware of, protecting this place and his boss, Gemini. The stairs went down two floors with no doors until the lowest level. Gemini had to have at least two other secret exits out of this bunker. No way was this the only door in and out.

At the bottom, he entered a spacious office with a mahogany desk, couch, and plush chairs. Animal heads and hunting trophies covered the walls, and a long marble bar ran along one side.

Gemini, the only name he'd ever given, sat behind the desk, flipping through a stack of papers. He glanced up. "Ah, Frank, have a seat. I just need a moment." Dressed in a khaki canvas hunting jacket and shirt, he looked like an adventurer in a 1930s movie. Neatly trimmed silver hair and mustache completed this picture. With long, slender fingers, he flipped through a stack of pages, studying each for a moment before turning to the next.

Frank glanced at his watch as he eased into a chair and set the box on his lap. It was the middle of the night and Gemini was still working. Frank collected these puzzle pieces, wishing he had a more complete picture of the man. Over the last few years, he'd made some careful inquiries, and only discovered that Gemini occasionally went by the name of Selik. Other than that, he was a ghost.

Gemini stacked the papers and set them aside. "Is that it?"

Frank nodded and handed over the banker's box.

"Will they miss it?"

"I doubt it. There were other boxes—I gave them to Bruno—but we burned the place. It'll look like a tragic gas fire."

The older man lifted the lid, sifted through the contents, and looked up, his eyes narrowing as he smiled. "This is perfect. Let's have a drink." At the counter, Gemini lifted a decanter and poured the dark liquid into two cut crystal glasses. "And Houk?"

Frank shrugged. "Died in the fire."

"Good." Gemini shook a paper from the box. "This is exactly what we needed. Our senator won't be able to resist it. When I leak this information to him, I believe he'll set sail within a week. Are your men ready for the chase?"

Frank took a sip, savoring the expensive single-malt Scotch, and nodded.

"Good. I had a special bomb created. My man was adamant that the only residue would be gasoline—that even the Quantico lab wouldn't be able to tell it was an explosive. I have a fast ship, one no one will miss, waiting for you in the Bahamas. Everything should be in order."

Frank frowned. How to phrase this? "Forgive me for saying so, sir, but this plan seems awfully complicated. I don't like complicated. If you want this senator dead, there are a million easier ways to accomplish that and make it look like an accident."

Gemini sipped his drink. "Of course, you're right, but you only understand half the objective. Do you know how this organization got its start?"

Frank stopped with his glass halfway to his mouth. In the three years that he'd worked here, no one had ever offered him any details. That seemed like a good thing, and he wasn't sure he wanted to know more now. "No, sir."

"Our founding fathers were at least tacitly involved in some secret government research projects. Projects that would change the world and secure America as the preeminent power." He waved a long-fingered hand dismissively. "Because of some unfortunate failures and silly moral concerns, they stopped them. Our benefactors thought they were too important to abandon, so they created this organization to continue that work." He swirled some of the Scotch around in his glass. "To do this, we need to recover some items from the original research. As you might expect, we aren't the only interested parties. The senator is one, and in some ways, he's ahead of us. Especially on one critical piece." Gemini took a sip.

Frank waited.

"I want you to follow this senator until he gets to his destination, which we think will be somewhere east of Puerto Rico. I believe the information you got from Houk is the last clue the senator needs to find this place. As soon as he has this clue, I believe he'll go for it, and I want you to find out where he goes."

Frank finished his whiskey in a long swallow and set it on the counter. This felt messy.

Gemini continued, "But—and this is the key part, Frank—when he gets there, you must eliminate him immediately. Before he takes possession of anything there. We have it on good authority that he won't have any security with him, and he'll be in international waters when you catch him, so it should be simple. But he *cannot* get what he's after, and he cannot return home alive."

Frank made a circle on the bar top with his glass. "This is a U.S. senator we're talking about. Are we sure we're ready for this?"

Gemini smiled. "We're ready. We have people in the CIA, the FBI, even on the senator's own staff. Trust me. There's no one left who can help him."

CHAPTER 1

Once you've been on the run, you always feel hunted. You never get over it. At least, that's how it was for Eddie. He still looked over his shoulder, half expecting to see someone when he did.

Heat waves shimmered across the asphalt as the small side road smoldered in the midday Miami sun. Like the oil fires he'd seen years ago in the Gulf—a foreboding thought for sure.

He pulled to a stop, checked the BMW's rearview mirror, and waited. Damn, it was hot. He turned the air conditioner up another notch and checked the road again. Empty, but he didn't like it. Some instinct scratched at the edge of his mind. Trouble was coming. He could feel it.

Luis lounged in the passenger's seat, watching him through dark glasses. "Seriously, man, who're you looking for? We're no longer wanted men. Even the FBI isn't interested in us anymore."

Eddie eased the car forward again. "The government never stops being interested in you, Luis—ever."

"You don't trust this guy we're meeting?"

Eddie shrugged. "I don't know him."

"But Jeff does."

"No, like always, Jeff knows someone who knows him. That's not the same thing. Hell, Jeff knows everybody. That doesn't mean I trust them all." The steering wheel slid through his calloused hands as he turned. If they had a tail, they were very good. Luis may have thought he was being paranoid, but Eddie noticed his friend kept an eye on his side mirror as well.

He hated what he'd become. Where was the driven-but-lighthearted boy from west Texas? The question irritated him. When had he changed so much? It wasn't the war. He knew he'd never be the same after that. Who would be? This sense of gloomy paranoia came after, however, and Eddie was getting sick of it.

He pulled up to the third level of a garage at an outdoor mall and parked near the elevator. The button-up shirt and jeans emphasized his slim hips and broad shoulders. He stretched his long, lean frame and closed the car door. His dark hair was short and just a little disheveled.

Luis was shorter than Eddie, with the olive skin of his Cuban heritage, and jet-black hair tied back into a short ponytail. Like a coiled spring, all tension and potential.

Eddie was glad to have someone with Luis' skill set along, while hoping they wouldn't need it. He slid into a blazer, covering the shoulder harness beneath his left arm.

The mall was abuzz with activity. Anyone not seventeen, tan, and laughing stuck out like a sore thumb. It was the perfect location to spot a tail. A young girl passed, and Eddie turned as if admiring her, which gave him a view of the stores on the far side. No one caught his attention or looked out of place.

Luis performed a similar task on his side. This practice was second nature for them, but it still irritated Eddie. It could all be for nothing. Luis was more than likely correct—it was just baseless paranoia. Even if it wasn't, who should he be watching for? The Bureau and the Agency had very different tactics and approaches, and very different rules of engagement.

Halfway across, they split up without a word and took different meandering paths to the far side.

Eddie chastised himself. Don't just go through the motions. It's always the one time you don't take countersurveillance seriously that trouble happens. Concentrate on the task at hand. No one looked out of place in the mall, however, and no one loitered on the street out front.

He turned and met Luis coming from the opposite direction.

A bright green Jaguar XKRS pulled up to the curb as they exited. Neon yellow rims matched a stripe running up the hood and over the car's roof.

Luis jumped in the back as Eddie slid into the passenger's seat and the car pulled smoothly away.

Eddie fastened his seat belt. "Very subtle, Jeff."

The driver, a short man with ginger hair that clashed with his large, crimson Chicago Bulls jacket, glanced over with a half-smile. "I borrowed it from Charlie Nixon."

Eddie shook his head. "I don't care where you got it. Didn't it occur to you that you could spot this car from space?"

Jeff shrugged, causing the big jacket to jump up around his ears. "You said, get a car no one is tracking and isn't connected to us. So that's what I got."

Luis grinned. "You have to admit, Eddie—who would expect someone to show up to a clandestine meeting—in a neon car driven by a man in a bright red winter coat—in Miami in July? We're like ninjas." He shook his head and chuckled.

Jeff shrugged again.

Eddie grinned despite himself and then shook it off. This was a perfect example. Instead of laughing with his friends, he was worried and agitated. It just wasn't who he was, which bugged him. The damned Agency had broken him. He was just into his thirties—much too young to feel this way. "I'm just nervous about this meeting."

Jeff glanced over. "Why?"

Eddie watched children playing in the front yard of a house. "I don't know. I just have a bad feeling."

Luis leaned forward, resting his arms on the back of their seats. "Seriously, Eddie. Why's this one got you so spooked?"

Good question. He wasn't sure. He just still felt unsettled and couldn't acclimate to this new life. It lacked direction, purpose, and ambition—things that had always anchored Eddie—and now they were gone. The CIA had turned everything upside-down, made him into a wanted man, and abandoned him. Even after resolving everything, his life never really regained a footing he recognized. They'd even taken her from him—indirectly—and he still hadn't gotten over that, either. Maybe he never would.

Eddie shook his head. "I don't know. I just worry about how long we can do this. South Florida's secret Robin Hood white knight gang isn't really a thing, you know?"

Luis shrugged and sat back. "Nothing we've ever done has been a thing. We just do it anyway. We do good for people."

Jeff nodded as he turned at a light. "If we didn't help the people we do, who would?"

Eddie didn't really have an answer for that. True, they were helping, but it was all—well, temporary was the only word that seemed to fit. That's not how he normally did things. The car's flawless paint job reflected everything they passed. A good metaphor for his life as of late—racing by and not really in focus.

Jeff pulled up to a restaurant. More of a shack, really. Squat and shabby, surrounded by a gray, weathered deck filled with picnic tables.

Eddie just couldn't shake the feeling that he was playing hooky. Exactly what he was playing hooky from, he couldn't really say, but it didn't reduce the feeling.

The area looked clean. No parked cars or loitering garbage men.

A Black man, sitting ramrod straight in a crisp white Coast Guard uniform, was the only customer.

Jeff said, "That's our guy. Commander Nathan Williams."

As they stepped out of the car, Eddie studied him—probably in his early thirties with dark, intelligent eyes and a wary posture. He liked the look of him and had to admit he was curious.

Nathan stood as they approached and shook hands with each as Jeff introduced them.

They sat and Eddie said, "Jeff here says you need some help. What's the problem?"

Nathan pursed his lips. "Were you in the service?"

Eddie tilted his head toward Luis. "We were in the Army."

Nathan nodded. "Then you know how it is in basic training. You make friendships that are—*different*. I met Malcolm at Cape May, and we became friends right away." His forehead creased. "He has problems with addiction, and it finally washed him out of the Coast Guard. For a while, I thought it'd kill him, and I'd lose my friend." A faraway look shadowed his eyes. "Every time we came back into port, I'd go see him. Check up on him, you know."

Eddie nodded.

Nathan sighed. "He hit bottom, and I got an email while at sea that he'd checked into rehab. It stuck, too, and for the past two years, he's been clean. Got his life together, got a job on the docks here in Miami."

Sweat trickled down Eddie's neck. How did Jeff and Nathan both sit here in jackets and seem completely unaffected?

Nathan continued, "But now some bad men are, I guess, blackmailing him about stuff he did and people he owes money to. They want him to let certain containers come in and out of the port without having to go through customs, stuff like that. He doesn't want to get in trouble, and he can't lose this job."

Eddie asked, "What bad men?"

"A guy named Enrique Gomez."

Eddie exchanged a look with Luis, and they said simultaneously, "Suavé."

Nathan leaned forward. "You know him? Can you help?"

Eddie leaned back. "We know *of* him." He studied Nathan. "How clean is this guy Malcolm? Are we just postponing the inevitable?"

Nathan held his gaze.

The wind tossed the fronds in a tree behind the building. The air smelled like old fish-fry grease, and Eddie wrinkled his nose as he waited.

Nathan said, "He was drunk and hit a car, almost killed a little girl. Malcolm went to the hospital and wouldn't let the cops take him away until he was sure she was okay. She lived, but just barely. Her father told him God had just given him a second chance, and he'd better take it. He's been sober ever since."

Eddie sighed. He liked this guy, and they might be able to help. If so, wasn't it their duty? Whatever changes the Agency and war had wrought on him, they hadn't altered this part of him, his desire to do the right thing. "All right. We'll look into it."

Nathan's shoulders sagged, and he stood. "I don't have much money."

Eddie waved the thought away. "Don't worry about that. I make no promises, but we'll ask around and see what we can do."

Nathan shook his hand. "Thank you, sir. I won't forget it. We sail out the day after tomorrow, but Jeff knows how to get in touch with me."

Eddie asked, "You based out of Miami?"

"Yes, but we're only here in port because some senator has his yacht anchored offshore, so the powers-that-be thought we should be around and visible while he's here."

Eddie said, "Oh yeah, it'd be awful if we lost a politician, wouldn't it?"

Nathan grinned, bright white teeth contrasting with his coffee-colored skin.

Eddie smiled back. "Stay safe out there. We'll be in touch."

As Jeff pulled away from the restaurant, Luis asked from the back seat, "What do you think? Muscle this bad guy?"

Eddie shook his head. "I don't think so. I'm afraid Enrique would just escalate things. We need some sort of angle." He put on his sunglasses and watched the palm trees pass. "We need to do more than intimidate Suavé. We need to find a long-term solution. Some way to solve this permanently. Really scare him and end this problem once and for all."

CHAPTER 2

Loren stopped mid-stride, noticing the three-year-old thoroughbred gingerly favoring a front foot. She turned, pushing a blonde lock behind one ear, and called over to the trainer, "Paula, *Surge* is limping."

The horse's hair felt coarse as Loren lifted a leg and examined the foot.

A stocky woman with a dark ponytail approached and pointed to a purplish section. "Stone bruise. I swear he seems to get these awfully easily. I think his feet are too flat—"

The dull thud of someone turning off the main road in the distance distracted Loren. The trainer's words faded to the background as she tracked the car coming down the long dirt road. Unusual for someone she didn't know to venture all the way out here. She touched Paula's shoulder and nodded toward it. "Let me see who this is."

The fine hairs on the back of her neck tingled. Like an echo from the past, an instinct from another time in her life. The yard smelled of sweet hay and horse manure as she passed through the gate to the parking area between the barn and her small, framed house. Faded blue jeans accented her long legs and round hips as she leaned against a post and waited.

A nondescript, blue sedan that looked like a rental. It could only be one person, and now the hairs stood up on her forearms as well.

Her former CIA boss, Craig Black, stepped out. Incredibly, he always looked the same. Short and square with salt and pepper stubble, and dark, untidy hair. The same jeans, blue blazer, and penny loafers that were like his uniform.

The corners of his narrow mouth pulled down, and his dark hooded eyes seemed somehow sad as he held out his arms. "You don't have a hug for your old boss?"

Loren pushed off the rail and hugged him. "I'm happy to see you, Craig, but I don't for a second believe this is a social call."

He pulled away and nodded. "Let's go someplace where we can talk."

During the deepest and most dangerous part of her Agency mission, Loren had dreamed of a place just like this. A pleasant piece of Virginia land, a bright sunny sky, and horses. She hadn't even known anything about the graceful animals then, but she swore that if she made it home, she'd settle in and learn. Her light at the end of the tunnel. The one thing that no one could take from her. She believed it was one reason she'd survived.

Craig's sudden appearance caused an unexpected thrill inside her, however. Did she miss the danger? That was too simple. She missed the sense of importance, the stakes, doing something that really mattered. This revelation surprised her but rang true. She thought she'd had enough adventure for a lifetime, but somehow, maybe she hadn't. She wanted to hear the story he'd come to tell and unpack whatever puzzle it contained.

The house's main room was a cozy area filled with four large, dark leather chairs. The only decoration was an expansive painting of a foxhunt above the fireplace, and she inexplicably felt embarrassed by the stark, almost masculine quality of the room. Why was that? This man always made her second guess herself. She sat, pulled her legs up under her, and waited.

Craig took a seat with a sigh. "We've had a group watching Senator Sam Hawthorne for the past three months."

Crap, that wasn't what she'd expected at all. Thoughts of doing important work and puzzles blew away from her mind like dry leaves in a fall wind. Sam was in trouble? Her friend and maybe the closest thing to a proper father she'd ever had. A knot tightened in her chest. "Why?"

Craig said, "I'm friends with the head of his private security team, and he called me with some—I don't know, concerns, I guess you'd say. Worries about the senator, and for him."

"What kind of worries?"

Craig shifted in his seat. "I don't know what he's up to, but yesterday he took a secret meeting in Fairhaven, Massachusetts, with Selik. You remember that name?"

She shrugged one shoulder. "A person of interest. If I remember correctly, not a good guy." She furrowed her brow, trying to remember the details. "I had a side mission to find out anything I could about him if the situation presented itself. It never did."

Craig pursed his lips and nodded. "We don't know much more than that now."

Selik was almost like a ghost in those days. It surprised Loren that that was still the case. Worry spread up over her chest and shoulders. There had to be some explanation for this. She couldn't believe Sam was bad. He loved his country and already had more money than he knew what to do with. No denying how it looked, though. "Well, that's not good."

"I know, so I called him."

Loren raised her eyebrows. She'd forgotten how direct Craig was. "What'd he say?"

"Some cock and bull story about a rare World War II plane crashed in the Caribbean somewhere. That Selik had information on its whereabouts and that he didn't know that Selik was a person of interest. It was all crap." He pursed his lips. "Sam and I have been friends a long time, Loren. It was a lie. A blind nun would have seen it. Then, right after the meeting, he arranged a trip on his boat for the day after tomorrow. Supposedly to go after this plane." He narrowed his dark eyes. "And he told his security team he was leaving them home."

In politics and espionage, the appearance of impropriety was almost as damaging as the real thing. Loren understood and believed that, but she knew Sam. What made him tick. No way he was doing something illicit. There had to be a logical explanation, but until revealed, this looked bad. "What're you going to do?"

Craig sighed. "I don't know. I like Sam. He's one of the few people on the Hill who gets it. To better answer your question, I'm trying to give him the benefit of the doubt and help him if I can. The son of a gun won't trust me, though."

Not surprising. Sam Hawthorne was too smart and too experienced to trust Craig completely. "What do you want from me?"

He scratched at his stubble again. "I want you to do two things for me, actually."

Her eyebrows rose again expectantly.

Craig said, "I have two problems. The first is, what's Sam up to? I need to figure this out before anyone else does. The second is, because of his meeting with the senator, for the first time we have a line on Selik. We know where he is, and at least one of his aliases."

Loren crossed her arms.

"We don't know why, but the day after tomorrow he's off to the Dominican Republic, awfully close to where the senator is heading on his boat with no security."

"Don't we have people there?"

Craig clasped his hands together, rested his chin on them, and measured his response. "We do. However, whatever they find will be official, documented, and beyond our ability to control. It could be devastating for Sam."

"Or it could all be nothing."

Craig shrugged. "Maybe. But this looks bad. What I should do is escalate this to my boss, and he should report it to the president and the FBI. But I'm willing to drag my feet a little if you'll help me."

There it was. The bastard move she'd been expecting from Craig. "So, if I don't help you, you're going to make trouble for Sam?"

Craig shrugged again. "Sam created this trouble for himself, not me."

"But you're making it my problem."

"Look, Loren, I'm giving you a chance to help your friend. A friend who helped you when you desperately needed it."

Loren uncrossed her arms and clenched her fists. "That's a low blow."

He nodded. "I know. But it's true."

"I can't just leave this place, Craig."

He shrugged. "I'm not asking you to abandon your farm here. Take three or four days, go down and see what this Selik character is doing. Then, boom, you're back here with all your horses. If you ask me, it's a simple job and a small price to pay to keep Sam out of trouble."

Bastard. She had no good argument against that. This was how it always turned out when talking to Craig. Selik was a dangerous customer, however, and she'd been a deep undercover asset, playing a role, not a field officer. Trailing agents in foreign, unknown areas where potential violence was at play was outside her training and experience. She frowned. "How hot of a situation are we talking about?"

Craig shrugged. "It's most likely just a meeting. Selik doesn't know who you are, does he?"

"I don't see how."

"Then it should be a simple surveillance job."

Was that the entire story? Probably not, coming from Craig. It didn't serve any purpose for him to put her in danger, however. And if she didn't do this for Sam, people might get the wrong idea before all the facts came out, and the senator had stuck his neck out for her in the past. "All right, but I'm going out on a limb here, Craig. Don't leave me twisting in the wind."

He raised thick bushy eyebrows. "Good. I won't."

Her heartbeat quickened. Craig always led with the simple request. Just to take her temperature. "What's the second thing?"

His eyes were dark, like deep pools of oil.

This one must be a doozy. Her stomach clenched.

He frowned. "I don't like Sam going on this trip with no security whatsoever. He won't trust any of my people, and *you're* going to check up on Selik."

A lump formed in her throat. He wanted her to talk to Eddie. She could see it in his face. Not like this. Not out of the blue with Craig, of all people, in tow. Please no. Let it be anything but that. "Who?"

Craig shrugged. "It has to be someone not connected to the Agency, but who you and I trust. Someone we know can't be bought or coerced."

Her forehead creased. "But I haven't seen him since—"

"I know. Look, I'm not thrilled about asking him, either, but who else would you send? Who else do you think you could convince Sam to take? They're fellow Texans. He's the obvious choice."

She leaned back and covered her mouth with one hand. She wanted to see Eddie so badly it hurt, but not like this. Everything had ended so abruptly, even before anything between them had ever even really started. And so much time had passed. "Where is he? What's he doing?"

Craig rolled his eyes. "He's in Miami playing at being Robin Hood."

CHAPTER 3

Eddie drove through the iron gates and down the palm-lined drive of his property in Coral Gables. Two stucco structures and a four-car garage surrounded a circular brick parking area. The mustard walls and barrel-tile roofs were typical Miami architecture, and fruit trees dotted the five-acre compound.

It still didn't feel like home, which added to his unease. The damn place was too large and ostentatious for a simple boy from west Texas. He hadn't even spent any time of note in most of the rooms, keeping primarily to the kitchen, den, and one bedroom. He'd taken the house as a sort of payment at the end of what he now thought of as "the Agency screw-up."

It was a fortress, though—difficult to storm or breach, with a tunnel between the two structures, poured concrete walls, and bulletproof glass. His first thought when he saw the place was that it might come in handy. Especially in what his new life had become. Against his better judgment, he'd accepted the house. He really didn't have anywhere else to go, which was a depressing truth all on its own.

He'd never felt comfortable here, but it was an excellent base for doing dangerous work. Maybe that was the problem. It was good for work, but not really a home. He wondered for the hundredth time why he stayed here. He had no connection to Miami, no real ties here, and enough money to live anywhere.

Staying here also meant that the Agency knew where he was—or at least Craig did. Those two weren't always the same thing. So why not just sell it and move on? Eddie sighed. Maybe tomorrow.

Perhaps he'd lived too long in the shadows. It finally felt good to be out in the open like this. Maybe if he didn't make the CIA search for him, they wouldn't be as interested—fat chance. More than likely, he stayed here because he didn't view any of this as permanent. The house was a placeholder until he moved on to the next phase in his life—whatever the hell that was.

Eddie parked in one garage and then, as he and Luis crossed the courtyard, Jeff's Porsche purred down the driveway. The three of them entered the main house through the kitchen door.

Inside, Eddie grabbed each a beer and asked Jeff, "How do you know this Coast Guard guy, Nathan, again?"

He shrugged. "I know the Murphys and their daughter is dating the—"

Eddie held up his hand. "Forget it. I should've known better than to ask. You know, you can't just collect people like books."

Jeff frowned. "Says who?"

Luis raised his eyebrows. "Whether or not you think he can, he seems to be doing it."

Eddie shook his head. "I still don't understand how, even after all these years."

Jeff shrugged. "It's a gift. Besides, what else would I add to the team?"

Eddie wasn't feeling the humor of the conversation, but he should be. He loved these guys, trusted them, and would go anywhere with them. Circumstances had thrown them together, and they'd never parted, but how long could that last?

Was this an after effect of years on the lam, on his own, not depending on anyone else? Partly, but that wasn't the entire story. He leaned back and pushed these unsettling thoughts to the back of his mind. "I liked him."

Luis nodded. "I did, too. Seemed like a straight shooter. I want to help this guy."

Eddie asked, "What do we know about this Enrique Suavé?"

Luis took a sip. "He's a nasty little cockroach, but he's smart. Word is, he has some connection to the Olivos brothers, but I don't think he'll run to them if we just rattle his cage a bit."

Eddie frowned. "Do you think these containers are for the brothers?" He hoped not. They were big-time drug smugglers and a completely different situation, probably bigger than Eddie's team could handle.

Luis shook his head. "No. They have their own internal distribution. They don't entrust that to anyone."

Eddie glanced at his watch, calculating London time. "Let's see what Piper can dig up on this guy." He dialed and put the phone on the table.

"'Sup, mate?" Piper's voice projected from the phone.

Eddie grinned. "What's our favorite limey hacker up to tonight?"

"Breaking the encryption on the new jet-set phone."

Eddie's smile faded. "Piper, we agreed you'd stay out of trouble."

"I'm not *doing* anything to it. Just flexing my mental muscles a bit, is all."

Eddie shook his head. "Well, we have a mission, and we're going to need your help."

"Okay, shoot."

"We've got a Miami punk named Enrique Gomez, aka Suavé. I'm sure he has a criminal record. I want everything you can get on him—money, houses, warrants—everything."

Piper said, "I'm on it, give me a few," before hanging up.

Eddie bounced his fingertips against one another. He turned to Luis. "What's this guy's firepower?"

Luis shrugged. "He has a small group of muscle and one merc named Alvarez. Ex-military. We need to pay attention to him."

Jeff leaned back, frowning. "You don't think we should just scare this guy off?"

Eddie shook his head. "I don't think so. That would just put Malcolm in jeopardy. Like he ran off and tattled on these guys. No, it has to be something that puts the focus off of him and onto us." He turned to Luis. "What if we acted like Malcolm was already ours, and they were horning in on our territory?"

Luis raised an eyebrow and shrugged. "It could work. We blow in there like we're super well-connected and know everything about him."

Eddie said, "Exactly, like we already have our claws into Malcolm, and we don't appreciate the competition."

Jeff looked through Eddie. "It would draw Enrique's attention to us and away from our man. That's an interesting idea."

Luis slowly nodded. "I like it. How do you want to play it?"

Eddie frowned and scratched his chin. "Why don't you go talk to the Cuban street mafia and see what you can find out about this guy. See if you can dig up anything we can use." He turned to Jeff. "We know anyone connected to the docks?"

Jeff frowned and drummed his fingers. "Yeah, I know some people."

Eddie stood. "Good, go talk to them. See what you can find out. Make us look really connected and powerful. I'm going to see this guy, Malcolm. See what I think of our client."

• • •

The street in front of the squat cinderblock house was empty in the midweek afternoon. The area was poor, but the yards were clean and well maintained. City folk would call it blue collar, like the town he'd grown up in. The type of place Eddie had killed himself to escape, but now longed for.

He hoped he liked Malcolm. It would make this easier. It all seemed straightforward, but something about it still bothered him. This was why he'd come here. To see where this guy lived. To look him in the eye and get a feel for him. Eddie judged a man from his gut, by his look and his handshake, growing up in a place just like this street. He still operated this way despite all his Agency training on nonverbal cues and eye movements. He trusted his intuition, and it rarely let him down.

As he stepped out of the car, the house's faded gray door opened a crack, and a shotgun barrel snaked out. "Can I help you?" The voice was deep and steady. Calm, not confrontational.

A good sign. At least this guy was paying attention. "I'm a friend of Nathan's. He thought maybe we could help you."

The gun lowered, and the door opened another few inches. Malcolm was a big man, with broad shoulders and heavy-lidded eyes. He wiped the sweat from his bald head with a rag. "What's your name?"

"Eddie Mason."

"Come on inside." He sat in a beat-up chair and motioned Eddie to a plaid couch, one corner propped up on a concrete block. He clasped big, calloused hands together and frowned. "How do you know Nathan?"

Eddie leaned back on the couch. "I don't. He's a friend of a friend. He seems like a good guy, though."

Malcolm nodded slowly. "He is. The best. Suavé is a tough customer. Do you really know what you're getting into?"

A good question. Not based on blind hope, but in the real world. An inquiry of commitment and situational understanding. Eddie respected it. "He is, but so are we."

Malcolm's gaze darted back and forth on Eddie's face. "Who's we?"

If he were in Malcolm's shoes, he'd want that answered too. After all, this was a risk for them both. "I have a group of friends who have certain talents and connections, and I guess you'd say we help people. I think we can rattle Enrique."

For the first time, Eddie sensed fear in Malcolm.

The big man's brow furrowed. He pulled his head down into his shoulders and lowered his voice. "You know, it's not just the situation I'm in. There's lots of weird shit happening at the docks the last couple of weeks." He smiled weakly. "I mean, it's Miami, so there's always something going on, but not like this. Lots of odd containers loaded late at night, all headed to the Dominican Republic."

Eddie didn't like the sound of that, and the nagging at the back of his mind intensified. "What does Enrique want you to do? Could he get someone else to do it?"

Malcolm nodded slowly. "Yeah, they already have guys that do this kind of thing for them. They're just using this as an excuse to add me to their crew." He furrowed his brow. "You really think you can convince him to stop?"

"I do. Push back on Enrique. Make it seem like you're more afraid of us than him. Say things like, 'you don't know these guys, and they'll kill me.' Stuff like that and leave the rest to us."

Malcolm raised a thin eyebrow and smiled. "You want it to look like I'm already someone else's stooge?"

Eddie nodded. This guy was smarter than he looked. "If they think you called in muscle, they'll just bide their time and try again later. Answer with bigger muscle. But if they think they've stumbled into something they want no part of, they'll leave you alone. Hopefully for good. It moves his attention to us."

Malcolm pursed his lips and nodded.. "Okay. I can do that. I can't thank you enough."

"You working tonight?"

Malcolm nodded. "I go in at 6."

"Do you expect Enrique to pay you a visit?"

"Oh, yeah."

Eddie stood and handed him his card. "We'll be there. Call me if something changes or if you need anything. Don't worry, we'll take care of these guys. You just keep on the straight and narrow."

Malcolm took the card. "I will, and I'll never forget this."

Eddie clapped him on the shoulder and walked out the door.

He kept one eye on his rear-view mirror as he took an unorthodox and unpredictable route home. They should be able to bully this guy off of Malcolm. What worried him was, why did Enrique want this help now? What other groups were at play here and did Eddie and his team have a good read on the situation? And, most importantly, why did someone want to send so many illicit containers to the Dominican Republic?

CHAPTER 4

Loren stared out the window, absentmindedly playing with the small gold cross around her neck. Yesterday, she'd never have believed that anything could convince her to just pick up and leave. Yet here she sat on an Agency jet bound for Miami. Another sign of the ruthless effectiveness of Craig Black. She sighed. She was on her way to visit two of her favorite men in the world, and yet all she felt was trepidation. How had Craig found such easy leverage over her? Because Sam was the force that had pushed her life of destruction onto a different path, that was why.

Loren was fifteen when she first realized her father was a conman and a crook. By then, her mother had been dead for years, so it wasn't like she could really have done anything about it. Right? This question still nagged her on sleepless nights. Where would she have ended up if her father hadn't been foolish enough to try to con Senator Sam Hawthorne? That one decision changed the direction of her entire life. So, now she would never really know what would have become of her. Other than a stint in prison, at least.

Loren shook her head. Her dad was a good conman, but Sam was miles out of his league. Taking him on was definitely flying too close to the sun. By the time they arrested Loren and her father, she was two weeks past her eighteenth birthday.

She spent three days in that stinking Dallas County jail cell. She could still remember the water stain on the ceiling shaped like Australia. The stupid faucet that would never stop dripping.

The first day was a blur of worry, regret, and anger, broken only when the chief guard, Linda, took her to meet her public defender. She quickly understood just how bad her situation was after spending only thirty seconds with that incompetent man. On the second day, they told her that her father had committed suicide. She lost that day to sadness, loneliness, and anger.

Right after lunch on the third day, three guards came to tell her she had a meeting. Three guards. Not a good sign. A severe-looking Latina guard she'd never seen before cuffed her. Handcuffs were definitely a bad sign.

They left her in an interview room alone, her shackled hands resting in her lap and her heart hammering in her chest. How much worse could it get? Much worse, something told her.

As her dad planned his con on Sam, she'd seen the senator from afar. When he strolled casually into the room and sat opposite her, however, she was completely unprepared for the power and presence of the man. His carriage was erect, and his movements were unhurried. He was clearly a man accustomed to other people waiting for him.

Why on earth he was here? On instinct, she ran through a quick information collection. Her father would be so proud. The overall impression was wealthy. No, that wasn't right. Everything about him spoke of quality. From the gray fabric of his suit to the simple chunky, dull gray chronograph at his wrist. Even his socks were the nicest she'd ever seen.

When she met his gaze, his attention was steady and unwavering. A small crease formed next to one of his eyebrows that seemed more curious than angry.

He said, "Ms. Malen, I'm Sam—"

"I know who you are."

The corners of his mouth lifted a fraction. "I suppose you do. Forgive me, I meant no condescension. I was sorry to hear about your father and his unfortunate choice."

Loren narrowed her eyes. "Yeah, thanks. What do you want?"

Sam pursed his lips. "Your father chose his punishment for his part in this crime. That only leaves us with what to do with you?"

Maybe the tough-girl approach wasn't the best play. It might be time to stop antagonizing the one man who held her life in his hands. His being here meant there was at least a slight chance of avoiding jail and destruction. She raised her eyebrows and tried to flush away any attitude from her face. "What are my options?"

Sam raised one eyebrow in an expression she interpreted as appreciation, though she wasn't sure what she'd done to deserve it.

He pursed his lips and stretched out his long legs. "I'm not sure. Did you know he was trying to swindle me?"

A weird question. How to answer it? Her public defender, no matter how useless, wasn't here. That had to violate her rights. Was this a ham-handed attempt to get her to admit guilt? She didn't think so. Something in his unwavering blue eyes prompted her to tell the truth. She swallowed and nodded.

He nodded back, again seeming pleased with the answer. "I really am sorry your father killed himself. It was cowardly, and it left you in quite a pickle."

She couldn't have said it better herself. She loved her father, but in the last month she'd come to see that she didn't respect him. That realization was both surprising and sad.

Sam sighed. "You're a bright girl. You think quick on your feet. Are you opposed to working for a living?"

She sat up a little straighter. "No. I've been on my own with my dad for most of my life." She lifted her cuffed hands and then dropped them back in her lap. "It's not like I've been holding out for a management position."

His eyes widened, and he actually laughed softly.

She shrugged one shoulder and smiled. Not too obviously. She added just a little interest, and then let her smile fade. Don't overplay it. "I don't have a resumé that too many people are going to find very compelling."

Sam arched an eyebrow, but his eyes clearly communicated that her pretty-girl charms were having no effect. "You might be surprised."

Given a thousand guesses, she would never have predicted that response. Or, for that matter, what happened afterward.

Loren smiled at the memory as her thoughts returned to the present. The next day, Sam introduced her to Craig. And she made the easiest choice in the world: The Agency or prison.

Sam was like a proud father after that. Keeping tabs on her training. Giving her equal measures discipline and praise as she grew as an agent and a woman. He became the father she should've had, and they grew closer over the years.

But yesterday, Sam was hesitant when she called and only reluctantly agreed to a meeting. He'd been nothing short of enthusiastic at the prospect of seeing her before. What was going on with him?

And then she would drop in on Eddie. And this was almost more than she could wrap her mind around, for she was a jumble of feelings about their relationship—if you could call it that. Although she dreaded the circumstances of this meeting, she still ached to see him.

She couldn't bring herself to do it over the phone, so she decided to just go see him. Not even call and give him a head's up. Hopefully, that wasn't a mistake.

He wasn't going to like her just showing up with Craig. It would cast a light of suspicion on her, and that broke her heart. She sighed heavily. There was nothing she could do about that now.

Craig sat across the aisle, flipping through pages in a thick manila folder.

How much did she trust him? He was emotionally blackmailing her, after all. Despite that, she thought Craig actually cared about her, and she believed he cared about Sam. But things were never quite that simple with her old boss. He was always playing more than one game.

She was angry at him, but part of her was grateful that he'd maneuvered her into helping. Not giving her an actual choice was a blessing. Not that she was going to forget his tactics. "You shouldn't have talked to his security people without Sam knowing. He was bound to find out, and you had to know that would piss him off."

Craig set down a paper, leaned back, and frowned at her. "He's my friend too, Loren, but think about it. He's the Chairman of the Senate Intelligence Committee. If he's bad or caught up in something bad, it could be devastating. So, even though he's my friend, my first duty is to protect this country." He jutted out his jaw and fixed her with his dark, implacable eyes. "That's the thing that you, Sam, Eddie, and everyone else never seem to get. It's not personal, but I'll do whatever I need to do to protect this country. I could've done a lot worse to him, but I haven't. Instead, I came to get *your* help, don't forget that. I'm giving him every benefit of the doubt I can."

Typical Craig answer—true, but not quite the entire story at the same time. She nodded reluctantly.

Craig scratched his chin. "I've been thinking about this, and I don't think it'll work if you just suggest that he take Eddie along. He'll still seem like one of my stooges. I think you should say that Eddie is a man for hire and that you think Sam should hire him."

Loren asked, "Why? You think he's more likely to trust someone he's paying?"

He shrugged. "It can't hurt. And it can't be cheap. It needs to be something like twenty thousand a week to make it seem legitimate."

She nodded and looked back out the window. It made sense, but she didn't enjoy deceiving Sam. She might try that, but only as a last resort. Please, God, let everything be normal when she saw him. And let none of this be necessary.

A knot formed in her stomach, and her shoulders tightened as her mind wandered back to Eddie. Why did everything with them always end up so complicated?

They'd parted in the heat of the moment, under great stress, and hadn't seen each other since. If only there were another way to see him again. Perhaps this was how it had to be. Left to their own devices, neither had found their way back to the other. Maybe fate needed to lend a hand, even if it was in a sucky situation.

She took a deep breath. Eddie and Sam were so alike and yet so different. Similar makeups, but very different backgrounds. What was the best way to approach them? No good ideas had presented themselves yet.

• • •

The building where Sam had finally agreed to meet Loren was not what she expected. Miami was usually a casual place, but the people coming in and out all wore professional attire. She felt a little self-conscious in jeans, a girly tee, and tennis shoes.

Getting into the building wouldn't be a problem—she'd always been able to overcome a situation with posture and attitude. This place made her uncomfortable, however. Clinical and unwelcoming—he'd never met her at such a place before. Was that on purpose? She'd not known Sam to be so Machiavellian, but maybe she'd just never had a reason to look for it before.

She gave the guard a confident smile, and he only half glanced at his clipboard before passing her through. Pushing a lock of golden hair behind one ear, she closed her eyes, and willed her heartbeat to slow. Relax. Sam was her friend, and she was here to help him.

The elevator doors opened to a vast expanse of windows overlooking miles of calm, blue water stretching off into the distance. For a moment, the magnificent view entranced her.

Sam appeared and held out his arms. "Loren. It's good to see you." He was tall and slim in an expensive gray suit with a bright yellow tie.

She hugged him, then stepped back and studied his deeply tanned and lined face. "How are you?"

"Good." His light blue eyes were hard, and he jerked his head for her to follow him down a hallway covered in a plush navy-blue carpet. They passed fine, expansive offices with antique desks and bookshelves before arriving at a conference room at the far end.

He carefully closed the heavy wooden doors, and they sat on the couches. "So. Now Craig has invited you into his worrying-about-Sam club, is that it?"

"That about covers it." He was trying to make this conversation light, but it seemed forced and false.

Sam adjusted his jacket and shook his silver head. "I should have known."

Loren leaned back. He was angry but trying to hide it. Maybe as angry as she'd ever seen him. "You seem surprised and irritated at a situation you caused yourself. Aren't you always telling me that perception is reality?"

He shot her a look before raising one thick eyebrow and smiling. "I taught you well."

She crossed her long legs. "Yes, you did. Now, what're you up to?"

Sam's smile faded a fraction, and he threw up his hands. "You know how I like to collect things. I think I've found a rare plane. That's really all there is to it."

He was lying. She would've known it even without all her training and experience. And he'd never lied to her before. It kicked up her sense of dread, but also made her a little sad. "Is that what the meeting with Selik was about?"

He sat back hard against the couch. "Yes. I didn't even know he was a person of interest. Really, Loren, this has been blown way out of proportion."

"I agree." Loren said, "So, why are you making it worse by going on a trip and leaving your security detail behind?"

His eyes flashed, and then his shoulders slumped. "Because I can't trust them anymore. I have to send a message to them and the Agency. Why can't I take a little trip on my boat without security? Normal people do it every day."

Loren looked down her nose at him. "You're not a normal person, and you know it. What would you tell *me* if our roles were reversed?"

Sam blew out a breath. "Probably the same thing you're telling me now."

She shrugged. "You know more about playing the image game than anyone I've ever met. You know this looks bad. It doesn't matter if it really is or not. Especially since it would be so easy to defuse the situation."

He narrowed his eyes. "You have a suggestion?"

"Actually, I do."

Sam's eyebrows shot up. "I'm listening."

"I know a guy here in Miami. You'd like him—he's from Texas, ex-CIA, and he hates Craig. A man for hire, I guess you'd call him. I think I can convince him to go along with you on your trip. It would be a simple thing to do, and it would shut everybody up."

The eyes remained narrowed. "How do you know he hates Craig?"

Loren snorted. "Because he used to work for him."

Sam tucked his chin to his chest. "You really think this is necessary?"

She shrugged. "It can't hurt. You can afford to hire him for a week, and it gets everyone off your back. Why wouldn't you? Look, just meet him and see what you think."

"What's his name?"

"Eddie Mason."

CHAPTER 5

Eddie sat on a tower crossbeam at the edge of the port, watching the last slice of sun melt into the horizon. Harsh blue lights lit up the great cranes overhead, making them look like a menacing, mechanical army that had waded ashore to lay waste to Miami.

Naturally, Jeff knew someone here at the port who got them access. So they'd spent the last couple of hours scouting the place. They'd found no signs of Enrique or his people, which was surprising. No sign at all. He was turning out to be the amateur Eddie had hoped he was. Any pro would have at least sent someone to scout the area before the meeting. Still, Luis was out there somewhere prowling, just in case they'd missed something.

The docks were immense from this vantage point above the shipping crates. Eddie could just barely make out Jeff parked at a side entrance in a nondescript sedan, ready if they needed a quick getaway. Everything was in place.

The day had been productive. Piper discovered two outstanding warrants on Enrique Gomez, a.k.a. Suavé—one in Texas and one in Nevada, as well as a comprehensive list of everything the gangster owned.

Jeff somehow uncovered the names of two dockworkers already under Enrique's thumb. How Jeff always seemed to know everyone, or why they shared these kinds of things with him, was still a mystery to Eddie.

Luis had heard rumors that Enrique was afraid of the Russian Mob, so maybe they'd use that. He figured that should be enough for a good bluff.

In the hour since Malcolm's arrival, he'd remained inside the office with the other workers. Now the waiting game—always the hardest part of an operation for him, but over the years, Eddie had learned to manage this stage. He pushed his concerns to the back of his mind and turned his attention to the little things around him. The gentle lapping sounds of waves hitting the pylons. A pair of seagulls flapping across the sky. The port was quiet tonight, with only one crane moving in the distance. Eddie rested his hands on his thighs and stretched out his legs. He rolled his neck, tucked his square chin into his chest, and let everything but the mission drift away.

Across the way, the door to the office opened. Malcolm and a handful of other workers emerged and fanned out across the port.

Eddie watched him move into the canyon of shipping containers before turning his attention back to the main entrance. No sign of Enrique yet. He lifted his binoculars and focused on his getaway car. Jeff eased the seat back, pulled out a massive bag of pistachios, and ripped open the top. He cracked open a nut and tossed the shell out the window. Eddie shook his head and grinned. His earpiece cracked, and Piper's voice floated in all the way from England. "Hey, Eddie, we have a problem."

His smile faded. "What's up?"

"I can see someone at the house on the security monitors."

Eddie frowned. "My house? Where?"

Piper said, "At the front gate. Hold on, I can answer the intercom from here."

Eddie's pulse ticked up a notch as the seconds passed.

"Uh, Eddie—it's Loren. Loren Malen."

Eddie's brow furrowed. That certainly wasn't what he'd expected. "Is she okay?"

Piper said, "She says she needs to talk to you."

Eddie swallowed down a lump in his throat. Why was she here? And why now, after all this time? Running a hand through his untidy brown hair, he squeezed his eyes shut and forced his mind back to the situation at hand. They couldn't miss this opportunity with Enrique. "Tell her to wait. I'm in the middle of a job, but I should be back in about an hour."

"Got it," Piper replied.

Luis' voice came over the earpiece, "You okay? You want to push?"

Eddie shook his head. "No, I'm fine. Let's get this over with. Jeff, if this goes south, get out of here."

Jeff replied, "10-4."

Eddie had neither seen nor heard from Loren in years. Circumstances forced them apart before what they had took on any kind of shape. Or even really began. She had to do what she had to do. At the time, he wasn't sure how real his newly minted exoneration was, so he'd run. Their agreement at the time was that when she was free, she would reach out. She never had.

Understandable, really. Their relationship had been a series of encounters amid stress and danger. Not really the basis for something obviously long term. But everything came rushing back now and a shroud of worry settled over him. He had to shake it off and keep his mind on the task at hand. He would deal with Loren, and whatever her arrival meant, later.

Two black Mercedes sedans pulled through the front gate. One stopped, and a pair of goons stepped out and disappeared among the shipping crates.

Luis would handle them. Through the binoculars, Eddie tracked the first car as it continued deeper into the port. Alvarez, the mercenary, driving with Enrique seated next to him.

Eddie said into the radio, "Showtime, two bandits loose in the playground heading south."

Luis said, "Hunting time."

Eddie pulled the holster with his Sig Sauer 9 mm closer to his hip and climbed down the ladder. He wore fine navy suit pants and pulled on the matching jacket as he crossed the main yard. He had decided that this is what Enrique would expect a fellow gangster to wear, but he felt ridiculous in it.

Row after row of containers stacked four and five high created eerily silent canyons. He kept his hand near his pistol as he scanned the tops and blind alleys, moving deeper into the yard.

Rounding a corner into an open area, he found Malcolm facing the two men. Enrique was short and stocky, with a big nose and stubby limbs. He wore his black hair slicked back and rocked on his heels like he was late for an appointment.

Entirely different, Alvarez was tall and lean with long arms and legs. His body was like a coiled spring, and his attention darted in every direction. When Eddie arrived, Alvarez put his hand on his pistol and moved Enrique behind him.

Earlier, Piper had forwarded pictures of the two men, but they didn't do them justice.

Enrique still rocked on the balls of his feet, seemingly unconcerned, as he took Eddie in. In that shiny suit, he looked like some type of fancy bird.

Alvarez was bigger than Eddie had expected and looked capable, dangerous, and uncomfortable in an oversized blazer.

Malcolm's shoulders slumped as he noticed Eddie approaching. He pointed and said something to Enrique that Eddie didn't hear.

Enrique turned, cocked his head to one side, narrowed his eyes, and studied Eddie as he approached. "And just who the hell are you?"

The clothes, gold watch, cuff links, and posture were almost comical; this guy obviously viewed himself as a gangster character straight out of a movie.

On the far side of the clearing, Luis appeared and quietly moved toward them from behind. Careful not to look at him and give away his presence, Eddie focused on Enrique.

Luis slid his pistol out and held it down and ready.

Alvarez kept his head on a swivel, however, and quickly caught sight of Luis and pushed Enrique away, creating a distance between the two men. Smart move. Make himself and Enrique into two targets instead of one. Alvarez was a pro.

Enrique flinched as he registered Luis's presence and finally seemed to recognize his situation. He put his hand on the pistol at his waist as well.

Eddie and Luis continued to close the gap until they were fifteen feet away, flanking the group.

Alvarez took a few more steps back to protect his blind side while shooting quick glances up at the surrounding crates.

Luis still held his pistol casually at his side. "Your friends aren't coming." His tone was calm and neutral. "They're tied up."

Eddie resisted, shaking his head. The corners of Luis' mouth twitched. His friend thought that the terrible action-movie line was a riot.

Enrique recovered from his shock, found his voice again, and turned to Luis. "And who the hell are you?"

Eddie said, "That's my associate. My name's Eddie Mason, and I've come to ask you to leave Malcolm here alone. He belongs to us."

Enrique adjusted his suit cuff. "Well, maybe we'll just take him off your hands."

Alvarez's brow furrowed. He glanced over at his boss before turning most of his attention back to Luis.

Eddie said, "Listen, Enrique, I don't think you understand the situation you're in."

The shorter man chuckled derisively. "So, why don't you enlighten me?"

Eddie said, "We're motivated to keep what is ours. Motivated enough to cause you trouble if we have to."

Enrique looked down his nose at him. "What kind of trouble?"

Eddie shrugged. "For instance, I can let my friend at the sheriff's department know about your warrant in Nevada or the one from Texas. How the hell do you get arrested in Pecos, Texas, anyway?"

Enrique's face blanched. His oil-black eyes darted from face to face before he squared his shoulders and tried to reassemble his mantle of false bravado. "That's bullshit. You're messing with the wrong guy, and you're going to regret it." He turned to his gunman. "Deal with this."

Alvarez frowned at Eddie and then gave Luis a long look before shaking his head. "I don't think so, boss. I think maybe this isn't the kind of mess we want to get involved in today."

Enrique's close-set eyes widened. He frowned at his henchman, then turned back to Eddie. He thrust out his chin. "You don't know who you're dealing with. The people that want these crates are not the kind you want to disappoint."

Eddie shrugged. "So, use Diaz or Melton. Those guys are under your control already, I believe. You don't need Malcolm."

Enrique took a step back, his jaw working. He looked over at Alvarez.

Time to go for the kill. Use Enrique's movie-fueled imagination against him. "Look at me, Suavé."

Enrique snapped his attention back to Eddie.

"We don't want trouble. But my boss Nicolai doesn't share. So, take care of your powerful customer with someone else, and then you and I don't have any trouble."

For a moment, Enrique visibly vacillated between running and attempting to maintain his tough-guy image.

Eddie said quietly to him, "Do we have an understanding?"

Alvarez nodded. "We do." He stepped over and took Enrique's arm.

The shorter man turned to pull free and then looked up at his gunman with surprise. Alvarez's expression was stony, and Enrique swallowed. He glanced over at Luis, straightened up, and with a last blast of hot air, said, "This idiot isn't worth all this trouble. That's for damned sure. Come on."

As they walked away, Alvarez kept looking from them to the surrounding crates and back.

Eddie leaned over to Luis. "Follow him and make sure he doesn't take a parting pot shot at us."

Luis nodded and trotted after them.

Eddie swept the area once again for anything of concern. Unlikely that these guys had some unexpected backup, but you could never be too careful.

Malcolm shook his bald head. "Damn. You guys are badass."

"He was easy. Call me if he hasn't gotten the message."

Malcolm stuck out his hand. "I swear to you, Mr. Mason, I'm doing everything I can to keep straight. I'll never forget this. If you ever need anything, call."

Eddie shook it. "I might just do that."

Eddie's mind was a jumble as he walked toward the car. What was Loren doing here? For so long he'd waited for her to call, then he accepted the truth. Their relationship, if you could call it that, was born out of danger and circumstance. Like a comet, never really meant to shine on night after night. Even though everyone said he was no longer a wanted man, he'd run like he still was. Did he really expect her to run with him? Part of him had, but the rest of him knew that was selfish.

It was months before Eddie finally allowed himself to believe that no one was after him anymore. By then they were here in Miami, doing whatever you called these missions. She'd told him she would reach out, and she never had. That was the fact that mattered. But she was here now, and he didn't believe she just happened to be in the neighborhood. In his bones, he knew this visit wasn't about the two of them.

Luis fell back into step beside him and said with a grin, "Nicolai?"

Eddie chuckled. "It was the only Russian name I could think of." He looked sidelong at his friend. "They're all tied up? Who are you, Schwarzenegger?"

Luis' smile widened. "Come on, that joke was begging to be told." His grin slowly faded. "Think it worked?"

Eddie shrugged. "He's a little rooster, but I think Alvarez understands the score."

Luis nodded, then the corner of his mouth quirked up. "Nicolai doesn't share. Classic."

• • •

When Eddie, Luis, and Jeff made it back to the house, Loren was waiting at the gate. She followed them into the courtyard and stepped out of her car.

Eddie studied her from across the bricked space. The thought that came to him now was the same as the first time he ever saw her—that she was effortlessly beautiful. Not like a model, or even an actress, not glamorous or jaw-dropping, just a type of easy beautiful that got to him every time.

Her eyes were alert and her posture cautious as she stood waiting.

He understood her hesitation. What to say?

Craig Black stepped out of the other side of the car.

Eddie's mouth twisted. "I didn't know you brought him."

She pushed a lock of blonde hair behind one ear. "I didn't want it to be like this, either, but I didn't really have a choice. I just need you to give him a minute."

Luis pulled his jacket aside, exposing the pistol on his hip, and grinned. "Want me to go all Wild West?"

Eddie's gaze never left Craig as he shook his head. "No. But be ready. Later, I might tell you to shoot him in the knees."

Craig scratched at his salt and pepper stubble. "I see you kept the entire crew together." With a nod, he added, "Luis. Jeff."

Eddie held his gaze. "What do you want, Craig?"

"I want five minutes. Surely you can give me that?"

His attention traveled from Craig back to Loren. Her eyes were steady, but the way the skin crinkled around the edges looked like worry. "It's good to see you, Loren. I'll give him five minutes for you."

She stepped forward and gave him a hug.

Her smell, with its hint of jasmine, caused a million memories to flood his mind like a dam bursting. Why did she affect him like this?

She whispered in his ear, "Thanks, Eddie. I appreciate it. It's good to see you."

The group filed into the house. Luis and Jeff walked through to the refrigerator and grabbed a beer and remained in the kitchen, out of the way, as Craig, Eddie, and Loren sat in high-backed chairs in the living room.

Eddie held Loren's bottle-green eyes for a moment and then turned to Craig. "What do you want?"

The older man adjusted his coat and sighed. "I need a favor."

"Of course you do. What kind of favor?"

"Do you know who Senator Sam Hawthorne is?"

Eddie didn't like this at all. Anything to do with Craig and a U.S. senator was something he definitely wanted to avoid. "He's the senior senator from Texas, chairman of the Senate Intelligence Committee."

The corners of Craig's mouth lifted a fraction. "He's also one of the good guys. He gets it, and he's rich enough to be free from special interest loyalties—"

Eddie said, "Good for him. What does that have to do with me?"

Loren leaned forward. "He's a very dear friend of mine. You might even say he saved my life." She hesitated. "And now, it at least appears like he's in some sort of trouble."

The time he'd spent with Loren totaled all of two weeks, at the most. How little he really knew about this woman. Never in a thousand years would he have guessed that she knew a multi-millionaire senator. Even more alarming was why this involved the CIA, or at least Craig? "What kind of trouble?"

She met his gaze. "Do you know who Selik is?"

The name meant nothing to Eddie, and he shook his head.

Loren continued, "He's a person of interest with the CIA. Not a good guy."

Craig sucked his teeth. "Sam had a secret meeting with him yesterday afternoon."

So, his old boss also knew the senator well enough to refer to him by his first name. "About what?"

Craig shrugged. "Sam's a big collector, especially artifacts from World War II, and apparently Selik knew the location of a rare experimental aircraft from that time. Or at least that's the line of bull he's feeding everyone."

Loren nodded. "He says he had no idea who Selik was and that it's all a misunderstanding."

Eddie arched an eyebrow. "You don't believe him? What do you think he's doing?" Against his better judgment, he was curious, but that sense of dread over the last couple of days was now a roar in his ears.

Craig said, "We don't know, but something's up, and he's making noise that he's going to sail his yacht down off the coast of South America, supposedly to look for this lost plane. He's going without his security detail, and I don't like it."

Eddie leaned back. "Who cares if you don't like it? And again, I ask, what does this have to do with me?"

Loren answered, "I want you to go with him."

Eddie's eyes widened. "Wait, what? Why? Look, if you think he's in danger, you should send a few people like Luis. I'm not a gun for hire."

Luis nodded from the kitchen. "I know a few guys I could get. We could watch his back."

Craig shook his head. "Thank you, Luis, but that's not—"

Eddie said, "That's not the whole story. What a surprise. How do you know any of this, anyway?"

Craig hesitated. "The head of the senator's security detail told me."

Eddie shook his head. "You're unbelievable."

Craig held up his hands defensively. "I'm not spying on him. His security guy knows me, and he's worried about the senator."

Eddie snorted. "No wonder he doesn't want his detail with him. He's probably figured out they're compromised."

Craig scratched at the salt and pepper stubble on his chin again. "Probably, but I think it's a bad idea for him to take this trip alone. I think Loren can convince him to take you along as an extra set of eyes. Someone who can watch for trouble."

Eddie held Craig's gaze. "This all sounds like Agency business. I don't work for you anymore."

Craig said, "I know, but he won't accept help from the government right now."

Eddie shrugged. "I don't blame him, and I don't see why I should get involved with you, either."

Craig furrowed his brow and, with an edge to his voice, said, "Clearly, this can't be anywhere near as important as playing Robin Hood down here with the money *I* gave you." He dropped his head and sighed.

Eddie tightened his jaw. Craig obviously regretted the comment, but Eddie didn't care. "Well, now. Isn't that just a classic example of a Craig Black half-truth?"

The older man lifted his head. "You're right, I'm sorry. I don't want to be here, but you should know I wouldn't come back unless it was really important."

Eddie stood and walked into the kitchen. "Actually, I think you *do* want to be here. I think it was your plan all along to get me set up here so I could do off-the-books jobs for you." He reached into the refrigerator, pulled out three beers, and returned. He handed one to Craig. "I think you've been looking for the perfect opportunity to reel me back in." He handed the second bottle to Loren.

Craig opened his beer and took a swig. "You're right, I have, but this isn't it. I would've preferred to wait until I could've brought you something simpler. Something you and your little group of Boy Scouts would see as noble. But this came in, and I'm desperate."

Eddie turned to Loren. "Now, that's the first thing he's said since he arrived that I actually believe. And why are you here? I didn't think you worked for him anymore, either. Are you just here to soften me up?"

Loren stiffened, anger flashing in her eyes, and then she leaned back with a long sigh. "I wanted to see you, and…" she faltered, "and Craig has lured me in just like he's trying to do to you, I guess. Some of this involves me as well."

Eddie narrowed his eyes first at Craig and then back at Loren. "What part involves you?"

Craig's phone buzzed. He glanced at it and stood. "Look, I have to take care of a few things, and you two have a lot of catching up to do." He stood. "Believe it or not, I get your hesitation. I also know that if you do this, it will be for her, not me."

Eddie said nothing.

Craig continued, undaunted, "I'm a lot of things, Eddie, but I don't invent drama. You know that's true. This is important." He glanced at his phone again and then at Loren. "Listen, go get a drink and catch up." He turned back to Eddie. "She'll fill you in on the details. She understands what's at stake here and she's agreed to help. Listen to her." He started toward the door and turned. "Regardless of what you think of me, you know I wouldn't be here, hat in hand, if it wasn't important." He walked out the front door and closed it behind him.

CHAPTER 6

After Craig's exit, Loren stood and wrung her hands. That could have gone worse.

An awkward moment of silence passed with Eddie standing with her in the living room.

Jeff cleared his throat and announced, "I think Luis and I are going for pizza."

Luis nodded rapidly. "Yeah, pizza. We'll see you guys later."

Loren hugged each of them before they hastily exited.

The house was suddenly cavernous and still. Eddie's square jaw tightened, and his brown eyes narrowed as he searched her face.

So much to say. So much to explain. Where to begin?

Eddie's brown hair was just slightly disheveled, and Loren had to fight back a smile and a sudden urge to fix it. She really wanted to keep this professional—at least until this situation worked itself out. But before really thinking about it, she kissed him slowly, easing her body into him.

What was it about this man that drew her in like this? The tide of the moment threatened to wash her away, so with some effort, she pulled herself back. "Not yet."

Eddie's mouth tightened, but he nodded, searching her face.

Flushed, she tucked her hair behind one ear as she walked into the kitchen, making a show of admiring it as she cooled down. "Nice house. Do Jeff and Luis live here, too?"

Irritation flashed in Eddie's eyes, but he quickly quelled it and shook his head. "The second building has four apartments. They each have their own place there. How's the horse farm business?"

"Good." Loren held his gaze and then looked off toward the living room. "You know, when I was deep undercover, I told myself, if I ever made it home, I'd be happy the rest of my life. If I just had a place where I could sit in safety and security and watch the sunset."

He crossed long arms, but his dark eyebrows lifted expectantly.

She ran a finger along the marble countertop, her nails short and unpolished. "It turned out not to be true. Not completely, at least." She shrugged. "Much to my surprise, I miss the action sometimes, even though I thought I'd had enough of that to last me a lifetime. I..." She faltered again, and the moment stretched between them.

His face was implacable. She couldn't tell if he understood or if he was thankful to be out of the business. It was sometimes scary how little she knew him. How vulnerable she was with a man she'd spent little significant time with.

Eddie pushed off the counter and opened the fridge. "Hungry?"

"Starved," she answered with a smile. Although grateful for the change of subject, she was still unsure how to proceed with him. She'd never had trouble dealing with any man before, really—even when she was younger. They'd always shown an interest in her, and she'd always been able to use that.

Not so with Eddie. He found her attractive, she could see that easily enough, but he never ceded control of a situation. That was unusual, and simultaneously irritating and exhilarating.

Eddie carved up a chicken breast. "It's been a long time."

She paced around the kitchen, taking in different details but not looking at him. "It has..." she trailed off and glanced over.

He shrugged and lifted his gaze to meet hers. "I wasn't sure if we'd ever see each other again."

Loren frowned. Why would he think that? Then she realized that she'd been quiet too long, and she opened her mouth but wasn't sure what to say.

Eddie pulled out a frying pan and placed it on the stove. "You like mushrooms? There are some in the fridge."

Changing the subject again. He was letting her off the hook and playing nice. She opened a cabinet and pulled out a white bowl decorated with little blue flowers. Had Eddie picked these out, or did they come with the house?

He cooked, and she helped in companionable silence. When dinner was ready, he placed a plate in front of her.

She took a bite and smiled. "Wow. Very nice, Mr. Mason. This is good." He never ceased to surprise her.

"I have my moments. All right, what's the story? How'd Craig drag you into this?"

She didn't want to return to this subject. She wanted to talk about how Eddie really felt. Did she haunt him the same way his memory hung around in her mind like smoke after a forest fire? She understood, however, that none of that could happen until he knew why she was here. She swallowed and focused. "I know Sam from way back,"

Eddie asked, "Sam? You two are on a first-name basis?"

"Uh-huh. He's a good man. I owe him, he—well, I just owe him. He saved me. I have, I guess what'd you call a checkered past. It's a long story. I'll tell you someday, when the time is right. Let's just say, indirectly at least, he's how I ended up in the Agency."

Eddie nodded, eyebrows raised. "I would not have guessed that. Okay, we'll add that to the list of things we should probably talk about some day."

She smiled ruefully, and forced herself to avoid thinking about the past, or what was going on with Sam, and focus on the present. Going there would just bring sadness, and she would not be sad today. "Anyway, when I was on my mission, I had a list of men I was to get close to, get information from." She pushed a lock of hair behind her ear. "And mostly, I did. Selik was on that list, but I never interacted with him. I saw him twice, once in Paris, but that's as close as I ever got." She looked up at Eddie. "Craig has photographs of Sam's meeting with Selik. I saw them."

Eddie asked, "Why was the CIA watching him? Do they think Hawthorne's dirty?"

"I don't think so, but it doesn't look good."

Eddie wiped his mouth carefully. "I'm guessing Craig knew that you and Sam know each other?"

"That's why he enlisted my help."

Eddie searched her face. "Have you talked to Sam?"

She nodded. "This afternoon. He was very guarded and upset. Now he's going off on his yacht and leaving his security behind. It looks bad, and I'm worried about him. There has to be more to this story." She let a slow breath out through her nose. "He's very important to me."

Eddie said, "So why would he take me along?"

"I asked him to."

Eddie barked out a laugh. "You must've been pretty confident that you could convince me to go."

She shrugged. "I had to ask him first. Besides, I thought you might do this favor for me."

Eddie looked at her through narrowed eyes. After a long moment, he shook his head with a half grin.

It filled her with warmth and gave her hope. Even with the horrible timing of this situation, and the involvement of Craig, some part of him remained connected to her.

Eddie said, "Why don't you go with him? You're smart, well trained. You could watch him."

"I would, but when the CIA got a line on Selik after the meeting with Sam—well, it was the first time they knew where he was. He's supposed to land at La Romana airport in the Dominican Republic the day after tomorrow. He has a reservation under an alias at a hotel. Craig wants me to go down to see if I can find out what he's doing."

"And you agreed to just leave your life and run down and check it out? You can't miss the action that much."

"You know how Craig is. He's—"

"Blackmailing you."

She shrugged one shoulder. "Yeah, kind of—emotionally, at least. If I don't do this, he'll have to make things difficult for Sam."

Eddie narrowed his eyes and set his jaw.

Loren could feel his anger and concern for her.

Eddie snorted. "Craig really is a bastard." He shook his head. "You can't tell me the Agency doesn't have someone already on the ground there. Why send you?"

"Craig wasn't lying. He likes Sam, and if this is something that would put him in a compromising position..." She shrugged. "If he sends me, it keeps whatever I find in the family, so to speak, until Craig can decide what to do with the information. It makes sense." It sounded like she was trying to convince herself. Was that the case? It was logical, but Craig's maneuvering still pissed her off. She couldn't let too much of that show, though. Not until Eddie made this decision, at least.

He leaned back, the muscles in his cheeks bulging, his voice hoarse and low. "I don't like any of this, Loren. You're not a field officer. This Selik sounds like bad news. Craig is putting you in a compromising position."

She nodded. "Oh, he is, but it doesn't mean that this isn't the best option."

Eddie uncrossed his arms, stood, and paced a few steps away. "Why don't you go with the senator, and I trail this Selik guy?"

She shrugged. "I thought about it. I'm not being foolish about what my capabilities are. Something in my gut tells me Sam is the more dangerous mission. More in line with your skill set than mine."

He turned back toward her, eyebrows raised. "The last time we saw each other..." His eyes darkened.

Last time they'd fallen into each other's arms, and it had been wonderful. She ached for that closeness again. She could feel his desire for her. It was both thrilling and frightening. "I know." She walked over and kissed him softly. "I want to, but I don't want that to play any part in what I'm asking you to do."

Eddie nodded, ever so slightly. "I don't like this, Loren. It all makes me nervous."

She grabbed his hands. "I know. At least have lunch with Sam tomorrow. I think you'll like him, and it'll make this easier for you. Okay?"

"I'm going to regret this. I can feel it."

She smiled. "It'll be fine." Her phone buzzed, and she looked at it. "Craig's here. We'll talk tomorrow after you meet with Sam. It'll be fine, you'll see."

CHAPTER 7

The gated entrance was off the main road, and Eddie assumed it led to an exclusive neighborhood, but no sign or any other marker was visible.

As he pulled up, a guard stepped out of a small building. "Can I help you, sir?"

"Eddie Mason here to see Senator Hawthorne." He counted eleven cameras trained on him from the wall, trees, and metal posts.

The man looked down at his tablet, asked for and checked Eddie's ID, and then nodded. "Have a good day, sir." He gave a thumbs-up to the central camera, and the gate opened.

As Eddie drove on, he continued to replay the conversation with Loren over and over. Last time there'd been immediate fire, but yesterday she'd kept anything physical in check. Were things not the same for her? Maybe her desire for him had cooled. He pushed this thought away. She'd been hesitant, but he saw the longing in her eyes as well. The crappy situation had just cast a pall over the entire conversation.

The driveway wound through dense foliage and landscaping before crossing a wide-open manicured lawn. An expansive three-story house stood at the edge of the water, and a marina filled with gleaming boats lay beyond.

Maybe he was thinking about this all wrong. Last night wasn't a social visit. Loren was on a mission, and she couldn't afford any distractions. He should've recognized that before. Was he already on a mission himself? If so, he'd better get his mind back in the game. Even if he didn't accept the role, something wasn't right here. He needed to keep his wits about him.

At the front, a red-vested attendant ran out, opened his door, and took his keys as a petite, dark-haired woman in an elegant, moss-colored suit appeared at the top of the stairs. "Mr. Mason?"

Eddie nodded.

She smiled. "Welcome to the Sand Dollar Club. Follow me, please." She led him to the rear of the structure and through a polished wooden door.

A panorama of boats at their moorings was visible through tall, narrow windows set into the far wall. Senator Hawthorne sat behind a table covered with a pristine tablecloth, reading the *Wall Street Journal* and sipping coffee from a china cup.

He stood and smiled. "Mr. Mason. Glad to see you. Do you mind if I call you Eddie?"

Tall and very lean, built like a marathon runner. Beneath crisp, bleached shorts, his tan legs were slim and corded with muscle.

Eddie shook his hand. "No, sir, that's fine."

"Great, please just call me Sam. Have a seat."

The senator sat erect, his graying blond hair perfectly groomed, and his alert eyes were the color of old blue jeans. He had the air of command, as he frankly considered Eddie. His voice, however, was calm and inviting. A man in charge who was happy to listen to your concerns and worries. Did it come naturally, or was it a long-rehearsed façade?

Sam smiled. "This is a bit of an odd meeting, isn't it?"

"Yes, sir."

Sam pursed his lips and then asked, "You used to work for Craig?"

"I did," Eddie replied

"But you're no longer part of the Agency?"

"I'm not. I'm a private citizen now."

Sam poured Eddie some coffee and looked sidelong at him. Trying to appear casual, but not quite keeping the underlying interest from seeping through, he asked, "And you know Loren from your time with Craig?"

"Yes, sir." He could sense this man's protectiveness of her.

A moment of awkward silence stretched as the conversation stalled, and then Sam leaned back and asked, "So, what did Loren tell you?"

How to answer that? Mentioning the meeting with Selik seemed unproductive. Better to act as if the senator's cover story was the only thing going on. "You're going to sail down after some rare aircraft, maybe into international waters, and everyone is concerned that you're leaving your security detail behind."

Sam raised a thin, barely visible eyebrow. "Everyone?"

Eddie shrugged. "Loren and the CIA, or I guess Craig, might be more accurate."

Sam nodded and rocked his head from side to side. "That's mostly true. What did you say to that?"

Eddie shrugged. "My first response was, who cares? You're a grown man, you can do what you want."

A faint smile brushed Sam's lips. "What changed your mind?"

Eddie sighed. "Loren."

Sam nodded. "That's the same reason I agreed to meet with you."

Eddie didn't enjoy pinning all of this on her. He felt defensive of her, which surprised him. "You should know that when Loren came to see me, Craig came with her." Eddie couldn't quite keep the irritation out of his voice.

Sam's eyes widened. "Really? I didn't know that. You didn't like that?"

Eddie shrugged. "I don't trust Craig, and he's manipulating her."

Sam's jaw tightened, but he shrugged one shoulder as if it wasn't a big deal and tried to cover his reaction by taking a sip of water. "I think he is, too, but she's a big girl."

Eddie said, "She is, and she's no fool. That doesn't mean I have to like it."

Sam smiled, but the amusement never made it to his eyes. "What did you say to Craig?"

"I asked him why it was any of his business."

Sam snorted. "I'll bet he didn't like that."

Eddie shrugged. "He wanted me to do this, so he put up with it."

"Did he try to justify his position?"

"Of course. He said he was simply concerned about your safety. I told him that if he just wanted someone to guard you, he should go get some gunman he trusts. That's not really what I do."

A knock sounded, and a waiter in a jacket and tie leaned into the room. "Are you ready for lunch, sir?"

Sam looked up and smiled. "Yes, Miguel." Turning to Eddie, he asked, "Is shellfish okay with you?"

Eddie nodded.

Sam turned back. "Yes. Thank you."

Four waiters wheeled a cart in, set the table, left plates of lobster and shrimp, and then disappeared in a quick, organized dance.

Sam gestured. "Please, eat. If you're not a gun for hire, then what are you?"

Eddie shrugged again. That was a good question. Both for his cover here and for his life. How to answer that? "Capable man for hire, I guess you'd call it."

Sam raised his eyebrows. "You get many calls for that kind of thing?"

He snorted. "You'd be surprised. Why did Loren tell you she wanted you to take me along?"

"For appearances, and I suppose another set of eyes. Someone to help keep me out of trouble. She said it would be a simple thing to do to make all the questions go away." He studied Eddie. "She also said if I needed someone watching my back, you'd be her first choice. That's unusually high praise from her."

Both pleased and embarrassed by her admiration, Eddie wasn't sure how to respond.

Sam shook his head. "She's probably right. She's presented a simple solution to this situation that I find myself in. Very like her."

Eddie added dryly, "And very like Craig as well."

Sam frowned. "What do you mean?"

"He has a talent for framing situations where the only logical course left to you is the one he wants you to take. It's a real gift."

Sam chuckled and folded his arms. "Loren says you don't trust Craig very much."

Eddie shook his head. "Not particularly. Craig's always playing his own game. A game played for his benefit and his benefit alone."

"Well said. My sentiments exactly." Sam unfolded his arms, took a bite, and chewed, all the while studying Eddie. "But you do trust Loren?"

Eddie hadn't expected the question, but he nodded almost automatically.

Sam wiped his mouth with a linen napkin. "She also tells me you're from my neck of the woods. Where exactly?"

"The middle of nowhere. A little place called Dickens."

"I know of the place. Not too far from Lubbock, correct?"

Eddie raised his eyebrows. Surprising and impressive knowledge. "Yes, sir." Then he realized that as the chair of the Senate Intelligence Committee, Sam probably had an entire dossier put together on Eddie before this meeting, and that it probably included his elementary school report card. This small talk was all bullshit, probably along with this man's knowledge of the state of Texas.

Sam took a sip of water. "I like places like that. If you ask me, they're the best parts of America."

Eddie nodded. He agreed, but from this guy it sounded like a campaign sound bite.

Sam gazed out over the ocean and frowned. "I find myself in a bit of a spot. I've accidentally created a situation that has the attention of Craig and, by extension, the CIA. So, my simple trip is now under the microscope. If I don't accept some sort of help, then everyone is going to assume I'm up to something bad."

"Are you?"

Sam's eyebrows shot up again. "I guess that's a fair question. It's not anything illegal or anti-American, if that's what you're asking. I'm looking for something. That's all there is to it."

"A plane?"

Sam nodded. "A Helldriver XSB2C-2, a rare dive-bomber on floats. I think there's only one left in the world."

"That would be something. How'd you find out about it?"

Sam waved a hand dismissively. "I'm a bit of a World War II nut. I belong to all the associations, sit on all the museum boards. A fellow collector brought me the information."

Eddie kept his face a mask as he took a drink of water. That was a lie. Even if Eddie hadn't already known it, his gut and his training could tell. "And where do you think it is?"

The senator hesitated. "Not too far from the Turks and Caicos. That's why I don't understand the concern. It's not like I'm going to sail around West Africa or some other pirate hotbed."

"But you're leaving your people home. You must have a reason."

Sam sighed. "I suddenly find that maybe I can't trust everyone on my security team. I can't tell you how disconcerting that is. It's that simple." He took a sip of water. "Speaking of whom to trust and how far, how does one find himself on both the FBI's and CIA's most wanted lists?"

Eddie paused, his fork halfway to his mouth. The question caught him by surprise, but he chided himself for that. He'd already guessed that the senator had checked up on him. With the connections Sam had, he could probably answer that more thoroughly than Eddie could. "That's one reason I don't fully trust Craig. He didn't prioritize protecting and vouching for me when suspicion fell on me, because he had his own agenda. In fact, he didn't help me at all until I could prove my innocence to him." He took the bite and chewed.

"But in the end, they cleared you." A statement, not a question.

Eddie nodded. "Eventually." The bitterness in his voice irritated him.

Sam's eyes narrowed and his voice hardened. "Your frustration is understandable, Eddie. I feel the same way about this situation, and I don't like any of these people being in my private business—Loren included."

Eddie shrugged. "So, tell them to butt out."

Sam's eyes widened, and he grinned. "I see why Loren likes you." He chewed deliberately as he considered this and then wiped his mouth. "That seems unwise and, frankly, a little petty. Craig's heart is usually in the right place, and I really don't want to alienate him. The prudent thing to do is accept this offer from people I consider friends." He fiddled with the stem on his water glass. "It doesn't hurt that I also realize that I really don't have a choice. Hell, if Loren trusts you, then it might be nice to have a little company on the trip, and you get a few days out on the ocean. What do you say?"

Eddie considered the offer. It might also be unwise and a little petty for him to turn this down. He could go along for Loren and maybe get some bargaining chips with Craig. It couldn't hurt, and, like the senator, he wasn't sure he really had much of a choice. Craig had once again put him in a situation where the only reasonable way forward was his way. And it would be unwise to make an outright enemy of the man. He sighed. "I'm inclined to do this for Loren as well, and as you say, it probably isn't wise to aggravate Craig."

"Then it's settled. This should be fun. Loren says that your standard fee is twenty-five thousand a week?"

Eddie didn't have any kind of standard fee. Why had Loren said he did? Where had that come from? "That'll be fine." He nodded out at the boats beyond the window. "Is one of these yours?"

Sam scowled and shook his head. "No, no. We'll leave in a launch from here tomorrow and take it out to my *Morning Star*. I like to get going early. Does 6:00 work for you?"

Eddie wiped his mouth and nodded.

Sam slapped the table with his palm. "It's settled, then. Maybe this will get everyone out of my hair once and for all."

CHAPTER 8

As Eddie drove out through the Sand Dollar Club's winding driveway, he marveled at the situation he suddenly found himself in. Once again, Craig had deftly steered him into a position that forced a quick decision without a lot of options. Into a dangerous situation between the CIA and a powerful and wealthy senator, of all places. How had he done that? The obvious answer was Loren. Was she an accomplice or a pawn herself? That was the question.

The sudden appearance of Craig and Loren, as well as the senator's inquiries, dredged up memories of when everything went to hell. Eddie's role for the CIA had been simple. When an asset, any asset, was on the run and needed immediate extraction or protection, Eddie was there in Europe, waiting. Over seven years, he saved fifty-six agents and secured many more secret packages and deliveries.

During this time, his mission, and to some extent his life, became intertwined with Loren's. She was part of an Agency Operation called Clay Pigeon, which placed five female agents with high interest targets in Saudi Arabia. It was a high-risk assignment, and before it was all said and done, four of the five came to Eddie on the run.

Loren was the first, but it was with Nikki, the second Clay Pigeon, when everything went to hell. Where Loren was careful and calculating, Nikki was brash and aggressive. The worst part was that Nikki thought she was smarter than she actually was. As his mind wandered back to her, he still felt a surge of irritation, even now, years later.

She set a meeting with Eddie between 2 and 3 p.m. at the Café Du Pain Et Des Idées in Paris. Her directions were specific. Sit outside at one of the wooden tables, with three books, two with bookmarks.

She was one for the details, that's for sure. Eddie sat enjoying a pastry. He didn't like the location, however. It was at a "T" intersection with four-story buildings on all sides. A hundred windows overlooked the spot. Too much exposure, too little cover to speak of, and no clear escape routes.

Usually, agents on the run made him wait, observing and only contacting him near the end of the time window. Using every available minute to ensure it was safe. But at 2:12, his phone rang. He turned it over, studied the number while taking a bite of a pastry, and answered. "Oui."

Nikki's voice was husky and laced with irritation. She said in English, "You didn't answer the contact number."

Eddie studied the pastry and brushed off an imaginary particle. "You take precautions and so do I."

Nikki was silent.

Eddie took another bite.

"Okay, we're going to meet at five tonight."

Eddie wiped his mouth. "Not now? How hot is your situation?"

"Not bad at the moment. They don't know I'm gone yet. So, I think being careful is more important than fast."

He glanced around casually. She had to be near here watching. Studying his body language. He shrugged. "Okay. When and where?"

"At five o'clock sharp, start walking along the Rue de Rivoli from the intersection at the Rue Malher."

Not an awful choice. A busy one-way road. Lots of cross streets. Difficult to tail someone in all that mess. He tried to picture the exact corner.

"Start walking along with the traffic, near the curb. Wear dark slacks and a gray blazer. Carry a pink shopping bag in your left hand while you walk."

Eddie frowned. Too many details. Simpler was always better. Besides, where would he find a pink shopping bag?

He opened his mouth, but she rushed on. "Just be there and keep walking toward the Tuileries Garden. Got it?"

Eddie pursed his lips. "Got it."

She hung up.

Eddie sighed. His instincts were flaring, but the meeting was set. No point dwelling on the problems now. He stood and went in search of his props.

The September wind was cool, but by the second block walking the Rue de Rivoli, he was hot and uncomfortable. Soon he would pass his car and begin moving away from it. He considered it his primary asset. Number one, if they used his car, then he'd be the driver, and number two, it was full of hiding places, equipment, and parking-garage access cards that would be useful in a getaway.

He passed street after street until the park was visible ahead on the left. How much further? The road ended near the Place de la Concorde. What then?

A black Mercedes screeched to a stop next to him. The door opened and Nikki leaned across.

Eddie stooped and looked in the open window.

Deeply tanned, with black curls hanging around her oval face, Nikki looked back with narrowed eyes. "What's your code name?"

He furrowed his brow. "Lighthouse. What's the code phrase?"

"Red leaves on a fall wind. Now get in."

Eddie straightened and studied his surroundings. She wasn't alone in the car. It was the right phrase, and it was his job to get in and help her, but he didn't like it. If someone wanted him dead, however, they would have just shot him, so he opened the door and climbed inside.

Nikki put it in gear, let out the clutch, and the car lurched forward, closing the door with the momentum.

Eddie felt the cold steel of a pistol against the base of his skull. He'd expected as much. He looked sidelong into the back seat, moving his head as little as possible.

A woman obviously related to Nikki, but not nearly as pretty or glamorous, her light brown hair pulled back into a ponytail, held the gun. Her eyes were steady. Resolved but not panicky. Thank God for that, at least.

Nikki said, "This is my sister, Miranda, and just in case you're not sure if she knows how to use that thing, I assure you she does. She's a cop, so just behave." *Nikki flashed a self-satisfied smile. She wore a short, clingy, black dress which rode up her muscular legs.*

He could just make out a barbed-wire tattoo circumnavigating her right thigh.

Nikki asked, "Do you have a gun?"

Eddie held her gaze. "I do."

"Why don't you give it to Miranda real slow like."

"I'm supposed to be your protection—"

"Well, as you can see, we don't need much protection, just an escort. So, hand it over or get out."

Should he refuse? See if she was bluffing. If not, would she contact him again? This was his job, so he gritted his teeth and reached into his jacket.

The pistol pressed harder against his head.

"Easy." *He pulled the Sig from his holster and, holding it by the barrel, handed it into the back seat.*

Nikki nodded and made a turn.

Eddie noted the Castiglione street sign. Heading northeast. Deeper into the city.

Nikki kept glancing into the rearview mirror. She sped up, weaving in and out of traffic. "Got any others?"

Eddie shook his head. "No. It's not good for my cover to get caught with guns."

Nikki said, "Well, we'll see about that. Now, how does this usually work?"

"When I've secured a runner, I set up an exchange."

She looked sidelong at him. "With who?"

"Art Tullis. My contact."

"Always the same contact?"

Eddie nodded.

"For how long?" *Nikki asked.*

"I don't know. A long time. Years."

She pursed her lips. "Where do you usually meet? Here in Paris?"

"If it's appropriate."

"Well, it ain't this time. Where else?"

He'd recently spent some time on the coast. He knew a dependable retired doctor in that area and had access to a boat there. Options were always good. "Honfleur is out of the city, but not too far away."

"Normandy, huh? All right, I think that'll do." As she spoke, she kept touching a small, beaded, black clutch next to her hip. Whatever she'd hidden there was important.

With both women watching him like a hawk, Eddie called his contact and set up the meet.

The three-hour drive passed mostly in silence. He tried a few times to engage them in conversation, but after a few terse answers, the conversations stalled. Out of the corner of his eye, he could see the tension in Nikki. No matter how she tried to mask it, her fear was obvious.

They parked near the designated meeting site, and as they stepped out of the car, Eddie got his first proper look at the two women. Miranda was in jeans, a flannel shirt, and work boots. Practical and stoic. Nikki was in the stupid dress and high-heeled pumps. She wouldn't be able to outrun anyone, but she'd look good until they caught her. He shook his head.

Nikki picked up the little, sparkly purse and gripped it in one fist. Tossing the keys on the driver's side floor, she said, "We won't be needing Khali's damned Mercedes anymore. Someone's going to get a nice car."

Miranda's brow furrowed, and her attention darted between Eddie and Nikki. She clearly didn't like the situation either, but held her tongue.

Nikki turned and started walking.

Miranda met Eddie's gaze and then motioned him forward with the gun.

They crossed the street and headed down a murky side road. The starry sky was calm and clear, but the smell of coming rain was on the wind.

Eddie said, "Give me my gun back. I'm not going to be much help to you unarmed."

Nikki turned to him, her eyes dark pools in the shadows. "If this meet isn't on the level, your gun isn't going to make a damn bit of difference." Her tone was an odd mixture of resignation and defiance.

"It might not be a bad idea," Miranda said.

Nikki shook her head. "Trust me." She turned back to Eddie. "I appreciate your help but until I look into the eyes of someone I know, and trust," she nodded toward her sister, "she's the only one carrying a gun."

Eddie ground his teeth. Again, she knew he wouldn't refuse.

They turned and made their way down an alley to the park and stopped across the street. It sat raised above the road, the streetlights painting lines across the stone square at the center. Quiet.

With a nod from Nikki, Eddie crossed the street. He felt naked without a gun and his heart thudded in his chest. With one last check in both directions, he climbed the small staircase.

Art sat on a bench on the far side, wearing a ball cap—the all-clear sign. He nodded.

Eddie returned the gesture and motioned Nikki and her sister up the steps.

Art stood and started forward. A bullet hole appeared in his forehead, like a trick of the light. It just appeared without a sound. Art stumbled, stepped back, and fell heavily on the bench.

"Get down!" Eddie shouted as he grabbed Nikki's wrist. He twisted to grab Miranda, who stood legs apart, pistol out, moving jerkily back and forth at the empty darkness.

Two soft spurts.

The pistol flew from Miranda's hand. She faltered a half step toward Eddie and then fell, landing on her back. A dark stain spread across her shirt from two holes just below her collarbone.

Nikki screamed and lunged toward Miranda, yanking Eddie around behind her.

Eddie fought to regain his footing. Where was the shooter?

Nikki continued to scream, staring down at her sister.

Eddie grabbed her, trying to pull her down when a searing pain striped his side above his hip. At least he now had a sense of where the enemy was. He steadied himself, grabbed Nikki around the waist, and pulled her over his hip as he lay back. He needed her behind him.

Her scream turned to a bloody gargle as a bullet struck her in the throat. It exited through her back and whistled by his ear.

He growled. Another bullet struck him below his right rib cage, then a second bullet hit her in the head, and he let her go, falling back against the hard brick ground.

Nikki folded, and her lifeless body fell on top of him.

Keeping his head still, he scanned the ground for Miranda's snub nose revolver. It couldn't be far. Should he feel around for it or lie here and play dead?

He strained to hear anything above the wind rustling the leaves. His right hip was on fire, and he could feel blood running down his side. Nikki's body was limp and lifeless. Craning his neck, he slowly scanned the mottled interior of the park. Nothing moved. Were they coming to finish the job, or had they fled?

Someone laughed a short distance away, followed by muffled conversation. Time to move. Coming witnesses would drive the killers to act now or flee. Either way, Eddie had to get going.

He twisted and made it to all fours, and felt something hard under his knee—Nikki's sister's pistol. He shoved it into his waistband, then searched for the clutch that had been so important to Nikki, finally finding it under her left leg. Thrusting it into his pocket, he pushed off the ground and forced himself to his feet. His right knee tremored and threatened to buckle. Blood flowed out between the fingers he had clamped to his side.

The bodies of the two women lay in awkward, lifeless positions. He gritted his teeth. Damn it. He collected his bearings and then hobbled out of the park, then stopped and leaned against a wall to gather his strength. He'd never lost an agent in his custody before. Some were already dead by the time he reached them, and a few had simply never showed up at a meet, but this was the first one killed on his watch. He squeezed his eyes shut and swore.

Back at the Mercedes, he stopped to check his injuries in the light of a streetlamp. One bullet just caught his side, leaving a long channel through his skin. A nasty cut, but nothing worse. The second had gone through him clean between his ribs and hip.

He would live, but he needed to stop the bleeding. He pulled out his cell phone. Wiping sweat from his eyes, he dialed his CIA contact number, and it rang twice before a mechanical voice announced in French that this was not an active line.

Eddie stared at the phone. It was the right number. He tried again, once more hearing the recorded message. Exactly how wrong were things? His side throbbed.

Ten minutes later, Eddie pulled the Mercedes up in front of the cottage belonging to Doctor Alphonzo Gomez. His head swam, and he steadied himself, grabbed the pistol off the seat, and stumbled to the house.

The rotund doctor answered the door in his bathrobe. "Eddie! My God, what happened?"

Eddie flinched from a stab of pain. "The less you know, the better, Doc."

He stepped aside and motioned Eddie inside. "Come in. Come in."

Later, after the doctor dressed his wound, and he'd regained some of this strength, Eddie drove the Mercedes to within a block of the sailboat. Nothing moved on the dark road. Not surprising at 3 a.m. He looked in the back and found a stack of fashion magazines. He lit them and placed them under the driver's seat. Within minutes, the interior of the car was ablaze.

Eddie turned and hobbled down to the docks. The ground moved as if he was already on the boat, and he stopped twice to collect himself before pushing on. When he finally reached the craft, he leaned on the rail, and then hauled himself aboard. His side burned and his vision swam. He stumbled down into the cabin. Groaning, he rolled over onto his back and closed his eyes.

• • •

Now, years later, his anger at the memory still surprised Eddie. He learned well after the fact that the information Loren brought back the prior year was devastating to whomever the Clay Pigeons were working against. This time they were more prepared, and by the time Nikki ran, they already had a mole in the CIA.

Eddie still had to remind himself that it didn't matter what he or Nikki did that day. Whatever precautions they employed. The mole was still going to pass on the location of the meeting, so inevitably, the gunmen were there waiting. As an additional protection, the mole disconnected Eddie's contact number that night as well.

It was just their good luck that Eddie spent eighteen hours passed out on the boat. By then, the authorities discovered Nikki and Miranda's bodies, and no one had heard anything from him. The mole had plenty of time to plant the seed that it was Eddie who killed them. Why else hadn't he checked in? Why else had he disappeared?

This was the part that bothered Eddie the most. Craig should have known that he was innocent. Or at least given him the benefit of the doubt.

When he finally got through to the CIA, the mole intercepted the call, set up a meeting no one else knew about, and tried to kill Eddie. He almost succeeded, too.

Eddie found himself cut off from the CIA, and wanted for murder in a foreign and suddenly hostile land. They'd trained him well, and he'd always been good on his feet. So he ran. With his training and resources, they would never catch him. At least, that was what he believed then. However, Fate wasn't done with him yet. But that was another story.

Ironically, it was another Clay Pigeon who brought Loren back into this life and produced proof of his innocence. But he was on the run a long time before that happened. He rubbed his face as if he could scrub all the terrible memories away.

Now Craig and Loren were back, disrupting his life again. This time they dragged a U.S. senator into the picture, just to up the stakes. A senator who had just tried to deceive him. If Eddie believed Loren and Craig, then Senator Sam Hawthorne had lied to him about the plane and how he'd come across the information.

What did that mean? Nothing obligated Sam to explain himself to anyone, especially Craig. Maybe everyone was blowing this out of proportion.

Eddie shook his head. The whole situation stank. Hopefully, he could simply ride along for a week, and then this would all be over. Probably naïve, but he desperately hoped it was true.

CHAPTER 9

When Eddie returned to the house, Jeff and Luis were sitting at the kitchen counter eating sandwiches. A funny pair—one dark and muscular and the other pale, short, and skinny.

Jeff asked, "How'd it go?"

Eddie sighed. "I guess I'm going to take a boat ride around the Caribbean."

Luis put down his sandwich. "You trust this guy?"

Eddie grabbed a chip off a plate. "He definitely wasn't telling me the whole truth. I mean, he's supposed to be this big World War II buff who discovered a rare airplane, but he didn't ask me if I knew anything about the war, or that time in history, or aircraft. Usually, people like that want to talk about their hobby, especially a big new discovery, but he just threw out the plane model number as if checking off a box. It didn't ring true."

Luis frowned. "You worried?"

Eddie said, "Only a little—at least so far. But I do have a favor to ask."

He narrowed his dark eyes. "Anything."

"While I'm with the senator, Craig is going to send Loren down to the Dominican Republic to find out what she can about the senator's contact. She's smart and capable, but she isn't trained to do that sort of thing, and I'm not sure I entirely trust that she's being straight about all of this. I want to send you with her if that's okay?"

Luis shrugged. "Sure, no problem. You think she'll agree?"

Eddie nodded. "I'll make her. I appreciate it." He turned to Jeff. "Can you find out who we know down in Haiti or the Dominican? We need to get Luis some firepower. The senator and I are supposedly headed down that way as well. I might need an escape plan. We'll need some guns and maybe someone we can count on in that part of the world."

Jeff said, "No problem."

Eddie took a seat. "It makes me nervous to be on a boat in the middle of the ocean with no way home. It puts me at the senator's mercy, and I don't like that. So also see if you know someone who has a big boat or a plane nearby that we can borrow or rent or something if we need it."

Jeff nodded. "I'll make some calls and see what I can come up with."

Eddie turned back to Luis. "Where are the tactical bags with the hidden bottoms?"

Luis stood. "I think they're in the storage room in the garage. I'll find them."

A beep sounded.

Jeff glanced up at the monitor. "Looks like Craig and Loren are back." He moved toward the door. "I'll let them in. I need to go get my computer and start calling people, anyway."

A moment later, they entered, and Loren studied Eddie. "How'd it go?"

He shrugged. "As well as can be expected, I guess."

Craig furrowed his brow. "Are you going?"

Eddie held up two fingers. "On two conditions."

"I'm listening."

"One, Luis goes with Loren to the Dominican. I want someone I trust watching her back and close enough to help me if I need it."

Craig looked over at Loren, bushy black eyebrows raised.

She studied Eddie and then nodded. "I don't suppose you'll give me a choice."

Eddie shook his head. "Correct."

Craig gave a quick nod. "What else?"

Eddie said, "You give me some intelligence support on the stuff I do here. If I need a background check or some information that only you can get, you help me out."

The skin around Craig's dark eyes crinkled. "You could've always asked for that. I would've helped you."

Eddie snorted. "Maybe this just makes it more palatable to me, and less like I'll owe you something in return."

Craig shrugged. "If that's how you want it to be, then we have a deal. When do you leave?"

"Tomorrow."

Craig nodded. "I appreciate it, Eddie. Watch this guy's back until I can figure out what's going on."

Eddie turned to Loren. "When do you fly out?"

"Tomorrow, mid-morning." She frowned. "I guess we need to get another ticket."

Craig rubbed his hands together. "I'll go take care of that and get some other things going." He turned to Loren. "Want to stay here while I get the ball rolling?"

She raised her eyebrows at Eddie.

He looked into her eyes and nodded. "Yeah, I'd like to catch up."

Loren walked around Eddie's bedroom as he packed clothes into the small tactical bag Luis had found for him. "This place doesn't really feel like you. It's way too fancy."

Eddie snorted. "Oh, it is, but it serves our purposes. It's like a damn fortress."

"How'd you find it?"

He rubbed his neck. "Let's just say it was part of my separation package from Craig. I guess the person who owned it before me did—I don't know, off-the-books work for him."

Loren frowned. "What happened to them?"

He'd wondered that many times. "Whatever it was, they didn't need the house anymore." He reached underneath the bag and held his finger at a certain spot, and a drawer popped out of the hard-plastic bottom.

Loren's green eyes widened. "Very nice."

Eddie grinned. "I had these made last year." He placed two Sig Sauer pistols, a few clips, two satellite phones, and a lock-picking kit into the compartment and snapped it closed.

She looked from the bag to him. "You're certainly fully prepared."

He shrugged. "That's the problem. I'm not really sure what to prepare for."

She walked over and stood very close to him. "I do appreciate this. More than I can tell you. You know that, right?"

Eddie nodded.

"Take care, Sam and yourself, okay? When this is over, we can talk for real."

He looked down into her eyes. "Not now?"

She stepped away. "It's all too raw. You know, when we finally talk about what happened, we're going to have to sort through some stuff. It'll distract us. We need to keep our heads clear until this is all worked out."

Eddie frowned. "I suppose you're right. It's not the time or place." His brows drew together. "How exactly did Craig blackmail you into this?"

She shrugged. "He said if I didn't help, he'd have no choice but to make things difficult for Sam. Expose his actions to the powers-that-be."

The fact that Craig was pressuring her made it easier to accept somehow. Less like she was just taking advantage of him. "How the hell do you know Sam Hawthorne?"

She looked over, a crease in her forehead. "I wasn't always..." She lifted and dropped her hands. She shrugged. "I have a bit of a past."

Eddie raised his eyebrows. "So you said before. Not only is that not an answer, it just adds more questions."

She ran a finger along a carving on the headboard. "I promise, I'll tell you all of it. Just not now. Not before we have to go on these trips. I made some poor decisions, and Sam could have made life very difficult for me. But he made another choice." She looked over at him. "Let's make this pact. When this is over, no matter what happens, we will meet someplace and talk."

"I wanted to last time, I just didn't..."

She walked back to him. "I know, me too." She stood up on her tiptoes and kissed him gently. "We need to see each other without all of this intrigue, so we can figure out if this is real, you know?"

"Yes, I do," he said and kissed her again.

CHAPTER 10

Just after sunrise, Eddie and the senator left the Sand Dollar Club in a sixty-foot Hatteras fishing boat. Eddie sat in one of the rear chairs, his bag on the deck between his ankles. The early morning air was cool, and the ocean was calm. The sunrise and the salty sea air, however, failed to calm him. Why was he doing this? What did Loren mean by a checkered past? So many questions.

Craig was playing him. Hell, he was always playing some kind of game. The senator was almost certainly playing him as well. Was Loren playing him, too? That was the key question. Not only for this mission, but maybe for his life. These doubts kept fluttering around his brain like moths.

Sam was in the cockpit with the captain, driving the boat out himself. The man liked to be in control.

The hull sliced easily through the water as it raced away from the Miami skyline. Sam had been polite, but brisk, at the club—ready to get going. "Here she is." He pointed ahead at the stern of a large yacht, the name *Morning Star* stenciled across her transom in white, block letters.

As they came alongside the craft, Eddie whistled.

Three decks stood stacked above a navy-blue hull that stretched on and on. Sam was much wealthier than Eddie had realized. "How long is she?"

Sam grinned like a schoolboy. "Two hundred and thirty feet. She's something, isn't she?"

Eddie nodded. The resources this man had access to, combined with his power and influence as a senator, were staggering. Just how far in over his head was he? A new thought suddenly weighed on his mind. It was a simple thing to make a body disappear at sea.

A staircase unfolded and stretched down to the water. As they approached the ship, Sam grabbed a worn leather bag, narrowed his light-blue eyes, and said, "Just to make sure we're on the same page, you work for me, right? I mean, I know you are doing this to placate Loren and Craig, but you're here to help me. Is that correct?"

Eddie cocked his head to one side. An important question with a complicated answer, which surprised Eddie a little. He was here as a favor for Loren and Craig, but they wanted someone to look out for Sam. "It's your money and your boat. They want me to help, but I work for you."

"Okay, then here's what I want. I've already discovered that I can't trust my security people. It makes me wonder just how compromised I am." He looked up at the massive ship towering above them. "I gave most of my people the week off, so we're down to a skeleton crew. You have free rein on the ship. Keep an eye on everyone. Anything you need, or if something just seems wrong, you come tell me right away. Got it?"

Gone was the genial host from yesterday's lunch. In his place was the man used to giving commands and having them obeyed.

Eddie nodded. "Yes, sir."

"Good." Sam stepped up onto the stairs and climbed.

Eddie grabbed his bag, jumped nimbly over, and followed.

At the top of the staircase, the captain, tall and Nordic looking, stood at attention in a crisp, white uniform complete with shoulder boards and gold braiding. Behind him, five shorter men wearing light blue uniforms stood in a military at-ease posture, hands clasped behind their backs.

Sam smiled and greeted the captain and crew.

As part of his Agency mission, Eddie spent a great deal of time around very wealthy people, and in his experience, most fell into two categories when it came to "*the help*." They were either rude to the people serving them or didn't notice them at all.

How Sam interacted with the waiters at the club and the crew here said something about his character. He was respectful and attentive as he addressed each of them by name.

Eddie grew up in a place where manners and integrity defined a man. He didn't believe someone could fake that, and the senator's behavior impressed him.

Sam turned. "Captain Jon Hoksrud, this is our guest, Eddie Mason." He gestured to include the rest of the crew in his comments. "He has free access to the ship, understand?"

The blue-uniformed crew members were short round-faced men, with coffee-and-cream-colored skin. They appeared so much alike that Eddie wondered if they were related. All raised dark eyebrows at the statement but nodded without comment.

Why the surprised reaction? Was it unusual for someone to have this type of access? Or was one or all of them a conspirator? Was something sinister really at play here, or was this all being blown out of proportion? There was just so much Eddie didn't know, and if he wasn't careful, this ignorance was going to cause him to see everything as suspicious.

Sam introduced the members of the crew quickly. Each nodded in greeting, their expressionless faces revealing nothing. He motioned for Eddie to follow. "Come on, I'll give you a tour."

As they walked along the deck, Eddie asked, "Is that everyone on board right now?"

"Afraid so. It's enough to keep her moving, but that's about it. We have a cook, but no waiters or other nonessential personnel." He turned to Eddie with a half grin. "We'll be roughing it a bit."

Eddie tucked this piece of information away. By leaving his security detail behind, and then most of his crew, was Sam reducing the number of witnesses, or possibly the number of people to eliminate? Or was there truly cancer within the senator's organization? Maybe all the above?

Of course, the other possibility was that Sam was just trying to prove a point to the CIA. This all could be just some sort of power play between the senator and Craig. He was, after all, dealing with two colossal egos.

Eddie's attention slid over the decking. Brass screws in laser perfect lines pinned down small two-inch wide planks one after the other into the distance. He'd worked construction as a kid, and he knew precision, artisan work when he saw it and marveled at the care and attention even down to this little detail.

The opulent interior was even more impressive. Room after room of marble floors, dark wood paneling, and theatrical lighting. It had a pool, media room, and gym. Eddie moved Sam's category from very rich to crazy rich. The senator was clearly proud of the craft, but his tour was swift, business-like, and focused more on the layout than the accoutrements. Eddie was an employee, not a guest.

The master suite was located off the main living area and larger than Eddie's first apartment in college. Sam set his small bag on the bed, then led Eddie back into the plush living room. He was about to head downstairs when he halted. "Hold on a second." Sam hurried back into the bedroom, closing the door behind him.

Eddie waited, looking out the windows at the ocean beyond, when he heard a metallic click from the bedroom. He turned as the senator reemerged. What was that sound?

Sam said, "Sorry, I thought I forgot something. Come on. I'll show you where you're sleeping."

At the waterline level, they entered a small living room with four suites beyond. "It's only us, so pick whichever one you like."

All were enormous and over-the-top, like they'd leaped from the pages of a magazine. Eddie dropped his bag on the bed in the nearest, and they continued the tour.

In his time in the military, Eddie had seen a thousand cockpits on crafts that floated, flew, and drove—all crammed with high-tech gadgets and gear. Still, the *Morning Star's* command center shamed them all.

The room was a semicircle with a backlit stained-glass ceiling depicting Neptune flanked by mermaids. Two plush leather captain chairs sat in front of a grand, polished wooden wheel. The dashboard was full of scopes, lights, and computer monitors. A screen at least fifty inches wide sat to one side, displaying a map with a radar representation of every vessel in the area moving in real time.

Eddie whistled.

Sam nodded with just the hint of a smirk. "We have all the latest technology."

They continued down to the engine room and lower levels and then came up on the bow of the incredible ship outside the master cabin. A small Zodiac inflatable boat sat strapped to the deck.

Eddie had not seen one piece of equipment he assumed one would use to locate an aircraft on the ocean floor. No air tanks, small robotic submarines, nor any other type of specialty gear. They weren't off to search for a submerged plane. So, where were they actually going, and why?

He turned to the senator. "I'm not sure what I'm supposed to be doing."

"Look for any sign that I have a mole or someone else I can't fully depend upon. Watch my back. Beyond that, I guess look for anything that might be a threat."

Eddie cocked his head to one side. "Like, maybe the CIA itself."

Sam half grinned. "Maybe." Then his smile faded. "Do you think they could've bugged or tracked *The Morning Star*?"

Eddie frowned. "I wouldn't put anything past the Agency."

"But wouldn't we be too far from land for them to receive some sort of transmission?"

"Probably. I don't know much about that kind of technology, so I can't be sure. They can do all kinds of things with satellites, though, and there are devices that simply record and store, to be retrieved and examined later."

Sam's brow furrowed. "Of course. I should've thought of that. If someone planted such a device on *The Morning Star*, could you find it?"

Eddie shrugged. "I'll do my best. It's not really my specialty, but I'll look around."

Sam said, "I don't want to be a fool. See if you see anything unusual. I know most of the crew, but then again, I thought I knew my security detail. If you see anything I should be worried about, let me know. If not, we'll tell Craig to relax when we get home, and maybe he'll get off my back." A muscle pulsed in his cheek.

Eddie nodded. "I can do that."

"Good, get started. I'm going to go get us underway."

Eddie looked back at the distant Miami skyline. Were Craig and the Agency overreacting? Or were they sailing toward real danger?

CHAPTER 11

Frank tried to keep the rolling to a minimum as he piloted the dark tactical boat through the swells. It wasn't an overly large craft, and they were in the real grown-up ocean now. He'd trained on boats, but this was at the edge of his capability, and he had a healthy respect for the unrelenting power of the surrounding water.

He'd never done an assault at sea before, and he mulled over the pros and cons. The remoteness was the primary advantage. Little chance someone would stumble across the scene. It would just be them and the senator. Also, no place for his quarry to hide. Of course, that was true of the hunter and the hunted, and that was a worry if this somehow all went south.

A flash of lightning lit a mass of clouds on the horizon, and then a second followed suit. The bolts highlighted their outlines, making them look like Portuguese man o' wars.

Frank traced the blue path on the GPS, leading to his prearranged destination. It should take him well south of the storm and into calm waters. He pushed the throttle forward and picked up speed.

Mack made his way back to him adjusting his equipment belt and sat in the copilot's seat.

Frank leaned down and spoke over the engine. "You ever do a job at sea before?"

Mack shook his head. "Only in training."

Frank said, "We need to be fast. It has to be over before they know what hit them."

If the shit hit the fan, it would be a son of a bitch to get away clean. All that water would work against him. That was definitely a con. Frank didn't like missions without clear, easy escape routes.

The sun passed behind a cloud, and for a moment the sea darkened. Waves rose and fell like muscles rippling beneath a black, oily skin, and the vulnerability of the situation made him feel exposed and nervous.

Frank switched his thoughts back to the positive. He had the element of surprise. Gemini had assured him they would have superior speed, and he had an excellent team with him.

His men sat back-to-back down the middle of the craft, their heads down, hunched forward against the salty spray. They waited patiently for the call to action—seasoned soldiers of fortune and experienced killers, the lot of them. Again, they were probably overkill, but Frank held to the concept of victory through overwhelming firepower. And he believed at his core that you can never have too many men.

He glanced over at Mack. Once again, the kid looked like he was ready to leap overboard just to get into battle a second sooner.

Frank suppressed a smile and shook his head. Many men under his command had died over the years. They were soldiers, just as he was, and soldiers died in combat; that was the way of things. He lived with them, trained them, took pride in them, and drank a toast to them when they fell.

His smile faded. Twice in his career, however, a soldier stood out and became like family. The first was during the original Gulf War, a stupid redneck out of Mississippi named Charley. He was from some piss-water, backwoods town no one ever heard of, but he was a hell of a soldier. When he died, it was so stupid. So pointless.

The enemy had only been shooting at Frank's squad to harass them. He didn't think they were even aiming. One round made it through the slit in the Humvee's metal window, a million to one chance, and found Charley's neck between his helmet and his flak vest—a billion to one shot.

It was the shot that changed Frank forever. If that was how life was going to be, then he was going to be that way back. It was suddenly clear to him that you had to take your piece out of the middle before the Grim Reaper got you. From that moment on, things stopped being about duty and honor and were more and more about himself.

He remained isolated from the men after that, and for the better part of a decade, they were just his soldiers. Then he met this pain-in-the-ass Mack. Probably the only man in the world who Frank really thought of as a friend. This crazy, talented, hotheaded, impulsive kid who never all-the-way listened. Probably as close to a son as he was likely ever to have. He and Mack had worked together ever since.

Frank lit another cigar and coaxed it to life. He let all these negative thoughts float away. Time to settle into this calm before the storm. The ebb before the wave.

For over an hour, they motored southeast along the line of the Bahamian shelf on the edge of the real deep water.

Mack shaded his eyes against the sun. "We're getting close. What exactly are we looking for?"

Frank shrugged. "Some kind of boat." Then he noticed a dark shape off to his right. "What's that?"

The younger man lifted a pair of binoculars. "It's a ship. Low slung. Man, she's big, at least a hundred feet."

"Gemini to Crossbow," came a voice over the radio.

Frank lifted the mic and responded, "This is Crossbow, go ahead."

"Right on time. This is your ride; keep to the shadows and stay frosty. Gemini out."

Frank checked the surrounding sky. Where was he? How was it he could see them but still be out of sight? When no obvious answers presented themselves, Frank put it out of his mind, for now.

The ship sat at anchor, dark and quiet. Mack was right. She was big, with a low profile and a slanted back. She looked fast as hell. Frank drove a circuit around the expensive-looking craft before approaching from the rear, the tactical boat jerking back and forth in the swells.

He leaned down to Mack. "Heat up and get everyone unstrapped and ready. I don't like just pulling up here with our pants down." Frank doubted there would be any trouble, but he'd learned a long time ago to assume that nowhere was safe.

The younger man nodded, pulled his sidearm, and lurched forward, making a twirling motion with one finger. The men stood, checked their gear, and took positions.

Frank brought the nose up slowly to the stern, and one soldier leaped on deck with a rope.

Right behind him, Mack and two other men boarded the craft, weapons drawn and ready.

Frank remained at the wheel but reached down and unsnapped his Glock.

The two boats bumped into each other with a hollow sound, and a salty spray shot up between them.

He studied the quiet ship, his shoulders tense and his senses alert.

Mack reappeared and gave the all-clear sign.

Frank let some of the tension out of his body. He killed the engine, moved forward, and leaped onto the yacht's back deck. Extravagant, the craft appeared to be in the middle of a refurbishment; cabinet doors were missing in the kitchen, dark glue lines zig-zagged the bare living room floor, and the hallways were half painted.

Frank took in his surroundings and barked, "Mack, go find the cockpit and make sure this thing has keys or whatever it needs. Mike, go check the engines and the fuel supply. José, secure our boat and give it enough rope so that we can tow her. The rest of you find out where we can store this stuff and bunk everyone."

Frank opened the refrigerator and grinned. It was full of beer. He pulled out a can, opened it, and took a swig. He had to admit he rather enjoyed working for Gemini.

A short, muscled man came into the kitchen. "This baby has two Lycoming gas turbines, three water jets, and enormous tanks."

Frank looked down his nose at him and tossed him a beer. "What does that mean to me, Mike?"

Mike grinned. "She can go real, real fast, for a long time."

Frank nodded. "Good."

Most of the rest of the men gathered in the kitchen and Frank distributed cans to them as well.

Mack arrived. "We can take her for a ride whenever you're ready."

Frank nodded. "Then let's see what she can do."

Before Mack could move, however, a deeply tanned bald man stuck his head around the corner. "Hey, Cap, you should take a look at this."

They followed him into a large area in the bow. In the middle of the vacant room was an aluminum tubing sled about four feet long. At its center was a polished silver cylinder with wires and lights attached to it. Two red plastic five-gallon gas cans sat strapped to either end.

Frank grinned. "Be careful, boys, this is our bomb. We're going to kill a senator and an important one at that, and it has to look like an accident. I'm told if we set this next to the engine, then the marks on the wreckage will look just like a tragic engine explosion, even to a lab."

He looked at the men, making sure he had their full attention. "Remember, this has to look like an accident. If at all humanly possible, don't shoot anyone. Leave no evidence. According to Gemini, the senator isn't supposed to have his security detail with him. This should be a milk run. But you men know nothing's ever as easy as the generals think it is, so stay frosty."

They grinned.

Frank fixed them with a steely gaze. "If we do this right, we're going to head down to Brazil afterward. Have a little fun." He liked the group's expression and body language. The men looked ready to go. "According to our intel, the senator set sail this morning. We already have a device hidden on his vessel. Every seven minutes it pings. So, we'll know exactly where he is, and we're just going to slide in a few miles behind them, wait for our moment, and then help him have a little engine trouble."

The men chuckled.

Frank continued, "Do this job well, boys, and we'll get a well-earned rest in Rio. So, who wants to bunk with the bomb?"

CHAPTER 12

Loren met Luis at the airport and once again found herself on a plane, leaving her life further behind. He was like a panther—dark and quiet, moving with a kind of fluid grace that spoke of athleticism and danger. Maybe more like a loyal dog, waiting for the order to attack. Unsettling thoughts. She wasn't in a position to refuse Luis' company, but she didn't like it.

Luis barely spoke, which was both welcome and unnerving. Loren didn't really know him. She didn't really know Eddie all that well, either, but Luis was like a black hole, offering nothing but taking in everything around him.

Additionally, Eddie, a very capable and deadly man, spoke of Luis as another level of lethal. Also, both reassuring and terrifying. Loren wasn't afraid of Luis, but she found him unsettling, and now she was on her way to a foreign country with a stranger. She felt manipulated by Craig, and to a lesser extent Eddie, and she was getting sick of it.

At least with Eddie, she knew he was just trying to protect her again. She smiled, remembering the first time he saved her. He was different then. More innocent somehow. Good at his job, though. Thank God, because she'd been in trouble.

The thought of that gloomy little park in Paris, all those years ago, still made her shiver. Nestled in a canyon of skyscrapers, it was a foreboding dreary place, particularly once the sun fell below the buildings. She couldn't even remember why she'd chosen to meet there, of all places, especially at night.

The minute Eddie entered the area and moved in her direction, however, there was something about him. He radiated calm capability. She studied him in the pool of light from a lamppost. Right on time, and right where she asked him to wait.

Just as she was about to step out, the hair on the back of her neck stood on end and she turned. At the far end of the park, Dami, her mark, and one of his henchmen, Abar, entered.

After all these years, she still thought of her targets as marks, no matter what nomenclature the Agency used. How did they find her?

Out of the corner of her eye, she saw Eddie melt back into shadows about ten feet from her. He recognized and understood the threat.

She'd scouted the area carefully beforehand. Ahead was the main entrance, but three other exits lay behind her.

The two men stopped in front of the sculpture, eyes to the front, standing maybe twenty-five feet away with their backs to her. They knew this was the rendezvous, so all they needed to do was just stand there. Their presence alone would prevent the meeting. That was bad enough, but if they caught her...

She tensed and gathered herself, ready to run, when Eddie floated slowly toward her. He stopped a few feet away and held up his hands. She could just make out a pistol in one. With exaggerated care, he slid the weapon into his waistband. Again, he held them up, palms facing out. He glanced over at the two men still standing with their backs to them, then eased over beside her.

In a whisper he said out of the corner of his mouth, "I'm the Lighthouse." His posture alert but not tense.

Loren's gut said to trust him, not that she had a lot of options at the moment.

He held his hand out to her, and after a hesitation, she took it.

Did Eddie have any idea how dangerous and motivated the two men not thirty feet away were? She hoped so, because her life depended on him now.

He led her through the foliage, away from Dami and the main entrance.

So, he'd done his homework as well. She cursed the stupid dress and pumps. Not exactly ideal for an escape, but she hadn't had a lot of time or options.

A short metal gate with a chain and padlock blocked the pathway out. Eddie leaped nimbly over and then turned, once again offering her a hand.

She lifted one leg and the awkward angle made her twist her foot in the damned high heel. She bumped it, causing the lock and chain to clang. Eddie caught her with one hand and with the other snatched the lock before it could hit again, but the damage was done.

She kicked off both shoes and vaulted over the gate. They ran along the passageway and down the staircase at the end.

The chain clanged again behind them. Dami was coming.

At the bottom, they burst out onto the street. Eddie let go of her hand and pointed to a dark BMW parked down the block on the other side of the street.

Loren nodded and sprinted. Her feet slapped on the pavement, still damp from an earlier rain.

A shot rang out and Eddie returned fire.

She yanked open the passenger door and leaped in.

Eddie jumped in just after her. He started the car and threw it into gear. It slid sideways, caught, and shot forward.

A large black Mercedes sedan zoomed out of a side street into their path.

Eddie braked. The car skidded forward on the wet pavement, stopping barely a foot from the other vehicle. He jammed the BMW into reverse, swung the nose around, and shifted again. The acceleration pushed Loren back into her seat.

Dami was in the middle of the road. He tried to level his pistol, but Eddie and Loren were too close. His shot went high as he dove out of the way.

Loren turned. The Mercedes collected Dami before racing after them.

Eddie held out his pistol. "Cover us."

She nodded and took it.

He put his hand back on the wheel and immediately turned, and she had to brace herself on the door as the tires squealed in protest. Two cars in their path screeched to a halt, and Eddie shot between them. He glanced at the rearview mirror. "They're motivated, I'll give them that."

Loren looked over her shoulder and noticed the Mercedes a few cars back, gaining fast.

Eddie turned again onto a boulevard with a concrete divider down the middle. At the first gap, he braked hard and pulled a U-turn in front of oncoming traffic. The tires spun, spewing blue-gray smoke as the car slid around.

The Mercedes made the turn too late, slamming into the median.

Eddie ducked down an alley. He made another immediate right and downshifted. Looking sidelong at her, he said with a smile, "I'm Eddie, by the way."

She grinned back. "I'm Loren. Do you think we lost them?"

Eddie nodded. "For now." He slowed and pulled into a parking lot.

A sense of dread washed over her. "What're you doing?"

"Making sure we really lose them." Reaching into the back seat, he hauled a leather satchel into his lap, opened it, and flipped a red toggle switch inside. It hummed and then whistled. He swore and turned it off.

"What's that?"

"Tools of the trade. It means you have a bug, a tracking device somewhere on your clothes."

In a panic, she looked down at herself. Suddenly every inch of material felt like wool. It itched, and she wanted all of it off.

Eddie reached into the back seat again and retrieved a paper shopping bag. For the first time, he looked stressed. His forehead creased, and he rubbed the back of his neck. "I'm sorry, ma'am, but you have to get all of your clothes off and change into these." He gestured to the shopping bag, and half shrugged. "Everything."

Ma'am? Loren fought back a smile. He was embarrassed. She'd spent the last two years around men who leered at her. Touched her. Treated her like property. Then this. Where was this guy from?

Her dress had three buttons on the back at the top. She yanked them open, and lifting her bottom, pulled it over her head.

Eddie stared straight ahead as he pulled back out into the traffic again.

Loren tossed the dress out the window. The bag contained a dark blue sweatshirt and a pair of sweatpants. She pulled on the top and, reaching underneath, undid her bra.

She could almost imagine a bead of sweat running down his temple as he forced himself not to look. How cute was he?

She wriggled out of her underwear and pulled on the pants. One by one, she tossed everything out the window. The new clothes were huge, and she swam in them.

Finally, he darted a quick look at her. "Get the satchel and check again."

She nodded and complied. This time, when she flipped the switch, there was only the hum and no whistle. "Does that mean we're good?"

He glanced up at the mirror again and shook his head. "No more bugs, but we have other troubles."

She whipped her head around. Two more black Mercedes were rushing up behind them.

"They really don't want you to get away, do they?"

Loren swallowed and said half to herself, "If they knew what I know, they'd burn half of Paris down to get me back."

Eddie downshifted and turned again suddenly. Looking at her out of the corner of his eye, he said, "They'll have to do more than that to take you away from me now."

He said it evenly with conviction, not bravado, and Loren believed him. She pulled her legs up and hugged her knees to her chest.

Eddie swerved onto a busier road with multiple lanes of traffic and stoplights. He veered into the middle lane and glanced at the mirror. At the next intersection, he feinted right and pulled the car hard to the left.

The momentum threw Loren against the door, and she felt the suspension strain, but Eddie completed the turn and raced down a smaller street.

Glancing off another car, the first Mercedes slammed into the side of a building, its rear end lifting before it crashed back down.

After making the turn, the second pursuer caught up with them.

Eddie navigated back onto the busier highway and slowed.

The Mercedes raced up behind them and braked just feet behind their bumper. Loren studied the silhouettes of the men inside, but couldn't identify them.

Eddie maintained the slower speed, keeping them close, then abruptly accelerated before slamming on the brakes and turning. The move surprised the car, speeding to keep up, and it shot past. Eddie shifted, turned again at the next light, and took off.

The rain started falling again. Would that help or hurt?

Loren glimpsed another Mercedes on a side street. Were they chasing them as well?

Eddie said, "In the glove compartment is a plastic box with a bunch of key cards in it. Find the one labeled Travail."

The box must have had thirty cards in it, but she quickly located one with the name handwritten on blue painter's tape.

Eddie made a few more turns before pulling into a large three-story parking garage. He held the card up to the reader. After a beep, the arm lifted, and he sped inside. Remaining on the ground floor, he drove to the rear and parked in front of a waist-high concrete wall.

Sheets of rain fell now, but Loren could just make out the shapes of buildings behind the parking garage. Eddie remained in the driver's seat, the engine running, his focus on the entrance.

Her heart pounded in her chest, but no pursuers materialized.

After a moment, he shut the car off and turned to her. "It's going to be hard setting up a meeting in this. I have a place nearby where we can lie low for a while, okay?"

Until she was inside a CIA building, she would not believe she was safe. But what choice did she have? "Okay."

At the edge of the wall, they studied the alley. Lightning flashed and reflected on bottles and broken glass strewn across the ground. She glanced down at her bare feet.

Eddie followed her gaze. "It's not far. I'll carry you."

With a sigh, she nodded.

He took a deep breath and then pommeled over.

She hiked the pants up to her ribs and then pulled the drawstring tight and tied it.

He turned and held out his arms, and she climbed up and into them. His eyes were dark, and there was a shadow of stubble on his chin. His arms and chest felt strong and reassuring, but the smell of rotten food was overwhelming, even in the rain. One of these buildings must be a restaurant.

At the end of the row of businesses they stopped in front of a small two-story building with an outside staircase. Maybe a second-floor apartment?

Eddie set her down gently on the concrete in front of a wooden, single garage door secured with a combination lock. Rainwater ran down Loren's face and soaked her clothes. "Keep an eye out," Eddie instructed before stooping to work the lock. He wiped his eyes several times before he could get it open. Lifting the latch, he rolled the door up halfway and ushered Loren inside. Eddie turned on the light, lowered the door, and slid the two bolts into place.

A neatly made cot stood against one wall with a short refrigerator and stove opposite. Two large footlockers sat stacked in the far corner.

Loren stood in the center of the room, shivering. The wet shirt clung to her. Remembering she no longer wore a bra, she crossed her arms over her chest.

Eddie flinched at her movement and pulled a blanket from the bed. "Sorry," he said as he handed it to her.

Thanking him, she wrapped it around her shoulders.

He gestured to the bed. "Have a seat. We're safe here. Would you like something warm? I have coffee and let's see—yep, some tea as well."

"Tea, please," she replied and sat on the bed. Who knew she was here? No one. She still held the pistol. That was something, at least.

He put the pot on the small stove and opened a box of tea bags. "We should probably wait until morning. Let them spin their wheels out there for a while and spend all their energy. Then we can set up a meeting and get you to safety." In one sudden motion, he whirled around.

Loren leaned back, bracing herself, and tightened her grip on the pistol.

"I'm sorry." He chuckled in embarrassment. "I'm just a simple Texas boy sometimes. It just dawned on me the position you're in. You don't have to worry, you're safe now. I'd never take advantage..." He shrugged. "I understand you've been through a terrible ordeal—if you want, I'll try to set up a meeting as soon as—"

Her eyes flew open wide, and she laughed. A deep, tension-relieving laugh. He was too much. So earnest and unexpected.

Eddie faltered. "Ma'am, are you all right?" His Texas accent suddenly showed through.

Her chuckle turned into a wide grin. "Yes." She shook her head. "I'm fine." Her smile faded a bit. "I'm sorry, it's just that I haven't been around polite, *southern boys in a long, long time. In fact, I can't remember the last time I was around anything really American."*

Eddie nodded. "Actually, neither can I. Where are you from?"

With no real hometown from a life on the road, she lied. "California. Santa Barbara." She and her father had spent a summer there once, which was an eternity for the two of them, and she'd liked it.

"It's beautiful there. I took a trip down the coast once when I was at Stanford."

Loren raised her eyebrows. "Stanford, huh? I'm impressed."

"Thinking happens in Texas, too, you know."

She grinned wider. "I visited Texas once, a long time ago. I loved all the horses."

He pulled down the two cups from a crate beside the stove and placed a tea bag in each. "So, what kind of place were you at?"

"What kind of security clearance do you have?" she asked in a half-joking tone.

"Probably not high enough for any specifics."

"A place where there were a lot of men who think their dogs have a higher position than their women."

He narrowed his eyes.

That made him angry. She was really starting to like this guy.

"Sounds like a strange place to find a beautiful young woman."

She shrugged one shoulder. "Well, it's a little strange to be saved by a Texan in Paris, too, I have to tell you."

"Touché." He sipped his tea.

Something about him and his situation resonated with her. His role was an extended mission, just like hers had been. "How long have you been in place?"

He frowned. "Five years."

Wow. That was a long time. "Two for me. It's hard."

"It is."

They drank in silence.

"You know," she said, "this may be the only time we can have a conversation like this for the rest of our lives."

Eddie's brow furrowed. "What do you mean?"

"When we get back to America and return to normal lives, we won't be able to tell people what we really did before. It will be the same layer of lies, just for a different reason. Constantly guarding our tongues."

"That's a depressing thought," he said lightly.

She chuckled without humor and her mood darkened. "It's true, though, isn't it?

"Probably." He looked past her, digesting the idea.

This was a weird place, between her mission and the rest of her life afterward—whatever that was. This moment, with this man, took on a different meaning. For two years, the mission had dictated what she did with her body. And every relationship she had from now on would never truly be this honest again.

She wanted to seize this moment. To mark it and make it part of her. The thought took root. The situation and this rugged, polite Texan moved her somehow. "I've done a lot of things that I pray God can forgive me for. I hope He understands why I did what I did. I hope it was right, and now I have to ask His forgiveness one more time."

His body tensed at her sudden intensity, but his attention remained riveted on her face.

"I've spent years lying with men that I detested, men I loathed. I'd stare at the ceiling and send my mind somewhere else." She turned away. The heat of the sudden anger and shame surprised her. There was more buried deeply within her than she'd even realized. She felt her eyes sting. Damn it. She fought back the tears, but a single drop escaped and rolled down one cheek.

Eddie half stood, a crease forming in his forehead.

He was so cute and concerned. She smiled weakly and motioned for him to sit back down. "I'll try to spend the rest of my life a good and moral person. My duty is done." She swallowed and held his gaze. "Tonight, I want to be with a man that I choose. On my terms."

Eyes widening, he shook his head. "It's not right—"

"I'm a big girl, Eddie. I know what I'm doing. I need some, I don't know, honest comfort. I need to be close to a man who makes me feel safe."

She pulled off the blanket. The wet shirt clung to her. Eddie's attention darted to her breasts and then back to her face. His brow furrowed and his eyes took on a pained expression.

The fact that he didn't want to take advantage of the situation made her want him even more. "I'm not really a damsel in distress, Eddie. I'm a trained agent on the run. Let me have this one last thing before I come in from the cold."

Eddie set his cup down on the stove, stood, and walked over to the bed. He kneeled down in front of her. She kissed him fiercely, with passion.

•   •   •

Loren sighed and forced her mind back to the present. The memory of the rest of that night still made her smile. The next day, Eddie passed her off to his contact and her life went on without him. He was always in the back of her mind after that, but she thought she'd never see him again. Fate kept bringing them back together, however.

She appreciated Eddie wanting to protect her once again now, but it wasn't the same this time—or at least she hoped not. This was a covert reconnaissance mission. A task already outside Loren's comfort zone as it was, without bringing his friend along. Looking over at Luis, she recalled he hadn't even worked for the CIA. He was in some military branch. Army, she thought. Did he even understand what such a mission required? She sighed. No point in this line of thinking. He was here, and nothing was going to change that.

Her mind wandered back to Eddie's current mission. His situation was much more tenuous than hers. She closed her eyes. Please let him be okay.

CHAPTER 13

Eddie wasn't sure where to start. The yacht was enormous. Passageways crisscrossed the interior, with nooks and crannies everywhere. With no proper direction, it made sense to begin with the worst-case scenario—someone wanting to put the senator in a watery grave. Hard to come up with something worse than that. So, what would it take to do that?

The engine room seemed like the most logical place to him, so he started there, going over the entire area, including instruments and storage lockers.

The two crew members present nodded a greeting and then appeared to ignore him. Seemingly unconcerned with his activities as he prowled around. Nothing in their mannerisms caught his attention. Was that a bad sign? He didn't know. Not having a clear aim was making him paranoid.

A green light appeared on a panel, and one crewman started the two massive diesel engines.

The steel flooring vibrated under Eddie's feet, followed by a deep rumble. Must be raising the anchor.

He continued searching the room for anything unusual or out of place. At the rear of the compartment, he stumbled across a wide set of metal drawers which contained schematic drawings of the entire ship. He flipped through blueprints for plumbing, fire control, and electrical.

He paused on the last but didn't see any closed-circuit televisions or the like. There appeared to be only two cameras near the front of the ship, both facing backward, and wired to the cockpit. He'd noted them on the tour but hadn't seen any others onboard. Sometimes cameras were out and visible, and sometimes hidden. Each served its purpose, but this drawing seemed to confirm just the two.

Was it unusual for a ship this big and expensive to have so few cameras? Was Sam avoiding a record of whatever he did on this boat? Was that also the reason he left the security detail behind?

The next sheet showed the internal layout and construction diagram. Blue lines traced the walls and passageways of each level. He noted a container in a master suite wall. Was that the click he'd heard when Sam went back into his bedroom? If so, what had the senator hidden there?

Deck two contained two small rooms Sam hadn't included on the tour. What were they? They might be a good place to put a central control unit for a hidden camera system, one not listed on the blueprints. He added the rooms to his mental list, as he flipped through a few more drawings, but nothing else caught his eye.

Eddie frowned. If he had an enemy on this boat, was it the senator, or a member of the crew, someone ahead on their journey, or all the above?

Eddie's mission for the Agency had been protecting the actual professionals, not doing any genuine type of spy-craft. Everything he knew about surveillance and tracking, he'd learned from the Dove brothers at the Agency. The thought of them and their odd training methods brought a smile to his face. He rarely let his thoughts go back to his early days at the CIA. Unfortunately, the way his time at the department ended would always taint the beginning. A real shame because he really had enjoyed his time there.

Especially the Dove brothers. They drilled central tenets into him. Trust no one. Always assume someone's watching you. Everything is bugged, and everyone is being tracked. And finally, always know as much as your enemy knows.

Only three places on the ship remained a mystery to him. The senator was piloting the craft, so he had a moment to rectify that situation, starting with the wall box in the senator's room.

Eddie closed the drawer and strode to his cabin, retrieved a lock pick, and moved quietly upstairs and out onto the deck until he could see into the bridge. As expected, the captain stood to one side, and Sam was at the wheel, piloting his pride and joy.

Eddie glanced at his watch. It seemed reasonable to assume he had a few minutes that were safe. He moved down one level, entered the master bedroom and got his bearings, then went to the wall where the plans showed the recessed box should be.

His heart pounded as he searched for the hidden area. The moment it took him to find and open the hidden panel felt like forever. Inside was a square, metal door with a standard keyed lock. Eddie cocked his head and listened. All seemed quiet, but the rumble of the engine and the sounds of the waves outside left a doubt. As soon as he started, he'd be in a compromising position, difficult to explain.

Eddie took a deep breath and then inserted the pick. He quickly opened the door and stopped short. A small, brown bottle sat beside two thick white rags and a white surgical mask. Eddie picked it up and read the blue label: Anesthetic Ether. Next to these were bottles of Versed, a syringe, and an I.V. kit.

He stared at the contents with a dull feeling in his chest. It was everything you'd need to knock someone out quickly and keep them under for a day or so. There were no other first-aid items in the box. Hard to come up with any other explanations that weren't insidious. Was this why Sam had gone back into his bedroom earlier? Did he put them here, or was this stuff already on board?

Eddie closed the door, locked it, and left the room. His limbs ached from the adrenaline as he stumbled back to his cabin.

What had he learned? First, if the drugs were for him, then they didn't intend to kill him. Nor had they planned to poison or drug his food. You used ether like chloroform in the movies, only much faster and more effective. So, meals weren't the danger, sleep was.

He was out at sea with a man he didn't know. A man with a locker full of drugs on a cruise whose purpose Eddie was certain was a lie, with days at sea ahead. Eddie couldn't go a week without sleep.

Back in his room, he examined his door and considered ways to secure it. Had he seen anything on the tour of the ship he could use? He remembered empty pallets stacked in the back of the main storage room below. Maybe a piece of that could work.

Eddie ran down the stairs, found them in a back corner and sorted through the scraps until he found one shaped like a wedge and carried it back to his room.

With some work, he changed the angle until he could force it in between his door and the jamb. It wouldn't stop someone forever, but it would make enough noise to alert him to an intruder.

Throughout his professional career, Eddie had been both the hunter and the hunted. Often, he went from being one to the other without warning, and this was feeling like one of those times. What the hell had he gotten himself into?

CHAPTER 14

Once they landed in the Dominican Republic, Loren rented a car and drove Luis out of the airport.

She asked, "You're sure these contacts of yours are dependable and can get us a gun? Are we sure this is even necessary?"

Luis nodded. "It is, and Jeff knows these people. We're cool."

What the hell did that mean? Probably no point in having Luis along if he wasn't armed. Hopefully, Jeff's contacts wouldn't cause them any kind of trouble. That was the last thing they needed.

Following Jeff's instructions, they drove to the Marina Zar Par in the town of Boca Chica on the coast. The blue three-story building fronted rows of gleaming watercraft spread out in the ocean behind it like splayed fingers. A beautiful resort area that seemed like the last place on earth where they would find someone with illegal arms.

"Are you sure this is the place?" Loren asked with a sideways glance at her companion.

Luis grinned. "Pretty sure. With Jeff, you never know where you might end up."

She followed him around the building, past a tall metal structure storing small boats at multiple levels. They strolled down one of the long docks, between sailboats and fishing vessels, to a substantial cabin cruiser at the end. A young woman of about twenty lay sunbathing on the deck in a bright pink bikini.

Luis shaded his eyes from the sun. "Hello."

The girl sat up, looked down at him, and smiled. "Can I help you?"

"I hope so. My name's Luis, I'm looking for Chad?"

The girl nodded and yelled, "Chad, someone's here to see you!" She turned back and studied Luis' lithe, muscular form. "I'm Stacey."

Loren frowned. The girl wasn't exactly being subtle. Had she been any different? Yes. By that age, she'd already been more sophisticated and effective at manipulating men. Well, all of them except Sam and Eddie.

Luis grinned. "Nice to meet you, Stacey."

Smooth and confident. A mature and standoffish kind of flirting. Acknowledging the girl, but nothing about his posture invited any sort of escalation. Luis was clearly used to female attention and adept at using it. Why hadn't he ever tried any of that on her? Maybe there was more to him than met the eye.

A man, also in his mid-twenties, appeared from below. In khakis and a button-up shirt, he looked like the last person on earth who would have a gun.

The preppy smiled. "Oh, you must be Jeff's friend. Hold on." He went below and reappeared with a wooden box with the name Barcelo Rum stenciled on the side. He smiled. "Having some party, huh?"

Luis grinned. "You might say that." He thanked him, gave the girl a last smile, and then led Loren back the way they'd come.

Once in the car, he pried open the lid with a knife from his bag. Inside were two Springfield XP .45 pistols and several boxes of ammunition. Luis pulled one out, checked it, and grinned. "Jeff comes through again."

Loren shook her head. "I'm guessing Mr. Blazer back there had no idea what was in the box?"

Luis shrugged. "That seems like a safe bet. Probably just a courier. Jeff knows a lot of people."

This was the most talkative and relaxed she'd seen Luis. It humanized him and oddly made the whole situation feel better, or at least more comfortable. She could work with him. What a relief to turn her full attention back to the mission.

According to the Agency's information, Selik was staying at the Hostal Nicolas de Ovando. They checked into a small hotel down the street, but close enough to monitor their target.

After dropping their bags, they met at a small cantina next door. While waiting for their food, Loren studied Luis, who was once again cool and aloof. "It surprised me that after everything that went down, you stayed with Eddie."

His even, oil-black eyes held her gaze as he shrugged, revealing the jagged edge of some tattoo peeking out of his shirt collar. "I'm a soldier. Soldiers need someone to follow."

Strange answer. "Eddie seems like an odd choice."

Luis frowned. "There are a lot of guys who can look at the facts and make the right choice under pressure. Hell, you can even find people with the basic aptitude and train them to do that. Eddie is one of the rare men who can see through the facts, beyond the tactics, to the truth. It's not something you run into very often." He shrugged. "If I'm not going to be in the service anymore, he's the kind of man I feel comfortable following."

Loren moved a lock of hair behind her ear to conceal her surprise. That succinctly described how she felt about Eddie. At a more generic level, at least. "Why didn't you just stay in the military?"

His jaw tightened a fraction.

"I'm sorry, was that an indelicate question?"

Luis took a sip of his beer and relaxed. "No, it's okay. I was injured in Afghanistan on a mission with my unit. I was the only survivor and..."

"I'm sorry. I didn't mean to—"

Luis held up a hand. "It's okay. You didn't know. I just couldn't see myself starting over. I was in the hospital for months." He shrugged. "When they assigned a new soldier to our group, I remember what it was like. I didn't want to be that guy. Then all that shit went down with Eddie, and as they say, the rest is history."

"Is it okay to ask what your unit did?"

"Recon. So, what do we know about this guy we're supposed to—what, follow?"

An evasive generic answer and a subject change. The war and what his unit did were not topics for discussion, it seemed. What kind of injury? He certainly looked fit and healthy now. She leaned back in her seat and checked her surroundings. "Nothing so specific, that's the problem. I'm just here to find out what he's doing and pass it on."

Luis took another sip of beer. "They didn't even classify this guy for you. I mean, is he a terrorist, arms dealer, or a slave trader? I'd handle each a little differently, especially if I were you."

His gaze remained steady on hers—he was just being a soldier. Looking for the rules of engagement. The entire concept of a person of interest was foreign to him. "It's not slave trading women. I know that much, at least."

He smiled briefly. "Well, that's good to know. Do we think he's dangerous?"

Another soldier's question. She was pretty sure that he meant hand to hand. Trying to decide the capabilities of his enemy if this became a firefight. Smart of him, and relevant to his role. Loren was much more worried about the other dangerous, the kind that could destroy everything you love with a phone call. She suspected Selik was the second type. "I think we should be very careful with him."

Luis nodded and then shook his head with a wry smile.

Loren furrowed her brow. "What?"

Luis shook his head. "This mission, it's so CIA."

Loren arched her eyebrows. "Know a lot about Agency missions, do you?" She said it playfully, but seriously.

Luis' smile faded a bit. "My brother's in the Agency. I followed him into the Army, but your friends plucked him out." He shrugged. "I did some missions in the Gulf that had some Agency people in them, and they even tried to get me to join, but I said no thanks."

Wow. "I didn't know that."

"I know. I just told you that to make you relax a little. I know how to handle myself on a mission like this. I got your back."

Perceptive. Do *not* underestimate this man.

After a quiet dinner, they turned in. Right before he entered his room, Luis said, "If you get into any trouble, just yell."

His eyes were steady and almost distant, but there was no flirtation or friendly banter in the statement. It was merely shoptalk to him. Yell, and he would kill anything threatening her. It made her feel safe and sent a shiver through her at the same time.

Lying on her bed, she stared at the ceiling, her thoughts and emotions in a knot. She tried to work through them and settle her nerves.

Was Sam up to something bad? She'd known him a long time and had trouble believing it. No denying he was acting strange, though.

She thought back to her first dinner with Sam. He literally flew her in a private plane from the jail in Texas to New York, where they sat at a small table in the dark corner, and she couldn't stop staring at him.

It felt like a con. An elaborate set up. How could she go from facing prison, straight to becoming a spy? Do not pass go, do not collect $200. Skip jail all together. Why would he offer her such a choice?

Finally, Sam set down his fork and leaned back. "All right, out with it."

Her eyebrows shot up. "Out with what?"

"You look like you're waiting for stormtroopers to bust through the door and drag you back to your cell."

She held his gaze. "In my experience, something that appears too good to be true always is."

Sam barked out a short laugh. "Too good? Let me be clear, my dear Ms. Malen, I'm offering you a way out of jail. Don't for a second think it's going to be easier. You have debts to pay for your wrongs and I promise you, working for the CIA, you will pay them."

Well, that sucked. At least it was honest, and it certainly didn't feel like a con. "Then why would I do it?"

Sam carefully folded his napkin and wiped his mouth. "We are more alike than you might think, Loren. I don't believe in a free lunch, either. It will be hard. But I like you, and I see something in you. So I'm offering you a gift, freely, with no strings attached. Even though the CIA will be difficult, you'll be able to use your considerable talents for good. You'll be able to make a difference. Trust me, I have all the money in the world. Nothing feeds the soul like doing something important that matters."

Loren bit her lower lip. She was tired of just surviving. She'd never imagined a life like that. "Why me?"

Something crept into his light blue eyes that was softer. "You know that in my job, I'm connected to the CIA?"

She nodded.

He smiled. "Well, the skills you've developed in your life of crime are very similar to those of spy craft. You've had a lifetime of training in deception. Playing a part. Reading people." His eyes twinkled. "Sometimes in life, it's not what you're doing, but why and for whom. You have impressive skills that I admire, Loren. I'm just asking you to switch sides. Become one of the good guys."

One of the good guys? She'd never really thought of herself as a bad guy, but her hands weren't exactly clean either. What would it be like to be doing good for once? She returned his smile. Especially if it meant she could still do some of the fun stuff. "I think I'd like that."

"I thought you might." He lifted his wineglass to toast. "Welcome to a life of importance."

He was right, and she'd never been the same since that day. She owed him a lot, and if she had to, she'd protect him and maybe even cover for him—if it wasn't too big. But there was a limit to what she would do to help him. A boundary. This realization surprised Loren.

She sighed. She also had very mixed emotions about letting Craig talk her into involving Eddie. It was good to see him. When she first laid eyes on him, a warm glow passed over her. He had just the right mix of confidence and innocence that drew her in. She desperately hoped that she hadn't gotten him into something dangerous.

The next morning, before first light, they took up positions on either side of Selik's hotel.

Loren sipped her coffee and studied the old stone building from across the street. It harkened back to a different time, an era of Spanish forts and the wild, untamed Caribbean. Not what she'd expected. Most of her Agency targets, in her days on the job, stayed in fancy places or hidden dives. This place was discreet and just a little out of the way.

She glanced over and caught sight of Luis seated at an empty table at the far end of the block, reading a newspaper. He blended in down here much better than she did, and she reflexively stepped back deeper into the dark alley.

More than an hour passed with no sign of Selik. Was this the correct approach? This wasn't her expertise, and she'd never planned a mission like this before.

What if he never showed? How long should she wait, and if he didn't appear, what was the next move? Trial and error was the only way she knew to do this. Not an encouraging thought.

Why had Selik and Sam really met? Was Selik's trip here somehow connected? What did Craig hope she'd discover?

She took another a sip of coffee and collected her thoughts. An endless parade of questions was getting her nowhere. Loren preferred missions with clear-cut objectives. She didn't like this figure-it-out-as-you-go approach.

Finally, just before nine o'clock, Selik walked out the front door and stopped to speak to the bellman. Loren had only seen a black and white long-range photograph, but she recognized him immediately. His silver hair was neat, and his thin mustache and khaki clothing gave Loren the impression of a British explorer from the turn of the century.

She lifted a hand and wiped her brow.

Luis noticed the signal and calmly stood, prepared to hail a cab, then paused.

Selik finished speaking to the bellboy and then turned and walked down the road, away from the sea.

They hadn't expected him to leave on foot.

Loren began walking in the same direction but stayed on her side of the street. She finished her coffee and tossed the cup into a garbage can as she passed, using the act to check on Luis. He'd crossed to Selik's side of the street and was now walking casually about a hundred yards behind him.

Selik continued on steadily, making no obvious attempts to check his surroundings. By outward appearance, he was simply a man enjoying a stroll on the warm, cloudless morning.

She sped up a bit, so that she was ahead of him a while, before stopping to look at a stand on the sidewalk, and naturally falling behind him again.

Was his destination the Don Diego Terminal on her side of the road?

Selik patted his breast pocket as if he'd misplaced something, then spun, and headed back toward the hotel.

Loren held her breath, but Luis was cool and continued past him without even breaking stride.

So, Selik *was* taking in his surroundings. His street craft was natural and impressive.

Loren paused and looked at a rack of postcards. She knew the play. Her mark would come back.

Selik retreated a block before turning again on his heel and settling back onto his original course.

She glanced up the road. Luis was nowhere in sight. Selik continued past the terminal, and after a moment, she followed, just keeping track of him.

Had he made them? She didn't think so. Up ahead, Selik crossed the street and disappeared down a side road. At the point where she thought Selik turned, the road was empty.

Her heartbeat quickened as she looked down each alley. Nothing. Should she double back? She noticed Luis standing in a doorway.

He nodded, beckoning her forward, leading her down another road to the edge of the Orzama River. Standing on the seawall, he tilted his head to the left. Selik walked up the gangplank of an ancient freighter moored a few boats down.

Written in white letters across the vessel's rusty, black stern was the name *Voodoo III*. Why did everyone involved in this need a boat?

CHAPTER 15

Frank marveled at the massive craft's speed. The ship effortlessly sliced through the water, the big jet engines producing an odd whining sound that added to the surreal quality of the ride, while Marco, a short, squat man, kept her on the prearranged heading.

Mack sat in the back row, a laptop across his knees. "We got a message from Gemini. *Morning Star* left at first light, heading southeast. He confirmed that his security team stayed behind. All clear."

Frank took in and let out a slow, deep breath. "So, he should be a sitting duck."

Mack grinned. "Let's go get him."

Frank waved a thick-fingered hand at the empty seat. "Get out the tracker and let's make sure we can follow him."

Mack pulled a tablet from the plastic case beneath the chair and turned it on.

Frank leaned over his shoulder. The ten-inch screen displayed a GPS map of the Caribbean, an hourglass tumbling over and over as the system searched. He shifted his feet as the seconds passed. If the tracker didn't work, there was no Plan B.

A blue blip lit up on the screen and then slowly faded. A moment later, it reappeared.

Mack grinned. "Got him." He scrolled through the menus and announced, "One hundred and seven miles to the south, southwest of us."

"How fast is the senator's ship traveling?"

Mack frowned. "A little over eighteen knots. He's pushing her about as fast as she can go."

Frank glanced at their digital speedometer, noting their current speed of forty-two knots. "So, we should be on top of her in a little under three hours." He scratched at the puckered scar on his neck. "Since we're so much faster, let's slip in a few miles behind her and match her speed. I'm not sure how far she's going, and I want to conserve fuel."

Mack raised his eyebrows. "It'll be dark when we catch her, and she'll be in deep water—why not get it over with?"

A line of lobster buoys flew past the craft like a breadcrumb trail home.

Frank turned to the man at the wheel. "Marco, take a break. I'll take over for a while. What do I do?"

Marco nodded and stood. "Just keep the compass at one hundred and thirty degrees, boss." He grinned. "You can't get lost." He headed below.

Frank settled in behind the wheel and motioned Mack to the seat next to him. "The job is more than eliminating the senator. We need to know where he's going and report it back."

Mack's blue-gray eyes narrowed. "But we aren't supposed to get whatever he's after?"

He knew where the young man's thoughts were heading. Youthful and ambitious, he didn't want someone else getting his spoils of war. "After we mark the spot, another crew is going to take care of that, but I wouldn't sweat it."

Mack was a bright kid, and his eyes widened a fraction as he realized how transparent his thoughts were to Frank. He half grinned. "Why's that?"

Frank pulled a cigar from his pocket and stuck it unlit in the corner of his mouth. "Because it ain't gold bullion, and I have a powerful instinct it would be much better for our health if we didn't know anything about it. These guys don't skimp on our reward. Let's waste the senator and leave the trouble to someone else. Let them deal with the complicated stuff."

"I get it. Greedy men are dead men." Lowering his voice and glancing around, he asked, "Aren't you a little curious about what everyone is so interested in?"

That was the question Frank had toyed with for weeks, but he wasn't about to tell the kid that. Mack was too young to understand that the really dangerous stuff wasn't treasure or money—it was information. If the organization and Senator Sam Hawthorne were this interested in something, then Frank didn't want to know anything about it. He looked down his nose at Mack. "Curious men usually end up dead men, too."

The roar of the engines and the whistle of the wind filled the cockpit as the men surveyed one another.

Mack broke eye contact first and asked, "Where do we think the senator is heading?"

Frank shrugged. "Somewhere near the Turks and Caicos is everyone's best guess."

"And this other team, the cleanup team, where are they? They have to be waiting somewhere nearby."

Frank looked at the razor line of the horizon. He didn't like Mack's line of thinking, and it must have shown on his face because the younger man held up his hands defensively. "I'm just curious. When we hit the senator, they have to be somewhere nearby. This could get sticky, is all I'm saying."

Frank didn't entirely buy this explanation and decided to answer the question and change the subject. "I believe they're in the Dominican Republic. Also, Gemini says we need to get the bugs back."

Mack's shoulders slumped. "The ones we planted on the senator's yacht. Really? Why? He'll be dead."

"I don't know, but he wants all twelve of them. This has to be clean. Get in, take charge, shooting no one if possible. Then get the bugs, blow the boat, and get out of Dodge."

Mack rubbed his mouth. "They're pretty well hidden. It's going to take a little time to get them all."

Frank grinned. "Luckily, we're in the middle of the ocean, so that shouldn't be a problem."

This seemed to satisfy him, but Frank's mind unwillingly turned back to the team waiting in the wings in the Dominican Republic. He wasn't so different from the kid. He also wanted to know what everyone was actually after.

CHAPTER 16

Loren had seen the newer, larger ships moored in the main commercial port when they landed. The *Voodoo III* was not with them but docked here in the older and seedier area upriver. Why was that? It certainly seemed suspicious.

As they worked their way nearer, Loren kept close behind Luis, who appeared tense and ready. They studied the vessel and the gangplank. All seemed quiet, but this wasn't a good vantage point, and she was resistant to get any closer. She led Luis away from the water, street by street, studying the rooflines until she noticed a church tower.

Luis spoke to a plump, elderly man who kept darting his watery dark eyes at Loren as he listened.

Loren pointed up at the turret and asked in Spanish, "Can we get up there? I'm a photographer, scouting locations."

Luis raised his eyebrows, clearly surprised that she knew Spanish.

Loren smiled inwardly at his reaction. She'd always been good at languages.

The man smiled and nodded vigorously, then pointed up at the ceiling. "*Si, si.*"

Luis and Loren climbed the curving staircase to a trapdoor opening onto an area atop the tower. A waist-high brick wall enclosed the space, offering an unobstructed view of the *Voodoo III*.

Luis carried two small wooden chairs up from the building, and they settled in to watch.

Loren pulled a pair of binoculars from her backpack and studied the ship and its surroundings. She handed them to Luis. "What do you think?"

"I see three gunmen, probably local muscle. They don't seem like pros."

Loren nodded and forced back a smile. She'd noticed the men as well, but her question was more about the setup. "Lots of crates going on. At least ten fifty-five-gallon drums of gas in the hold and there are more on the deck. That's a lot of fuel."

Luis swiveled the binoculars back to the ramp. "That last crate says Generac on that side, that's a big commercial generator. Nothing obviously illegal. Other than the muscle, it looks pretty innocent."

Loren frowned. Was it reasonable to assume that whatever Selik was doing here was necessarily something wicked? More importantly, did this ship have anything to do with Selik's meeting with Sam? "I don't know. But if Selik is involved, I doubt it's something legitimate."

He looked back at the ancient freighter. "The way Selik was dressed, I half expected him to load jeeps and lion cages onto the boat."

She grinned. He did look like someone on safari in a 1930s movie. She removed her hat and fanned herself against the heat as the time passed.

Luis said, "So, if you don't think the senator is sailing down to find some plane, what do you think he's doing?"

That was the question, wasn't it? Luis had probably been waiting for a good time to ask since they left Miami. The period of inactivity up here on the tower had worn away at his patience. "I've no idea, and I don't know if Selik's being here has anything to do with it." She shrugged. "That's part of the problem."

Luis pulled two granola bars from his bag. "Your senator and Selik both have boats, one here, and Hawthorne is supposedly heading toward us in one. That can't be a coincidence."

Loren accepted the snack from him. "True, and somehow it just feels connected."

He narrowed his eyes, looked back at the boat, and took a bite. His forearm was smooth and dark, with a spiderweb of veins. "You think the senator is dirty?"

"I don't think so. I hope not."

Luis chuckled dryly. "I hope not, too." He looked upriver and then down the other direction, the skin crinkling around his eyes.

She knew Luis didn't entirely trust her, and she could understand that. He was worried about Eddie and the danger he might be in. The same anxiety curled in her belly like a snake.

At midday, they climbed down and ate at a nearby cantina before returning to their vantage point. The afternoon crept by, and the ancient freighter only baked in the heat. Shadows stretched across the rooftops, and the colors faded as the sun slipped toward the horizon.

Loren leaned back against the wall. She needed to shade her eyes against the setting sun to see the ship now. This was fruitless. She didn't think that doing this again tomorrow was going to produce anything useful, either. Now the question was, what was her mission objective?

She'd located Selik and discovered that his activities centered on this freighter. She knew the name and location of the vessel. Technically speaking, she'd completed her mission. She could return home with this information.

That would help Craig, and maybe Sam, but she couldn't shake the feeling that it wouldn't help Eddie and that he was the one in the most immediate danger. The most in need of *her* help. No. This wasn't enough. She needed to increase the stakes a little. Eddie's life could depend on her. She turned to Luis. "You said earlier that the gunmen look like amateurs to you?"

Luis shook his head. "Nah. They don't move; they never check their six or the far bank. I think they're mostly for show. Why?"

Loren bit her lip and studied the area. Possibly she could tilt the situation toward something that better fit her training. "We need to see inside that ship. If I get in there, and there's trouble, do you think you could get me back out?"

Luis' dark eyes held hers for a beat, and then he turned his gaze toward the boat. "Why?"

"Because I think the best way to figure out what's going on is for me to be seen. Get them to invite me on board," she added with a smile.

A crease formed in Luis' forehead. "That sounds dangerous. I'm supposed to keep you out of harm."

She shrugged. "This is the kind of thing they trained me for, and I can take care of myself. Just be ready if I need you." His expression was stony and unreadable, but she felt his discomfort.

"I don't know."

"It's the only way we can make sure that Eddie's safe. Are you going to help me do that or not?"

He frowned. "How are you going to get noticed?"

She smiled. "It'll be easy. I guess you could say this is more my skill set. This is the very thing they trained me to do."

CHAPTER 17

Around noon, one of the crew silently served Eddie and Sam shrimp salad sandwiches, chips, and lemonade.

Eddie masked his concern and suspicion. He needed to act like everything was normal, but his adrenaline was pumping as he covertly studied the senator. Was this man planning to drug him? Sam seemed normal, which made Eddie second-guess himself.

The older man wiped his mouth and asked, "How goes your search?"

Eddie shrugged. "I looked through the engine room, and the lower decks. Nothing appeared out of the ordinary. I'm just working my way up."

Sam nodded. "Good. Let me know if you find anything. I have some work to finish up. I'll recap with you later," he said with an air of finality before standing up and leaving the table.

Eddie stood and quietly followed at a distance. The senator locked himself in one of the two rooms not on the tour earlier. He frowned, returned to the table, and took another bite of sandwich. He had to get into that room, and the sooner, the better. Was this somehow being disloyal to the senator? Turning on his employer too early? No, he couldn't just ignore the locker full of drugs. He sighed. Where did his loyalties lie? Eddie wasn't sure he trusted anyone in this entire situation.

This lack of moral clarity was the one constant that had plagued Eddie's life since Craig Black enticed him out of the Army and into the CIA. After that, it was never simple again. Hell, Eddie wasn't even sure whose side Craig was on in this situation. Of course, you never really knew exactly where Craig stood on anything.

He remembered the first time he learned that lesson, his thoughts wandered back to a parking lot on a picturesque tree-lined side street in a Paris suburb.

Two days earlier, Eddie received a call from an asset named Carlo. Panicky and in near hysteria, fear had consumed the man.

When Eddie finally calmed him down enough to understand him, he learned that he and his companion were on the run from a man named Utu Corsicona. That Utu had caught Carlo's partner and cut out his tongue before killing him. Carlo's current state seemed more justified once Eddie learned that. They agreed to meet in the town of Nancy, far from Paris and, hopefully, unnoticed. Utu was there, however, hot on Carlo's heels. Eddie saved his contact and delivered him to his handler, but it had been a very close call. He gritted his teeth at the memory.

After passing Carlo into the hands of the Agency, Eddie started looking for Utu. This was an enemy he needed to know. Especially once he discovered the man also lived in Paris. In this quaint little neighborhood in the house Eddie now watched.

Did the neighbors have any idea what kind of thug lived here? Maybe thug was the wrong word. The man was smart and capable, but Eddie thought of him as a thug because of his brutality. Eddie and Carlo had barely escaped with their lives, but not before Utu killed at least two innocent bystanders. The savagery of his response shocked Eddie.

Once he discovered Utu's location, he decided a little surveillance was in order. He parked in front of a closed shop, just down the street from the house. It was dusk, but he had a good view of the upper rooms from here. They looked dark and vacant. He wasn't sure who this guy worked for, but he needed to know more about him. In his gut, Eddie suspected he might come up against him again.

Right before dark, a lone figure appeared, walking toward Eddie from the direction of the house in question. A short and stocky man. Something about him was familiar. Eddie wrapped his hand around the handle of the Sig in his lap and studied him.

The figure looked both ways and then crossed the street, and Eddie recognized him. Craig Black! Son of a bitch. Eddie had not seen or heard from the man in the three years he'd been on this mission. Not since his training. He didn't even have a way to contact him, yet now he was walking down the street in front of Utu's house, of all places.

Craig opened the passenger side door, gave him a nod, and slid inside, rubbing his hands together. "It's cold out there." *He looked sidelong at Eddie.* "How've you been, my boy?"

Eddie narrowed his eyes. "I'm fine. Long time no see. What the hell are you doing here?"

Craig scratched at the stubble on his chin. "You've been doing a good job, Eddie. I've been pleased with your work."

Eddie snorted. "Is that why I haven't heard a word from you all this time?"

Craig scowled. "Of course that's why. What, are we dating? With me, no contact is always a sign that you're doing good work."

So, if Eddie had not heard from him since things had been going well... "Then to what screw up do I owe your sudden appearance?"

Craig clucked his tongue. "Don't be so negative. I'm not here because of any screw up. I just want to discuss Utu."

And there it was. "You mean the eastern bloc bastard who tried to take me and my agent out?"

"Yes. There's more at play than you know. I need you to not kill him."

Where did that come from? "First, I'm not an assassin. Second, what's he to you? That guy's an animal."

"What are you doing here if you're not going to kill him?"

Eddie shook his head. "I'm just checking him out. I'm not a murderer, and you didn't answer my question."

"Let's just say he's part of something else I'm working on."

Eddie raised his eyebrows. "Well, I'm not here for that, but if I need to kill him to save one of my runners, I will."

Craig pursed his lips and nodded. "Agreed."

Eddie frowned. "How did you even know I was here?"

Craig opened the car door. "I always know, Eddie," *he replied with an enigmatic smile and got out of the car.*

"What, that's it, you're leaving? I haven't seen you in three years and you show up just to tell me not to murder this asshole?"

Craig stepped out and leaned back into the car. "Yes. I've got things to do, and I think it's better that you and I don't have a direct line of communication. Keep up the good work." He closed the door and walked back the way he'd come.

Eddie shook his head at the memory. That entire exchange was a perfect example of what it was like to work for Craig. It was a long time before he ran into Utu again. But that night was the first time he really understood how Craig operated. The first of several times his boss thrust Eddie into something without giving him the entire story or even a clear definition of who the good guys and the bad guys were.

Now Eddie had to add this situation with Sam, and this damned boat, to that never ending list. He didn't like this feeling at all. He saw the world as black and white—there were people you trusted and people you didn't. There were good people and right things, and bad people and wrong things. Craig swam around in a murky grayness, like this damned situation, which made Eddie very uncomfortable.

He returned to searching the massive ship. Was someone tracking her, or maybe bugging her? If so, they wouldn't know how long she'd be at sea. Listening and recording devices took power. To work around the clock for an unknown number of days took a lot. He needed to prioritize probable locations for a listening device.

He walked downstairs, entered the senator's bedroom, and examined everything that used electricity—each wall plug, the clock radio, and every light.

The overhead light looked clean, as did the standing lamp by the door. He unscrewed the shade on the bedside lamp, studied the naked lightbulb, and frowned. It sat up a little high. He took it out, sat down heavily on the bed, and let out a slow breath. A small, very high-tech recording device with a flash memory sat in a fake bottom of the light socket. Quality work. Was it CIA or someone else?

Everything changed with this discovery. Now he had proof. This wasn't just people being paranoid. Someone was spying on a U.S. senator. The mission and the danger were suddenly real.

Eddie stood, pulled the pick from his pocket, and once again opened the metal box in the wall. He removed the can of ether, the item that posed him the most risk. Covering his mouth, he poured the contents into the sink downstairs in his bathroom and hid the can in the cabinet. That done, he returned to hunting for bugs.

For the next four hours, Eddie meticulously searched the ship, discovering nine listening devices in all. Four in bedroom lamps, four in wall sconces, and one attached to the icemaker at the bar. Whoever installed the last one needed time and privacy.

Who would have such an opportunity? Possibly the crew. A well-trained team of two could've placed every bug on the ship in maybe a half an hour, which was an eternity for this kind of work, unless they had the run of the ship.

He frowned at the pile of devices. Nine seemed like a decidedly incomplete number. Most likely, he'd missed at least one and needed to make another sweep. Someone with sophisticated tools and access to this yacht was spying on the senator. Did that show that Sam was the victim in this situation? Did that make him a good guy or mean that Eddie could trust him? Doubtful. He rubbed his face. He'd really only established one thing conclusively. The senator wasn't paranoid. Something was definitely at play here. He walked up to the bridge, one of the few places he'd yet to examine, and found the captain alone at the helm.

They exchanged a nod.

Through the windshield, long pink brushstrokes painted the horizon as the sun slid into the sea. The first stars were just pushing through the fading blue overhead.

Eddie looked under the dash, not seeing any obvious place to hide the type of devices he'd already discovered. He was resistant to search further in the captain's presence. Who could he trust in this situation? He studied the big color radar screen. A representation of the *Morning Star* sat in the middle of the monitor, and the outlines of islands scattered across the digital ocean. "How far is this image?"

"Roughly twenty miles on every side."

A small black line sat six inches behind the center, and Eddie pointed to it. "What's that?"

"Another ship."

Eddie's brow furrowed. "Behind us? How long has it been there?"

He shrugged. "Maybe a half hour. It's not unusual. The larger vessels take the same sea lanes through here. I follow a line of ships all the time. Why go through unknown waters?"

Something about it bothered Eddie. "How far behind us is she?"

The captain moved the mouse and after a few clicks said, "One point six nautical miles."

A knot formed in his stomach. He looked at the tall man, his hair so blond it was nearly white. "How long have you been with the senator?"

He shrugged. "About five years, give or take."

"Is this the first time he left his security detail behind?"

He shook his head. "Mr. Hawthorne is always doing something unexpected."

That wasn't really an answer. Eddie's attention traveled back to the screen. "I'm probably paranoid, but will you please keep an eye on that ship? And let me know if it does anything unusual?"

The smile stayed on the captain's lips, and he nodded. "Of course, but why?"

Eddie shrugged. "Just a hunch." As he walked back into the main area, he could tell that he couldn't depend on the captain. He didn't believe that the possibility of a threat was real.

The senator was at the bar mixing a drink when he arrived back in the living room. He glanced up. "Find anything interesting?"

Eddie poured the pile of electronic devices onto the polished marble surface.

Sam's face darkened, and he narrowed his eyes. "Where were those?"

"All over the ship. I doubt that's all of them."

His pale eyebrows drew down. Through gritted teeth, he asked, "Who do you think planted them?"

Eddie shrugged. "No idea. Could be someone on the crew, or someone else more sophisticated. They're professional. I'm guessing someone snuck on board, probably at night, put them in, and slipped away. How hard would that have been?"

Sam frowned. "Probably not very hard. At anchor in the middle of the night, it would be easy enough, I guess. I also had work done on her a few months ago. So there were plenty of opportunities. You think it's the Agency?"

"I've been thinking about that. I don't know. They're definitely Agency quality. But if it were Craig, he'd have to know I'd find them. He's not stupid. If they were his, I think Craig would've told me about them or retrieved them. Why risk pissing you off more?" Eddie studied the pile of devices. "Would your security detail have looked for things like this? I'm wondering how long they've been here."

Sam laced long, thin fingers in front of him. "Probably not. They're more concerned with threats. They have a bomb-sniffing dog, things like that."

"So, they could've been here for who knows how long." Eddie studied the older man. "I would say there's no reason to think that these are only here on the ship. I doubt they could get into your office on the Hill, but what about your house or your car?"

Sam's eyes widened, and then he shook his head. "I don't know. I know I have a problem with my security. The question is, how big a problem. If these are here, I think it's safe to assume that they're everywhere."

The ship keeping pace a mile behind them still bothered Eddie. "If someone could get these on board, I don't see why they couldn't get a tracking device on here as well."

The senator's eyes hardened, and he stared off into space before looking back at Eddie, his jaw set. "That would be unacceptable. Check the ship again. We cannot be followed."

CHAPTER 18

As Loren and Luis descended from the church tower, she asked, "Can you disappear, but keep an eye on me? Be close in case I need you?"

His brows drew down, and his gaze darted around her face. "I don't like it."

"I get that. But can you do it?"

He rubbed his lips with one finger. "Yes, but if you go inside that boat, I might not see you. If I can't see you, I can't help you."

"I understand. I'm pretty good at taking care of myself. Just be ready if I signal. And, Luis, don't do anything until I do. Got it?"

He frowned before nodding reluctantly. "Be careful."

"I will."

Luis gave her one more searching look, then turned and walked away.

Loren took a long breath and then started back toward the ship. She made a few passes, making no attempt to conceal her presence. The guards, amateurs that they were, didn't appear to even notice her. Darkness was settling on the river, and she was hot and sticky. She wanted a shower before dinner, so she decided to call it a day and return to the hotel. By tomorrow morning, she would have a better plan of attack.

She wondered if and when Luis would reappear. Would he stay away completely until she called for him? Is that what she wanted? Was that part of the plan? She sighed. As she strolled back to her room in the settling darkness, there was no sign of him.

She had higher hopes for tomorrow, but if something didn't come of this by midday, she would report to Craig that she'd located Selik and connected him to a ship named the *Voodoo III*. And then she'd go home. That was something for the Agency to work on, and maybe it would help Sam in the long run. What about Eddie, though? The ache of worry still constricted her chest every time she thought of him. She desperately hoped he was okay.

In the years after Eddie saved her in Paris, she thought about him all the time. But it had been one night—under charged circumstances. How real could it be? Sadly, at the time, she thought she'd never see him again. She left the Agency and didn't know about Nikki's murder, nor that Eddie was on the run.

When the FBI finally lucked onto Eddie's trail, they asked Loren for help. She did it to help Eddie, not the Bureau, and if she was totally honest with herself, as a chance to see him again. Once they resolved that situation, they had to part ways again.

Now, once more, she'd contacted him, this time to convince him to help the CIA. Worse, to help Craig. From Eddie's point of view, every time she reached out, it was to help some agency to use him. A troublesome cycle. It was not at all what she intended, but certainly a reasonable conclusion on his part. It didn't put her in the most trustworthy light.

She rubbed her face. This whole situation sucked, and Eddie was in danger. She could feel it in her bones. And the circumstances of their last meetings had to be driving a wedge between them. Another entry on a growing list of things she would deal with after all of this mess was over.

The air conditioning in her room was glorious, and she was reaching down to pull her shirt over her head when she froze.

Selik walked out of the bathroom and smiled at her. "Please, don't let me stop you."

Act surprised or play it straight? She read his cold, gray eyes and decided it was too late to play the innocent. "Why are you in my room, Selik?"

He tsked. "Not a good name to use here, Loren. I'm sure you know I'm checked in down the road as Klaus. We should use that one. I came to take you to dinner. Get some clothes and shower. I don't mind waiting."

If he wanted her dead, he would've tried already. Where was this going? What did he want? She purposely provoked him by waving a red flag, so it shouldn't surprise her she received a reaction. "Am I some sort of prisoner?"

Selik smiled. "Of course not. I only want to make sure we have time to talk."

Loren didn't believe that for a second. How to stroke this mark? She studied him out of the corner of her eye as she pulled some clothes from her bag.

Selik raised his eyebrows as if he'd just remembered something. "My men saw you for just a moment near the docks today with some man. Is there someone else we should invite to dinner?"

She shrugged and forced herself to sound airy. "He was hanging around the lobby earlier. I gave him fifty bucks to translate for me today. I don't speak Spanish. He might still be there. Do I need him?"

Selik narrowed his eyes and studied her before shaking his head. "No, I don't think so."

She entered the bathroom and closed the door. She was out of practice. When she was with the Agency, she would've started taking her shirt off before the door closed completely. As if he was accidentally getting a glimpse.

This made Loren stop. She wasn't a spy anymore. She'd done her time, and she was through. Just how far was she willing to go to help Sam? Not that far.

When she left the Agency, she swore she would never sleep with any man she didn't want to ever again. She was done with that life, and her body and her choices were her own now. That was a promise she wouldn't go back on for anyone—not even Sam.

She turned on the water and undressed. Where was Luis? Would he understand this was part of the plan and stay in the shadows, watching? She sighed, hoping so. This was why you didn't go into the field with someone you didn't know well or hadn't worked with before.

Fighting back a surge of adrenaline, she stood under the water, prayed, and sent mental messages to Luis—wait and be ready. Afterward, she quickly put on a lightweight, yellow sundress and stepped out of the bathroom, still combing her hair. "Where are we going?"

Selik shrugged. "I've discovered a little place down the road, not fancy, but good. I thought I'd introduce you to it if that's okay."

Loren nodded, trying to appear unaffected and casual. "That sounds good to me."

Luis was nowhere in sight as they strolled down the street to the restaurant. She glanced casually around. Two men were following at a distance like shadows. As they passed under a streetlight, she noticed more details about them. Large and capable looking, one with a blond ponytail and the other with a thick black beard. Her heartbeat stepped up a notch. These weren't the amateurs who'd been guarding the boat earlier. These looked like pros, maintaining a respectful distance, eyes everywhere. The stakes had clearly changed.

She just hoped if things got dicey that Luis was as talented as Eddie said he was.

They sat at an outside table. Selik still wore khakis with a stiff safari jacket and didn't seem a bit affected by the heat. Loren fanned herself with her menu. Ugh, the humid air was oppressive.

The waiter poured wine, and they ordered. After he left, Selik lifted his glass. "To Senator Hawthorne."

Loren kept her face a mask and only showed a fraction of her surprise. She lifted her glass. "Do you know Sam?"

Selik shrugged. "We are both great collectors. Men such as us are bound to run into each other from time to time."

She studied him. Play the innocent or play along? Selik wouldn't buy a routine. He seemed completely at ease, and impossible to read. "Are you after the same plane Sam's interested in?" Sam had fabricated the plane as a cover, Loren was sure of it. If that were true, then Selik would know nothing about it. He didn't bat an eye at the question, however.

"No, I'm not interested in any of that. My interests are in pre-Columbian artifacts—art and weapons. The senator and I trade tips when we come across something that might interest the other."

All of that was a lie, but to what purpose? Also, this statement seemed to indicate that the meeting with Sam was not a onetime incident. It spoke of a relationship, if only a casual one. This wasn't improving Sam's situation, or her faith in the man. "Is that why you're here? Going after some artifact?"

His gunmetal gray eyes were steady, and his lined face set. "Something like that."

Their food arrived.

Selik took a bite, chewed slowly, and then wiped his mouth carefully with a napkin. "So, why don't you tell me what you're doing here?"

She hadn't really expected to actually end up interacting with Selik, so she wasn't as ready as she should have been. At least this situation was closer to her training and experience. "I'm on vacation."

His expression didn't change, and he took a sip of water. "My sources tell me you're no longer with the CIA, so Sam must have sent you here."

She held his gaze and said, "No one sent me here. I'm on vacation." What sources did this man have that could connect her to the Agency?

Selik returned to his meal. "And your sightseeing led you to old freighters on the river?"

"Of course not. I saw you on the street and recognized you from long ago." She shrugged. "I guess my curiosity got the best of me. Sometimes I miss the old life." She kept her voice light and conversational. "What *are* you doing with that old ship, anyway?"

He shrugged. "Business. Buying here and selling there—it pays the bills." He took a sip of wine, his attention never leaving her. "Have you seen Sam recently?"

This kind of question could be a trap. She just met with the senator, but how on earth could he know that? She shook her head. "Not in over a year—at least not in person. He texts me now and then."

Selik asked, "Is that how you know about the plane he's after?"

Loren nodded. "I only know he found one, not a lot of details. He's a busy man these days."

"He is that."

They finished the meal and sipped their wine, making small talk.

He was still curious about Sam, but seemed to put that aside for the moment.

She had to probe gently and carefully. More questions from her about the ship or Selik's activities would be too much.

Selik pulled a cigar from his jacket pocket. "Do you mind?"

"Not at all. Go ahead." She glanced around. No one else remained eating on the patio. Time to thank him and get out of here.

Before she could move, however, two men walked up and sat at a nearby table. Loren looked over her shoulder. They weren't the same men who'd followed them from the hotel. Those remained down the road.

Selik puffed on his cigar and narrowed his eyes. "I'm very sorry Sam got you involved in this."

Two more men approached and also took seats on the other side of Loren and finally the pair down the road approached, bringing the number of trained guards to six.

The man with the ponytail walked into the light and pulled back his jacket, showing her his pistol in a holster.

Selik calmly blew out a long stream of smoke. "I'm afraid you're going to have to come with us."

CHAPTER 19

As Eddie sat down for dinner, he tightened one calloused hand reflexively. Having no proper read on the situation made him nervous. The captain and Sam joined him at the glass dining table. The senator seemed distracted and irritable since Eddie's discovery of the bugs. He gazed off at the sea as he ate, the muscles in his jaw clenching between bites.

The captain seemed unaffected by this silence, quietly eating with a smile.

Eddie surreptitiously studied Sam's every move and expression. Separating paranoia from genuine concern was a muddy mess. He was working for a man he was pretty sure planned to drug him or someone else later on the trip. Finding the bugs or perhaps a tracking device, however, would be mutually beneficial. It made sense to continue with that part of the mission. If the senator was in danger from outsiders, then so was Eddie.

They ate thick, delicious steaks in near silence. As soon as he finished his dinner, Sam folded his napkin, declared he was turning in, and left the dining room.

The act made Eddie feel more than ever like a mere employee. They remained, drinking brandy, and listening to the ocean outside, before Jon said, "All very wealthy and powerful men are a little eccentric. How could you have so much and not be? Everyone I've worked for is like this."

Eddie took a sip. "My experience is that everybody's a little weird when you get down to it."

The captain nodded. "Yah, this is true as well. Do you have a moment? I wish to show you something."

The two men took their snifters and walked up to the bridge.

"When you asked me about that ship behind us today, it piqued my curiosity. So, I looked at it and discovered something odd."

He gestured to the large monitor still displaying the islands and other ships. "This device acts as our black box, if you will—like they have on airplanes."

Eddie nodded.

"So, we can rewind it." The captain worked the controls and the ships on the screen reversed course as time moved backward. He pointed at the craft trailing behind them as it moved away from the *Morning Star* toward the top of the screen, where he paused it and then let the image move forward again. "This is that ship entering our space. What is odd is that we've been doing a steady eighteen knots since we left Miami. That's about as fast as she will go, but we can keep up that speed for days."

He pointed at the black line on the screen. "This craft behind us is big. I don't think as big as us, but a decent-sized vessel." He hovered the mouse over the other ship and a number indicated that the craft was moving at forty-two knots. "That is quick. Some yachts now have water jets and can really move. This one races down and then, when she gets about a mile behind us, settles in at our same speed."

Goose pimples raced down Eddie's arms and his eyes widened.

Jon held up a hand. "It may be nothing. Maybe they were showing off and then fell to a more economical speed once they reached the shipping lanes. It takes a lot of fuel to move a big vessel at over forty knots."

Eddie studied the small boat icon as it raced down the monitor. "Jon, where are we headed?"

The tall, slim man hesitated. "Mr. Hawthorne told me to sail to Mayaguana. It's an island in the southern part of the Bahamas. He said he'd give me more specifics then."

Eddie asked, "What time will we make it there?"

"Somewhere around noon to one o'clock tomorrow."

At least he still had some time to work with. The trailing ship could easily overtake the *Morning Star*. They were holding back for a reason. Maybe they were waiting to attack under cover of darkness. More likely, they planned to follow them to their final destination and then act. Maybe this wasn't about killing the senator. Maybe it was just about discovering where the hell they were heading. Or both. "Who drives the boat at night?"

Jon studied him with bright, cornflower blue eyes. "I will until around midnight, and then Carlos will take a shift. You seriously think we're in some kind of trouble?"

Eddie shrugged. "I'm not sure, but I want you to do something for me. And tell your man Carlos—if for any reason, we slow down or if that boat behind us gets any closer, I want you to tell me immediately. Do you understand?"

The captain nodded.

"This could be life and death important."

"I understand. I'll let you know."

Eddie walked out on the deck and felt the wind on his face as he gazed out at the horizon. The briny smell of salt was heavy on the air. Without the land's light pollution, it was amazing how densely the stars speckled the sky. In all directions, it was just darkness, with only the faintest twinkle here and there in the distance.

They were miles from help, security, or a safe port. Even this mammoth craft didn't prevent him from feeling vulnerable in the endless black swells. He looked to the rear, wondering about the ship trailing them. Who were they?

He found a deck chair and sat until the senator's cabin darkened. He glanced at his watch. Nine p.m. He waited a full half hour to make sure Sam was asleep, before tiptoeing down to his room to collect his flashlight and lock pick. Then Eddie headed up to the locked room the senator had used throughout the day. He paused outside the door in darkness and listened. When convinced the coast was clear, he picked the lock.

The room was only slightly larger than a closet. Stacks of packages, manila envelopes, and boxes sat piled along the walls. Three thick folders and a laptop sat on top of a wooden table in the center. Using only his small flashlight, he opened one and paged through it.

Eddie wasn't sure what he expected to find, but this wasn't it. It was a stack of shipping manifests, purchase orders, and invoices from dozens of companies. The items on the papers seemed ordinary—pipes, fittings, some kind of lab equipment, and raw materials.

The only odd thing was brief notes and drawings in the margins of some pages. Lists of numbers, grids with letters or symbols in the squares handwritten here and there.

He looked past these at the contents of each and noticed Project names like Pegasus, Ergot, and Afterimage, but none of them meant anything to him. Nothing appeared sinister or even out of the ordinary, other than that they all were from years ago. He saw the name Apenno Technologies as a supplier a few times, the only vendor to show up more than once. He didn't remember ever hearing the name before. Nothing else struck him.

A thump sounded outside. Eddie froze, holding his breath. His heart pounded, and he stood stock-still, waiting for the door to burst open. Another thump. Eddie exhaled. Just water hitting the hull. He slowly relaxed and then closed the folder. Nothing here was worth the risk of staying any longer.

He slipped out, walked back down to his room, closed the door, and wedged the wood into the jamb as best he could. Pulling out his cellphone he checked in vain for service—nothing. What did surprise him was that now there was no wi-fi either. Had the senator turned it off? Not that it mattered—who could he reach out to that could help him now? Still, it wasn't a great sign. He pulled a pistol from the bag and lay down with it. He had to get some sleep. Tomorrow was going to be the day.

CHAPTER 20

A car pulled up to the curb, and Ponytail pushed Loren into the back seat. Selik slid in beside the driver, and they pulled away.

They wanted her alive, so she would go along for now and see where this led. As they turned the corner, she was simultaneously hoping that Luis was keeping pace somehow and willing him to stay away. Now was her opportunity to really learn something. She looked at the back of Selik's head and asked, "Where are you taking me, and why?"

He didn't turn, but said over his shoulder, "We're just going to go somewhere and have a chat. Don't worry."

Continue to play the innocent? "Don't worry? You're taking me somewhere at gunpoint! That seems like something to worry about." She analyzed the direction they were traveling. Heading toward the old freighter. This was her mission, and the only way she was going to get aboard that ship, but a small voice questioned how she was going to get back off. She'd figure something out. She always did, but she once again hoped that Luis was as capable as Eddie thought he was.

Selik half turned. "This is for your own protection. Sam has involved you in something very dangerous. I'm simply making sure you don't accidentally wander somewhere that could get you hurt. I'm confident Sam told you to expect such a thing."

They stopped at the bottom of the gangplank, and Selik got out and walked up ahead of her. Jamming the barrel painfully against Loren's lower back, Ponytail gestured for her to follow him.

The main hold was open and dim, with only a few evenly spaced bulbs emitting a weak, orange glow. As they passed, Loren saw the crates she'd noted earlier, as well as several others. She followed Selik up a set of metal stairs and down a short catwalk to an office. Ponytail shoved her down into a wooden chair with a dirty, green cushion.

Selik sat at a rusty metal desk facing her. Behind him, a large window opened to the far bank of the river. "I'm sorry, but I can't have you running around for the next twenty-four hours. Soon this will all be over, and if you behave, then you can go."

Make this worthwhile. Get him to talk. Anger seemed like a reasonable response. It was easy to dredge some up, for that's truly how she felt about her treatment. Her eyes were wide and her jaw set. "So, I'm a prisoner? For what reason?"

"Don't be so dramatic, dear. I'm just keeping you out of trouble for a little while. Sam made a mistake sending you here. One of many, I'm afraid. You can't make something as big as Mendelson's work just disappear. And now his arrogance has been his undoing." He sucked on his teeth and narrowed his eyes. His voice turned quiet and menacing. "I'm going to ask you this once, Loren, and I highly recommend you answer me with the truth. What kind of container is Sam after, and how do we transport it?"

Loren's head spun. Selik assumed she knew much more than she actually did. She'd never heard of Mendelson or any kind of container. Selik didn't believe that Sam was after some airplane, either. What had the senator gotten himself into? The confusion on her face was real, however, as a crease formed at the top of her nose. "I've no idea what you're talking about. What container?"

Selik bore into her with implacable gray eyes for a long time before he blew out a breath. "Maybe Sam was smarter than I thought. But if you really don't know anything, then your friend put you in a very perilous position." He rubbed his face, considered her, and then said mostly to himself, "Why would he have sent you here?" His eyebrows rose. "Unless it was your previous employer." A muscle tremored in his cheek. "You'd better hope it wasn't the CIA, Ms. Malen. That would very be messy." He shook his head.

"It doesn't matter. This will all be over soon. We'll get what we're after, and then Sam won't be a concern for us anymore."

Her arms and legs felt numb. Sam would cease to be a concern because they would beat him to the punch or because they were going to kill him? "What're you saying?"

A look of smug self-satisfaction spread across Selik's face and then disappeared as he stood. "The last piece of information I need is the canister's location. Once I have that, we win. So, is there anything you want to tell me? Anything that might mean we don't need to follow the senator? Something that just might save his life? If so, now's the time."

Loren played up her fear and indignation and tossed in a little dumb blonde. "What are you saying? That you're following Sam? For what? I don't know anything about any of this."

Selik said in an icy voice, "We shall see." Glancing at his watch, he said, "I have things to take care of. I insist you be our guest tonight." He gestured at a black vinyl couch against one wall. "Tomorrow, we should settle all of this, and then you and I will have another talk." He stood and turned to the man at the door. "Two of you guard her all night, understood?" To Loren, he said, "You've no idea what you're up against, my dear. If you did, you'd have never come." He turned off the light and left the room.

The men followed, and one guard locked her in from the outside. Through a window in the door, she saw her sentries lean against the wall and light cigarettes.

Frustration billowed inside her, and she squeezed her eyes shut and tried to calm her mind. This had to do with something called Mendelson. She memorized the name and then moved on. There was some kind of canister as well. Sam and Selik appeared to be looking for the same thing. What could it be? Selik didn't know much about it, and he was hoping she did.

She clenched her jaw. Why keep her here? Who could she tell, and what could she tell them? Sam was the only person connected to this, and how on earth could she even contact him in the middle of the ocean? She didn't know whatever number they used on Sam's yacht. Her primary form of communication with him had always been through text. Not very useful hundreds of miles from the nearest cell tower. She'd cross that bridge once she got out of here.

Standing, Loren turned on the desk lamp. She stood at the window and studied the murky shapes across the river, indistinct and blocky. A pinprick of light blinked twice. Luis, signaling her—it had to be. Holding her hand in front of her chest, she gave a thumbs-up, her body blocking the gesture from the men in the hall outside.

One flash of acknowledgment.

Relief washed over her. She wasn't alone. Luis was out there, watching and waiting for a signal. Suddenly exhausted, she turned off the lamp, crossed the room and lay on the couch.

Letting out a long breath through her nose, Loren turned her thoughts to the part she didn't want to think about. Selik claimed his men were following Sam and that he was in danger. Was that a bluff? She didn't think so, but she couldn't do anything for them now, regardless.

She had to trust that Eddie would keep them alive until she and Luis could help. Eddie was an incredibly resourceful man—possibly the most capable she'd ever known. If she could've picked anyone to protect Sam and bring him home, she would have chosen Eddie.

She'd depended on him the last time she had a friend in trouble. Amy, the third Clay Pigeon, also ran to him. He'd come through for her then, too.

The memory still nagged at her as her mind wandered back to France so long ago.

The city of Rouen was cool and busy that day. Loren wasn't sure why Amy had chosen this place to meet.

It rained that morning, and she remembered the smell of wet concrete that hung in the air as she stood across the street from the church of Jeanne d 'Arc. She studied the architecture and glanced at her watch. The church's namesake reminded her a bit of Amy. Small but feisty and often underestimated. The prearranged meeting time had passed, but Loren still believed she would show. She had to.

Eddie nodded to her, and they crossed the street and stood in front of the building. Tourists milled about the church and the local lunch traffic congested the street. Loren surveyed the crowd and cars as they passed. Eddie held the red book at his side where it was plainly visible, as they'd agreed.

Loren glanced at her watch. Twenty minutes late now. Where was she? She glimpsed Amy's red hair a few cars back in a powder blue Citroen. The traffic was still dense, and she started and stopped in rhythm with the other cars.

As she pulled even with them, Amy looked over, shook her head once, and then motioned over her shoulder with her chin. A black Mercedes rode her bumper, two large men in the front seat.

Eddie stepped out into traffic right behind Amy's car, as if he was an oblivious tourist. The driver slammed on the brakes and laid on his horn.

Eddie feigned fright and dropped his book. As he reached down for the book, he snatched the pistol from his waistband and fired a shot into the front tire. He quickly tucked the pistol away again.

Loren rushed forward, trying to draw attention to her and away from the sound of the gun. In French, she yelled and lectured Eddie, calling him a fool and that he was going to get himself killed. She grabbed Eddie's arm and ushered him to the other side of the street.

Narrowing his eyes, the driver turned and raced at them.

Eddie pushed Loren one way and leaped the other.

She hit hard on her right palm before she gave way to her training and ducked into a roll, searching for Eddie as she came back up to her feet.

The car careened off a short wall lining the street. Eddie appeared from the other side. He held his pistol low with both hands as he circled behind it.

The driver tried to leave, but the car only lurched forward before stopping. Something was clearly wrong with the front wheel.

A red Ford roared past them. Two more men also chasing Amy? If they lost contact with her now, they'd have to start over, wasting time and prolonging Amy's exposure.

The passenger from the Mercedes threw his door open and stepped out, pistol drawn.

Eddie fired twice. The man doubled over and fell back behind the car.

Tires screeched, and Amy skidded to a stop between them. "Get in!" she yelled.

She must have circled the block.

Eddie pointed Loren to the front seat and dove into the rear.

As Amy raced away, the red car rammed them from behind, driving them into a light pole.

Loren shot forward, and her forehead slammed into the ceiling just above the windshield. Her ears rang, and she felt a trickle of blood on her forehead.

Eddie scrambled off of the floor of the back seat, his brows drawing down as he saw her.

Loren shook her head. "I'm fine. Are you okay, Amy?"

Amy rubbed at her collarbone. "Yes, I'm okay."

Eddie leaned out the back window and fired twice at the red car behind them, then yelled, "Drive!"

Amy grabbed the wheel and mashed down on the gas. The car and the post stayed connected for a second before finally breaking apart and they shot down the road.

Eddie yelled over his shoulder, "Keep going!"

Loren turned. Spiderwebs of cracks stretched across the glass at the edges, surrounding a gaping hole in the rear window. How many shots had they used? There couldn't be that many left.

The other car roared back into pursuit.

Eddie said, "Amy, when I tell you to, I want you to slam on the brakes. Got it?"

"Stop?!"

"Yes, when I tell you."

"Okay."

The red Ford closed the gap.

Amy's attention darted from the road to the rear-view mirror.

Eddie yelled, "Now!"

Amy slammed on the brakes, causing the little car to fishtail. The red car skidded in response and turned.

Eddie leaned out and fired three shots into the car's side window and windshield before the pistol clicked empty. He turned and yelled again, "Go!"

Amy's car lurched forward.

The red car stayed in the middle of the road, not pursuing.

Loren let out the breath she didn't realize she'd been holding.

Amy slowed. "Where do I go?"

Eddie glanced behind them. "Just keep driving." He turned to Loren. "Now's your part, Loren. We have Amy, but who can we trust? Where do we take her?"

He wasn't going to like her answer, but it really was their only option. "I've got to call Craig. He can help us."

Eddie sat back heavily. "You couldn't prove that by me. I'm a wanted man, Loren."

Loren reached back and took his hand. "I know. But he knows more now. It's different. Trust me, okay?"

After a long moment, he nodded.

• • •

Loren rolled onto her side on the greasy green couch in the gloomy office. That was a strange memory to creep into her mind now. It was another time Eddie had figured a way out of a tight spot. He could do it again.

Did he understand he was sailing into a trap? That was the question. Selik would never have told her this much if he were going to leave her alive. He meant it to scare her into cooperating, but it was a bluff.

She took a deep, cleansing breath and willed herself to focus. What was everyone after? How could she help, and did Eddie know he was in trouble yet? She closed her eyes, said a quick prayer, and tried to send a mental warning to him.

CHAPTER 21

Eddie jerked awake for the tenth time. Dim sunlight streamed in through the small portal. He glanced at his watch: six-thirty. No point trying to sleep anymore, so he sat up and raked his fingers through his hair. Most of the night, he'd spent sitting up in bed clutching his Sig Sauer 9 mm to his chest, fading off now and then before popping back alert.

He stretched, swung his long legs off the bed, and laced up his boots. According to the captain, they should reach their destination today. He pulled the wooden wedge free from the door, tucked the pistol and holster into his waistband, and headed topside.

One of the ever-silent crewmembers set a coffee pot down at the main dining table as Eddie took a seat.

The senator's plate was already clean, and he poured himself a cup. "Good morning. Have some food." Sam said it without meeting Eddie's eyes. He concentrated a little too much on sugaring his coffee, like an amateur, building up his courage before a difficult or distasteful task?

Sam took a sip and then rose, cup in hand. "I don't mean to eat and run, but I'll catch up with you in a little while." Without a backward glance, he turned and walked back to his stateroom.

Eddie said to himself, "He was going to knock me out right now." He could feel it in his bones. He stood, raced down and collected the empty can of ether. Pulling his pistol, he jogged back upstairs and into the senator's stateroom.

Sam stood at the wall box, the metal door open, staring at the interior.

Eddie pointed the Sig at him and held up the bottle. "Looking for this, Senator?"

Sam paled, blue eyes wide, and jaw hanging slack. He lifted his hands in a placating gesture and said, "You don't understand. I meant you no harm, but this secret is too dangerous. I was trying to protect you."

Anger rose inside Eddie, but before he could speak, the engines wound down and the craft slowed. "Why are we stopping? We aren't supposed to get to Mayaguana until mid-day."

Sam hesitated, so Eddie lifted the gun higher and said in a low, menacing voice, "Why are we *stopping*?"

Sam said, "That was a ruse. I told Jon not to tell you. We're here."

Eddie's anger melted into fear. "Sam, this is a life or death question, so don't lie to me. Are you meeting someone here?"

The older man's eyes narrowed and his jaw set. "No. Why?"

"Damn it." Eddie turned and ran from the stateroom.

Sam pounded after him down the stairwell. "What is it?

Eddie burst into the cockpit.

The captain turned, his face ashen and drawn. He pointed at the screen. "You were right."

Sam looked at the display. "Right about what?"

Eddie gritted his teeth. "A ship has been following us since yesterday."

On the projected map, the distance between the *Morning Star* in the center and the approaching craft shrank rapidly.

A crackling pop sounded, and they all jumped. The three radios released a wisp of foul-smelling smoke.

Eddie swore. He'd been so busy looking for bugs, it never occurred to him to look for the sabotage of the communications equipment. He turned to Sam. "Can I trust you? Because we're about to be boarded."

The senator's eyes were wide, and his mouth still hung open. "I don't understand."

Eddie said, "Whoever you've been dealing with has double-crossed you." He turned to the captain. "Can we outrun them?"

He shook his head. "No way."

Eddie raced from the room and flew down the stairs to his own cabin. He opened his case's false bottom and pulled out the second pistol and two extra clips. Only forty-eight rounds. The captain thought the ship following them was large, but not as big as the *Morning Star*. Hell, even something a third of that size could easily hold fifty men. He was likely out-manned, outgunned, and with no help for five hundred miles in all directions.

Sam rushed into the room, his lips blue, shock still prominent on his face.

Eddie asked, "Do you have any weapons or ammunition on the ship?"

The senator shook his head and then stopped. "There are some skeet shotguns at the rear and some birdshot."

Better than nothing. "Where? Take me to them."

As Sam led him numbly to the rear, Eddie asked, "Can you shoot?" He still didn't know if he could trust the man, but he was running low on options.

This question seemed to revive the senator. He licked his lips, his spine straightened a bit, and he said, "Yes, both that Sig and the shotguns."

They came up on the rear deck, and Eddie asked, "Who's coming?"

Sam said, "I'm guessing commandos who work for a man named Selik. We're all looking for the same thing. I have the location, and he doesn't. Or I guess he does now, damn it."

Eddie grabbed his arm. "Can I trust you?"

Sam said, "Yes. I was trying to keep you out of this, but that's all over now. You can trust me."

Eddie handed him a pistol. "Let's get those shotguns."

As they continued out onto the open deck, a lounge chair splintered into pieces. The crack of a gun echoed a second later.

Eddie turned. A long, sleek yacht motored a few hundred yards behind them, with a tactical boat full of black-clad soldiers racing ahead of it. He leveled his pistol and fired one shot, aware of his ammunition situation, and pulled Sam down. Before he hit the floor, he saw the tactical boat swerve and turn away from the ship. Well, that bought them a minute, at least.

Sam crawled back inside the cabin. "I guess we can't get to the shotguns now."

Eddie asked, "Is there anything on the boat they want?"

Sam clenched his jaw. "I don't think so. They just needed the location. My guess is that their orders are to eliminate us."

Eddie rubbed his face. He needed some advantage, and quickly. Maybe he'd get another chance to go for the shotguns while the bad guys were regrouping. He inched forward, leaned around the corner, and saw the flash of a sniper rifle from the flat top of the larger enemy vessel in the distance.

CHAPTER 22

Frank spun the wheel of the tactical boat and chomped on his unlit cigar. He'd read all the plans and schematics of the senator's big ship, so when the two men appeared heading to the rear of deck number four, he knew they were after the two skeet shotguns.

Man, they reacted fast. How'd they determine they were at risk so quickly? Was it when they'd blown the radios? That certainly got their attention, but to go from there to the shotguns was a leap. More was going on here than Frank knew. He could feel it. He hated nothing on earth more than walking into a place unprepared—especially one filled with layer after layer of confined spaces.

Frank had ordered the warning shot, but he'd been completely shocked when the unknown man with the senator returned fire. Who was he? The old man was supposed to be alone. Frank lifted his radio and called Nelson, his sniper on the ship. "No one gets to the skeet cabinet." By the sound of it, the unknown man had shot at them with a 9 mm handgun, so he then moved out beyond reasonable pistol range. Who was this guy—and was he the only one?

He scanned the unremarkable, craggy little island with a rise in the middle ahead to the left. What on earth could be so valuable here, of all places? His secondary aim was to discover the senator's destination—at least he'd accomplished that part of the mission. Should he pull back and return to his ship? No. The primary objective remained. He could not let the senator get away alive. He scratched at the white puckered scar on his neck.

Why did things always get so complicated so quickly, and why didn't the people upstairs ever understand that?

His immediate concern was the gasoline bomb strapped to the front of the tactical boat. He didn't need this party-crasher hitting it with a stray round and ending this whole affair before it began. The longer he stayed out here in no-man's-land, however, the longer his enemies had to prepare. Aggression was his only actual choice.

Frank shouted to his men, strapped in down the craft's centerline, "All right, we obviously have at least one unexpected hostile. Remember: don't shoot anyone unless you have to, but if they fire at you, drop their ass."

The men nodded.

Frank touched his radio's throat mic. "Nelson, cover us. I'm going to approach from the rear and rush this bad boy."

Over the radio he heard, "10-4."

Frank pushed the throttle forward, swung the craft around in a wide arc, and raced up to the *Morning Star's* rear. At the last minute, he killed the engine and coasted into the ship with a bump.

The oval outline of a door was visible here just at the waterline. Mack stepped forward and molded a small plastic charge to the metal where a handle would normally be. He retreated a few steps and then squeezed a button. With a deafening blast, the door launched inward.

Frank yelled, "Team one, get on board and make sure the way is clear. The rest of you get that bomb to the engine room."

Two by two, the soldiers leaped onto the craft, pivoting back and forth with their submachine guns, before moving forward onto the ship.

The sniper rifle cracked in the distance as Nelson squeezed off two more rounds at someone, somewhere.

Frank gritted his teeth in frustration. Holding his pistol level, he leaped onto the vessel's deck. Two reports sounded from deep within the ship.

He heard Mack's voice in his earpiece saying, "Two men down. Earl is gone, and Flip is hurt badly."

He pulled out the mangled remains of his cigar and threw it on the deck. Two shots—two hits—whoever they were up against was very capable, low on ammo, or both. He keyed his neck mic. "Mack, the top priority is the bomb. Get it to the engine room."

"Roger."

A pair of his troops stood at the rear, guarding the tactical boat. If this got worse, it was their only retreat option.

Frank nodded at them as he ducked through the door and inside the craft. She was amazing, and a small part of him regretted that in a few minutes she was going to be gone. What a waste.

Two of his men reappeared, dragging what had to be the captain between them. His hands and feet were zip-tied together, and gray tape covered his mouth. They dropped him in one corner of the room. More of his men returned, dragging five crewmembers dressed in light blue and trussed the same way as their captain.

Mack was the last to return, half dragging, half-supporting an injured soldier. Bright blood ran out between the fingers of the man's hand clamped onto one thigh. Mack eased him down to the deck, and another of the soldiers treated the wound.

Frank studied it. If you wanted to incapacitate a man and force his buddies to carry him, but weren't sure if he was wearing a vest, the thigh was a smart target. Hard to hit, though. A skillful shot. Who the hell was this stranger? He looked around the room. "Where are the senator and our unexpected guest?"

No one answered.

Frank touched his throat mic and called Nelson. "Has anyone left the ship?

Nelson replied, "Not that I've seen."

Frank gritted his teeth. He hated this. It was much too tricky a place to go in after them. "Screw it. Come on, let's get off, and we'll blow this thing sky high."

CHAPTER 23

Eddie leaned into the master cabin, pistol ready. Empty.

The senator peeked into the bathroom. "Clear. What was that thing they were carrying?"

Eddie scratched at one cheek. "My guess is a bomb."

Sam's eyes widened. "Are you serious? Then we need to get off the ship."

"I agree." Eddie gestured toward the bow. "There's a boat just through there, right?"

Sam said, "Yes, the Zodiac, for emergencies."

"I think this qualifies." Eddie opened the door and looked out onto the bright white bow, where the small inflatable craft sat secured in place.

Keeping low, they stepped out and released the straps holding the boat down.

Sam asked, "Won't we be vulnerable out there in the ocean, though?"

Eddie said, "One problem at a time, Senator." He snuck a quick peek behind the ship and saw the tactical boat motoring back to the other craft. He turned to Sam. "Over that side, and let's get moving."

They pushed the inflatable to the rail and back as far as possible. Their only hope was making it into the water unnoticed. Eddie stooped to lift the craft over.

Sam suddenly turned. "Wait, I have to get something."

"Not now," barked Eddie.

The older man ignored him and raced back into his cabin.

Eddie's heart pounded as the seconds ticked by before Sam reappeared. He clutched a key in one hand, which he quickly shoved deep into his pocket.

Eddie lifted the Zodiac and turned it, blocking the foolish man from his view as he prepared to hoist it over the side.

With a sudden roar and a wave of heat, the inflatable boat and Eddie flew into the air. The *Morning Star* heaved and shattered from the inside with a deafening concussion.

The rubber boat slammed into Eddie as it raced into the sky like a kite. He held onto the handles for dear life, the rope scraping the skin from his fingers. It flipped suddenly and one hand came free, then he and the boat tumbled toward the ocean.

Burning debris flew off in all directions. A piece hit Eddie's left cheek, and a bright light of pain surged through him.

Eddie crashed into the ocean. As he went under, the boat wrenched free from his hand. He kicked toward the surface, gasping. His whole body felt singed, and every nerve reported pinpricks of pain. His head seemed stuffed with cotton, and his rapid heartbeat thudding in his ears was the only sound making it to his brain.

The massive craft listed to one side, the entire back blown away and spewing flames. The ship seemed to sit back and then slide below the surface.

Eddie looked back and forth, searching for the Zodiac. Splinters of wood littered the ocean and larger objects sprouted flames as they bobbed atop the waves. The senator floated face down a short distance away, and Eddie pulled hard at the water, swimming to him as fast as he could. He turned him over, and Sam coughed. A gash crossed his forehead so deep that Eddie thought he could see part of his skull.

Eddie put one arm around Sam's chest, keeping him afloat, and looked around again for the little boat. Nowhere in sight. At the top of a wave, he glimpsed the island in the distance. Fighting against the swells, he made painfully slow progress toward it.

A high-pitched whine floated in on the wind. The tactical boat! He reached into his waistband. The pistol was gone. He gritted his teeth. The second pistol he'd given to Sam! He felt around the man's midsection until his hand closed around the handle of his other Sig. Thank God. He scanned for the enemy.

Blood poured from the side of Eddie's face. What would kill him first? The bad guys, a shark, or maybe his leaden legs would give out under Sam's weight, and they'd just drown. He looked over his shoulder at the island, still maddeningly far away, and kicked for all he was worth.

The whine changed pitch. The menacing black boat sped around toward him. Should he shoot or lie low? No point in giving away their position, but if he waited too long, he'd be a sitting duck.

A sudden ripping sound answered the question as bullets struck the water in a line that just missed Eddie's head. He felt a stinging burn on the top of his left arm just above his elbow and blood drifted away from there as well.

Great. Automatic weapons on top of everything else. Eddie lifted the pistol, aimed as well as he could, and squeezed off two more rounds. They must have been close because the boat swerved away. He checked the senator, who appeared no worse than before. Eddie's head was getting fuzzy. He willed his legs to kick one more time and then another.

The senator coughed and moaned.

Eddie could still hear the tactical boat. He jerked back and forth, trying to locate it. His visibility was severely limited, and he couldn't find it anywhere in his field of vision. He kicked again.

The enemy craft whizzed by about a hundred yards away. Another line of bullets dotted the water toward him, just missing to his left.

Eddie squeezed off two more rounds as it passed. How many shots did he have left? He wasn't sure, but some still functioning part of his brain told him it didn't really matter. He kicked once more and then a second time.

The boat flashed past again, further away this time. Smart move by the bad guys. Let Eddie wear himself out first. No point risking the men and wasting ammo.

He scissored his legs another time, but each stroke was harder, the interval between them longer. Energy ebbed from his body. A swooshing sound from behind made him turn. To his relief, a large stone was taking the brunt of a wave. Eddie's limbs were stiff as he navigated past it. The water surrounding him was turning scarlet. He sluggishly steered around several more rocks before he could find a flat place. He dragged Sam up on the narrow rocky slope and flopped onto his back. His whole body buzzed with pain, and his heart hammered in his chest.

He lifted his head. The tactical boat raced past. A big man stood at the wheel watching him. Eddie lifted the pistol, and his hand shook as he tried to level it. At least ten men were on the boat as it turned and came back for another pass, closer this time. He knew he didn't have ten bullets left.

Eddie willed the fog from his mind. Think. He staggered up onto all fours. The senator was limp, but his chest rose and fell. Eddie couldn't just leave him here. Maybe if he crawled up to a better location, he could keep the men at bay until dark, but that was a long time from now. Rivulets of crimson ran down his right arm. With an effort of will, he steadied himself and then rolled into a sitting position.

The driver of the tactical boat killed the engine. It drifted to a stop a hundred yards from shore, the black-clad men all staring in his direction, measuring him. Wondering how close to defenseless he was—and if it was time to swoop in for the kill.

Eddie's head swam. The craft out on the water shimmered, separated, and then merged. He squeezed his eyes shut and willed the double vision away before laboriously lifting his pistol in nothing more than an act of defiance. He would die shooting it out, rather than pass out and wait for them to come and execute him.

A crack tore through the air, and one man on the tactical boat slumped forward. The sound was earsplitting and close, and Eddie flinched with the shock of it.

The big man at the wheel ducked, started the engine, and threw the throttle forward.

Another shot rang out, deafening in the quiet morning air.

Eddie turned and looked up the rocky slope. It was gray with only a few pale stubborn plants insolently poking out from the sand here and there. A dark figure stood silhouetted against the sun—a featureless form, holding a long rifle off to one side. Eddie's last thought before he faded into oblivion was that it was an awfully odd-looking angel.

CHAPTER 24

Loren flinched as heavy footfalls banged on the stairs outside, and she sat up just as Selik burst into the room, two of his henchmen on his heels.

Narrowing his eyes, he demanded, "Who's with the senator? Who's protecting him?"

They were alive, and Eddie was giving them trouble. Thank God. Loren shrugged. "He said he was taking a friend, that's all I know."

Selik slapped her. Pain shot through her head and stars danced in front of her eyes.

"Don't lie to me!" Selik said in a low, menacing tone. "There's at least two of them."

What was he talking about, two? "I don't know anything about that. He didn't tell me anything about anyone else."

Selik asked, "Who is the one, then?"

Loren looked up into narrowed, flat gray eyes that were burning with rage and frustration. A muscle bulged rhythmically in Selik's cheek. "I don't know. Everyone was worried that he wasn't taking any security, so he told me he was taking a friend. That's all. What happened?"

Selik's jaw stayed rigid, and his aggressive posture didn't ease a bit as he said through clenched teeth, "An inconvenience, nothing more. They will not deny me."

A boom tore through the air. The ship rocked with the explosion. Loren felt it through the floor, and the sounds of men shouting rang out.

Selik stood and stared at the ceiling, listening. He turned to the man with the black beard, who now stood in the doorway. "Lock her up." Then to one of the other goons in the room, "If she moves, shoot her. When she's secure, come help." At the door he encountered Ponytail and barked at him, "Have the Beaver brought around to Boca Chica, get the other men, and go help Frank."

Loren dropped her head in what she hoped looked like a docile and defeated posture as the black-bearded man pulled her hands behind her back. She glanced up through her hair, straining to hear the conversation at the door.

Ponytail stepped back, allowing Selik to leave the room. "What about the trouble here?"

Selik said, "We'll deal with this. It'll take time to gather the other men. Helping Frank is the most important thing right now."

What did that mean? It seemed like a safe bet Eddie was about to have more trouble. The black-bearded man tightened a pair of handcuffs painfully around her wrists.

She looked up into the cool brown eyes of the second man with the gun. They were calm and resolute. He would kill her without hesitation.

Using a second pair of handcuffs, the first man anchored her bound hands to a steel pipe running up the wall, then the two of them hustled out the door.

Had she underestimated the situation this badly? Her pulse pounded in her ears. She took a deep breath and pulled. The cold steel of the bracelets dug into her wrists, forcing her arms into an uncomfortable angle. She bent and strained against the pipe with both arms. The metal cut into her skin and hurt like hell, but the pipe moved a fraction before she stopped and flexed her fingers. Sweat stung the abrasions around her wrists. She needed to find something to use as a lever. She pulled her feet from her sandals and was feeling around the floor for something to use when the second explosion came.

Loren reflexively jerked against the pipe again and winced as the cuffs pressed against her bones. Leaning forward, she pulled with her back, shoulder muscles, and all her strength. The pain was almost more than she could bear, and her arms trembled. Just as she was at her limit, she felt a small pop as the conduit moved a fraction.

She leaned back, let out a sigh, and flexed her wrists back and forth, rubbing them against one another. A tear leaked out of her eye and slithered down her cheek. The pain was a pulsing fire.

She heard Selik shouting in the distance as Loren leaned forward, gathered her courage, and pulled on the pipe again. It resisted and then moved just a quarter of an inch before she was out of breath and had to stop.

It took her three more tries, and her hands were slippery with her own blood when she finally pulled the handcuff free and stood. Her thighs twitched, her shoulders ached, but she stumbled toward the door. Her hands remained shackled behind her, so she had to turn to open it. Once able to work the knob, she eased the door open a few inches with her head. The dimly lit cargo was empty. A man raced by carrying a large fire extinguisher, then all was still.

Luis eased into the room. He moved slow and graceful like a cat. His pistol held in both hands low in front of him.

She stage-whispered, "Up here."

His dark eyes and weapon tracked up in unison, and he locked onto her. He raised his eyebrows and gave her a thumbs-up.

She turned and showed him her cuffed hands.

He nodded. Then spun and fired two shots to his right. The blasts were earsplitting in the closed metal interior. Loren flinched with each round.

He ran up the stairs, grabbed her upper arm, and propelled her down the catwalk. A bullet whizzed above them and ricocheted off some part of the ship.

Luis fired two shots blindly behind them and then pushed her behind a large column. "Can you swim?"

Panic rushed up inside her at the thought of trying to keep from drowning with shackled hands, but she nodded.

Luis said, "Okay, hold your hands out as far apart as you can stretch them."

She pulled the handcuff chain tight, squeezed her eyes shut, and held them away from her body.

Luis aimed the pistol and then with a boom, her hands shot apart, burning hot slivers of metal striking her arms. She rubbed them and then ducked as another round struck near them.

Luis fired back. "As soon as you see the water, jump. No hesitation."

She nodded. "I'm ready."

They turned and ran down the catwalk and through an oval door. They burst out onto the deck between two surprised men.

Luis shot the closest in the chest, and Loren threw herself over the rail.

They were higher than she'd expected, and she fell and fell before plunging into the cold, inky water.

CHAPTER 25

Eddie snapped awake, disoriented, adrenaline surging through him. An I.V. dripped into his arm, and in a panic, he reached to pull it free, remembering the drugs in the senator's room.

A soothing voice said, "Hold on. You've lost some blood, and this is helping."

Eddie looked up to see a man of about thirty with an average build and a patient and friendly face walking briskly toward him. He held a pistol down at his side, but his posture wasn't threatening, more like a man approaching a large dog he didn't know well, slow and keeping his voice neutral and even. His hair was light, and he wore simple wire-framed glasses. He made a gentle motion for Eddie to sit back. Setting his pistol on the counter, he grabbed a glass of water and offered it to Eddie. "You must be thirsty."

If this man intended to harm him, he'd already had plenty of opportunity. Eddie's attention strayed to the pistol. Where was his own weapon? He gratefully accepted the cup and gulped the contents down. As his wits returned, he realized they were in a small apartment. He was lying on a couch in a living room, with a narrow kitchen beyond.

He sat up slowly, letting his head get comfortable with the idea. His arm ached. A clean white dressing encircled his left bicep. He touched his aching cheek and his fingers encountered a bandage.

In a matter-of-fact voice, the man explained, "The bullet just grazed you, but it was deep. Other than that, just a lot of scrapes. You were damn lucky."

Eddie straightened with a start. "Where's Sam? The other man who was with me?"

The man pointed toward the rear. "He's in the bedroom. He's pretty beat up and unconscious, but his vitals are steady."

Eddie swung his legs around and set them on the floor. "I think I'm good now." He pulled the needle from his arm and got to his feet. "I want to see him."

The man nodded and moved, putting his body between Eddie and the pistol on the counter. It was subtle—and again appeared more defensive than threatening. He motioned Eddie to walk ahead of him through the narrow room to a door in the rear.

Eddie hesitated, not wild about turning his back on the stranger, but not seeing any other choice. His legs felt leaden, and he lumbered into the room, passing the couch and shelves of books. He glanced over his shoulder, but the man remained a respectful distance back and made no threatening moves.

The door opened into a simple bedroom, containing only a bed, a dresser, and a side table. Sam lay on the mattress, eyes closed, covered with a blanket except for his right leg. Long wooden splints, secured with tape, ran up both sides, and a white bandage covered most of his calf below the knee. Another encircled his forehead.

Eddie studied the dressings, clearly applied by someone who knew what they were doing. The senator's face was alarmingly pale, but his chest rose and fell steadily. "Did you fix him up, too?"

"Yes."

"I really appreciate it. You saved our lives. What happened to his leg?"

The man grimaced. "A bad compound fracture. The bone poked through the skin in two places. Maybe as ugly a break as I've ever seen."

Eddie held out his hand. "Thanks again. I'm Eddie Mason."

The sandy-haired man paused, and his eyes narrowed ever so slightly for a fraction of a second. Almost as if he knew Eddie from a long time ago and was trying to remember where. It was just a flash before he took Eddie's offered hand and said, "Pleased to meet you. That's Senator Sam Hawthorne, isn't it?"

Eddie nodded. How many people could identify a senator, even a famous one, that easily, especially in this disheveled state? Eddie also noted he didn't offer a name in return.

The strange man studied Sam. "He's on the list of good people. Is it your job to protect him?"

List of good people? What was that? The man had no accent, and it wasn't as if he sounded robotic, but his cadence was odd. Like he was trying to remember words he hadn't used in a long time. Eddie rolled his injured shoulder, testing it. "Sort of. For now it is, I guess."

The man cocked his head to one side. "So, protecting him is your mission?"

An odd question. Mission wasn't a word most people used to describe a task. At least for civilians. "You could say that." His head was clearing, and his wits were returning quickly now. "How'd we get here?"

"I brought you."

Eddie remembered the beach and dragging Sam out of the water. "Were you the one with the gun? At the shore?"

The man nodded.

"Thanks again. You definitely saved our asses. If I remember correctly, you're a pretty good shot."

The sandy-haired man shrugged sheepishly. "I'm competent with the rifle."

Once again, Eddie found that phrasing odd. "Were you in the military?"

The man removed his glasses, pinched the bridge of his nose, and dropped his head.

Eddie knew men who, when they returned from the Gulf, didn't want to talk about it, and he figured that was the situation here. Hell, Eddie didn't love talking about his time in the war, either. He looked away. It felt like he was intruding on a painful, private moment of grief. He scanned the apartment. Something seemed wrong, but he couldn't quite put his finger on it. There were electric lights and normal switches and plugs, but also kerosene hurricane lamps. Something about the place didn't seem right. The clock beside the bed looked like it was wind up. He turned to his host. "What did you say your name was?"

The man looked up and drew his eyebrows together. "I didn't." He squeezed his eyes shut as if he was going to be sick. "It's a difficult thing to say."

Eddie's pulse beat faster as he studied him. He walked into the living room. Something was very off. He was nearly positive he'd never seen him before—so why would his name matter? Hell, he could make one up, and Eddie would never know the difference. He turned back.

The man was taking long slow breaths, as if fighting back nausea.

Eddie asked, "Difficult? Could my knowing your name cause you trouble? Or me trouble?"

The man grimaced, and his gaze dropped to the floor. Swaying slightly, he reached a hand up to the doorframe and steadied himself.

Eddie looked away from the internal struggle, inexplicably embarrassed again as if he were watching something private. He glanced around the room. Maybe he should talk about something else for a minute. "Where's my pistol?"

The tension in the man eased at the change of subject, and he looked up and motioned to a table in the corner.

Eddie's Sig lay there on a kitchen towel.

The man said, "I assure you, you aren't in any danger."

Eddie picked it up and popped the magazine, which held three rounds. He pulled back the slide far enough to see the bottom of a brass casing in the chamber—cocked and ready to fire.

His mind continued to clear, and more warning bells kept tinkling in his head. Then he realized. His jeans were still damp. How was that possible? "How'd we get here again?"

The man answered patiently, "I told you, I brought you here."

"How?"

"It wasn't easy."

How were his jeans still wet? How much time had passed? Eddie's gaze swept over the kitchen. Everything was in cans. There were no jars, plastic bottles, or bags. Just cans. Nothing perishable.

Eddie looked back at the man standing at the edge of the living room. A sudden wave of panic crashed over him. Eddie rushed through the apartment, flung the front door open, and took two tentative steps out into the bright sunlight. It opened halfway up the rise on the island. Two poles sticking out of the rock held a canopy of camouflage netting. Through it, Eddie could see debris from the *Morning Star* floating on the ocean, and beyond it anchored out at sea, the large boat that had followed them.

Eddie turned. Built into the cave's mouth was the door to the apartment he woke up in. The frame was rough here, with no attempt to make it look finished and normal like the interior. Boards overlapped and fit together like puzzle pieces, filling the space between the cave edges and the door. He looked through the opening at the apartment beyond like it was a portal to another world. How in the hell was this place in the middle of the ocean on an island, of all places? How was this guy living here like this? The mysterious man was still standing in the center of the room, simply standing there, motionless, returning Eddie's gaze with raised eyebrows and a bland expression.

CHAPTER 26

Loren swam deeper into the cold, opaque river, while bullets from men on the freighter punctured the water, making plunking sounds above her. She dove with all her might and then leveled out, fighting the swelling urgency for air, and scanned the bright surface for cover. Ahead to the right, a dark rectangle jutted out into the river. Praying it was a dock, she rose to it, her lungs burning. The surface seemed so far away, and she had to assert control over the panic rising inside her.

Finally, Loren burst out under the small structure. Razor-sharp oyster shells crusted the thick legs. She gasped and pulled in a massive lungful of air. Her focus darted around for any immediate signs of danger. She was safe, at least for the moment. She regulated her breathing. Her heart still hammered in her chest, but her mind settled and returned to the situation.

She peeked around the edge at the freighter a short way down the shore. A man on the deck spotted her. She ducked back just as his bullet splintered the wood and shells.

From behind the dock's protection, she swiveled around, searching for any sign of Luis. Had he made it off the boat? Was he safe? If she lost him, how would she ever find him again?

With a rush and a splash, Luis surfaced next to her and grinned. "You okay?"

"Fine, thanks for coming."

He shrugged. "That's my job."

A second shot rang out and impacted the dock above them.

Luis ducked and then scanned the river. "What do you think? The small blue boat next to that sailboat over there?"

She looked at the craft maybe thirty yards further down river and nodded.

He submerged below the surface and disappeared.

Loren took a deep breath and dove after him. At once, the surrounding water thrummed with gunfire, louder and closer than before. Thin columns of air formed as the bullets passed through the water, making fine, two-foot needle stalactites on the surface. She dove deeper and kicked forward. Ominous dark shapes reached out from the bottom, and she navigated the space between the dangers until she saw the blue boat and pulled toward it.

They moved like this, diving from cover to cover until the two of them stopped under another dock to catch their breath. Wiping the thick wet hair from her face, she leaned out around the edge and studied the far shore, as Luis scanned the near bank.

Loren spotted a gunman on the far side and dragged Luis under the water as men fired at them. Bullets whistled past, just above them.

They swam further on to the next cover, moving shorter distances back and forth, playing cat and mouse with the men tracking them from both sides.

Under the boom and netting of a fishing boat, Luis said, "They really don't want you to get away."

Loren shook her head. "I don't know why. I don't know anything, and I don't see how I could be a threat to them."

Luis held up a finger and grinned. Sirens wailed off in the distance, growing louder. "It's about time all this shooting attracted someone's attention."

On the far bank, Loren recognized the man with the black beard who'd cuffed her on the ship. He looked up, clearly listening to the sirens. He checked up and down the river once more before he put his pistol into his coat, pulled up his collar, and then slipped away between two buildings.

Loren pointed. "That's one of them from the ship leaving. The police seem to have spooked them."

Luis said, "Okay, what do you think? Maybe three long swims upriver to get away from this area?"

Loren nodded. "Let's go."

Her heart was pounding, and her lungs ached, but she matched him length for length until they discovered a boat ramp angling down into the river.

Loren's thin cotton dress clung to her, and black-green algae oozed up between her toes as she minced up the slippery slope. At least they were on solid ground.

Her wrists burned, the saltwater irritating her scrapes from the handcuffs, the bracelets that still encircled her arms biting into her skin. She scouted the area, and when it seemed safe, searched the ground for something to pick the cuff locks and free herself. She spotted a wire and stooped to pick it up as they walked.

They emerged on the edge of a shantytown. The skeletons of buildings lined the river, and makeshift housing stretched away into the distance. They ducked into an abandoned warehouse and out of sight. The remains of the collapsed roof lay heaped in one corner.

Luis and Loren stood motionless, water dripping from them, heads cocked, listening for any sounds of pursuit or danger. All was quiet.

Loren inserted the wire into the handcuff lock on her left wrist, and after a few twists, released the catch and the metal clanked to the floor.

The corners of Luis' mouth quirked up in a half smile.

She smiled wistfully, sighed, and rubbed her arm with relief. Her thin dress clung to her, and her sopping hair clumped together in sections. She ran her fingers through it to get the worst of the tangling out.

Luis was wet, but his hair was still tight in his short ponytail and his damp shirt merely accented his physique. The water may have made him look even better. So unfair.

Loren removed the second handcuff bracelet, then closed her eyes and rubbed her arms, thankful to still be alive. She was safe, at least for now. Hopefully, Sam and Eddie were still safe as well.

CHAPTER 27

Eddie walked back inside the apartment/cave, his pistol leveled at the fair-haired man.

He stood calmly—one hand lifted, palm out, but keeping a firm grip on the pistol he now held at his side. "I'm not a threat to you. Whatever it takes to support the mission to protect the senator, you can count on me." His words were calm and measured, like he was talking to a frightened child.

Eddie noted yet another reference to a mission by this odd character. What the hell was going on? Why was this man living in an apartment in a cave on an island in the middle of the ocean? A thousand questions collided in his brain.

This man *might* be a danger, but the men outside definitely were very much a threat. Eddie's back was against the wall, so he analyzed the situation and prioritized his concerns. He felt weak and his head was pounding, but he didn't believe that this man had drugged him. That meant that he'd saved him and the senator and even patched them up. He had little choice but to trust him, at least for the moment, for he had to deal with the well-armed mercenaries anchored just offshore before anything else. "How long was I out?"

"Two hours."

Eddie felt the rush of adrenaline in his system.

It must have shown in his eyes because the nameless man said, "Twice those other men tried to approach, and I chased them back with a few shots. They moved the smaller boat to the other side of the island and left the bigger one where it was. They don't know the lay of the land or our strength, so they're waiting, but we should get back outside where we can keep an eye on them." He said it calmly, but with a hint of urgency.

Eddie nodded and motioned with his pistol for the other man to go first. After a slight hesitation from his host, the two of them walked back out into the sun. Eddie scratched his chin as he studied the yacht and then turned his attention to the tactical boat. He could see men in the smaller craft, but couldn't make out any movement on the larger one. He said, half to himself and half to his companion, "We can't go anywhere, and they have us surrounded. If nothing else, they can just wait for dark."

The man nodded. "I agree. Swim ashore in multiple groups and hit us from both sides."

It was an experienced tactical observation. No amateur, he clearly had some sort of military experience. Eddie glanced back through the cave mouth into the normal-looking apartment. It was like some bizarre special effect in a movie. What the hell was going on here, and who was this guy?

They were standing on a flat area outside the cave mouth that was about ten feet by ten feet, maybe thirty or forty feet higher than the water below. Narrow sandy paths snaked between rocks and short, stout vegetation, down to the beach on each side of the island.

Two long poles held up a sophisticated camouflage netting the likes of which Eddie had never seen. They could see through it, but he guessed by the faint markings that the men in the boats could not. Velcro held a slit doorway closed on each side at the top of each path.

Eddie said, "Let's go back to the beginning. What's your name?"

The fair-haired man looked pained, his brow knitted, his eyes almost pleading. "I'm not trying to evade your question. I'm really not." His tone was breathless and strained.

Eddie believed him. The response looked genuine, and there was no reason to dodge the question. "Let me ask you this. Do you not want to tell me your name or do you not know it?"

The question also appeared to confuse him, and he said, "If I had an answer, I'd give it to you. I promise." His posture and voice were very earnest.

"And you live here in this cave?"

He nodded.

"For how long?"

Again, the frustrated hesitation. He seemed to want to answer, but was unable. Finally, he gave a small shrug; the skin crinkling around his hazel eyes.

Eddie sighed. This man was stuck or stranded here for who knew how long and didn't appear to have any practical knowledge about his situation. Did he have some sort of amnesia? Maybe, but that wouldn't explain the apartment. "Okay, we'll cover that later. For now, I'll just call you—I don't know—Caveman, is that okay?"

The sandy-haired man smiled slightly and nodded. "I guess it works as well as any other for now."

If you didn't ask him anything personal, he seemed almost normal. Eddie studied the camouflaged canopy. "What does this netting look like to them?"

Caveman shrugged. "Vegetation. It's very convincing even through binoculars."

Eddie shook his head. This situation just kept getting weirder. So many questions that would have to wait until later. He gestured at the rifle leaning against the edge of the apartment door. "Other than that, do you have any other equipment to speak of?"

Caveman frowned. "You mean equipment to help us with the mission?"

"Yes. That kind of equipment."

"Some."

"Good," Eddie said. "Let's see what you got."

Caveman walked to the edge of the camouflaged netting and glanced down each trail to make sure it was clear, before motioning Eddie to follow.

He led Eddie through the living room and into the bedroom, where he opened a dresser drawer and pulled out three boxes of sniper rifle ammunition, as well as a case of .45 ammo for Caveman's Glock.

Neither of the weapons used the same ammunition as Eddie's pistol, so his hope for more bullets faded. He studied the items and looked up at the man. "Why?"

Caveman shrugged. "Necessary for the mission."

Everything here was bizarre and wrong, and it was giving Eddie the willies. "So, you have a mission, too?"

Caveman cocked his head to one side. "Yes, but this equipment can help with both."

Eddie frowned. "Both, meaning mine and yours?"

Caveman nodded.

"What's your mission?"

Once again, the strain returned to the odd man's face and, with some effort, he answered with odd delays between the words. "To wait here for further instructions."

What the hell did that mean? They were on an island in the middle of the ocean. "Why would that require weapons?"

Caveman opened and then closed his mouth a few times before saying with effort, "I have to wait here." He squeezed his eyes shut. Opening them, he focused on Eddie and continued, "Even if someone were trying to make me leave."

This statement gave Eddie goosebumps. It wasn't a threat, but the conviction was complete and ice cold. "Does my mission come into conflict with your mission?"

Caveman smiled faintly. "I don't think so. Not now, at least."

Not now. Eddie said, "If I remember correctly, you took down at least one of them with that rifle. Just how good are you with it?"

"I'm competent with this equipment," Caveman replied matter-of-factly.

There was that phrase again. "Just competent?"

Caveman shrugged. "Expertise takes time."

True, but it was still a weird way to answer. More concerns for later—if they made it that long. He nodded, lowered his pistol, and stuck out his hand. "All right then. Partners?"

Caveman studied it for a moment before taking it. "Partners."

Eddie asked, "Do you have any other ammo?"

Caveman shook his head. "Not 9 mm, sorry."

Eddie considered taking the Glock from him. Securing the pistol with the greater store of ammo. But he didn't know this man or his capabilities.

He was on Caveman's turf and needed him for everything. Eddie tried to evaluate how weak his body was and decided this wasn't the time.

They walked back outside. Stepping a little further away from the cave but staying under the camouflage, they could see both vessels sitting offshore.

Eddie asked, "This netting is really that good?"

"Very much so," replied Caveman. "If we stay under it, they can't see us. That's what's keeping them at bay, I think. They can't tell exactly where the shots are coming from."

Eddie nodded. "You think they're trying to surround us?"

Caveman shook his head, took off his glasses, and polished them on his shirt. "My guess is they want to make sure we don't escape."

An odd conclusion. Eddie went back over everything he knew. Why had the senator come here? What was he after? Presumably, it was the same as these mercenaries. Did that mean that Caveman's mission was to guard it? Eddie glanced over at him, trying to decide how to proceed. "You know we aren't here by accident, right?"

Caveman raised his light-colored eyebrows. "I supposed not. The last few hours have been such a blur, I haven't really thought about it much. Why *are* you here?"

Eddie shrugged. "I don't know. The senator came here looking for something." He nodded out to sea. "These jokers followed us. I'm guessing because they want it, too. Sam didn't want to tell me what it was, so all I know is it's some big secret. And, frankly, I don't want to know," he turned to Caveman, "but they're going to come for it, and we're in the way."

Caveman stared back at him with his normal calm and almost serene air. "I can't imagine what they want. There's nothing here but me."

CHAPTER 28

Frank stared at the island baking in the afternoon sun and frowned. How many people were up there, and how well equipped were they?

They now knew the senator's destination, and the man himself might be dead. He had been limp and lifeless when mystery man number one carried him to shore. Who was he? He was a tough son-of-a-gun, he'd give him that.

Then there was mystery man number two, who appeared from the island, of all places. Where did he come from? They didn't see any kind of vehicle, so he must have been here waiting. The senator was obviously a step ahead of where they thought he was, that's for sure. At any rate, Hawthorne didn't look so good, so if he wasn't dead yet, every hour here without medical care was finishing the job.

Therefore, the mission parameters originally given to Frank were on their way to being complete, despite terrible intel, unknown hostiles, and every other damned problem.

Yet when he reported in, Gemini's overwhelming concern was that no one got off the island. Frank was to make sure that no one escaped before reinforcements arrived. Why did it matter? The obvious answer was, so they didn't take whatever was here off the island with them.

He pulled a Cuban cigar from a small leather case in his shirt pocket and smelled it. The wonderful smokes were a gift from Gemini, and Frank savored each one.

Mystery man number two particularly unsettled him. Was he in place to meet the *Morning Star*? Was he another interested party who'd beaten everyone here? He'd already badly wounded one man with a pretty good shot from the island. That made three men down on Frank's team.

He sighed. Both parties had guns and didn't hesitate to shoot. Not a good sign. Everything about this job was messy. Were there more hostiles up there? There wasn't much room, but nothing about this made sense.

He stuck the cigar in his mouth, uncut and unlit, and drew his brow down. He felt completely unprepared for this new objective. Sam was a billionaire senator. Who knew what resources he had at his disposal? It was too far to come in a helicopter, but hell, he could have some submarine sitting off the coast waiting to take possession of whatever everyone was so damned interested in.

Sam also had access to the military and the Coast Guard. Why wasn't he using them?

Frank frowned. This seemed like a secret, though. Sam hadn't even involved his own security team, so more official resources seemed unlikely. Was he dirty?

Regardless, the unofficial resources this man had access to had to be nearly endless. Hence the idea of the submarine.

What would he do if he wanted to get something off the island and had access to such a thing? He'd wait until night and just slip into the water. There was no way his men could watch every inch of land in the darkness, even with a boat on either side.

Frank glanced at his watch and frowned. Almost two hours had passed since he'd filled in his boss on the situation here. He'd expected another communication before now.

Frank picked up a satellite phone and dialed.

Gemini answered, his gruff voice sounding impatient and haggard.

That made Frank pause more than anything that had happened so far. His boss had always been as cool a customer as Frank had ever come across, and that was saying something. "Problems, sir?"

"No. I'm sorry, soldier. You're not the only one who had some unexpected guests today."

Frank chewed on the cigar. During his entire association with this organization, they were always two steps ahead of everyone else. Who in the hell could've gotten the drop on them here and there? "Everything all right?"

Gemini sighed. "We had someone snooping around, and we lost them. Which is bad, but the good news is we have their passports, and I know the police here very well. So, they're stranded here and now the most wanted people on the entire island. The even better news is it doesn't appear they know anything of any consequence. I had the Beaver serviced, and my men are flying it to the coast now to pick up another crew. I'll have ten highly trained soldiers to you in the next two to three hours. What do you want me to send with them?"

Frank moved the phone to his other ear while he considered that. "I'm worried that the people of the island might have a submarine or something else that I don't have the manpower to deal with."

Gemini was silent a beat before responding, "I don't think we have to worry about that."

Frank said, "Then send some night-vision equipment for all the men and get them here by dark. We can take the island just after sunset."

Another hesitation. "Frank, is that the only way to secure the location? Do you have to take your men onto the island?"

What the hell did that mean? "I don't see any other way, sir."

"Very well. I'll come with the team. Hold the fort. We're on our way."

The line went dead.

Frank clipped the end of the cigar. Gemini *really* didn't want anyone on that island without him. He lit it, picked up his encrypted radio, and called Mack. "Crossbow to Badger."

"Go ahead."

Frank said, "How're things on your side of this damned place?"

"Boring. I don't like it at all. Rocky cliffs with only two worn paths up to the top. If they're ready for us, this is going to be ugly."

"Agreed. Gemini is sending trained reinforcements and night vision."

"Good. You know what, get him to send some gas as well. Maybe we can smoke these guys out. They have at least one wounded."

Frank grinned. Now that was a good idea. He was still worried about what he didn't know, but he had these bastards trapped. He clicked the mic. "I think I have some over here. I'll check."

Frank walked back the length of the yacht to the rear. He was a paradoxical mixture of patience and a need for action—a trait he attributed to an effective soldier. Most of his men were resting, long practiced at grabbing sleep between calls of duty. He stood at the back, looking out at the miles of ocean in the distance—endless and empty. He called over his shoulder to his two ex-Seals, "Corey. Miller."

A bald, broad-shouldered man and a tall, wiry man with a hooked nose stood and trotted back to him.

Frank said, "Frog up and check the back of the island. Stay away from the front. I'm pretty sure they could pick you out and take a shot from that ridge if you swim too close."

The two men nodded and shrugged out of their flak jackets.

Frank watched them pull air tanks from a box on the deck, then added before turning back to the cockpit, "Make sure we're alone, and there isn't anything underneath that we don't know about."

The two men nodded, sat on the side of the boat, pushed off, and fell backward into the dark blue water.

CHAPTER 29

Eddie and Caveman sat in camp chairs on either side of the apartment's entrance, keeping watch over the enemy. Eddie held his pistol on his lap and glanced at the SR-25 sniper rifle across the other man's knees. He wanted to go check on the senator but didn't like the thought of turning his back on this unknown armed person, nor leaving him unsupervised. Caveman was here, presumably to protect something, and had the equipment and firepower to complete the mission.

Eddie's presence had to be a problem. He ran his hand through his short dark hair, feeling it stick up at odd angles. Sand crusted his jeans and blood spattered his ripped tee shirt. He shook his head. What a mess. The only thing he had going for him right now was that Caveman probably needed him as badly as he needed Caveman. The heavily trained men sitting just offshore were a serious threat to both of them. After they neutralized them, however, all bets could be off. Of course, that was only a problem if they survived, and currently, the odds weren't looking too great. Eddie announced, "I'm going to check on Sam."

Caveman nodded without comment.

Eddie glanced over his shoulder as he moved through the apartment, but the quiet man merely looked back once and made no move to follow.

Sam was white as a sheet. He needed medical attention—and soon. Eddie placed a hand on his forehead. Cold and clammy. At least he didn't have a fever yet.

Eddie returned to his position at the mouth of the cave, his long fingers wrapped tightly around the pistol's grip. The coiled spring of tension inside him was sapping his already low reserves of strength. He had to find some balance. Who knew how long it would be before Eddie was on friendly ground again? Maybe never if he didn't keep his head. "Our friends do anything interesting while I was gone?"

Caveman shook his head. "Nope. You think they're waiting for reinforcements?"

Eddie shrugged. "I don't know. Where would reinforcements even come from?"

Once again, Caveman appeared uncomfortable and almost embarrassed.

Eddie had a sudden, shocking revelation. Caveman didn't know where he was. He held up his hands. "Okay, let's do this. Don't worry about things you can't answer. If I ask a question that gives you trouble, just say 'I don't know.' Can you do that?"

Caveman nodded, the creases in his forehead smoothing out and his shoulders sagging a fraction. "Thank you. I'll—I'll try. I know it's weird." An awkward moment of silence stretched between them. "So, you don't know what the senator was after? Why he came here?"

Eddie shook his head. "He told me he was looking for some old, crashed airplane."

Caveman took off his glasses and wiped them on his shirt. "But you don't believe him?"

How to answer this? Was this business still just between himself and Sam, or did the current situation change things? Or, more to the point, did the fact that the senator intended to drug him mean all bets were off? "I don't. I think that was just a cover story."

Caveman said, "Yet, you're still protecting him?"

Eddie shrugged. "I think he's basically a good guy and people I trust seem to trust him. They asked me to watch over him." He shrugged. "So, that's what I'm gonna do. I guess that's my mission."

Caveman merely nodded, not appearing to see the humor in Eddie's comment.

How much should he ask or push this man? Was the risk worse than the alternative? He doubted it. "Do you mind if I ask you a few questions while we're waiting?"

Caveman shrugged, his brow furrowing. "I suppose that's only fair."

Eddie asked, "How long are you supposed to be here?"

"Until the mission is complete."

Eddie stretched his long legs out in front of him. That answer was quick. No pained expression or struggle at all. "Can you tell me what the mission is?"

The crease returned to Caveman's forehead, and he hesitated before answering. "To wait here until further mission details are available."

This question was clearly more of a struggle. What was it that made a question about mission details more difficult than the mission's duration?

The camouflage netting rustled in the breeze. The response about the mission itself sounded like Caveman was reciting lines, a pat answer he'd memorized. "How long are you equipped to stay here?"

Caveman's face lit up. "Nearly indefinitely. The containers had seeds. I have a small vegetable garden in a hidden depression on the other side of the rise. It also included fishing equipment. The canned goods are just to supplement, but I'm pretty competent at feeding myself now."

He liked to use the words mission and competent. Was that just a quirk, or was this guy bonkers? "Containers?"

Caveman motioned toward the other side of the island with his head. "They put me here with all the items required for my mission." Caveman studied Eddie and frowned. "Do you want to see them?"

Eddie peered out at the two vessels offshore, still sitting quietly at anchor. "Why not? We're just waiting, anyway."

Caveman led Eddie down a path screened with plants and bushes, around behind the rise to a deep bowl-shaped depression behind the cave. It was maybe thirty feet across and a good fifteen feet deep. A taut roof of camouflage fabric, similar to the canopy over the cave entrance, covered the entire area. Something about it was slightly different. Designed to fool satellites, Eddie supposed. Clearly very high-tech stuff.

In the center of the depression sat two gray steel shipping containers. Rains had pushed the sand up against the edges and spots of rust dotted the hinges. They had to have been here for at least a year. He turned to Caveman, who looked back expectantly, with nearly the same bland, patient expression as before, but something was different now. This odd man hadn't followed Eddie into the depression but remained at the edge.

Eddie gestured at the containers. "Do you mind?"

Caveman shook his head. "No, go ahead."

Eddie pulled down the handle and had to kick some sand aside before he could open the door. Inside, stacked against one wall, were cardboard boxes gone limp and faded. One closest to him was from a standard, white bathroom sink. At the rear was a pile of power tools powdered with sawdust.

He looked back at Caveman. "Did you build the apartment up there?"

Caveman smiled. "Yes. I'm competent in carpentry, electrical, and plumbing."

Eddie shook his head. Unbelievable. Who would go to all the trouble to put this man here, and for what purpose?

Numbly, he moved over to the next container and, with a similar effort, opened it. Inside were several pallets stacked against the wall and a box for a portable generator. In the rear were two rows of fifty-five-gallon drums. That answered the electricity part of this puzzle. Eddie guessed there was some sort of solar power nearby as well.

A few more boxes sat stacked near the door. Eddie squatted next to one and pulled a paper from it. It was a shipping manifest for a crate of wood flooring.

He recognized the vendor's name, Apenno Technologies, but wasn't sure from where. He'd seen the name recently. Ah, on some papers from Sam's locked room aboard the *Morning Star*. This was the first thing he'd seen to connect those documents and this island.

That beautiful ship was now gone, along with all of Sam's folders and research with it. So sad.

Out of the corner of his eye, he noticed Caveman was watching him like a hawk. Why? What was he waiting for? Eddie closed the door, turned, and walked back.

Caveman relaxed just a fraction. Was he worried about Eddie looking through these containers? If so, why did he suggest coming here? He could have just not mentioned them.

They started up the path side by side, but Caveman stepped in front as it narrowed near the top. For the first time, the quiet man had intentionally put himself in a vulnerable position. He still had a tight grip on the Glock, with his finger up by the trigger, but something had changed. Eddie just wasn't sure what.

Maybe this whole little excursion was a test? An experiment to see how much Caveman could trust him. Eddie couldn't decide if that made him feel better or worse about the situation.

At the crest, they took a moment to verify that the two enemy boats were still in the same spots.

He was missing something. He could just feel it. "I'm going to check on Sam again."

Caveman nodded.

Eddie's pistol had three rounds in it. He was still armed, or at least enough so to fight off Caveman if he had to. The odd man wouldn't have returned his pistol if he was worried. He squinted down at the Sig and frowned. Holding it close to his chest, Eddie pulled the slide completely back, exposing the chambered round. His heart raced. Inside was just the casing, a spent shell.

Caveman had tricked him into thinking he had a loaded pistol ready to fire. If Eddie pulled the trigger, nothing would happen, and he would have to rack the slide again before the weapon would shoot. It was a clever deception, and in his foggy state, Eddie had fallen for it neatly. A thread of ice traveled up his spine. He looked over his shoulder as he entered the bedroom. Caveman stood at the door, staring at him, his brown eyes calm and unreadable.

CHAPTER 30

Loren and Luis waited in the abandoned building until the sounds of the police died away.

She turned to him. "We've got to move. I say we move *away* from the river."

Luis nodded, and they eased through the doorway and down an alley.

Loren picked her way around glass shards and twisted pieces of metal, carefully placing her bare feet in clear spaces. They were dirty and crisscrossed with scrapes, and one heel throbbed from some injury she didn't remember sustaining.

They continued deeper into the poorer section of town and down narrow paths between shacks.

She kept glancing over her shoulder, but there were no signs of the police or the men from the freighter. Probably none of them wanted to search a neighborhood like this without some kind of guide.

They moved continuously, only pausing once at a three-legged table beside a pile of rubble. Luis sat and took his pistol apart, wiping each piece on his shirt.

Loren asked worriedly, "Will it still fire?"

Luis frowned, then nodded. "It's not good for it, and it needs a good cleaning soon, but now that it's dry, it should be fine. Most ammo is pretty waterproof." He glanced up at her. "What got them so worked up this morning?"

She smiled weakly. "I think Eddie gave them some trouble. Selik wanted to know who was helping Sam, and he didn't like my answers." Her smile faded. "Eddie and Sam are in trouble."

Luis said, "How does he know Eddie is helping Sam? Does that mean they've already had a fight?"

"I don't know. Also, Selik said that two people were helping Sam. Besides Eddie, who could the second be? Weird."

Luis furrowed his brow. "Maybe he wasn't talking about Eddie at all, but someone else?"

Loren shook her head. "Who, though? And how would they get to the ship? No, I think it's Eddie. I can feel it."

Luis nodded and turned back to the pistol.

Loren closed her eyes and sifted through what she'd heard earlier. "They said something about a Beaver they were bringing to Boca Chica. That's where Jeff's friends gave you the guns, isn't it? Does Beaver mean anything to you?"

Luis stopped. "Yes. They probably mean a DeHavilland Beaver. It's a seaplane—a good one. Do you think they're trying to get reinforcements to the guys who are after Eddie?"

She shrugged. "I don't know, but we should try to stop them if they are. It's our only lead. What are our resources?"

Luis shrugged. "I have five bullets, thirty-two dollars cash, and a soggy granola bar. You?"

"I lost my purse, so I've got nothing, not even shoes. I don't even have a passport. This is going to be a shoestring operation." She glanced down at her bare feet. "Maybe worse than that."

Luis finished assembling the pistol, popped in the clip, and shoved it into his jeans. "We need transportation." He studied her with unreadable, nut-brown eyes. "Why didn't they just kill you?"

Loren could tell that Luis did not entirely trust her, and probably resented that she helped send his friend on a dangerous mission. She couldn't blame him, but it made her wonder how much she could trust Luis. "They wanted information from me, but I honestly didn't know what they were talking about. I think they were still hoping I could help them. I think my time was running out, though."

Luis studied her a beat longer. "Yeah, Selik was obviously unhappy. As soon as he hit you, I blew the barrels of gas."

Loren shook her head. "That was good timing. I'm not sure I thanked you properly."

Luis waved a hand dismissively but continued to study her with impassive eyes. "I'm just glad I could get you out of there."

It seemed like he was trying to decide if he bought the story. She understood his concern but didn't need to deal with his distrust now on top of everything else. Hopefully, Luis was more interested in helping Eddie than worrying about her.

He nodded before turning away and starting off again.

The tension in her shoulders eased a bit as she followed him.

They walked deeper into what was quickly becoming little more than a shantytown. People stared at them as they passed. Well, that wasn't quite true—they stared at her. Now and then, she'd see a face that appeared hostile or dangerous, but with one look from Luis, they'd melt away.

She looked down at the thin sundress, torn in places, dirty and wrinkled. She couldn't imagine what her hair looked like, but she must be a sight. Luis, on the other hand, looked reasonably normal. His short black hair was already dry, along with his clothes, and their rumpled appearance somehow seemed intentional. She shook her head.

He called over his shoulder, "What size?"

Loren asked, "What?"

"What size shoe do you wear?"

"Oh, eight."

Luis nodded and studied the people they passed. Finally, he started an animated conversation in Spanish with a young girl.

Loren understood it was some sort of negotiation, but she couldn't hear the details.

He reached into his pocket and pulled out a ten-dollar bill. The young girl tried to snatch it, but Luis was too fast and yanked it back, wagging a finger at her. She grinned and then disappeared into the maze of shacks.

A short time later, Loren walked out of the shantytown wearing the oldest and most worn-out pair of Converse tennis shoes she'd ever seen. She was happy to have them, though, and her appreciation for having Luis along grew with each passing minute.

At the edge of the slum, they emerged beside a busy road.

Loren asked, "You couldn't find some girl who had a car, too?"

Luis grinned. "Not with the cash we have."

"So, we need to steal transportation. This is probably the best area to find something easy."

Luis frowned. "Maybe we could borrow something."

She arched an eyebrow. "And just how would we do that?"

Luis motioned for her to follow. They walked along the edge of the shantytown. He spotted a group of boys with a motorcycle, and leveling his pistol at them, he walked over and spoke to them in Spanish.

Loren kept her distance, her head on a swivel, looking for police or other forms of trouble.

A few minutes later, he pushed the bike past her onto the road.

Loren fell in beside him, shaking her head. "What did you say to them?"

Luis grinned. "That I was with the CIA and I needed their ride. I told them before they went to the police, they should call a number I gave them and tell Jeff that Luis said we need to give them a brand-new bike."

Loren asked, "Will he?"

Luis scowled. "Of course he will. I'm not a thief." He started the motorcycle. "Come on, let's get to the coast."

Loren held on tight and ducked her head down as Luis weaved the little motorcycle in and out of traffic. He maintained a breakneck speed, and she tried to match him as he leaned into each turn.

He slowed and then shot forward between two cars. She wrapped her arms tighter around him.

Sam's trip had been to retrieve something—some sort of canister. At least it wasn't something obviously terrible, like drugs or a back-alley deal of some kind. What canister could someone hide somewhere in the Caribbean that all these powerful men wanted?

She remembered the crates in the hold of the *Voodoo III*. Was it plutonium or some sort of bomb hidden by some terrorist organization? If so, then why was Sam keeping it a secret? As a senator, he had access to that type of information and all kinds of resources at his disposal. Hell, why not tell Craig Black or send in the Marines? It didn't make sense.

Luis locked up the brakes, the tires skidding across the pavement. She snapped her head up. A long, dark van drifted into their lane as the passenger side window rolled down. Ponytail leaned out, leveled a pistol at them, and fired.

CHAPTER 31

Frank leaned back in the expansive leather captain's chair and watched the tactical boat motor over and pull up alongside. Mack and his other men clambered aboard. He did a quick head count. Including himself and Mack, he still had ten able-bodied men, two injured below, and one KIA. He turned back to the craggy, insignificant island and frowned. Messy was the only word for this whole damned situation, and it didn't appear to be getting any better.

He had a place in Colombia, near the town of Timbiquí on the coast. In exchange for training men for the drug lord, Cantor, he earned a nice little house on the water, well stocked and protected. It was his security blanket and possibly his retirement plan—always there waiting for him. Someplace he could live well on what he'd already put away. He didn't just want to settle for that, though, and he knew he'd miss the fight. He grimaced. No, he would just have to push through this damn situation.

Mack bounded onto the bridge and flopped down in the co-pilot's chair. "You called? Putting together a plan?"

"Maybe." He grabbed one of his meaty fingers with his other hand and popped the knuckle, not turning from the island. "The tactical advantage our enemy has here is the high ground. There are only two paths leading up to the point above with clear lines of fire down."

Mack leaned forward, resting his elbows on his thighs, and studied the strip of land. "Agreed."

"Well, what if that's also the tactical disadvantage?"

Mack tilted his head to one side. "I'm listening."

Frank handed him a stout pair of binoculars. "Look at the point where the two paths converge at the top. I've been looking at it all day, and I think it—well, it flutters. I think it's some sort of camouflage netting, a damn good one, maybe better than anything I've ever seen, but it doesn't look solid to me."

Mack focused on the area. "Yeah, I see what you mean."

"So what if we hit that spot with a grenade launcher? We've got a couple of 15s with attachments, right? If we pounded the crap out of it, you think it would give your people time to scale the beach before our mystery men could recover?"

Mack scratched his cheek, moving the binoculars over the island. "We'd have to move forward another fifty yards. You can't dependably hit shit with those launchers from too far away."

Frank nodded. "I noticed you passed by closer than that on your way over here and no one took a shot at you. I think we can get that close. How much ammo can they have? They'll try not to waste it."

Mack handed the binoculars back. "You're not waiting for the reinforcements?"

"No. I will if they come, but I've got a nagging suspicion that we're going to have to handle this on our own. This whole situation's giving me the creeps. I want to be done and out of here."

"So you want a backup plan?"

"Exactly. Nothing has gone according to design yet. Hell, this might be a good plan, even if reinforcements do arrive."

Mack studied him with even green eyes. "You really that worried?"

Frank shrugged. "I've never seen anyone get the jump on Gemini before. Ever. Sometimes ops just go bad, or maybe we've poked the wrong bear. I don't know, but I want to do my job and get the hell out of here. So, I'm going to blow the top of that little mountain open tonight, with or without help."

Mack grinned. "Sounds good to me."

"When you motor back over to the other side, this time anchor a little closer. Not enough to spook them, but enough to make it easier for us to get into place."

"Roger. We'll get a couple of launchers ready as well." Mack glanced back at the island. "That space at the top doesn't look that big. We drop a grenade on it. It's going to get real bad, real quick, for anyone up there."

Frank smiled grimly. "That's what I'm hoping."

CHAPTER 32

Luis swerved, and the shot whistled past Loren's ear. Ponytail disappeared as Luis ducked in behind the dark van and out of his line of sight. The vehicle slowed, forcing Luis to change direction and come out on the driver's side. Another pistol snaked out that window. Luis locked up the brakes, and the motorcycle shuddered to a stop in a cloud of acrid, white smoke.

A bullet broke the bike's front headlight.

Loren pulled the pistol from the waistband of Luis's jeans, leveled it, and fired once, chasing the shooter back inside. How many bullets did Luis tell her they still had? Four or five? One less now. She clung to him as he spun the accelerator and leaped forward again.

Luis cut between two cars and shot around another, trying to put some distance between them and the van.

Loren looked back. Their pursuers were falling behind but now passing the other cars on the shoulder. She leaned forward and yelled in Luis's ear, "They're still coming!"

He nodded and ducked between two cars. After gliding around a tanker truck, he shot forward.

They seemed to float back across all three lanes, and she glimpsed the sea, vast and blue, off to her right. They must be getting close to Boca Chica. The bike slowed. She snapped her head back, but she couldn't see any signs of danger. "What's wrong?"

Luis shook his head.

A tractor-trailer had pulled over on the shoulder. Luis continued to slow as they approached, then pulled over in front of it and stopped.

"What's up?" she asked.

Luis levered out the kickstand and the two of them stepped off the bike. "Those are the reinforcements headed to help the guys after Eddie, right?"

Loren shrugged. "It's probably a good bet."

Luis took the pistol from her and started back toward the edge of the expressway. "I'm going to slow them down."

The van approached, its engine roaring, the driver pushing it to the breaking point.

Her heart pounded. She peeked over the edge of the expressway's concrete wall. They were too high to jump. How many men were in the van? Probably more than they had bullets. If he didn't get them all, then they were sitting ducks. There was no place to hide. She looked inside the cab of the truck parked here, searching for any kind of weapon. Nothing.

As the dark shape blurred past, Luis pivoted and fired one shot.

The van's front right tire exploded, and the vehicle dipped. With a shower of sparks, the rim dug into the asphalt, forcing it to slow. The back end swung around, the height and weight too much, and in a spray of debris and twisted metal, it rolled.

CHAPTER 33

Caveman had given Eddie a pistol that he knew wouldn't fire. He wasn't sure he could blame him. They didn't know each other, and the hermit was in a vulnerable position. Eddie didn't think he was in immediate danger, for Caveman had, without a doubt, saved them and patched them up. The quiet man could have easily killed both of them, or simply not saved them in the first place.

Eddie forced himself to appear calm and unaffected as he checked on the senator. The older man's hair lay matted to his skull and bullets of sweat stood out on his forehead. Despite his other problems, he was really worried about the old man.

He leaned over as if checking Sam more closely and quietly slid back the slide on the Sig, dropping the spent shell onto the carpet and chambering a good round from the magazine. He only had three rounds, but at least now the pistol would fire. When this was all over, he definitely needed to add shooting Craig Black to his to-do list.

From the front door, Caveman watched him, his brown eyes alert and searching.

Despite Caveman's little trick with his gun, Eddie sympathized with the man. Now that he had a functioning weapon, he could afford to.

Eddie had also been on a mission all alone, without a real end date. It was one of many things that he still held against Craig. After a while, it got to you, and it made you a little paranoid.

He looked back at Sam. What kept Caveman from going crazy? At least no crazier than he already was. Eddie knew one thing that kept him sane, or at least distracted. His mind wandered back to his time with the CIA and the day Jeff collected him, just like he seemed to do with everyone else.

Eddie had just begun his mission and was attempting to establish his cover with surprisingly little help from Craig or anyone else in the Agency. Trying to get into an exclusive club in London to make a contact, he botched the job like the amateur he was. He was still such a simple kid from Texas then, despite all the Agency training.

An old soot-covered, red brick factory housed this club. If he hadn't noticed the well-dressed muscular men at the door, Eddie would have walked right past it.

As he approached, the bouncer with the clipboard met his eyes. "May I have your name, sir?"

Did not expect that. "Eddie Mason."

The large man frowned at his list. "I'm sorry, sir, I don't see your name."

How did the list work? This was way outside Eddie's sphere of experience. He pulled out his wallet. "How does one get on the list?"

The man narrowed his eyes. "Not like that, sir."

"Then what do you suggest I do?"

The bouncer shrugged massive shoulders. "I can't help you with that, sir."

Polite but implacable. Eddie held up his hands. "Okay, thanks anyway." He turned and ran into a short American man dressed from head to toe in a bright red that clashed badly with his ginger hair. Eddie studied the Adidas track suit and Chicago Bulls jacket. Everyone else coming in and out of this place was in an expensive suit. "Excuse me."

"You're American?" the short man asked.

"Yes."

He held out his hand. "Jeff Lansing, pleased to meet you."

"Eddie Mason."

"You going in?" He gestured toward the club's front door.

Eddie smiled wryly and shrugged. "Can't, not on the list."

Jeff snorted, waved a hand, and with a grin said, "I think I can solve that problem. Come on."

The wall of muscle parted for Jeff without a second look.

Jeff nodded over his shoulder at Eddie. "He's with me, boys."

The bouncers miraculously moved, and Eddie followed the red track suit inside.

He shook his head at the memory. Jeff really knew everyone. That fact had saved Eddie many times. It might save him now as well. Jeff was probably the only way Eddie was going to get off this rock.

As he walked back through the apartment, Caveman glanced over a shoulder back at him.

The smaller tactical boat now sat tied to the yacht. Eddie scratched at the stubble on one cheek and sighed. The mercenaries were up to something, and he was running out of time. He had to push concerns about his host to the back of his mind for now. "When did our friends get back together?"

Caveman's attention lingered on Eddie before shifting to the boats offshore. "A few minutes ago. Whatever they're doing, it can't be good."

"Nope, my guess is making plans." Eddie's pool of adrenaline was ebbing and a shroud of exhaustion was settling around him. The pain in his arm was now a rhythmic pounding. His head ached, and his patience was wearing thin.

The tactical boat took off from the larger ship, racing along parallel to the shore, much closer this time.

Caveman asked, "Fire another warning shot?"

Eddie said, "I don't think so. You think they're testing our defenses?"

"Could be. Or maybe they're just getting bored."

Eddie nodded. "I don't blame them. I know I am. You're sure that the bases of these two paths are the only places they can land?"

Caveman said, "Yes, everywhere else is steep and rocky."

Eddie rubbed his face and neck. Caveman's posture still seemed tense. The quiet man was capable, but Eddie felt like he could take the hermit even in his current state. Especially with a pistol that would now fire. "We need to get the senator to a doctor, and soon. I'm worried that he's still out of it."

Caveman said, "It's not as bad as you think. He was in a lot of pain, so I sedated him. I agree with you, though. He needs a hospital."

Eddie furrowed his brow. "How long do you think he's going to be out?"

Caveman shrugged. "At least until tomorrow morning."

Had Caveman mentioned earlier that he drugged Sam? Was that a concern? Sam was still breathing, so he didn't appear to have poisoned him. Did he drug the senator so he couldn't talk? "Why are you helping us so much?"

Caveman stared back at him with an almost blank expression. "He's on the green list." Then he added, almost as an afterthought, "And it's the right thing to do. Those men out there clearly mean him harm."

Caveman's phrasing always emphasized protecting the senator—never Eddie. Was that intentional or a slip? "You said that before. Green list. Like what, a list of good guys?"

Caveman adjusted his glasses and nodded hesitantly. "Sort of. Yes, that's probably the best way to describe it."

"Whose list? Who made it?"

Caveman's brow furrowed, and the pained expression came back into his eyes. "I'm not sure. I just know it, know the list, I mean."

He didn't want to push this subject too far, not now, at least. Sam's presence on that list might be the only thing keeping them alive. "And him being on the list, it makes protecting him part of your mission?"

Caveman scratched at his chin and shook his head. "No, not really. It makes it an acceptable side mission, is a better way of putting it."

What was the difference? Everything Caveman said sounded a little off, as if translated from another language.

The tactical boat reappeared and anchored in its original spot on the other side of the island.

Eddie studied it. Was it closer to shore than it had been before? Did that mean anything? He rolled his sore shoulder, then sat back in the chair by the door, placing the pistol in his lap.

Caveman studied the weapon and then looked up, his gaze meeting Eddie's. He tightened his grip on the Glock at his side. A long moment stretched before Caveman finally broke the silence. "You discovered the empty shell in your gun, didn't you?"

CHAPTER 34

Before the van stopped tumbling, Luis waved Loren back onto the bike, and they took off again. Through the vehicle's shattered window, she saw Ponytail wipe the blood from his face and look around in a daze as they passed. The men weren't dead, at least not all of them—only delayed.

When they'd first seen the *Voodoo III*, the few guards seemed unsophisticated, like local muscle. Then at dinner, there was a group of professionals, and now this van. It was a fifteen-passenger, but she wasn't sure how many people were inside. Just exactly what were they up against now? Selik would have ridden in the front seat, so since she didn't see him, she assumed he was somewhere else.

Was he with more men? Was he ahead of them? This group had to be heading to Boca Chica and the Beaver. It was too coincidental for them not to be. They were the reinforcements on their way to battle Eddie and Sam. If there were more with Selik, then they had to stop them, too.

The motorcycle slowed as Luis took an off-ramp and then circled back under the overpass before coming to a stop.

Loren climbed off the back.

Luis sighed. "This party just keeps getting bigger." He popped the magazine out of the pistol and looked at it.

She asked, "How many rounds do we have left?"

"Three."

Loren grimaced. "Any ideas on getting more ammo?"

Luis rubbed his forehead. "Not really. I guess we could find a phone and call Jeff, but I don't know what he can do on such short notice."

"We have to assume that there are more people ahead of us. It's also a good bet that there will be more than three of them."

Luis nodded wearily. "Agreed."

A small, white police car passed on the other side of the overpass, stopped, and backed up.

Luis noticed it.

The patrol car paused and then turned and headed in their direction.

Loren said, "Time to go," as she slid onto the motorcycle behind Luis.

He twisted the throttle, and the bike leaped forward.

The police siren pierced the air. She looked over her shoulder to gauge the distance. Widening, but the officer was surely on his radio.

The road led into a busy area with traffic lights and swarms of pedestrians intermingled with cars, trucks, and buses.

Luis slowed as he approached the congestion, maneuvering between the vehicles and then down a side street. Everyone was at a near standstill, and Luis painstakingly picked his way through the gridlock.

A second siren wailed above the whine of the engine ahead and to the left.

Luis turned right.

The traffic and press of people were getting worse. No escape this way.

Luis slowed, let the motorcycle fall at the side of the road, and side by side, they melted into the crowd.

Ahead, a police car with its blue lights flashing came to a stop, and two uniformed officers emerged and pushed through the crowd toward them.

At the next cross street, Loren glanced first one way and then the other. More police moved through the mass of people. Checking face after face, clearly searching for someone.

Luis tensed beside her, and they slowed, searching for an avenue of escape.

An elderly woman turned into an alley and mounted a steep set of stairs.

Loren grabbed Luis's arm and nodded in that direction. They turned and ran up the stairs after her and onto a long balcony.

Recessed doors lined one side and a wrought-iron railing mottled with rust and grime ran along the other. Beyond it, another congested road lay below, with police working through the crowd, their heads on a swivel.

Luis and Loren hunched low to stay out of sight as they hurried down the long outdoor passageway.

Loren frowned. Too many cops too quickly. This couldn't be about the car accident or even running from the first policeman. Either this was a manhunt for someone else, or Selik was already flexing his influence.

The elderly woman stopped at her door and watched wide-eyed as Luis and Loren rushed past her. Further on, a young woman in jean shorts and tank top flattened herself against the wall to get out of their way.

Loren glanced over the rail again. The officers on this street didn't appear to have noticed them yet.

The long walkway dead-ended into another similar corridor heading off to the left. They rounded the corner and skidded to a stop. This balcony stretched maybe twenty-five feet before coming to a dead end. Beyond a waist-high black rail was nothing but open space.

CHAPTER 35

Eddie took in Caveman's posture and the pistol at his side before holding up a placating hand. He was in the middle of the ocean, miles from help, and between two groups of trained killers. He needed this quiet, odd man in order to survive. "I did find the spent shell, but I don't blame you. You don't know me from Adam. So, as far I'm concerned, we're good. All right?"

Caveman nodded. A tense moment stretched between them. He opened his mouth as if to say something and then closed it. Both men stood on the knife's edge of indecision, unsure how to proceed.

A thump from the tactical boat broke the spell, and they turned in that direction, studying the craft. Nothing else happened, but it had deflated the tension.

Eddie glanced up at the sun. "We're burning daylight, and when the sun sets, I think we're in deep, deep trouble."

Caveman shaded his eyes and stared over at the larger of the two enemy boats. "I agree. Who knows what kind of equipment they have on a boat that big?"

Sam had brought them here looking for something, something that these gunmen were after as well. Maybe they could use it as leverage. He had to get Caveman to talk about it. "I need to know what you're guarding here."

Caveman shook his head. "I told you, nothing."

"Look, it has to be something. It makes no sense to take all the time and money to put you here. To provision you like this—just to wait!"

Caveman grimaced and shook his head as he turned and rubbed his forehead with the fingertips of one hand while he gestured with his pistol. "I don't know what you want me to tell you. It's just me here."

Eddie pointed at the ship in the distance. "They came here for a reason, Caveman! Sam came here for a reason! They're looking for something."

Caveman ran a hand through his sandy hair. "I can't imagine what it is. I can't even guess what it would be. I'm telling you, there's nothing here."

Frustration billowed inside Eddie. He closed his eyes and quelled his anger. He needed some answers, but he also needed Caveman's help. If he pushed too far, he could break this uneasy alliance upon which his life depended. "When you took me down to the shipping crates, you watched me closely. You wanted to see if I was looking for something. Why?"

Caveman stared at him with wild hazel eyes for a beat before shaking his head. "It was just a test. I'm not stupid. I knew you all were here after something. Obviously, you came for a reason. I don't know what it is. But I didn't know if I could trust you, so I wanted to see." His shoulders slumped. "You don't act at all like a man looking for something. Not in the apartment or in the containers."

"Because I've no idea what I'd be looking for. I'm just along to watch over Sam."

Caveman asked, "Then what does it matter, anyway?"

Eddie said, "Because I want to know, when the fighting starts, that the only thing we're protecting is the senator. We won't survive if I have to keep looking over my shoulder."

The crease in his forehead relaxed. "I'll do everything in my power to protect the senator and get the two of you off this island. I don't care about anything else. You have my word. That's all I can give you."

Eddie believed him, but this wasn't the entire story. The question was, did Caveman know it? "I appreciate that," he sighed, "and I'll have to accept it, but you have to admit—nothing about your being here makes sense. Don't you even question it?"

The crease returned, and the pained expression flooded back into Caveman's bloodshot eyes. He worked his mouth, as if he wanted to say something, but in the end, didn't respond.

Eddie shook his head and looked away. "I was in the CIA, and once a long time ago, they sent me on a mission without a clear end date. I didn't really think about it when I started, but over time, it really pissed me off." He looked back at Caveman. "I can't imagine what this has been like for you. How much longer do you think you can do it?"

Caveman shrugged. His forehead smoothed out, and he lowered his gaze. "I don't know. Even if I gave up and could make myself leave, I'm not sure where I'd go. Or even how I'd get there. I know it's odd, but my mind just doesn't want to think about it. It's—well, it's painful to think about, is the only way I can describe it. It's like I've been conditioned to avoid these thoughts, so—well, I do."

Just how mentally stable was he? When the men out there finally decided they'd had enough and came ashore, how much could he depend on Caveman? "So, now that you know I'm not here looking for whatever everyone is after, do you trust me?"

Caveman hesitated. He looked away, and then back at Eddie. "Yes. Some. But there's another problem."

"What's that?"

"I told you about the green list, right? Senator Sam Hawthorne is number thirteen on the green list."

Eddie frowned. "Thirteen out of how many?"

Caveman said, "One hundred and twenty-seven."

Eddie's eyes widened. What was inside Caveman's head? Who had compiled this list and what was it based on? "Who's number one?"

Caveman answered quickly, "Calvin Arturro."

Eddie had never heard of him. "Not the president?"

Caveman chuckled and shrugged. "He didn't make the list."

Eddie waited for the other shoe to drop. "And?"

Caveman held his gaze. "There's also a red list."

Goose pimples raced up Eddie's arms. "A bad guy list?"

"Yes. And number seventy-one on that list is Eddie Mason."

CHAPTER 36

Frank stood at the back of the yacht and chewed on an unlit cigar as he watched the two divers climb aboard and pull off their equipment.

The taller of the two stretched and said, "We didn't see anything unusual down there." He stopped to wipe saltwater from his eyes. "But we found a few places where we can wait out of sight before we charge up the two paths, especially on this side. Might save a few precious seconds and get us to the top."

Frank patted the man on the shoulder. "Good work." He leaned into the cabin and yelled, "All right, let's check our gear and get ready. Sunset is go time."

The men rolled off their bunks and silently got to work.

Frank walked back to the cockpit and picked up the encrypted radio. "Badger, this is Crossbow."

"Go ahead, Crossbow."

"I put two fish in the water to scout around and put together an assault plan. One's coming your way in a minute with the details, so don't shoot him."

Frank could hear the smile in Mack's voice. "No problem. We have two 15s rigged with M203s and twenty grenades, so we should be able to pound the hell out of them."

Good news. "Excellent." He glanced up at the sinking sun. "Tell everyone to check their gear. I want to hit them right at sunset, so the sun will be at our backs on this side. It will help us if they're staring into it. So, in a little over three hours, we pop this pimple and get out of here."

"Roger. Hit it from both sides?"

Frank spat overboard. "Yep. I say send them up two at a time—one pair from our side and one from yours right after the grenades. Then another two and so on. Hit them in waves."

"Roger."

Frank looked back at the island and narrowed his eyes. It was a small place. How many men and how much equipment could be up there?

CHAPTER 37

Eddie flinched. He had once been a wanted man, but being in the top one hundred of an official 'bad guy' list was a surprise.

Caveman's posture wasn't tense, and his hand was still loose on the pistol at his side.

Eddie said, "Your data must be about two years old, and if so, that would be about right. I was a wanted man then." No wonder the man wouldn't tell him anything. "I'm not now. It was a misunderstanding. I guess you'd call it, and I'm not wanted anymore."

Caveman nodded slowly before responding. "My lists have no context and no details. I don't know where they came from. I'm trying to reconcile your name on that list with what my gut tells me."

Eddie asked, "So, do you get any updates or changes?"

Caveman took off his glasses, cleaned them on his shirt, and shook his head. "No. My information hasn't changed since I arrived here." He hesitated, put them back on, and shrugged. "I haven't had any contact with anyone since then."

Eddie's eyebrows rose. This statement produced another avalanche of questions. "I was taken off the most-wanted list nearly two years ago. So, your information has to be at least that old."

Caveman shrugged.

Eddie rubbed his fingers across his mouth. "As far as you know, I could've been kidnapping Sam. I could've saved him just so I could get something from him. I didn't, but how can you know for sure?"

Caveman looked over at the larger ship offshore before turning back and meeting Eddie's gaze. "That's one thing I was looking for at the shipping crates. You don't seem like a man after something. You don't seem interested in anything but getting yourself and Sam off this island. But you're right. I don't know. It puts me in a tricky situation."

"I guess Sam is a public figure, but how do you know I'm the Eddie on the list?"

"I have a picture of everyone on the list—memorized them, I guess you'd say."

Eddie studied him. "In your head?"

Caveman rolled his eyes. "Yes, in my head."

Each new piece of information made the picture even more confusing rather than less. Eddie tried to rethink everything that had happened over the past twenty-four hours. Did Caveman trust him at all? For that matter, did he trust Caveman? Eddie did and still wanted to protect him. "Look, all I can tell you is that it was a misunderstanding and as soon as Sam is coherent enough to talk, he'll tell you that."

Caveman nodded noncommittally.

A worrisome response. Eddie continued, "I have to trust you, and you have to trust me. Otherwise, I think we're both dead men."

Caveman's attention darted around Eddie's face, and then he nodded. "The red list is what it is, but I still have my own brain and judgment. I believe I can trust you." Then he added with a sideways grin, "Beyond the fact that I have no choice."

Eddie chuckled. "Well, that's something, at least. We need to get ready for this fight." He rubbed his chin. "What if you were in trouble and needed help? They didn't leave you any kind of radio or anything, did they?"

Caveman was quiet for a long time. Then he shrugged sheepishly. "I have a satellite phone. Unfortunately, I don't think it helps. Who would we call, and how would they get here?"

A phone! Even though he had to agree that any help was a long way off. They had a phone! Eddie forced himself to appear calm, and he shook his head. "So, they gave you a satellite phone but no number to call in case of an emergency?"

Caveman took off his glasses again and wiped them. A wave of discomfort passed over his face, then he shrugged. "Yes. Doesn't seem to make much sense, does it? I'm supposed to keep it charged and turn it on every Tuesday night from eight to nine p.m."

Eddie raised his eyebrows. "Do you?"

Caveman said, "Of course." He tilted his head to one side and said, almost to himself, "I always do what I'm told."

"Did anyone ever call?"

Caveman chuckled without humor and shook his head. "Not so far."

This new trust was a fragile thing and if he wasn't careful, he could break it. "Do you mind if I use it? I know a few people who I think can help us."

Was it a mistake to ask? Would it somehow force Caveman's hand and make him act to protect himself? It was curious that the man didn't seem very secretive about anything. He freely shared that he had a mission. He was just very vague about all the details.

The wind rustled in the palm fronds a short way down the slope.

This time Caveman's face didn't look pained, merely thoughtful. It differed from his other interactions. What changed?

Caveman shrugged. "No, I don't mind. I think we could use all the help we can get."

Why didn't he offer the phone until Eddie specifically asked for it? "You don't have a helicopter, or a submarine hidden around here somewhere, do you? Something else for the mission, in case you need it?"

Caveman turned with a slight grin. "No submarine. Sorry."

Eddie nodded. "Just thought I'd ask." Something significant had changed inside Caveman. He wasn't sure what it was, but he answered more easily, and without the same pained expression or hesitation.

Caveman opened a drawer in the living room, pulled out a bulky device that looked like a two-way radio, and handed it to Eddie.

The look on Caveman's face was clear and void of expression. It was like interacting with a doll. Unnerving.

Eddie asked, "You sure you don't mind if I call and try to get us some help?"

"No. It's okay."

He took the phone and dialed Jeff, who answered on the second ring. "It's Eddie. Listen, I need you to call Luis. I'm in a little trouble here."

Jeff said, "Well, that's not good. I haven't been able to get in touch with Luis since yesterday afternoon. What kind of trouble?"

Worry ballooned inside Eddie. "I don't even know where to begin." He shot a look over at Caveman. "The senator is mixed up in something, I don't know what. Some men followed us, tried to kill us."

"What? Are you all okay?"

Eddie said, "I'm fine. Sam has a broken leg, but I think he's fine, too. Look, I'll tell you the rest later. These guys blew up the senator's ship and have us trapped on an island. They can't get to us for now, but we can't escape, either."

Jeff blew out a long breath. "Shit. What can I do to help?"

Eddie frowned. "Call Piper and have him work his computer magic and get a fix on this phone's location. Find someone you know with a seaplane or boat if you can. Anyone near or who can get here. We're going to need someone to come get us. Like now."

"Okay, I'm on it. You going to call Craig Black?"

Eddie rubbed his forehead. "I can't even if I wanted to. We need Loren to get in touch with him."

"You don't have his information from before?"

Eddie barked out a short, bitter laugh. "I never knew how to get in contact with him before. Even when I worked for him. That's just one reason I hate him so much."

"Got it. I'll call you back."

Eddie hung up and met Caveman's gaze. "I have some friends near here I was hoping could help us, but no one has heard from them since yesterday."

Caveman nodded. "I'm sorry to hear that. You think your friend on the phone can get us some other help?"

"Yes. The question is, how fast?"

Caveman frowned. "If we have to fight them back tonight, which seems likely, I thought of something else that might help us."

"What's that?"

Caveman led him back outside and gestured at the two paths. "Along each of these are grease pots. We might use them to—I don't know—to mess with their footing, or we could light them on fire and create a smoke screen."

Eddie chewed on that. "What are they for?"

Caveman grinned. "On the rare occasion that a sailboat anchored here, I dump them out on the paths. You'd be amazed. No one wants to walk up a trail of sludge. They quickly lose interest and sail on."

"You're kidding. And that works?"

Caveman answered proudly, "Like a champ. I've only had a few visitors. It's not a very attractive place, but it's kept me secret."

Eddie shook his head. He liked this strange man. His odd behavior didn't seem like an act. Eddie felt comfortable around him, and that wasn't a common thing. He hoped he wasn't falling for a masterful deception, and he reminded himself to stay alert and ready.

He shrugged. "It's worth a try. Smoke might be a big help, actually." He looked back at the larger ship and frowned. What was going on with Luis and Loren?

The satellite phone chirped, and Eddie answered it. A low pinging noise floated down the line. Piper working his magic, determining their location. The sound continued for several seconds, and then the line went dead.

Caveman returned to his seat beside the door.

The phone rang, and this time it was Jeff. "Okay. I don't have great news all around. I still can't reach Luis and Loren, and you are hell and gone from anywhere. I'll get someone to you as fast as I can, Eddie, but it isn't going to be soon. I even asked around about the Coast Guard, but no one is nearby. You're literally in the middle of nowhere. I probably can't get anyone to you until morning. I'm really sorry, man."

Eddie rubbed his face. "I figured as much. We'll just have to make it until then. Keep trying the others and let me know if you hear from them. Thanks, Jeff, I appreciate it."

"You got it. Good luck."

He hung up and turned to Caveman. Eddie no longer had the energy or the luxury to communicate gently with this man. The time of reckoning was here. "No one is going to make it here before morning."

The quiet man shrugged and leaned back. "I figured. I'm sorry about your friends. Do you think it's related to those men out there?"

Eddie nodded. "I do."

Caveman ran a finger over his lip as he stared off into space. "If you don't mind my asking, what are your friends' names?"

Eddie scratched his head. Why would Caveman want to know that? "Loren Malen and Luis Gutierrez."

Caveman smiled and shook his head. "Of course."

Eddie furrowed his brow. "Of course—what?"

"Loren Malen is number 111 on the green list."

CHAPTER 38

Loren studied the balcony. It ended at the edge of the building, and beyond the rusty black railing was the barrel-tiled roof of the building next door. A small alley ran between the two, and the other roof was three or four feet lower.

Luis turned to her. "What now?"

She looked over her shoulder. "Well, we can't go back. The only way is forward."

He grinned and held up the pistol. "Right. You go, and I'll cover you."

Loren climbed up over the rail, took a deep breath, and jumped. She landed on the roof below and tucked to roll, but the terracotta tiles began to shift and slide. She turned away from the sheet of moving clay and steadied herself on a stable part of the roof that strained to stay in place.

The pottery tiles she'd disturbed poured over the edge and crashed to the ground below with a roar.

She looked up at Luis, who checked both ways, then leaped after her. He landed solidly in the clear spot she'd created and offered her a hand. Loren grabbed it, rolled to her feet, then they gingerly stepped to the ridgeline before running along it. "Did anyone see us?"

Luis shrugged. "One cop looked up, but I don't think he saw us."

A large royal poinciana tree grew up against the structure at the far end. Loren jumped up to a branch and then slithered her way down.

An elderly man with a long, gray mustache leaned out of an ancient, rusted pickup, and observed her descent with wide eyes.

Her watch dug into the skin of her arm, which gave her an idea.

When Luis slid to the ground behind her, she said to the man in Spanish, "If you drive us to the Marina Zar Par in Boca Chica, you can have my watch." She held it up for him to see.

Luis frowned. "It's like a mile away. That's too much."

She cocked her head to one side. "You got something else to trade?"

He sighed and shook his head. "No."

The man frowned and examined the watch carefully.

Loren looked back and forth between him and the street, then spotted two policemen turning the corner at the end of the block and heading in their direction. She said to the driver. "Now or no deal."

The driver nodded and waved them into the front seat.

Luis and Loren squeezed into the cab next to the old man. She turned her face away from the policemen as the truck rolled past them.

It was late afternoon when the man with the mustache dropped them off in front of the marina. They hustled down the pier they'd followed two days ago. Was it just the day before yesterday? It seemed like ten years ago.

The girl with the pink bikini was still on the deck, today in denim shorts and a tee shirt. She looked up from her paperback as they approached, and her eyes widened. "What happened to you guys?"

Luis grinned. "We had an adventure. You don't happen to have a phone we can call Jeff with, do you?"

She didn't return his smile. Her brow furrowed, and her small dark eyes never left Luis' face as she nodded and called out, "Chad! His phone has international service." She looked over at Loren and her eyes widened.

Once again, the young man appeared from below, looking exactly like he had the last time they'd seen him. He studied them with a frown.

Luis said, "I need to borrow your phone."

Chad bobbed his head. "Of course." He ducked below and quickly reappeared with it.

While Luis dialed, Chad considered Loren. "Do you want lemonade or a beer or something?"

With a sigh, she nodded gratefully. "Some water would be great."

Chad disappeared below again. As Luis talked to Jeff on the phone, he no longer held himself with the same graceful ease. His shoulders were tense, and his dark eyes darted back and forth as he listened intently.

Pinpricks of worry crawled up Loren's neck and shoulders.

Chad returned with a glass of water for each of them. Loren thanked him, guzzled hers down in one long swallow, and then turned back to Luis.

Finally, he noticed Loren watching him. "Hold on a minute, Jeff." He said to her, "Eddie and Sam are stranded on an island a little over 300 miles northwest of here, and our friends have them trapped. They need help."

"How do we get there?"

Luis shrugged. "Jeff's still working on it, but he's hoping maybe Craig might be of some help."

"Get the details and give me the phone," she instructed him.

Luis turned to Chad and mimed writing on a piece of paper.

Chad ducked below again and returned with a pad and pen that he handed to Luis. He turned to Loren. "Hungry?"

She nodded with a weak smile.

He once again disappeared into the cabin.

Luis handed Loren the phone and a piece of paper with GPS coordinates written on it. "Hopefully he can help, or they're in trouble. Sam's injured. Jeff doesn't know how badly, but he's stable for now. They're running out of time." He picked up his glass of water and chugged it.

At least they were still alive. Her fingers were stiff and sore as she dialed Craig Black. She trusted the man more than Eddie did, but how far, she wasn't sure. She'd agreed to all of this for Sam, not for Craig.

The ring was the same odd tone she remembered from her years in the Agency. She recognized Craig's voice when he answered. "This is Loren. We have a situation. Can we talk on this line?"

Craig replied in a brisk, business-like tone, "We're clear. What's up?"

She glanced around and then walked a few steps away from the boat, lowering her voice. "Jeff says that Eddie and Sam are stranded on an island about 300 miles north of us. Sam is injured, and Selik's men have them trapped."

"How does he know they're Selik's men?"

196 THE CAVEMAN CONSPIRACY

Anger flared inside Loren. "I know because the bastard kidnapped me last night, and I heard him talking about Eddie and Sam. So, can you get the Coast Guard or the Navy there and help them out?"

"No." Craig's answer was flat, with no emotion or inflection at all.

For a beat, she stood speechless before blurting out, "*No*? What do you mean, *no*?"

"Look, Loren, I'm worried about him too, but Sam is obviously in some kind of trouble. If I send in the cavalry, then I have to explain how I know. Besides, Sam made me promise."

Loren cried, "Are you kidding me? You're worried about covering your ass? He could die out there, Craig. Eddie, too."

Craig said, "I know. I'm thinking. I'll find some unofficial channel to help them, but I can't do anything normal. How much time do they have?"

"I got the impression that they wouldn't make it to morning."

"Give me the coordinates."

Loren clenched her jaw and read the numbers to him.

A bright yellow plane flew over at low altitude, and Loren had to cover her other ear to block out the sound.

Craig asked, "Is there any way you can get to him?"

The aircraft banked around and landed on pontoons a hundred yards away.

She shouted over the noise, "I lost my passport, so I don't know how I'm going to—"

A wave from Luis caught her attention, and she looked over.

Luis smiled and pointed at the yellow aircraft, whose propeller was slowly winding down. "That's a Beaver."

The pilot stepped out and dropped an anchor overboard. She spoke back into the phone. "Craig, I'll call you back. I might have a way to get to the island, but you'd better have some help coming soon." She hung up.

Luis was about to say something when something caught his attention back on land, and his eyes narrowed. "Our friends are here."

Loren turned. Selik and a group of men came around the building and hustled over to a waiting boat.

A thousand scenarios and options ran through her head at lightning speed before she turned to Luis. "Can you fly that thing?"

He raised his eyebrows and nodded.

"Great, then we're going to steal it."

Chad reappeared with two sandwiches.

They each took one and then Loren said, "I'm very sorry, but I'm going to need to take your cell phone and your little boat for now. I'll get them back to you."

Chad nodded agreeably. "Sure, no problem. Anything for Jeff. Are you in some kind of trouble?"

She shrugged. "Not yet, but this is an emergency. Maybe a national security kind of emergency."

Chad nodded with little reaction and said, "I knew you guys were spies or something like that."

Loren ran toward the little skiff tied up to their boat.

Luis pulled the cord on the motor, and it chugged to life.

She untied the line, pushed off the dock, and perched in the bow.

He swung the skiff around and headed for the plane. "I take it Craig can't—or won't—help?"

Loren shook her head. "Not officially, he said Sam made him promise. He's going to try to help unofficially—whatever the hell that means. Anyway, we're all most likely on our own until morning."

He snorted.

Loren located Selik and his men back at the shore. They were also in a launch now and motoring toward the Beaver as well. Gauging the distances, she thought Luis would get them there first, but not by much.

Luis held the pistol out of sight down by his side. He leaned forward and said, "Get into the co-pilot seat as fast as you can."

Loren nodded and glanced back at Selik's boat. They'd been noticed; the men were pointing at them and waving their arms.

The pilot was leaning into the aircraft's open door. He turned as he heard Luis and Loren's approach.

Luis killed the motor and let the skiff glide the last few feet to the pontoon. He leveled his pistol at the man's chest and said in a calm, neutral tone. "Are the keys in the plane?"

His eyes widened. "Yes, but—"

Luis said, "Jump in the water right now."

The pilot shook his head. "You don't understand who owns this plane."

"Yes, I do. This is your last warning. Jump in the water, or I will shoot you."

The pilot leaped clumsily off the pontoon and swam away.

Shouts rang out from the approaching boat and its motor sped up.

Loren scrambled aboard and into the co-pilot's seat.

Luis slid into his seat and handed her the pistol. "Shoot if you have to." He put on the headphones and flipped switches and levers. The propeller turned jerkily before roaring to life.

Selik's boat was close now, but Loren hesitated, wanting to conserve ammo.

The seaplane moved forward, turned, and picked up speed.

Three cracks sounded from outside. Two bullets hit the plane with a hollow sound. The motor never wavered, however, and the aircraft kept speeding up. With a sudden surge, it lifted into the sky.

As they climbed, Loren asked, "Are we okay?"

Luis motioned to her headphones hanging on the back of the seat.

She put them on and then repeated her question into the microphone.

His dark eyes scanned the controls. He frowned and pointed at one gauge. "It looks like we have three fuel tanks and this one is emptying. They must have hit it."

Loren asked, "Will we make it?"

He shrugged. "I don't know. Put those coordinates into the GPS there."

After a few minutes of fumbling with the menus, Loren figured out how it worked, and hastily entered the numbers.

Luis kept the aircraft low over the water with the throttle forward. They really picked up speed.

The GPS completed its calculation and displayed the result.

Loren read it to him. "It's 342.7 miles, with an estimated travel time of two hours and ten minutes."

Luis grimaced and glanced at his watch. "Right about sunset. I don't love the idea of landing this thing in the dark."

She pulled out the cell phone and called Craig. "We stole a seaplane and are heading their way now. We're trying to make it there by dark."

"Very enterprising of you."

"Cut the crap, Craig," Loren snapped. "We still need help. Have you come up with anything?"

Craig said, "Someone I've worked with in the past is heading that way, but he probably won't make it until morning."

Loren asked, "Who is it?"

Craig hesitated. "His name is Tito. He's a smuggler, kind of a pirate, I guess you'd call him."

"A pirate? Named Tito?"

"It's not as bad as it sounds. I've used him before on Company business. No one pays any attention to his big old rusty freighter."

"And you're not worried about him talking about Sam?"

"Believe me—Tito hates publicity even more than the senator."

Loren shook her head. "I'm going to lose cell service before long, so if you get anything else that would be more helpful than that, call me back."

"I will. Good luck, Loren."

"Yeah, whatever." She hung up.

Luis looked over and raised his eyebrows. "Tito?"

She shook her head. "Yes. Apparently, he's a pirate Craig knows, and he'll be at those coordinates by morning."

Luis snorted. "This job just keeps getting better."

Loren punched Jeff's number into the phone.

He answered immediately. "How're you all doing?"

"Okay, I guess. We stole a seaplane, and we're trying to make it to Eddie and Sam."

"Any help from Craig?" Jeff asked.

"Very little. He thinks he can get a pirate named Tito to them by morning."

Jeff said, "I might have found one or two options, but I'm sorry, Loren, I can't get anyone there before morning, either."

"It's all right. Keep trying. We probably only have cell service for a short time, so call soon if you need us."

"I will. Good luck."

Luis glanced over. "The same with Jeff?"

She nodded grimly. "Tomorrow."

Luis shook his head and looked over his shoulder. "Go see what's in the cases in the rear. I'm hoping to God that there's some ammo back there."

She unbuckled and stepped between the seats and down the narrow fuselage. Three long black tactical cases lay across the very back seats. This looked promising. She popped the latches on the first. It contained a rifle she didn't recognize, two sub-machine guns she knew as MP5s, and twenty boxes of 9 mm ammunition and ten of .45. "We've got ammo!"

Luis grinned and gave her a thumbs-up.

She lifted out the rifle and turned it. An M39. She didn't recognize it, but her expertise didn't really cover rifles.

The second case contained flak jackets, and she removed two and set them aside. She awkwardly moved them onto one of the other seats. The last box was full of night-vision goggles—new and still in the box—and two hand grenades.

She shuffled back to the cockpit. "There are some MP5s, an M39 rifle, ammo, flak jackets, and night-vision goggles in the back. Oh, and two grenades."

He looked down at the GPS, then at his watch, and then eased the throttle forward a hair. He frowned. "I'm not sure we're going to make it before sunset."

"Can you land this thing in the dark?"

He shrugged. "I'd prefer not to, but I can. That's not what worries me. It will be a lot harder to help in the dark."

She jerked her thumb over her shoulder. "Even with the night-vision goggles?"

Luis frowned. "If it's dark, I can't use the rifle, even with the goggles. Of course, none of that matters if we don't get there in time."

CHAPTER 39

Frank's focus never left the island as he answered his satellite phone. Bad news. He could feel it in his bones. This entire mission had been snake-bit from the beginning.

Gemini's voice was tense and angry. "Our troubles continue here. Your reinforcements are going to be delayed, and it's possible that your targets have help on the way."

Frank couldn't recall ever hearing Gemini angry before. "What are my orders?"

Gemini's answer was quick and decisive. "As soon as you're ready, kill them all. I want everyone on that damned island dead."

Frank said, "You're okay with me sending everyone? Without you?"

"Yes. We no longer have the luxury of keeping things in silos. Take care of everyone, but I don't want your men to touch *anything* on that island. Do you understand me? Kill them all and wait for me."

He scratched at his scar. "The enemy has the high ground. It's going to be a bitch getting to the top. I'm going to lob a few grenades up there first. Any concerns that we'll destroy whatever you're after?"

After a long silence, Gemini asked, "Is there no other way?"

Frank sighed. "I don't see one. We're in a shitty spot."

"I see. Can you have the bombs land just short? Just enough to get your men up there?"

"We can try."

"It is imperative that we retrieve what is on the island. Please plan your attack to ensure that."

"Yes, sir. What kind of help could come for them?"

"I'm not sure. I believe two people, a man and a woman. They stole our airplane and could be headed your way. Even though I've no idea how they could know where you are, I'm through underestimating them. You should plan as if they're on their way."

"How soon?"

"A couple of hours, at least. And that's if they even know precisely where you are."

Frank had no doubt that they knew exactly where to come. He ground his teeth.

Gemini continued, "I'm working on other transportation, and I've put the word out for anyone we work with in the area. I'll get you help as fast as I can."

"Thank you, sir. Just how compromised do you think we are? When we're done here, do we proceed to the same rendezvous point?"

There was another long pause. "Just kill them, and I'll contact you with next steps."

"Yes, sir." Frank hung up and rubbed his chin. Now Gemini wasn't sure about the rendezvous site. Snake bit. He leaned back, closed his eyes, and calmed his mind. He adjusted his line of thought away from the mission and into self-preservation mode. It made sense to keep one eye on his own ass at this point.

He was happy the shackles were off. He could finish this mission in any way he saw fit. No restricting rules of engagement to make things worse. His experience was clear in this kind of situation. When things went south, the only way to fix it was to burn it all to the ground. Destroy the enemy and obstacles in a wave of violence. He reached down and picked up the encrypted radio. "Crossbow to Badger."

After a static pop, Mack answered. "Go ahead, Crossbow."

"Looks like it's just us now." A cloud passed in front of the sun, leaving Frank in the shadow. It muted the colors on the island and gave a moment's respite from the heat.

Mack whistled through his teeth. "Damn, your instincts were right again. So, what's the situation?"

Frank hesitated before answering. "The good news, at least, is no more pussyfooting around. We're going to go in and take these guys out."

"You want to go in after dark now?"

"I don't think so. We won't be getting the night vision now, so it would be a bitch. I'm still thinking about the sun setting right behind me. It sucks to fight with the sun in your eyes. I say we slip the men into the water and then just before sunset you ease forward and hit that spot with the grenade launcher, just like we talked about. Oh, except Gemini is really hung up on whatever is on the island. So, we go with the same plan, making sure we drop the grenades a little short of the top. Enough to send them back into cover without hurting anything up there."

"I understand. That's going to make it messier. The sun should give us help, though. They'll be blind."

"That's the idea."

"I buy it. Want us to get ready?"

"Yes. I'm so damned sick of this island. Let's kill these bastards as soon as we can and get out of here."

"10-4."

Frank set the radio back on the dash. He hated this island and the mystery guests who had given him so much trouble. It would be a pleasure paying them back in kind.

CHAPTER 40

So Loren was also on this "green list" stored inside Caveman's head. Something about him knowing Loren specifically bothered Eddie, but he couldn't quite put his finger on the reason.

After Caveman released this bombshell, he suddenly seemed embarrassed and dropped the subject.

Eddie tried to get his mind around the idea. Before he knew it, his own silence had gone on for too long, and an awkward moment stretched between the two men.

Caveman excused himself, presumably to use the facilities or perhaps to escape the tension.

The apartment had a toilet? Where did that empty to? Another entry on Eddie's growing list of questions.

Eddie kept seeing parallels between Caveman's situation and his own assignment as the Lighthouse. A long mission, with no clear completion date. He watched Caveman walk away through the apartment. Actually, it brought to mind both his mission and his time on the run. After Nikki's murder, he knew everyone assumed he would try to disappear off the grid somewhere like South America.

Instead, he made his way to a small town in southeastern Colorado and for a few years lived in peace. Well, apart from having to look over his shoulder every moment. He'd grown up in a small town. He knew how people who lived in places like that thought, and he could settle in and be as invisible as if he were in a Brazilian jungle. Until the FBI got lucky and found him.

That was the last time Eddie had felt this vulnerable.

He remembered driving into the feed store on that clear, chilly morning. The sheriff's son waved and headed in his direction. He was tall and lean, his blond hair sticking out at odd angles from beneath his cap.

Eddie glanced around the parking lot and up the road before putting his truck in Park and turning it off.

The kid wiped his hand on his tee shirt and offered it to Eddie.

Shaking it, Eddie asked, "What can I do for you?"

"Morning. My dad asked me to pass on a message to you."

"Okay."

Glancing around, he lowered his voice. "He told me to tell you that the FBI asked him to drive up to La Junta this morning. He wasn't sure what for, but he thought you might want to know."

The FBI? That was surprising. "Tell your dad I appreciate the heads up."

The kid nodded and ambled back across the dusty parking lot.

Eddie once again took in his surroundings. Nothing seemed out of the ordinary. He'd known that this day would come. That they'd eventually find him. The Bureau was not who he'd expected, however. He stepped out and grabbed a duffel bag from the passenger seat floor. Removing the cash, he tossed his wallet and IDs on the front seat. That identity was dead now. He glanced around, first in one direction and then in the other. All still seemed normal and quiet.

A large dirt bike stood tied down in the pickup truck's bed, and Eddie loosened the buckles. Everyone assumed he kept the motorcycle for running down a loose cow. No one suspected that he really kept it close at hand for situations just like this. He lowered a narrow ramp and rolled it down out of the back.

Eddie strapped on the duffel bag, started the motorcycle, and drove out of town. Heading east, he rode along a dusty dirt road out into the pastureland. He turned, crossing the wide grassy plain, and headed toward a spot in the fence that divided his ranch from that of his neighbor to the south. He found the section he'd doctored, unfastened the wires, and pushed the motorcycle through before hooking them back. Down a small slope he found another trail, barely more than a path that meandered on and on to the east.

Pulling onto Highway 109 an hour later, he headed south. This section worried him the most. If the FBI had a roadblock here, he would be in trouble. The landscape was flat and empty. He'd be easy prey for a helicopter. If he could make it to State Road 160, he'd feel a bit more comfortable.

He relaxed as he approached the junction. Should he take it west to Interstate 25, and then across 40 to Los Angeles? He had a solid escape route already set up there. Going that way, he'd be able to disappear again with ease.

The FBI's involvement bothered him, though. Why were they after him? Was it possible that they'd come to this little corner of nowhere for someone else? Not likely. What did they want? Knowing that might be useful if he wanted to stay a free man.

He frowned and decided to go 160 East to Interstate 27 and make his way toward San Antonio. He had a storage unit there with money and supplies. They had to have come for him—who else would they be after in such a tiny place? But he needed to at least check before over-reacting. He stopped in the little town of Springfield and pulled up to the narrow library building. It was a little after noon and the place was empty. Eddie nodded to the lady at the circulation desk on his way to the two computers on a table at the far wall.

He navigated to a page connected to a camera in his ranch house in Villegreen and entered his password. The image of the dim interior of the house loaded. Empty.

Eddie frowned and sat back. He watched it refresh one more time before closing the window and leaving. Was he being paranoid? What else would the FBI be doing there? The sheriff wasn't stupid. He'd passed on the information for a reason. After that incident with that idiot at the fair earlier this year, Eddie figured the sheriff knew there was more to Eddie's story.

How long should he wait? Down the street, he found a diner and had lunch, his mind racing the entire time.

He returned to the library. This time when he checked, his living room was full of people wearing windbreakers—FBI stenciled across the back in large yellow lettering. He frowned as he watched them mill around the small house. Son of a gun.

He hopped on the bike and continued heading south. When he reached Lubbock, he stopped at a roadhouse for dinner and called the lawman at home.

"Sheriff, this is your neighbor. Can you talk?"

"Yep. Everybody has flown the coop."

"I wanted to thank you."

The sheriff sighed. "No problem. I'm guessing I won't be seeing you again."

"Probably not."

"Well, whatever you've done, you were always a good neighbor to us. Mind if I ask you a question?"

"You've earned at least that."

The sheriff asked, "Were you a good guy or a bad guy?"

Eddie hesitated. "I was a good guy and something bad happened."

The sheriff said, "I figured it was something like that. I've never trusted those Washington types."

"Can you all split up the livestock? I want to make sure they're taken care of."

"I guess we'll have to. I'll see to it."

"I appreciate it, and I have one more question, if you don't mind."

"I'll answer it if I can."

"Who's the person who ordered my arrest? Not the agent here, but the man in charge?"

The sheriff said, "The warrant was under the name David Camden, FBI, DC office."

"Thanks."

"Why'd you want to know that?"

Eddie frowned. "This wasn't who I expected to come for me, and now I'm curious."

"Well, you'd better get going."

"Thanks again," Eddie said and hung up.

Northwest of San Antonio, he exited the interstate and drove into the town of Harper.

Eddie pulled into a rental storage place, punched the code into the front gate, and then drove down the aisle to unit 867. He dialed in the combination and rolled up the steel door.

Inside was a single bed along one wall. A small table holding a cell phone in its charger and a lamp stood beside it. Three steamer trunks lined the opposite wall. All his plans had centered on the CIA, or some assassin, coming after him. Powerful men still wanted the thumb drive Niki had been carrying in that stupid little sparkly purse.

They'd kill to get it back. Eddie didn't know what was on the drive. He'd taken it to his best underworld contacts. The encryption was unbreakable. So, he knew he had something people would kill for, but not exactly what it was. He figured it was his last bargaining chip when all this finally caught up with him.

The FBI's involvement completely baffled him, though. With what he knew, he could not see why they were interested, nor did he think they even had any jurisdiction. So, he had even less of the complete picture than he supposed he did. It was not encouraging.

He had a clear shot to freedom from here across the border. He knew a man near Mexico City who would fly him to Lake Atitlan in Guatemala. People knew him there. He could be in the wind in forty-eight hours. The thought of the FBI continued to gnaw at him, however. What did they want?

Eddie tried to make an objective evaluation of how cleanly he escaped. The Bureau was surely completely clueless about his current whereabouts. If they had any kind of line on him at all, they would've already tried to arrest him.

The only way they could catch him was if he didn't leave now. Disappear again into the great, big world.

He sighed. Would the question of the FBI nag at him? He frowned. It would. And knowing what the FBI wanted would make it easier for him to evade them. Was that a rationalization? The next day, Eddie called Special Agent David Camden.

• • •

Caveman returned, bringing Eddie back to the present. He sighed. What were the odds that the FBI agent he contacted just happened to have been the agent who debriefed Loren when she returned from her mission, after Eddie saved her? Fate just seemed to keep throwing them together.

It was odd, the things that paralleled Eddie and Caveman. For years, Eddie was alone and isolated with something everyone wanted. Just like

Caveman. Eddie never even knew what that something was, and if Caveman was being truthful, he didn't, either.

The connection really was weird. It made Eddie more sympathetic to Caveman and his current situation. Did that mean he was blind to the possible truth with Caveman? Eddie didn't think so, but he reminded himself to keep his guard up.

He shaded his eyes against the sun. It was sliding toward the horizon. They were gradually running out of time. He turned to Caveman. "I've been thinking about your grease pots along the path. Can we dump them out without being seen, while it's still daylight?"

Caveman nodded. "I can get to them unobserved. You think I should dump them out now?"

"I do, and I was wondering if you have something we could light them with, maybe from a distance. I think a smoke screen might be a big help."

He grinned. "I have flares. I'll be right back." He hunched down and then slipped off into the bushes.

Eddie looked back into the apartment, listening for any sounds from Sam. It was almost beyond belief that Caveman had built this. Shaking his head, he recalled the man's statement that he was competent in carpentry, electrical, and plumbing. Just how much information did his strange brain hold? He lifted the rifle just in case he needed to cover him.

Caveman returned from dumping the smudge pots and eyed the weapon in Eddie's hands.

He handed it over to him and frowned. "You seem to have a lot of skills you say you're competent at. Do you know how many?"

Caveman nodded and answered earnestly, "Of course. I'm competent at one hundred and seventy-eight core skills." His eyebrows shot up as if the answer surprised even him.

Eddie waited for him to smile and say he was kidding, but the light-haired man merely returned his gaze expectantly.

Eddie shook his head and said, "That's a large and very specific number."

Caveman shrugged and looked at the ground.

He tapped his chin with two fingers. "What else is in your head? Is it all just knowledge and skills?" He paused. It was too late for caution, so he might as well ask. "Do you know other things?"

Caveman's hazel eyes widened a fraction. "Like what?"

Then it finally hit Eddie. Why Loren's presence on the green list bothered him so much. Sam was a senator and a public figure of importance and power. Loren had been a deep undercover agent for the CIA. Her name in connection to anything important wasn't public. The people who created this list had to have access to classified information, and if that was true, it changed everything about this situation.

Eddie's status as a wanted man was probably at least somewhat public. But his mission for the CIA was another matter. It was absolutely top-secret. As far as he knew, none of it was public information to this day. "Do you know what Operation Lighthouse is?"

Caveman's eyes widened even more, and then he said in a near monotone, "CIA mission CXV234177-9043 Operation Light House."

Eddie's eyes narrowed. "That information is classified. How could it be in your head? How many CIA missions do you know about?"

Caveman licked his lips. "What type?"

"Any type?"

"Active Level-five missions, 3,764. Level-four operations, 523. Level-three operations, forty-four. Level-two operations, twelve. Six Level-one operations, and twenty-five experimental operations—"

Eddie held up his hand again. Holy shit, that had to be nearly every active operation the Agency was running at the time Caveman arrived on this island. He shook his head as it finally dawned on him. "It's you. *You* must be what everyone is after. The information in your head, even two years old, is crazy valuable to a lot of people."

Caveman paled and then turned a little green. "I can't be—"

"If you're really not guarding something else, it's the only explanation."

Caveman looked off in the distance, shook his head, and then sat down heavily and stared at the ground.

Thank God this had finally all come to light. Soon, Eddie was going to need Caveman's help. He gave him a moment to process this revelation before saying, "I know this is a lot to hit you with now, but I think it's important. We can deal with the implications of this information later, but our strategy will change if we know that it's you they're after. We're about to be in a world of hurt."

Caveman looked up, focused his troubled eyes on Eddie, then stood. Nodding decisively, he said, "I'll get the flares, and I have some more stuff I've been keeping from you." He cast a quick peek at the two enemy boats before leading Eddie back into the apartment.

The sound of them entering the senator's room awakened Sam enough that he thrashed once and moaned. Sweat covered his face, and his eyes fluttered open before closing again.

Eddie felt the senator's forehead—warm but not hot.

Two doors stood in the rear wall of the bedroom. Caveman opened the left one, exposing a shallow walk-in closet packed with supplies.

Whoa. Four pistols, several fishing rods, flashlights, toolboxes, and some diving gear. Boxes stacked up one wall marked ammunition, flares, and medical equipment. He turned back to Caveman, eyes wide. "Holy crap."

Caveman gave him a half smile. "Sorry, I didn't know if I could trust you before."

"What changed?"

He shrugged. "I don't know."

Eddie looked back at the closet.

Caveman pulled a box of 9 mm and handed it to Eddie with a shrug. "This is good, but it won't help us a bit if they drive us back in here. If they get close enough to lob in a few grenades, we're toast."

Eddie pulled a few flares from a box. "Then we'd better keep them on the beach."

CHAPTER 41

Loren sat hunched forward in the cockpit, her attention moving nervously between the sun melting into the horizon and the plane's gas gauge, which was following a similar path.

Luis reached up and turned some knobs on the dashboard. "It looks like they only hit the third gas tank. I've pumped all the gas out of it I could, but we lost a lot of fuel." He glanced at the GPS and clucked his tongue at the current range based on what remained.

She pulled out the chart and studied it. "Even if we make it there in time and somehow get Sam and Eddie off the island and out of there, it doesn't look like we'll have enough gas to reach anywhere safe."

He nodded. "I was wondering if we could land next to a boat or something like that. I don't know, I'm worried about the island first. If there are armed men on or near it, we're going to be awfully vulnerable landing. There's no cover or any way to approach in stealth. We'll be a sitting duck, and we'll be running on fumes."

Loren ran through options. She looked at the cell phone—no service. "Since we're listing negatives, I have another. Selik and his men are very well-financed. How hard is it going to be to get another seaplane and come after us? We could be the meat in an unpleasant sandwich."

Luis chuckled ruefully. "When do we start the list of positives?"

She shook her head. "I'm working on it." The endless dark ocean stretched out below, making her feel small and helpless.

"Who are these guys, anyway?" asked Luis.

She rubbed her forehead. "I've no idea. The Agency has been concerned about Selik for years, but I never heard any specifics about him, other than as a person of interest. They're all after something out here in the middle of the ocean, but I can't, for the life of me, figure out what. What's weird is they don't seem to know exactly what it is, either. Why would you be after something with such intensity if you didn't know what it was?"

Luis shrugged.

She opened the glove compartment and leafed through the papers before pulling out a sheet. "The plane's registered to the Maycock Company out of Tampa, Florida. Mean anything to you?"

He shook his head.

She closed it and sat back. Could they shoot at the bad guys from the air, or maybe drop something on them? "What if we flew slowly enough for me to drop into the water, and you kept flying to draw their attention? Maybe drop a grenade on them?"

Luis looked over, brow furrowed. "I can't—"

"Look, I don't know how to fly this thing, but I can shoot. As far as I can tell, it's our only option."

He shook his head slowly. "If we dropped the flaps and slowed her as much as we can, her stall speed is probably still close to fifty miles an hour. You'd hit the ocean like a missile. Maybe if we land just out of their range, you jump out, and then I take off to draw their attention. You could swim ashore, and then I could land further away."

She shrugged. "What other choice do we have?"

Luis shook his head. "None that I can think of."

CHAPTER 42

Eddie sighed and leaned on the apartment's doorframe, saving his energy. Injured, sore, and exhausted, he was running on fumes. He wasn't going to die here, at least not without a fight. Flexing his arm to keep it loose, he pushed a full magazine into his Sig. The cloud of paranoia and lack of direction that had plagued him for more than a year was gone. The rudderless emptiness of his life that had been his constant companion had evaporated.

He didn't know why exactly, but he believed in Caveman and felt protective of him. It gave him that sense of direction he yearned for. He would defend Caveman and help him figure out what had happened to him. The task aligned with his moral makeup. He shook his head and chuckled. How ironic that he'd finally found a reason to live again, just in time to die.

Caveman looked over at Eddie with a quizzical expression. "What?"

Eddie shrugged. "Nothing. I'm simply marveling at the absurdity of our situation."

"It is unreal."

He recognized this time of day from living in Miami. When the sun finally loses its grip, and the temperature drops a few degrees all at once. The wind rustled the palm trees. Eddie looked west, squinting at the larger ship and shading his eyes against the setting sun. This stirred in his mind like a dust devil, awaking his instincts. He considered the craft and then looked over his shoulder at the tactical boat. He turned to Caveman but stopped when the faint rumble of the boat's engines floated up on the wind. Eddie's adrenaline pumped. Was it moving closer? He couldn't tell, but he eased up off the seat and tightened his grip on the Sig.

Caveman noticed his movement and matched it, eyes wide.

A hollow thump pierced the air. A grenade launcher! He grabbed Caveman, and they dove into the apartment.

As they flew inside, a deafening roar crashed down upon them, followed by a wave of heat and debris.

Eddie's ears were ringing as he stumbled to his feet just in time for another explosion to knock him onto his back again. He coughed and looked for Caveman, who lay crumpled against the couch but stirring. "You okay?"

Caveman nodded, wiped dirt from his face, and put his glasses back on.

Eddie winced as he stood. "We need to light the oil. Get the flares!"

Caveman levered himself up on the coffee table and disappeared into the bedroom. He returned with two, and they stumbled toward the door.

Another concussion rumbled across the apartment. This detonation was a little further away.

Eddie turned to Caveman and shouted, "You ready?"

He nodded, handed Eddie a flare, and headed out the door. Outside, Caveman turned to the east side of the island.

Eddie faced the other way. He yanked the tab off the flare's end and squinted against the bright red shower of sparks, as they coalesced into a blazing ball of blinding light at the tip. He flung it end over end down the sandy path.

The flare bounced once and then stuck fast in the grease. It smoldered and puffed out a quick white cloud that rose into the air maybe fifty feet before the grease erupted into bright orange flames that billowed coal-black smoke.

Eddie turned to see a similar cloud rising from Caveman's side of the island.

Another hollow sound pierced the air. Eddie dropped to the ground and curled up into a ball.

The whole earth shook under him with the concussion as the grenade hit beyond the top of the hill.

Eddie scrambled to his feet.

The tattered remains of the camouflage netting waved in the breeze like the robes of the Grim Reaper himself, and the vegetation around the rim was red and burning.

Caveman rolled over unharmed. Thank God. The two of them dove back into the apartment.

Eddie stumbled to the remains of the entrance. "What are we going to do when those troops make it to the door and lob a grenade or a flashbang inside here?"

Sweat had carved lines in the fine powdering of dust that covered Caveman's face as he pursed his lips. "I don't know. We could pull the couch up in front of the bedroom door. It's a crappy place for a last stand."

Eddie ran a hand over his mouth. "No. I still think we need to engage them before they make it to the top. Come on." He took a few steps forward and leaned back out of the now gaping hole at the entrance to the apartment, the jagged edges of wood like teeth in a great, ruined mouth.

Caveman joined him and the two men stood back-to-back at the edge of the door, pistols ready.

Eddie said over his shoulder, "They've stopped shelling us, so they're coming."

Thick black smoke billowed up from each path and fluttered into the sky, leaving a dark line slithering to the south.

He squinted, but couldn't see any actual flames, and he wasn't sure if the oil was still burning or just smoldering. How long would it last?

A man in black tactical gear appeared out of the ash, his gas mask making him look extraterrestrial. How had he made it to the top so fast? He ran holding a submachine gun ready. A second man appeared behind him. The sun was just above the horizon, but the smoke acted like a curtain, keeping the light from blinding him. Eddie lifted his pistol and squeezed the trigger.

CHAPTER 43

Loren felt the engine reverberate through the cabin as Luis pushed the plane to its limit.

He pointed ahead, and Loren noticed the line of thin black smoke rising from the ocean just to the left of their destination as he eased the stick forward and began their descent. "You ready?"

She nodded. The ocean's color was now a deep, darker blue, as if the night was billowing up from below the surface. She closed her eyes and willed the craft to find just a little more speed.

The smoke ahead was the battle. Eddie and Sam fighting for their lives. But she was powerless to close the gap between them any faster. The propeller whirled. It pulled the craft with incredible force, but they approached the dark line at what seemed like a painfully slow rate.

Loren cradled one of the MP5s and the two grenades in her lap. She'd strapped on a flak jacket over the sundress, which she noticed was now a dingy brown, especially near the bottom. Her bare legs looked odd beneath it, and a line of dried blood snaked down from her right knee. She wiggled one visible toe in the torn Converse tennis shoes and shook her head. That was the only reaction she could muster to this ridiculous situation.

She would push forward as if Eddie and Sam were alive until she knew they weren't. They were fighting to stay alive until she could get there. That was all she would allow herself to think.

Gradually, the island took form. It was smaller than she'd expected, with a rise in the center.

Luis pointed to a ship just becoming visible on their left. "Is that Sam's?"

Loren shook her head. "No, I don't think so. His is blue."

He squinted at the other side of the island. "There's another smaller one to the east. I'm guessing that's not his, either?"

Loren swallowed. "I don't see Sam's boat at all." She'd assumed it had broken down. "Did something happen since we talked to Jeff? Maybe they got away."

"Then why would these guys have the island surrounded?" He adjusted their heading a fraction, aiming the plane at the smaller ship.

She looked over at the fuel gauge. So close to empty. Her heart ached.

They continued on a steady descent as they raced toward the island. A line of black-clad, armed men was just visible, fighting through the smoke to the top. Please, God, don't let it be too late.

Luis dropped some more and then banked a bit to the left, buzzing the smaller of the two boats.

Loren studied it. It looked empty, but then someone shot at them. Loren felt the two hollow sounds in her feet as the bullets struck the plane.

He pulled up and turned.

She glanced down. A circle of wreckage and debris covered the ocean floor just off the island. The structure of a yacht's main tower lay on its side. Her blood froze.

Luis straightened out and then banked around again. "Well, the guy on the boat isn't Eddie or Sam." He looked over. "What?"

"I saw Sam's boat on the bottom of the ocean. It's destroyed."

Luis's eyes widened, then hardened. "You ready?"

Loren nodded angrily.

He dipped lower and curved around on the south side of the island, a suitable distance from the two hostile boats.

The Beaver glided down toward the water. The pontoons touched. They bounced up and then settled into the waves again.

Luis turned the craft so that Loren's side was away from the island before shouting, "Good luck!"

She handed him the grenades and opened the door. "You, too." She leaped out into the black swells, landing feet first. The extra weight of the rifle and vest plunged her deep under the water.

Loren kicked for the surface. The plane's pontoons streaked across the surface and disappeared as it lifted off. The jacket was tight, and the gun and night-vision goggles were cumbersome, but her legs were delightfully free in the sundress. She kicked in long, powerful strokes. She broke through, located the island, and swam toward it.

A flash of yellow off in the distance caught her attention as the plane banked around. Hopefully, Luis had enough gas to harass them for a few minutes.

Loren put her head down and swam for the island with everything she had.

The swells rose and fell in giant rolls, and she rode them as best she could with long steady scissor kicks. As she neared land, the shore was rocky, so she swam parallel to it while searching for a way up.

In the rapidly fading light, the objects on the island were colorless and grainy. More gunfire erupted up ahead.

Finding a good spot, she trudged up onto the sand and raced toward the path she'd seen from the air. The smaller boat sat beached on the sand. Several men in black tactical gear prepared to run up a path that led to the top. A man with a short, bright-blond Mohawk stood at the back of the boat, scanning the sky. Looking for Luis. He lifted his pistol, aimed skyward, and started squeezing off rounds, then turned and leaped from the boat.

The Beaver flashed past, and over the tactical boat, before banking away from the island.

A small black object fell from the plane. It rattled around as it landed in the boat.

A concussion of fire and force lit up the sky. The grenade's explosion churned the water surrounding her, and the tactical boat launched skyward and split down the middle, the two halves somersaulting away in opposite directions.

A wave of heat raced past, and Loren took advantage of the diversion to move forward quietly in the near darkness, the wet dress clinging to her long legs.

The men on the beach recovered and ran up the path toward the top of the hill.

When she saw one stop to adjust a piece of equipment, Loren settled the stock against her shoulder, stared down the sight, and squeezed off a burst. The bullets caught the man in the forehead and just below his left eye. His head jerked around as he fell.

She pivoted toward the water. No one. She looked back and forth, trying to locate the man with the Mohawk who'd jumped into the water, but he was nowhere in sight. She backed into the foliage a step and held the MP5 ready.

The last light of day slipped away, leaving a shroud of darkness settling on the land.

She pulled on the night-vision goggles and scanned the green-tinted shore they presented to her. The fire burning on the path leading up the hill was bright, but the billowing smoke dampened the effect. A man, gun in hand, returned to the beach. Loren shot him and then pivoted back and forth, looking for others.

She continued down the shoreline, keeping her head on a swivel, searching for the man with the Mohawk. When she reached the bottom of the path, she checked her surroundings one more time and ran up. God, please have this path lead to Eddie and Sam.

CHAPTER 44

Eddie sat in the doorway facing one way, his pistol trained on the path in that direction. Caveman was still back-to-back with him in a similar position, covering the opposite side.

Another silhouette moved at the edge of the smoke. Eddie fired. The pistol jerked, the action moved, and the cartridge ejected, but he no longer heard any sound. Nothing but a dull roar filled his ears. His eyes were sandpaper, the lids heavy, and his head felt like it was full of cotton. Sweat rolled down Eddie's ribs, and his arm throbbed and felt stiff.

The light was nearly gone, with the oil having mostly burned itself out. Soon it would be dark enough for them to get a little closer. Close enough to throw a grenade and drive them back inside the cave for the last time.

Caveman's body jerked as he fired a shot at something on the other side.

Eddie wiped his eyes. They had to stay out of the apartment as long as possible. Once they lost this position, they would never come out again.

The surrounding plants became silhouettes. He squinted to see down the path now. A plane had passed over a few minutes ago, lifting Eddie's hopes that Luis and Loren had arrived. But after it landed and started taking fire, it took off again. It probably didn't matter. He and Caveman maybe had five more minutes, tops, before the gunmen overran their position.

Ammunition sat on the ground between them. Eddie took advantage of the free moment, reached back, grabbed a box, and thumbed a few rounds into a spent magazine. He called over his shoulder, "How you holding up?"

"Good. But I'm thinking we're just delaying the inevitable."

Eddie nodded and then said with a grim smile, "Then it's safe to tell me who put a bunch of classified stuff in your head."

Caveman barked out a short laugh. "Tell you what. As soon as I remember, you'll be the first person I tell. You have my word."

"See, now you've given me something to live for." He didn't entirely understand why, but Eddie felt content to die next to this man. One, he was surprised to discover, he thought of as a friend. He didn't know why this mattered, but it did.

The plane returned and banked just before the crest. A blast shook the island, followed by a small fireball.

"What the hell was that?" Caveman asked.

Eddie sighed. "I think it's my friends trying to make it safe to land."

"It's not going to matter. We're out of time."

A cylinder appeared out of the void, tumbling end over end as it arced toward them. Eddie glimpsed it out of the corner of his eye and screamed, "Grenade!" as he dove back inside, Caveman close on his heels.

With a thunderous detonation, the interior of the apartment lit up with white, hot light.

Eddie was facing away when the flash grenade went off, and he rolled, bringing his pistol up, and leveling it at the door.

A black-clad figure darted his head in and then quickly ducked back as they both fired at him.

Eddie scrambled forward. Pushing as fast as he could to make it back to the opening. Firing again and again before they could throw in another grenade. He desperately wanted to reclaim the door frame. Not to cede ground to the enemy. He fired twice more randomly as he rushed ahead. Reaching the opening, he swung his pistol out ready.

The man in black gathered himself, a grenade held in one fist. Eddie pivoted to fire. The man jerked and fell forward. Then a second burst of gunfire rang out. What the hell? He hadn't taken the shot.

Loren's voice came from the darkness, faint like it was from the bottom of a well. "It's Loren. A friendly. Don't shoot!"

Eddie sagged with relief. Was he hallucinating? "Come on." Then he thought he really had lost his mind. She climbed up to the flat area. In the faint moonlight, he could just make her out. She wore a torn and filthy dress, a flak jacket, and night-vision goggles, which made her head seem alien-shaped. He closed his eyes in relief. If it was a mirage, it was a good one.

CHAPTER 45

Frank stood on the bow, pistol down by his side, jaw set, staring at the island. The flickering fires gently illuminated the faltering curtain of smoke.

He clicked the mic and called again, "Badger, do you read?" The radio returned only a static crackle. Frank was reasonably sure the tactical boat was gone—destroyed by the damn plane. Had Mack perished with it? He tried again. "Mack!" Silence. He ground his teeth and focused on the island's crest above the light, shrouded in darkness, revealing nothing.

He spat into the ocean. These people were going to die. If it took him the rest of his life, he would hunt down every single one of them.

More gunfire floated in from the island. The smoke was really working against his men. How had they created that? And so fast? How?

The plane sounded on the wind again, faint but getting closer. He turned, sprinted back the length of the boat, and opened one locker, screaming as he went. He'd kept a man back in reserve, sitting ready in the rear. "Incoming! Pull the anchor! Turk, get us out of here."

He grabbed an H&K MR762 rifle and popped in a magazine. He scanned the beach with the night-vision scope and then looked back to the sky. The stars were just emerging. He strained to hear the plane again. Gemini mentioned just two people, and one was a woman. Hopefully that was true, and he would catch a break on something.

The deck beneath him rumbled as the engines started. He felt another vibration as the anchor rose. He was glad to be free and moving, but now he couldn't hear the plane.

Turk put the ship in reverse, and yelled, "Ahead at eleven o'clock."

Frank lifted the rifle to this shoulder and sighted down the barrel. He moved back and forth until he saw it and fired.

The plane dropped altitude and banked to the side.

He pivoted, firing another volley, as the craft flashed past. "Move it, Turk!"

The massive ship leaped forward and sped up. Frank ran back and took the wheel. He handed Turk the rifle. "See if you can knock him out of the sky." He pulled a wide turn. He was running blind in the darkness and didn't want to run into the damned island, so he powered out to sea a moment before coming around and up the other side.

The plane sped by again. Turk shot at it.

A small black ball appeared out of the darkness, smacked into the deck, and bounced over the rail. It exploded before it hit the water. The ship shook.

Frank gritted his teeth and swerved. He jammed his hand down on the ship's horn button. As it rang out into the night, he lifted the radio. "Retreat! Everyone back to the eastern beach. I repeat, retreat to the eastern beach!"

Turk fired a few more rounds. The plane didn't pass over again.

Frank slowed and monitored the depth finder. If he ran aground, they'd all be dead. When he was as close as he dared, he turned and faced the bow out to sea, and shouted, "Keep that plane off us until we get our men aboard! Toss out the anchor, but be ready to pull it!"

He walked back to the rear. On the beach, his men dove into the water. So few of them—two of the group of six he'd sent ashore. That was it? Frank swore and held his pistol ready in case any of these swimmers weren't friendly.

His men hauled themselves aboard. Just as he was about to get them the hell out of here, a whistle came from his right. Mack swam into view. He climbed up and collapsed onto the deck. Blood covered one side of his face and he gritted his teeth so hard that the muscles flexed in his temple. Still breathing, though.

Frank grinned, patted him on the head, and strode back to the cockpit. "Pull the anchor and let's move." He threw the throttle forward, and they raced out into the black sea and safety. They'd collect themselves, call Gemini, and then come back and kill these bastards.

CHAPTER 46

Loren appraised the strange unknown man and then Eddie with a shake of her head. He had a bandage on his arm and another on his cheek, sunken dark eyes, and deep lines etched his face, but he was still alive.

The other man looked at her curiously from behind round glasses that made him look professorial. The overall effect contrasted with the pistol held loosely but comfortably in his right hand.

She didn't see any sign of Sam, and a lump formed in her throat. She looked over her shoulder once to make sure there were no more hostiles before stepping forward and hugging Eddie. Everything was still green. She pulled the night-vision goggles from her eyes.

The man she didn't know ducked inside and returned with a gas lantern but did not light it yet.

Seeing Eddie again made her stomach clench. The dark stubble and grime somehow made him look even more masculine and rugged. It suited him. She really did love him.

Eddie gestured to the other man. "Loren, this is Caveman. Caveman, Loren Malen."

Caveman? She smiled and nodded at him.

The man with the glasses returned the gesture, looking down as if embarrassed.

Eddie asked, "Any more hostiles from the direction you came up?"

She shook her head. "I don't think so."

He nodded. "Where's Luis?"

Loren shrugged. "Landing the plane, I guess. He took out the smaller boat and then went after the big one."

Caveman said, "We saw it leave, so he at least chased it off. The question is, who did it leave behind?"

A horn sounded in the distance. Long and sustained. A second blast followed.

They all looked in that direction.

Loren pulled back down the night-vision goggles. "Watch my back. I'll check the other side."

Eddie told Caveman, "Stay here and keep your eyes down that side. I'll cover her."

He nodded.

Rifle to her shoulder, she then crept down the other path to the western side of the island, sweeping her gaze back and forth across the green-tinted world. She felt Eddie, tense and ready, close behind her.

The beach was empty. The only sounds were the waves lapping at the shore. Then the whine of the Beaver floated in on the wind.

She could just make out glimpses of the plane's silhouette in the moonlight as it approached the island from the west. The engine hesitated and then caught. It sputtered again as it touched down. It bounced once on the surface, and then settled in.

As it slowed, a bang rang out as something struck the craft. It shook and altered course, but kept coming forward, now listing to one side. The engine sputtered one last time, before finally falling silent. It glided forward and stopped with a jerk as it ran aground.

Luis stepped out. He was barely visible as he dropped the anchor, jumped in feet first, and then waded toward them through the water that reached nearly to his knees.

As Luis reached the shore, he gave Eddie a fist bump and took him in from head to toe. "You look like shit. What's the situation?"

Eddie grinned. "You two don't look like you're ready for the prom, either." He shrugged. "I think you chased off the hostiles for now. We have a friendly up top named Caveman, watching our back. Sam is injured and not ambulatory."

Loren said, "Caveman?"

He shook his head. "It's even weirder than you think. He's been—I guess—living here for a while. Maybe a couple of years. He isn't sure why, however, or at least won't say. Oh, and he doesn't seem to remember his name, either—so I named him Caveman out of necessity."

Luis shook his head. "Do you trust him?"

Eddie shrugged. "I don't know. So far, he's saved my life and Sam's, and let me call Jeff, but I guess you could say he needed me. He may not need me so much anymore. So we should definitely keep an eye on him. He's armed and more than capable." Eddie looked over at Loren. "I don't know what's on this damned island everyone wants so bad, but Sam planned to drug me once we got near here."

Loren shivered and, once again, the lump returned to her throat. "Are you sure? What happened?"

"I'm sure. They boarded us just as Sam was going to knock me out. They came in that big ship to kill us and blew up Sam's yacht. I don't know what we've gotten ourselves into, but I don't trust the senator all that much right now."

It didn't reconcile with the man she knew, but she trusted that this was the truth. How would this affect her relationship with Eddie? Ten thousand other worries immediately swallowed that thought and pushed it to the back of her mind.

Eddie gestured over at the plane. "Can we leave in that?"

Luis shook his head. "No way. We don't have enough gas left to even get airborne again, and I hit a rock or something on the way in, so it may not matter even if we did."

"All right, let's get back to higher ground and regroup."

They moved up the path, guns ready, with Loren in the lead and Luis bringing up the rear.

As they neared the top, Caveman appeared. He held his pistol ready at his side.

Eddie put a hand on Luis. "He's okay. Luis, this is Caveman. Caveman, this is Luis."

Caveman nodded a greeting. "Thanks for the help. I could just make out the men swimming to the large boat before it left. I think we're clear—for now." He kneeled and turned on the lantern to a very low light.

Loren caught sight of the cave mouth and stopped short. It looked like a regular apartment, but on this little island in the middle of nowhere. Jagged wood surrounded the entrance and there was no door, but other than that, it was just a normal apartment. She turned to Eddie, frowning.

He looked so tired as he shrugged, opened his mouth, and hesitated, before finally saying, "I don't know what to tell you."

Loren glanced back at the room, dim and empty, and asked, "Where's Sam?"

Caveman turned. "He's in the back room. I'll show you." He stepped inside and turned on a light switch.

She held Eddie's gaze for a moment, then followed. The room was long and narrow, covered with debris, but she marveled at the electric florescent lights.

Caveman opened a door at the rear and led her into a room.

Sam lay in the bed, looking pale and older than he had just a few days ago. Was that all it really was? It felt like years since she'd met him in Miami.

Caveman examined the bandage and splint on the senator's leg. "He had a nasty compound fracture, but if we can get him to a doctor soon, he should be fine."

The odd man's skill impressed Loren as he carefully and deftly changed Sam's dressing. The leg was horrible, and he was pale and sweaty, but he was clearly in expert hands. She looked around the room, then up at the ruined entrance. What the hell was going on? This obviously had something to do with what Sam was looking for, but it was all bizarre and beyond her comprehension. How was this place even here, in the middle of nowhere? How long had it been here and for what purpose? And what was so important that Sam would drug Eddie?

The senator's eyes fluttered open. He focused on her and winced. "How are you, my dear?"

She took his hand. "I'm fine. How're you doing?"

His voice sounded dry and scratchy. "Hurts like hell."

Loren lifted a cup of water from the side table and held it to his mouth. He took a few feeble swallows, lay back on the pillow, and faded off again.

Caveman said, "I sedated him until we can get him to a hospital. He was in a lot of pain."

She studied Caveman's open, unassuming expression and innocent eyes. Was this guy for real? It was all so weird. "What's wrong with Eddie?"

"He got thrown around pretty good when the ship blew up and a bullet grazed his bicep. He'll be okay. He just needs rest. Frankly, I don't know how he's still standing." He grabbed his first-aid case and led her back to the front of the cave.

She picked her way around splinters and chips of wood scattered across the floor. The sofa looked like it was from Sears. Not a picture in sight. Like a movie set designed by a man, except someone clearly lived here—and had for some time. There were faint wear marks on the carpet and scratches on the hardwood floor from the kitchen chairs. What on earth was going on here?

CHAPTER 47

Jaw clenched, Frank slowed the ship and killed the engine. Now, the enemy had resupplied, held the high ground, and, to top it all off, had a damned airplane. He didn't see a way to complete his objective, and he wasn't going to feed his remaining men back into that damned meat grinder of an island.

Mack shuffled up, looking like a drowned rat, a bandage covering one cheek.

"You okay?" Frank asked.

Mack nodded. "Whoever that bastard on the plane is, I'm going to kill him."

Frank studied the island in the distance. The landform was just barely visible in the moonlight. He never wanted to see that place again, except maybe to come back, scour it with napalm, and piss on the ashes. He picked up his satellite phone and dialed Gemini. The phone rang several times before his boss answered. Frank took a deep breath, then said, "Sir, we've failed our mission. Their reinforcements arrived before we achieved a beachhead. They destroyed the tactical boat, and we lost roughly half our remaining men. We're clear now, but our objective was not completed. Repeat, we failed our mission."

Gemini sighed. "Not to worry, Frank. They caught us all unprepared."

What did that mean? Who did he include in "all"? Just how bad was the situation? "What are your orders?"

"How many useable men do you have?"

Frank said, "Four, not including me."

Gemini said, "Head northwest towards Crooked Island. Understood?"

"Understood. Crooked Island."

"Wait there, regroup, and rest. I'll deliver these people right to you."

Frank felt the beginnings of a smile. This was why he worked for this group. Because they were bigger, meaner, and more organized than anyone else. "How's that, Gemini?"

"The people on the island think that help is coming to them in the morning, but it will actually be a smuggler we've used in the past. He's a tough little bastard named Tito, and he'll deliver them to you tied up with a bow."

"Very good, sir. Why don't we hook up with Tito now and be waiting for them on the boat?"

"Patience, Frank, there are still a few Coast Guard vessels in the area, and this is a U.S. senator. We need to maintain an air of deniability if something goes wrong. I've worked with Tito before. He's cunning and ruthless. Just get to Crooked Island, and he'll get them there."

"10-4." Frank hung up.

Mack wiped down his pistol with an oily rag. "Well, that sucked."

Frank rubbed his scar. "Gemini says they got the drop on them as well."

The younger man looked up. "You think we're on the wrong side?"

Good question. The question a survivor would ask, and Frank knew the two of them were nothing if not survivors. "Not yet. Supposedly, our people control whoever they've called for help."

Mack slid the action back and forth. "If they called for help, then who'd they call and how? And if they're waiting for help, does that mean their plane is out of commission?"

He sighed. "I don't know. Those are good questions. Maybe it's just out of fuel. We put a bunch of holes in it." He should start the engine and head in the direction that Gemini had instructed, but some instinct made him hesitate. His elation at Gemini's plan and confidence was ebbing.

At every step, the enemy seemed to do what no one expected. This ship was fast, and it would get them to Crooked Island quick enough if they needed it to. No, he would wait here and watch for a little while. Frank was not about to be caught unprepared again.

CHAPTER 48

Eddie stood at the edge of the light, scanning the area below with the night-vision goggles, but he was reasonably sure the enemy had bugged out—at least for now.

They'd discovered the bodies of three dead soldiers just beyond the rim. Two on his side, and one on Caveman's. Only three? He was sure he'd shot at least six. He sat on his haunches and studied one of the dead bodies. Flak vest, with at least two holes in it. Only a head shot was going to take these men out, and that was no simple task in combat conditions. Thank God Loren and Luis came when they did.

They carried the men down the path to the west side of the island, away from where the plane sat parked offshore.

As they turned to walk back up the rise, Luis said, "Let the animals have the bastards."

Back at the top, Eddie removed the headgear, sat down heavily, and leaned against the ruined doorframe, holding his pistol in his lap.

Loren sat down next to him.

He put his arm around her. "Thanks for coming." She was a mess in her torn dress and flak jacket, but still the most beautiful woman he'd ever seen.

She shrugged, studying his face, her brows drawn down, and a frown on her small mouth. She reached out and brushed a lock of dark hair off his forehead. "Sorry we didn't get here sooner."

Eddie waved his hand dismissively. "Better late than never. How's Sam?"

Loren shrugged. "He seems stable for now."

Caveman squatted down, opened his first-aid kit, and cleaned a cut on Loren's upper arm without asking.

She glanced over, unaware of the injury.

Luis leaned into the cave mouth and took in the apartment. He still held an MP5 ready, and his posture was tense and alert. He looked over at Eddie with a smirk and shook his head. Then he set one chair back on its feet and took a seat. There were bags beneath his sunken eyes.

Eddie's head pounded. A pain pulsed in his shin. Reaching down, he pulled a three-inch wooden splinter free with a quick jerk. He grimaced as a trickle of blood rolled down his leg.

The fires were mostly out, but an acrid smell still hung in the air. Eddie asked, "So, how are we going to get off this damned island?" He thought about the barrels of gas in the shipping container. It wasn't the type that would work in an airplane, however, so they were useless to them. "I think our friends will be back."

Luis nodded. "Agreed, and that plane was supposed to be bringing reinforcements. Loren and I discussed on the ride over that they're well financed and organized. They'll find another plane quickly. More bad guys are on their way. You can count on it."

"The ones who hit us here were pros. Well trained."

"Where we were, it was half and half—local muscle and then some mercs."

Eddie rubbed his face with both hands. "I'm guessing when they return, it'll be in force. They know the terrain, and they'll have a better plan this time." Eddie felt something hard beneath him, rolled to one side, and lifted the mangled remains of the satellite phone. He looked over at Caveman. "Sorry."

Caveman shrugged. "Better the phone than us. Besides, we've already established that I have no one to call, anyway."

When he finished dressing her wound, he moved to Eddie, and unwound the bandage on his bicep.

Eddie studied his friend. Staying busy. Keeping his mind off the current situation.

Loren met his gaze a moment before looking out into the darkness. "We called Craig, and he's supposed to be sending some smuggler named Tito to rescue us in the morning."

Eddie rolled his eyes. "But no Coast Guard, cavalry, nothing?"

Loren shook her head. "It pisses me off as well, and without a phone, we don't have a whole hell of a lot of other options."

Eddie looked over at Luis. "Tito? Some friend of Craig's? I don't like the sound of this smuggler at all."

Luis scratched his cheek. "I don't, either, but the plane's empty, so how else are we going to get off this rock?"

Loren added, "We talked to Jeff, too. He's still trying to find us help, but we're in the middle of nowhere. He blasted a communication to everyone he knows but says so far this has only produced a few options. But he doesn't believe any of them can get here before morning."

Eddie nodded and winced.

Caveman looked up. "How does it feel?"

Eddie sighed. "Fine, it's just stiff. I haven't been able to rest it much."

Caveman chuckled as he pulled off the last of the old bandage and studied the wound. "It looks pretty good." He applied antibiotics in careful and measured movements.

"So, you're competent at field medicine too?"

Caveman shook his head. "I'm expert level at most first aid." He said the statement with no expression. Then he seemed to realize Eddie was half-joking and grinned, his eyes wide with apparent surprise at the answer. His smile faded, and he grew thoughtful, as if trying to solve a puzzle.

Eddie gripped his shoulder and grinned back. "I'll add that to your resume."

Caveman snorted.

A crease formed in Loren's forehead. "I hate to say it, but I also don't trust anyone Craig would send right now. Hell, I don't really trust anyone who's not currently on this island."

Eddie raised his dark eyebrows. "Welcome to the club." He noticed some crusted blood on Caveman's upper lip and chin. During the fight, he must've gotten a bloody nose. At least that ruled out Caveman being some sort of alien. He bled red like a man, not a robot, or some other creature.

Amazing that this was even a question worth considering. Even more surprising to find that the revelation was a relief. How far down the road of weirdness had he wandered?

Loren reached over and cupped the side of Eddie's face. "I really am sorry."

Eddie took her hand. "None of us were given a ton of good options in this situation. I'm sorry for whatever this says about Sam."

Her shoulders sagged. "Me, too."

Luis straightened his goggles. "I'm going to do another circuit of the island. Keep your eyes open." He then slipped off into the darkness.

Loren gestured with her chin at Luis. "He's a character, but he definitely saved my life. Thanks for making me take him."

"I'm glad he could help."

Caveman stood and arched his back in a stretch. Dark circles ringed his eyes, and his shoulders drooped. He took a few steps away and looked out in the direction the big boat had taken.

Eddie held up a finger to Loren, then stood and walked over beside Caveman. He said quietly, "You know you have to go with us."

The pained expression returned to Caveman's eyes, and he took off his glasses and pinched the bridge of his nose. "I can't."

Eddie leaned in closer. "Listen, everyone knows you're here now. They'll come back. It's not safe, so your mission must change. If you aren't here to guard something, and I believe you aren't, then something is wrong. I give you my word that I'll take you someplace more secure. My friends and I are talented and well connected. We'll do everything we can to get you reunited with your mission."

Caveman hesitated. He looked down at the ground and furrowed his brow.

"Look at it this way," Eddie continued. "This isn't a change to your mission. It's just a change in mission parameters. I have friends who can set up the satellite phone number on another one. You'll be able to wait for a call every Tuesday. How can you continue your mission if you can no longer receive a call?"

Caveman half glanced over his shoulder at Loren and then said in a lower voice, "You know when you asked me about your mission at the CIA, and I knew it?"

Eddie nodded.

Caveman said, "Until you asked me, I didn't know I knew it. It's like your question triggered something, and I answered before I realized what I was doing. It's true about every other question you've asked me as well. That scares the hell out of me."

Eddie frowned. "Frankly, it scares the hell out of me, too. Who sent you here?"

Caveman stared blankly at him. "I don't know. It doesn't always work, but since I answered you the first time, it doesn't hurt as much when you ask me things. Even if I don't know the answer. Somehow, you changed something in me."

What did that mean? Regardless, Eddie didn't think it altered the situation. "You still have to go with us. Even if it's just to keep what's in your head away from the bad guys. It's your duty."

This gave Caveman pause, and he was silent a long time before shaking his head. His forehead drew together, and the skin crinkled around his eyes as he struggled. "I can't just leave."

He reminded Eddie of an autistic boy he'd met years before. The young man would exhibit a similar anguished expression when he was incapable of articulating what he felt. In just one day, Eddie had grown fond of this strange man and somehow felt responsible for him. "Listen to me. When you saved me and Sam, that wasn't part of your mission. You didn't even know it was Sam at first, did you?"

Caveman shook his head.

"Okay, so that was an independent thought, a judgment call. You saw something that wasn't right, something that needed to be done, and you did it. You're not a robot. If you stay, it's suicide. I don't think whoever took all the trouble to put you here would want that. They took great pains to keep you *alive*. Staying here to die can't be what they intended."

Caveman put back on his glasses, and then, with a deep sigh, nodded. "I suppose that's true. Our current location is compromised."

Eddie nodded. "Exactly. They put a lot of planning and resources into your well-being. Whoever did that can't want you to throw it all away."

Caveman sighed. He clamped his eyes shut and bent over at the waist as if he had a stomach cramp. He struggled this way for a beat before straightening. "I also believe I can't stay here any longer and complete my mission, but if I leave, my mission fails as well. Whatever I'm waiting for can't happen. No one will be able to find me."

Eddie took a deep breath. "I told you, we will set up the satellite phone again. But I think something has gone wrong with the mission. And, if you come with us, we'll try to find who you're waiting for. Seek them out and inform them of the situation. Get new orders. When I was in the military, that's what I would've wanted the men under my command to do in your situation."

Caveman blew out a breath like he was trying to quell nausea. He looked like he desperately wanted to take Eddie's advice, but still held back from taking the last step.

Eddie shrugged. "My friends and I really are uniquely qualified to help you do this. We have the contacts and the resources. If anyone can get your mission back on track, it's us."

Caveman's forehead smoothed out, and he nodded. "You can help me stay on my mission? You really believe you can do that?"

Eddie grinned. "I do."

Caveman grimaced one last time before heaving a long sigh. "Okay, I'll go with you."

CHAPTER 49

Eddie reached out and grasped Caveman's shoulder. Thank God he'd agreed to come with them. Out of the corner of his eye, he noticed Loren watching their interaction with intense interest. He leaned in and said to Caveman, "No matter what happens, you can't trust Sam yet. Okay? I know he's on your green list, but you can't trust him until we figure out what the deal is."

Loren stepped forward and opened her mouth like she wanted to protest.

Eddie said to her, "He was going to drug me, Loren. You asked me to keep him safe, and I did the best I could, and I'll do everything in my power to get him home. But Caveman here is my new mission. Maybe the mission I've been destined for, for a long time. We can't trust Sam. At least not yet."

Caveman looked over his shoulder at her as well, his eyebrows raised expectantly.

After a moment, she sighed. "I understand. I'm with you."

Eddie turned back to Caveman. "I want you to say you work for me. Don't let Sam know you were on the island."

Caveman said, "I'm still not sure I'm capable of actually leaving, but I understand."

Luis reappeared. Rifle held in the crook of his arm, eyes alert and wary. "The island looks clear. No sign of bad guys, but we're awfully vulnerable here in the dark. They could frog their way back to us from a long way off."

Eddie rubbed his face. "I guess we need to have a game plan for that. And another one if we have to go with this guy, Tito. There's ammo inside that we can use."

Luis nodded. "There's more in the plane too." He turned to Caveman. "Can you shoot?"

He shrugged. "I'm competent in a firefight."

Luis' eyebrows rose, and he looked over at Eddie, who held his hands in a "what can I say" gesture before saying, "Man, you look exhausted."

Luis scowled at his friend. "Have you looked in a mirror lately?"

Eddie smiled weakly and glanced at his watch: 9:30. It felt like it was well after midnight. He looked into Loren's eyes. "You look tired, too. Are you okay with taking the first watch with me?"

She touched the bandage on his cheek. "Of course. I couldn't sleep now if I wanted to."

He turned to Luis and Caveman. "We're a long way from home. Why don't you guys rest? Loren and I can take the first watch, and we'll switch at midnight."

Luis frowned.

"Listen," Eddie said, "I think we're going to need you fresh and ready tomorrow." He turned to Caveman. "Okay?"

Caveman rubbed his neck and nodded. He turned to Luis. "You can have the couch. I have a mat under the bed."

Loren and Eddie stood the remaining camp chair upright and sat side by side, staring out over the ocean. She reached over and pulled his hand into her lap.

He tilted his head back, closed his eyes, and thought about this woman, their connection, and how life kept throwing them back together. As usual, their relationship felt like it was at some sort of crossroads. Unresolved issues remained like the smoke still hanging in the night air.

For the millionth time, his thoughts wandered back to the last time they parted, like a bunch of crabs picking a fish carcass clean.

Everything in Eddie's life was about to come to a head. He was still on the lam. Loren popped back into his life and asked him to help her save Amy, the last Clay Pigeon. After rescuing her, they had no one to turn to. Craig was their only option. He closed his eyes and his mind wandered back to the last night of that time in France.

They arranged to meet him in Honfleur, of all places. The scene of the crime—Nikki's murder. It was nearby and Eddie knew it, but the irony was not lost on him. The same missions, people, and places kept cycling around in his life in some strange ballet.

He had to admit that Craig did in fact show up with the cavalry, which was good because they needed it. As soon as Amy and Loren were safe, Eddie slipped away in the confusion. He knew the town, so even at night he could disappear down the narrow maze of streets like a cat.

He'd done his job. Loren might trust Craig, but Eddie wasn't there yet.

As he hurried out of Honfleur and across a field, she kept catching in his thoughts like a thorn. He couldn't leave without at least saying goodbye.

Loren answered on the second ring. "Are you okay?"

"I'm fine. How are you and Amy?"

"We're safe. Why did you leave?"

Eddie rubbed his forehead. "I'm still a wanted man, Loren."

"I know but wait. Hold on." She spoke to someone off the phone in a muffled voice before returning to the line. "Eddie, the information Amy brought back— well, we're looking at it now, and it—well, I think it clears you. You can come in."

"Loren, listen—"

"No, Eddie, really! The CIA and FBI brass are here. You can—"

Eddie had opened his mouth to protest when Craig came on the line. "Eddie, it's Craig. It looks like I owe you an explanation. Tell me where to meet you. I'll come alone. Let me fix this."

Eddie squeezed his eyes shut. He could disappear from this spot, no problem. He knew their methods of pursuing him too well. What would that mean, though? Another small town in another place. Looking over his shoulder, waiting for them to find him again. Still better than prison, but not really living.

Where could he meet Craig and feel safe? The city map unfurled in his mind. "At the end of the Place Jean de Vienne is the Du Phare campground. Enter at the front gate and walk in on foot. Take the lane furthest from the ocean at the fork. I'll find you."

"When?"

Eddie glanced at this watch. "Half an hour."

Surrounded by woods on both sides, it would be nearly impossible to set up a trap at the campground in that amount of time. The area also offered a myriad of escape routes in all directions. When he finally saw him walking down the meeting place road, Eddie felt a surge of irritation.

Craig's gait was casual and calm, like a man out for a relaxing stroll. Not a care in the world.

Eddie could easily kill him and fade back into the foliage and disappear. Tempting. He stepped silently out of the darkness and fell into stride beside his old CIA boss.

The Agency man glanced over. "Good to see you, Eddie. I'm glad you're still alive."

Eddie grunted. "No thanks to you."

Craig let out a slow breath through his nose. "That's true. But you have to understand the way things looked from our point of view."

Eddie stopped walking. "You should have known me. That I would never do that."

Craig dropped his head, shook it, and then looked back at Eddie. "I've been in this business for many years, and in that time, I've seen people I never in a million years thought could go bad, turn up rotten. Enough times to make me doubt my gut. I've also learned this. If you were guilty, it would have come to light and if you were innocent—well, you were, and it came to light." He snorted. "I knew one thing. When they didn't find your body, I knew you weren't dead. I also knew we'd never find you."

"You could've tried."

"How?"

Good question, actually. Eddie rubbed his forehead. "Well, you could have taken me off the most wanted list."

Craig shook his head. "You ran from a crime scene where a key counterintelligence witness was killed. What did you want me to say? No, no, he's my friend? He'd never do that?"

Arguing with Craig was always like this. He presented a good reason for his Machiavellian ways—always logical and reasonable after the fact, and not quite the entire story.

Craig started walking again. "Look, I get it from your point of view. We left you out in the cold."

Eddie fell back into stride beside him.

"That's why this is the hardest job in the world, and we don't pick just anyone to do it. Shit happens, and this time it happened to you. What do you want from me? An apology? I'm sorry. I figured you'd find a way out of this mess, and you did. What do you want now? That's what you should focus on."

More Craig-speak. What did Eddie want? "I want my life back."

A faint smile touched his lips. "Now you're thinking clearly. I've given Loren a document clearing you of all charges and removing you from the most wanted list. It's signed by the deputy directors of the FBI and CIA." He stopped again. "Call her and see. She faxed a copy to a powerful friend of hers. You have your life back—in writing. Take it, Eddie. You've earned it."

Could this really be the end of the running? The end of looking over his shoulder?

Craig continued walking. "Call her and see. This is on the level, Eddie. You're free. She's at the Pasino Le Havre hotel in room 310. No one will bother you. Go see her."

Eddie made his way to the third floor of the hotel, and Craig was true to his word. No one bothered him at all. He'd called before, and Loren confirmed she held his exoneration in writing. He knocked softly on the door to room 310. She opened it a few inches before ushering him inside.

Amy lay in a fetal position on the bed, her body jerking with deep, wrenching sobs.

She'd been a rock through the entire ordeal. Kept her head and got the job done, so it surprised Eddie to see her like this. He raised his eyebrows at Loren.

She frowned, and a crease formed at the top of her nose. "The mission she was on. It was, well, it was tough. She thought she was going to die." She looked down at Amy. "That takes a while to get out of your system. I know, from personal experience." She looked back up at Eddie. "What about you?"

Eddie shrugged. "Let me see the paper."

She handed it to him.

It looked real. Something like this had to come with strings, though, didn't it?

Loren studied his face. "You don't believe them?"

"I don't know. I don't trust any of them. I can't stay here."

Loren looked back at Amy. "I understand, but I can't leave her, Eddie. She has no one else. I can't let these people debrief her without someone to stand by her. Someone to advocate for her."

The thought of parting from Loren again tightened around his heart like a fist. He understood, though. It was tough coming in from the cold and this woman, who cleared his name, was all alone.

He had to go, however. He needed some space from the men downstairs, and he needed to test their word.

Putting his arms around Loren, he hugged her. He couldn't remain, and she couldn't go. It was always the story of their relationship. He kissed the top of her head. "Afterward, get word to me."

Looking up into his eyes, she said, "I will. I promise," then leaned up and kissed him tenderly.

CHAPTER 50

Loren studied Eddie. A strange expression had crept over his face as he stared out at the ocean. What was he thinking about? She was not good at reading him yet and still didn't know his moods or rhythms.

Suddenly he stood. Using the night-vision goggles, he studied both paths going down to the beach and the ocean beyond.

Loren stood in a crouch, listening for danger.

Satisfied that the coast was clear, he turned back to her and pulled off the headgear. "When you first showed up a few days ago, I should have asked you how Amy is doing. I should have asked that first thing. I'm sorry. How is she?"

Loren leaned back. Unexpected and nice. "Much better now. It took a long time, though. A lot of sleepless nights, nightmares when she could actually fall asleep." She frowned. "But she came out the other side, and she's doing all right now."

Eddie rocked on his heels and nodded. "Good, I'm glad."

This led her back to when they parted last time. She suddenly felt defensive about her decision again. Even though she shouldn't. "I didn't have a choice. I had to go with her."

He took her hand. "I know." He studied their intertwined fingers and then looked up at her, his brown eyes searching her face. "Afterward you didn't reach out..."

What? "Yes, I did."

Eddie's eyebrows rose. "How? I never heard from you."

She shook her head. "No. As soon as Amy was settled, I called Craig..."

Eddie's brows drew together, and anger flashed in his eyes. "Are you telling me you tried to contact me through Craig? What did he say?"

This explained so much. Oh, man, Eddie was going to kill Craig, and she might help him. "I didn't know how else to contact you. He said that he passed the message onto you. But I thought you never reached out to me because..."

Eddie shook his head. "I never got it. That bastard."

What was Craig thinking? "Why would he do that?"

Eddie said, "Why does he do anything that he does? Because in some way we can't see, it served his purposes. All this time, I thought—"

"Me too." She grinned. "As much as that sucks, this is actually good news."

His eyebrows rose.

"It means we wanted to connect. We wanted to see each other. We just have a Craig Black problem."

A smile tugged at the corner of Eddie's lips and then faded. "We definitely have a Craig Black problem." His brow furrowed. "You've never left my thoughts since the day I first met you all those years ago. I don't know why. You just haven't."

Thank you, God. She squeezed his hand. "Me, neither. I was heartbroken when you didn't answer. I just don't understand what Craig thought keeping us apart would accomplish. Neither of us works for him anymore."

Eddie sighed. "I don't think Craig believes anyone ever really stops working for him. I'm so sorry. I feel like I've acted like a jerk now."

Actually, considering what he thought was true, Eddie had been pretty decent about the whole thing. "No, you didn't. It makes your agreeing to help with this even more meaningful. I really appreciate it. I'm so sorry for everything that's happened."

His smile returned. "I think this is where I'm supposed to be. I think helping Caveman is what I'm supposed to be doing. It's okay."

Dark rings circled his sunken eyes and stubble covered his jaw, but he was so handsome that her heart ached. He hadn't ignored her. He'd still been waiting for her call.

Eddie held her gaze. "I know it doesn't make any sense, and this is the weirdest relationship ever, but I think I'm in love with you. No. I *am* in love with you."

Deception and lies filled Loren's early life. Her father taught her to say what people wanted to hear, sometimes what they needed to hear. She never enjoyed doing that, but somehow it left her unable to believe what others said to her.

Especially that word. That most important of all words. Particularly from a man, a man she was romantically involved with. Not that her life, the way it played out, presented many opportunities for this problem. In her heart, though, she'd always dreaded this situation.

But now that the feared moment was unexpectedly upon her, she felt nothing but joy. She wanted to cry. She wanted to hug him. This man had changed so much about her in only a few brief encounters. She smiled. "Me too."

His eyes darted around on her face before he leaned in and kissed her. "We really have the weirdest relationship."

She grinned. "We do." Now the next big question. "What now?"

Eddie shrugged again. "I don't know. Let's get off this island first, and then see where that takes us."

Now that she understood where they stood, now that their relationship was clear and Eddie's actions had been explained, it allowed her to think about the physical side of their relationship again. She quirked a smile. "You know, if it wasn't for the possibility of an attack at any moment, I might make love to you right here on this hilltop."

Eddie grinned. "If it wasn't for the possibility of an attack at any moment, I might just let you."

The lighthearted banter was back. The fun she experienced with him blossomed like before and their interactions were effortless again.

She kissed him again, then stepped back and stretched. Putting on the night vision goggles, she checked the paths and ocean again. Ambushed while reminiscing—wouldn't that be typical for their relationship?

They sat again by the door, and she took his hand in hers.

Suddenly, she worried that the silence between them was awkward. She didn't know how to be with him yet.

He looked sidelong at her, eyebrows raised.

She shrugged. "I don't know where we go from here. How do we start?"

Eddie replied, "What do you say we start at the beginning, like normal people?"

A jolt of fear shot through her. This step was unavoidable, but part of her wanted everything to stay simple a little longer before becoming complicated.

His eyes were dark and intense. "Where do you come from, Loren Malen?"

She looked down.

Eddie's forehead creased. "Why that reaction? Look, I'll start. I grew up in Texas."

She looked up. "You don't say."

He continued in a low, husky voice. "My mom was French. She came here with her first husband, a German engineer working in the Texas oil industry. She didn't like him very much, but she did like America." He stretched out his legs. "She had a lot of wonderful qualities, but picking men wasn't one of them. Her second husband, my dad, was a drunk who left us before I was five years old. I haven't seen him since." He shrugged. "See, your story can't be much worse than that."

Loren looked down her nose at him. "My dad was a professional con man."

His eyebrows shot up.

Loren detected no condemnation, just surprise and curiosity. His reaction warmed her heart, and she pushed forward. "My mom died when I was eight. So most of my life I went from town to town with him." With her free hand, she drew a line in the sand. "Looking for marks, pulling cons, and moving on."

Eddie pulled their hands into his lap. "He *was*? What happened to him?"

"He committed suicide."

"I'm so sorry. Why?"

She met his gaze. "Because he was foolish enough to try to con Sam Hawthorne."

Eddie's eyes widened. "Wow. I take it that didn't go very well."

"You could say that. My dad killed himself in jail, but Sam offered me a choice."

Eddie nodded slowly. "I see. So that's how you ended up in the Agency?"

"It's a kind of screwed-up life story. So you see, I don't really have any experience with healthy relationships."

He shrugged with a grin. "Neither do I. We can learn together."

She touched his cheek. "I'd like that."

The next few hours passed in companionable conversation, and before Loren knew it, it was midnight, and Luis and Caveman emerged from the apartment. Caveman still looked somewhat haggard, but Luis looked refreshed and back to his intense, dangerous self.

Luis took the goggles from Eddie. "Anything?"

He shook his head. "Quiet so far."

Luis nodded. "You two go get some rest."

But before Eddie could answer, a dull thump sounded just offshore.

CHAPTER 51

Before Eddie could react, Luis had the rifle to his shoulder in a flash. Everyone held their breath, listening.

Another sound came from the western side of the island.

Eddie whispered, "Whoever they are, they aren't trying to be silent." Turning, he looked out over the ocean to the east. He was not about to run after one threat and leave his six open to a trap. "Could this be Tito?"

Loren shrugged. "According to Craig, he's not due to be here before morning, and he's supposed to be on some big freighter. Seems like we would have heard a ship like that arriving."

Eddie handed Loren his night vision goggles. "Watch the other side with Caveman here. Make sure this isn't a diversion." He motioned Luis forward, lowered his goggles and started down the path in the direction of the noise. He held his MP5 ready, scanning the ocean.

Eddie stayed close on his heels, and in the moonlight, he caught the outline of what looked like a massive trimaran sailboat anchored a hundred yards away. Not a freighter. He could just make out a dinghy coming ashore. Eddie touched his arm and pointed.

Luis nodded.

They came to the water's edge. Luis checked the beach up one side and down the other as Eddie watched the small craft approach. One figure slowly rowed the two oars.

Fifty feet from shore, the figure stopped, and called out in a deep male voice, "Jeff said I should announce myself or I'm likely to get shot."

Eddie considered this. "Are you armed?"

The man in the boat replied, "Not here in the dinghy."

Eddie said, "Come on, then."

He continued rowing.

Luis returned to Eddie's side, rifle ready.

The boat slid up onto the sand, and the figure leaped nimbly out. He took in Luis and his weapon while holding up both hands, palms out.

Eddie asked, "What's your name?"

"Scott. Jeff Lansing sent me to help you all out."

Eddie stepped forward and patted the man down. He was tall and slim, and Eddie could just make out a neat, full beard. He held out his hand. "I'm Eddie. Sorry about all this."

Scott shook it. "No worries, man. Jeff told me you all were in a bit of trouble."

"This is Luis. Come on. The rest of our party is up at the top."

Eddie led Scott up the sandy path, avoiding the larger pools of sludge, with Luis taking up the rear. He called out as they neared the top, "Loren, it's us!"

Another lantern now illuminated the crest. Further evidence of Caveman's impressive cache of supplies.

As Eddie introduced Scott, he studied the newcomer. He was lean and muscled, tan as a beach bum with longish, faded blond hair and a full snowy beard. Probably in his mid-fifties.

Luis blurted out, "You're Scott Cloud!"

Scott's bushy eyebrows rose as he shrugged. "I am."

Everyone looked between Scott and Luis in confusion.

Eddie asked, "Who's Scott Cloud?"

Luis' eyes widened. "You've never heard of him? He's the greatest surfer that ever lived—just incredible. My dad, my brother, and I saw you at the Bonsai Pipeline in 1998. You were *amazing*."

Scott took it in stride like a man used to fame. "Thanks, I appreciate it."

Luis looked over at Eddie, Caveman, and Loren expectantly. "You've never heard of Scott Cloud? Or Cloud Surfboards?"

A smile slowly spread across Caveman's face, as if he was remembering something from his childhood. "Wait a minute. 'Cloud surfboards let you fly,' right? Isn't that the saying?"

Eddie turned. It was the first thing he'd said that didn't sound stilted at all. Also, the first personal thing he'd ever heard him say.

Caveman started in surprise and then grinned. His smile slowly faded as a faraway look came into his eyes. He looked up at Eddie and shrugged.

Had he lived in the world at one time? Maybe someone hadn't grown him in a test-tube in a government lab after all. Or maybe they had, and it just meant that at some time in his life he'd watched television or read a magazine? What thought was too far-fetched for this situation?

Scott chuckled. "It used to be the saying a long time ago. Now I believe the New Yorkers have come up with 'Surf the Cloud.' I guess it's got a more minimalist vibe. I don't know, I sold the company ten or twelve years ago. They still use my design, though. They haven't messed that up, at least."

Luis shook his head. "I can't believe it. How do you know Jeff?"

Scott reached into his back pocket.

Luis' smile evaporated, and he snapped the MP5 up, ready to shoot.

The surfer froze. "Relax, man, just getting a picture."

Luis sheepishly lowered the weapon, but the alertness never left his eyes. "Sorry."

Scott pulled out an old snapshot and showed the group. It was a much younger Scott, bronzed and handsome, his arm around Jeff Lansing, who wore swimming trunks and a Bulls T-shirt with a long white stripe of zinc oxide on his nose. "I know Jeff from way back. He really got me out of a jam once. Cloud surfboards would have never existed if it wasn't for Jeff. I finally got his email a little while ago. I guess he's reaching out to everyone he can think of, and he remembered I sort of retired," he nodded out toward his boat, "to my *Cloud Dancer* there, to sail around the Bahamas a few years ago. I happened to be not too far away, so I thought I'd sail over and see if I could help."

Eddie shook his head. Jeff really did know everyone. "I really appreciate it. How big is your boat?"

"She's sixty feet. I can take all of you, no problem."

He rubbed his chin. Was this the best option? Tito the unknown smuggler, or this retired surfer? What a choice. "We have one other passenger. He's a U.S. senator, a famous one who's injured."

Scott's eyes were dark and inquisitive. He seemed to take the information in stride, however, and asked, "Where do you want to take him?"

Eddie shrugged. "The nearest safe port where we can get him a ride home."

The tension in Scott's body eased a fraction, as if he was afraid something more sinister was at play. He was a cool customer, this retired surfer, but no dummy.

Scott said, "We can get to Crooked Island, no problem. He can get help there."

Eddie glanced over toward Scott's craft anchored offshore. "Your boat is a sailboat? How long will it take?"

"She's a blow boat, but she's a Rapido, about the fastest sailboat there is, so maybe a day's sailing. Less, if we have good wind. If your other passenger is that important, why don't you just call the Coast Guard, have them come and get him?"

"Time is of the essence, I'm afraid. Some bad guys might come back, and we need to get away from here. After that, we can call whomever."

Scott looked at the group and frowned. "Jeff says you need help. I'll help."

Eddie turned to the others. "What do you think?"

Luis rubbed his neck. "We get out at sea in that boat, we're going to be sitting ducks. Especially if they have radar, which we have to assume they do."

Loren nodded. "Our only chance is if we can slip away tonight, unnoticed. Pray that they ran far enough away that by the time they come back, we'll just be another blip amongst all the other boats out there."

Eddie looked over at Caveman, who shrugged. He turned back to Loren. "What's the alternative, this smuggler Tito? Which option is worse?"

Scott's eyes widened. "Tito the smuggler? You don't mean Tito Flores?"

Loren shrugged. "I guess. I don't know his last name. He has some big freighter."

Scott waved his hands. "No way, man. That is one crooked dude. If he hasn't already double-crossed you, it's coming."

Eddie held Scott's eyes for a beat. "Men are after us. Well-armed men in a quick boat. If they catch us, they will do everything they can to put us and your boat at the bottom of the ocean."

Scott met the look and grinned, showing straight, bright white teeth. "You aren't living without a little danger now and then. We can slip out into the great wide darkness before these bad guys get here." He shrugged. "It sounds like a rush, besides, it's a senator, so it must be important. You can count on me." He looked over at Luis. "I could use a little adventure."

Eddie rubbed his forehead. He didn't know this Tito, a man loosely connected to Craig, who he definitely didn't trust. He also had the worry that the men on the ship might swim back ashore in the night and attack under cover of darkness. The longer they stayed here, the more vulnerable they were. Eddie weighed all the options. "Okay. I say, let's get Sam and get off this rock. Agreed?"

Everyone nodded. The wind picked up, and a lightning bolt struck the horizon off in the distance.

Hopefully, it wasn't an omen.

CHAPTER 52

Frank leaned back in the captain's chair and let the darkness press in on him. Most of his men had found a place to crash and recover from the day, but he couldn't sleep.

He tried to piece together the full original plan from his side. Gemini was looking for something. The same thing the senator was after. Each had pieces of the puzzle that the other didn't.

Gemini believed that the senator only needed one more data point that should lead to the whereabouts of whatever it was. So, Gemini leaked it to the senator, as if they were friends, hoping Sam would lead them here. That part of the plan worked like a charm.

Frank and his team were to follow the senator, eliminate him, and communicate the coordinates to Gemini. His boss had evidently been waiting for this call on an island nearby. Based on the time it took the Beaver to arrive, he guessed it was probably Haiti or the Dominican Republic. That was pretty far away, which showed that Gemini had only a general idea of Sam's destination. Then, after Frank's men eliminated the senator, Gemini's other team would race to that spot to get whatever was worth all this trouble.

He scratched at his scar and frowned. Problem number one, his boss' intel said that the senator would be alone, and Frank had never known the man to have bad information before. Never. Actually, on second thought, he amended this statement. Gemini's information said that the senator's security team had stayed home, and that was true. Gemini did not have incorrect information so much as incomplete information, which was sometimes worse.

Problem number two, someone also discovered and compromised whatever team Gemini had waiting in the wings. How was that possible? He was almost positive that this organization had infiltrated the CIA and just about every other agency that mattered. How then were they caught with their pants down so badly?

No government department could get the jump on them like this. It would take too many people to keep it off Gemini's radar. So, the only remaining option was a private crew. One man in the boat with Sam and one or two more on the island. Two more people stole Gemini's plane, so that was only four, maybe five, and the whole time Frank had them pinned down on the island, no other help came. Not what you'd expect from an agency or larger organization.

He fished in his pocket and pulled out a cigar. What did this discovery mean? It would explain why his organization stumbled into this situation. They had contacts across every governmental department. But counteracting a small, well-informed group was not really their design. That was probably what caught them so flat-footed. So, that left two questions. Who were they, and—maybe more importantly—how were they so well informed?

He lit the cigar, looked over the screens on the ship's bridge, and suddenly sat forward. Right next to that accursed island was a small radar contact. He glanced at his watch: twelve thirty. Way too early for it to be Tito, who wouldn't reach the island until near sunrise.

He bit into the cigar and swore. He'd been right to stay here. His gut had come through again. This group always did something unexpected, but this radar cross section looked small. Not like a Coast Guard ship or some freighter.

A smile slowly crossed his lined face. Maybe he had them now. He stood and walked into the ship's interior. "Look alive, people. I think our quarry is trying to slip away in the night and we're going to nail their ass. So get ready."

Mack rolled onto his feet and followed Frank back up to the bridge. "What's up, boss?"

Frank showed him the radar blip.

Mack narrowed his eyes and grinned. "It will be a hell of a lot easier to kill these guys away from that damned island."

Frank nodded and started the engine. "That's what I was thinking."

CHAPTER 53

Eddie led Caveman a few steps away from the others. "What do you mean, you're not going? I thought we discussed this."

Caveman dropped his head and sighed. "I can't. I don't know why, I just can't."

Eddie was developing a theory about Caveman. That whatever processes put the information into his brain also put in protections and possibly directives. A failsafe or a mechanism of control, but not absolute. Caveman's mission did not require him to save Eddie and Sam. In fact, one could say that doing so drew attention and endangered his mission. It was an independent act. So, he just had to continue to convince him that leaving this island aligned with his goals. "What's your mission? To wait? Forever? The fact that you're supposed to wait here means that whoever gave you the mission needs you to do something else after the wait is over. If you stay here, those men will come back, and they will kill you or take you prisoner. You won't be able to complete your mission."

Caveman looked up. "I know." He grimaced. "I know, but if I go with you, if I leave, what then?"

Eddie said, "You might live another day. And every day you're alive is another day that you might be able to complete your mission."

"What if the phone is not the way they plan to contact me? How else will they find me?"

"Who?" Eddie asked.

Caveman chuckled humorlessly. "I don't know. Whoever I'm waiting for."

"How are they going to find you if the bad guys get you? Your mission has been compromised. It happens, especially in the field. You adjust as best you can, and you move on. They gave you a phone. They'll use it."

Caveman's forehead smoothed a bit. "I don't know what I'd do off this place."

"Stay alive. You'd be with us. You're welcome as long as you need. Then, since your superiors haven't reached out to you, we'll find them." Caveman looked down, and Eddie rushed on. "I give you my word. We'll help you find whoever you've been waiting for. We'll fix this, but we can't do that on this damned island."

Caveman looked up, brow drawn down. A pleading look came into his eyes. "I don't know what it's like out there. I only have an impression, a sense. But I don't really know what it's like or how to behave. I see how you look at me sometimes. Like I'm saying things the wrong way."

Eddie grinned. "Of course I look at you strangely. You live in a cave in the middle of the Caribbean. It's strange."

Caveman smiled. "Even I know that." His smile faded. "Why don't you force me? It seems that to keep your mission, you should make me. I know you could."

Eddie looked away. "I don't know. Because I don't want to force you. I have a new mission, and that's protecting you. To help you find out why someone left you out here in the middle of nowhere. You make a good point. It might be smart for me to make you go, just to protect you from yourself. But I can only help you if you want me to. If you let me. You understand?"

Caveman shrugged and nodded, but there was still a cast of pain in his eyes.

"We have to go *now*, though. Every minute puts us in more danger." Eddie grabbed his shoulder affectionately and grinned. "Besides, we're probably all going to die, anyway. At least with us, you'd die among friends."

The lines faded from Caveman's face, and he straightened a bit. "If I do have to die, I'd rather it be among friends. I never thought about it before, but I don't like the idea of dying here alone."

"Then let's get the hell out of here."

CHAPTER 54

Loren held Sam's I.V. bottle as Eddie and Luis moved the senator onto the makeshift stretcher Caveman had created.

Sam grimaced as they jostled him passing through the front door, and she whispered to him in an effort to calm him.

Outside, they carefully eased him to the ground.

Scott took in the apartment with no comment, and only one raised eyebrow.

Loren stroked Sam's hair and comforted him until he settled back to sleep. He'd always been a vibrant, powerful man, but now he looked so much older. Was all this worth the price? She hoped so.

Eddie, Luis, and Caveman carried cases of ammo and equipment from the apartment's weapon closet and stacked them near the entrance.

Again, Scott seemed to take all this in stride. Loren thought he was some kind of man—handsome, calm, and almost Zen-like. She shook her head at Jeff's strange and seemingly endless network of friends.

Luis surveyed the equipment and stooped to pick up a large sniper rifle. "A 300 Win Mag, holy cow. Planning to shoot something a long way off before it made it to your island?"

Caveman shrugged. "I didn't pick the stuff. It was just all sent in the packing crate. I do like the Winchester a lot, though."

Luis nodded. "Well, whoever picked it has good taste."

Eddie crouched down, picked up a box of flares, and looked at Caveman. "I think we need to burn everything. I don't want to leave anything that will lead Selik's men back to you."

Caveman's eyes widened a fraction. "Selik? As in Anton Selik?"

Eddie looked up at Loren with raised eyebrows.

She shrugged. She'd never heard a first name used for him before. "I guess. Do you know him?"

Caveman said, "I don't know." He turned to Eddie. "Anton Selik is number thirty-six on the red list. Was it Selik's men who attacked this island?"

Loren nodded. How could this hermit know those kinds of things? And what the hell was this red list?

Caveman wrung his hands and looked down at the sand before saying to Eddie, "You're right. We need to burn it down. I'll go get what I want to keep." He walked numbly into the cave, looking stressed and almost sad.

Loren's heart went out to him.

Eddie turned to Scott. "I'm sorry to ask this. Can you please take Luis here back to your boat so he can check it out? I can't be too careful."

Scott said, "I understand. No problem."

Eddie nodded and turned to Luis. "You should probably also get whatever we can use from the plane."

The two disappeared down the path, and Eddie walked over to Loren. He looked manly with his one day of growth and tousled short, dark hair. That was what always struck her about him—he looked rugged and masculine. Capable. Someone who could change a tire, fix the kitchen sink, or dispatch an assassin, but not know if his tie matched his shirt.

This thought amused her, and she put her hand on his forearm. "It's always an adventure when we get together." She laced her fingers through his. They were long and strong, and she liked his hands very much.

He chuckled. "It is, at that."

She lowered her voice and leaned into him. "How does Caveman know about Selik?"

Eddie answered softly, "He knows about a lot of things, including you and me and our missions from our previous employer. I don't know how, and I don't think he does, either."

How was that possible? The situation was slowly morphing from weird to frightening. She pushed the thought from her mind. She'd deal with all that once they got out of this.

Loren pulled her hair back into a ponytail. It felt gross, and she desperately wanted a shower. She stretched and took off the flak vest.

Eddie bent over, touching his toes a few times before straightening back up with a groan.

Loren asked, "Why's it hard for Caveman to leave here?"

"It's like someone programmed him to stay here. I've never seen anything like it." Eddie smiled at her. "You're a sight for sore eyes."

He leaned down and kissed her lightly. Even in the middle of all this craziness, the kiss still gave her a thrill.

She subconsciously reached up and smoothed her grungy hair. Eddie really didn't seem to notice, and his expression didn't betray any deception. Even like this, he seemed to find her beautiful. What a man.

Caveman came out of the apartment with a small box. "This is everything I want. Let's burn this place and get out of here."

Eddie stooped, picked up one flare, and held it out to him. "Want me to do it?"

Caveman shook his head. "No, thanks. I need to do it." He broke the end, took a few steps into the apartment, and tossed the stick into the bedroom. Eddie handed him a second, which he lobbed into the living room. They backed out of the apartment as the fire grew and gained in intensity.

Eddie looked at the group. "This is going to be like a beacon. We need to get out of Dodge as soon as we're done."

Everyone nodded.

Soon, the heat from the flames licking out of the entrance forced them to retreat a few steps farther.

Eddie grabbed another handful of flares. "The crates, too. I think it's important that we don't leave them anything."

Caveman nodded and took them.

Loren followed Eddie and Caveman around behind the cave.

Two shipping crates sat in an open sandy area covered with some type of camouflaged tarp. Holy cow. This was more than just a weird hermit living on an island in the middle of nowhere. This looked like a conspiracy. It took money, planning, and connections. Meaning it was the government or a well-placed secret organization.

Loren sighed and put a hand to her forehead. This left one crucial question. Was Sam part of it, or was he trying to uncover it? The thought made her ache with worry and dread.

Caveman activated the flare and tossed it in the first container, then did the same with the second.

They hustled back to the cave. Loren said a silent prayer that no one was nearby watching.

CHAPTER 55

Scott's sailboat was a massive white trimaran with black and red stripes. He leaned down to flip on the lights, and Eddie placed a hand on his arm. "We need to keep hidden."

Scott nodded.

It was a bigger boat than Eddie had imagined, with long curved arms holding pontoons on either side—each the size of a small boat in its own right. The cockpit in the rear opened onto a set of stairs leading to the interior. The cabin ran down the middle with a narrow walkway on either side leading to the bow. He noted as he climbed aboard that there was no railing along the hull. This was a boat for experienced seamen.

Using a flashlight, they carried Sam aboard, downstairs, and along the central hallway. They put him in the first bedroom. Loren placed his head on a pillow and covered him with a blanket.

Eddie looked out a porthole. It wasn't a very good craft for getting into a firefight, but if they could get away clean, it should blend into a thousand boats out here on the ocean.

They gathered back in the cockpit.

Luis studied a chart with Scott. Gesturing at it, he said, "We have to decide. Head north towards Crooked Island? It's closer, but probably where they expect us to go. Or we could head south to Inagua, which is further and full of open water with very little cover. But it's not the obvious choice. It would be harder to find us if someone came looking."

Loren shrugged. "If we can get out of here without being detected, it's a big ocean to hide in."

Eddie said, "I agree. We can't go where they'd expect us to. So, if we are going to slip away, then we really need to do that." He turned to Scott. "South it is, then."

Luis went forward to pull the anchor, and the engine rumbled to life.

Scott handed Eddie a satellite phone. "Call Jeff. He's worried about you guys."

Eddied thanked him, put it on speakerphone, and dialed. After a long pause, it finally rang, and Jeff answered, "Thank God. I've been worried sick. Who got to you first?"

"Your friend Scott Cloud showed up in the nick of time. We're sailing south toward Inagua Island. Sam needs medical attention. Try to get someone to meet us there. The Navy, the Merchant Marine. I don't care who, but someone. Can you do that?"

Jeff answered crisply, "I'm already on it. I've called everyone I know for a thousand miles. I've got official and unofficial people converging on you. I'll let everyone know where you're heading. You all just need to make it to morning."

Eddie shook his head. "You're a lifesaver, Jeff. I appreciate it."

Scott pushed the throttle forward, and they pulled away from the island.

As Eddie watched it fall behind them in the darkness, a whirlwind of emotion stirred through him. He hated and loved that place. It was the reason they were in this mess, and it almost certainly saved their lives. Like a metaphor for Caveman himself. As much as he wanted off that place, Eddie knew it was literally a port in the storm. Offering shelter and protection. Away from here, they were naked and vulnerable.

An orange halo of the dying fire still crowned the top of the island. As it faded behind them, Eddie rubbed his forehead. They were now the mouse in the middle of the room. If the cat discovered them, they were dead.

CHAPTER 56

Frank pushed the throttle forward on the massive ship and then pulled back. Fire blazed at the top of the island in the distance. "Mack. Look at this." A much bigger fire than before. He lifted his binoculars and focused. The flame seemed to billow out of the opening in a cave. It roared and shimmered with heat waves.

He rubbed his chin. A cave. That explained a lot and certainly made the last twelve hours clearer.

Mack popped up from below.

Frank motioned at the scene and handed him binoculars.

Mack studied the island. "You think the radar blip was another hostile party and not a rescue?"

Frank scratched at his scar. "Or they got what we were after, and they're scrubbing it clean. It doesn't look likely that anyone's still there. Let's go take a look." He motored slowly toward the island and called out to the group, "Keep your heads down in case that sniper is still there."

With the moon well beyond its zenith in the sky, the fire was bright as a sun in the near total darkness. Just how far across the sea could it be seen?

Frank approached cautiously, but no shots came.

Mack trained the glasses back and forth on the island as they slowly circled it. "It's hard to tell if it was a fight or a flight situation. Or maybe even a 'burn the place down on the way out' type of scenario. I got to tell you, though, I don't know how another team could've made it to the top. Not without air support, not quickly at least. They'd have had the same trouble we did."

Frank agreed with him. "That means whoever set these fires was most likely helping the bastards who were here." What to do now? Crooked Island was out. Tito would arrive in a few hours and find an empty, smoldering shell. So, call Gemini or chase them down?

He looked down at the radar screen and studied the small dot heading south. He touched the menu and pulled up some information. The craft was doing thirteen knots. Really slow. Why so slow?

When Gemini found out this place was burning, he was going to be pissed. The entire mission was to get what was there. Probably every mission he'd done for the organization over the last two years led to this island. He'd not realized it before, but now he could connect the dots. Understanding how all the pieces fit with the benefit of hindsight. From the moment they asked him to hunt down and kill that scientist Henrich Stein, this was the goal.

Did that mean that they confined Frank's role to just this area, or that the entire goal of this organization focused on whatever was on the island? The thought gave him chills. Did this failure mean they didn't need him anymore? He glanced back down at the dot on the radar screen. It wasn't even five miles away yet.

Was the boat going slow because it had to, or for some other reason? If it was a super speedboat, then it could outrun Frank's boat, anyway. What was the range of a craft like that, though? How many men could a craft this size hold? "Mack, I'm going to stay back from whoever is ahead of us until sunrise. Make sure we know what we're dealing with. If it's nasty, we run."

"Run? From these guys, the mission, or this organization?"

Frank said, "I'm not sure. It depends on what we find."

Mack nodded and then grinned hopefully. "And if they're sitting ducks?"

He raised an eyebrow. "I'm thinking they wouldn't have burned everything unless they found what everyone is looking for. If we put them on the ocean floor with all those bastards on board, then we lose whatever was on the island. If that happens, our lives aren't going to be worth a plug nickel."

Mack's smile faded, and he rubbed his chin. "You think we're in trouble?"

Frank blew out his breath. "I think information is the most dangerous thing in the world. However, it's funny how that danger works. You have either too much or too little, and you're a dead man. You must find just the right amount, then you're golden. I've about decided that the safest thing for us, at the moment, is to get whatever everyone is after. If we get it, then everyone needs us."

Mack nodded. "That makes this more complicated. We can't just sink them. We have to board them."

Frank scratched at his scar. "I know."

CHAPTER 57

Eddie sat up and looked around. The sun was just peeking above the horizon in the distance, and the sky was a pale purple. At some point, he'd fallen asleep sitting in the cockpit. He rubbed his eyes and stretched. Every part of his body ached.

Loren lay on the seat beside him, wisps of blonde hair covering her face and one arm stretched over her forehead. As he eased up and stepped carefully over her, he noted that her skin was always a lovely honey color.

Scott stood at the wheel and greeted him with a silent nod.

Luis sat cross-legged on the bow, his rifle over his knees and his head down.

A cool wind passed, making the sails flap and giving him a pleasant shiver. Damn, he was glad to be off the island.

Scott held up a metal coffeepot and raised his eyebrows.

Eddie nodded and gratefully accepted a mug. The dark liquid smelled like heaven. He stood, stretched, and walked down into the cabin to check on the senator.

Caveman was sleeping on a couch. He stirred and put on his glasses.

Eddie held up the mug and pointed back toward the rear.

Caveman smiled weakly. "I haven't had coffee in forever." He stood and headed up.

Sam's eyes fluttered open as Eddie approached. He asked in a hoarse voice, "Where are we?"

"In the middle of the ocean, heading south."

The senator licked his dry lips. "How'd we get off the island?"

"My friend sent someone to help us."

Sam nodded. "And the people who were after us?"

"We chased them off and hopefully gave them the slip."

Sam's brows drew down. He studied Eddie with implacable light blue eyes, opened his mouth, then shook his head and let it fall back on the pillow.

The senator's expression added to a feeling that was growing in Eddie's bones. An instinct tugged at his mind. More trouble was coming. He could feel it.

Luis called out from the bow overhead. "Eddie!"

Eddie jogged up the stairs and stood on the deck, scanning the horizon. He turned to Luis, "Something seem wrong?"

He nodded.

The early morning haze limited visibility in all directions. The ocean was calm, and he couldn't see any danger. He was buzzing, though, and if Luis felt it too, then something was wrong.

Eddie turned to Scott and asked quietly, "Do you have radar on this boat?"

"Yes."

Eddie walked back and looked at the dashboard in the small cockpit. "Any vessels near us?"

Scott frowned. "A few."

Eddie studied the screen and shivered. Once again, he could see an object behind them closing fast. Coming up from behind, just like before. Eddie yelled, "Someone is coming!"

Luis jumped to his feet, rifle ready.

Eddie gestured aft. "Coming up behind us, you can't see them yet. Get the Win Mag."

Luis bounded down and disappeared below.

Loren stood, a pistol held in both hands.

Caveman stuck his head out of the cabin. "Trouble?"

Eddie nodded. "The big boat is coming."

"Can we outmaneuver or stay away from it?" Scott asked.

Eddie shook his head. "No. It's big, and it's fast. The only hope we have is to keep them back with firepower and buy some time."

Luis reappeared from below with the large sniper rifle and chose a flat space on the deck.

Eddie looked at the radar screen again. "They're coming up at about five degrees off the stern to the starboard. They're a little more than a mile out and hauling ass." Scott's boat was a light racing craft. Carbon fiber probably made up everything he could see. Bullets would go through this thing like tissue paper. He turned to the surfer. "Any propane or gas in the cabin?"

Scott shook his head. "Yes. There's a gas tank under my feet."

Eddie glanced down. "Can you vent it?"

Scott nodded. "I can." He reached down and pulled a ring in the floor.

Loren started toward the cabin. "Caveman and I will put something up around Sam and protect him as best as we can and bring back more guns." She looked over at Scott. "Can you shoot?"

Scott nodded. "Yes, ma'am. I have a shotgun downstairs, but it won't be much good at this range."

Loren shrugged with a slight smile. "We'll get you something more suitable."

Luis lay prone on the upper deck, his eye to the scope. "I got 'em. Are you sure they're hostiles?"

Eddie asked, "Is it the same blue boat as before?"

Luis concentrated on the image in the scope. "Yeah, I think so. I only saw it at dusk."

Eddie said, "Shoot a warning shot."

"Roger." The rifle bucked, and a fantastic boom filled the air. A moment passed, and the rifle kicked again. Luis grinned. "That got their attention."

Eddie shaded his eyes and looked at the horizon. "Are they bugging out?"

Luis shook his head. "Nope, but they're coming at us more indirectly."

Eddie shouted, "Keep moving! They have a sniper of their own. Make it hard for them to get a bead on you. Scott, you too, leave the wheel. Can you lock it?"

Scott nodded and strapped it in place.

Eddie pulled absentmindedly on the collar of his shirt. "Let's hold them off as long as possible." He and Scott hunkered down and moved around the side.

A bullet pierced the left pontoon with a small cracking noise, followed by the echo of a rifle.

Luis set up near the bow, returned fire quickly, then moved to a different spot. "This isn't going to work for very long."

Eddie ducked as another bullet clanged into the base of the mast. "I know."

CHAPTER 58

Frank banked the ship hard to the right and drove parallel to the sailboat. How the hell were these guys always so prepared and getting the first shot? "Mack, get a sniper rifle and return fire!"

They were in a frigging sailboat. Why the hell were they in that? It was definitely them, though. The bastards were already shooting at him. It looked fast, but hell, the fastest sailboat in the world was still the worst getaway vehicle imaginable. He shook his head and grinned. No way he would lose these guys now. He checked the fuel gauge. They could go all day and be fine, especially at this speed.

A bullet struck the top left corner of the windshield.

Damn, that was one badass shot. A thousand yards from a boat in a choppy sea. He almost hated killing someone so talented. "Turk! Amos! Pepper the crap out of that thing."

Mack lay on the deck and squeezed off rounds one at a time at a slow, measured rate.

Frank nodded. Good. Harassing fire played havoc with a pinned enemy's nerves. "Try to take out their sniper if you can. He's a pro."

Mack never took his eye from the scope. "I'm on it. You think it's the bastard from the plane?"

Frank grinned. "Could be."

Two more men appeared from below, carrying long rifles with large scopes. They took positions, one forward and one astern of Mack, and began shooting.

Frank gave a satisfied nod. It was working. The return fire from the sailboat had slowed to a trickle. After a few more minutes of this, he would move closer.

He glanced at his watch. No need to rush it. They had complete control of the situation. They'd be aboard in the next half hour. He called back to Mack, "Watch for white flags. I'd like someone alive. I still want what they have on that boat."

CHAPTER 59

Eddie and the others hunkered down and moved from one side to the other, away from the circling craft. The bullets made odd hollow sounds as they struck the taut carbon fiber body of the racing sailboat.

Luis rose and squeezed off three rounds quickly without aiming before ducking back down. "We've already lost the line of engagement!"

Eddie raised his head for a quick look at the horizon and squeezed off a round with a rifle Loren brought up from below. The ship was closer, but the son of a bitch was patient, and was staying just far enough away that they didn't really have anything to shoot at yet.

Loren called, "Do you want to abandon ship? Get in the water?"

Eddie shook his head. "What about Sam?"

Luis answered grimly, "He may already be lost. They'd have a hard time finding all of us in the water." He rose to shoot again, but a volley of bullets chased him back down.

Scott said, "We're a really long way from anywhere out here. I mean a really long way, and there's a pretty good current that would drag us even further into nowhere. It would be hard for anyone to find us, not just them."

Luis grinned. "Good point, Scott. Better to die quickly from a bullet than slowly drown in the ocean."

Scott shook his head but returned the grin. "That's not exactly what I was saying, but yes, that is the key point."

A bullet punched through the top quarter inch of Luis's shoulder near his neck. "Damn it!"

He slumped down, grabbing the wound. Blood ran down his back, bright red in the morning sun.

Eddie yelled, "You all right?"

Luis answered through gritted teeth, "Yeah. You were right, they were definitely keying on me."

Another bullet tore off the brim of Scott's cap, leaving the rest of the hat sitting at an angle, but still on his head. He ducked down further and chuckled. "I've always been lucky."

Eddie popped up and squeezed off a wild round.

Caveman shouted, "Give them to me! I'm what they want! Trade me for your lives!"

Eddie looked down at the ragtag team huddled here on the edge of the boat. They were running out of options, but he shook his head. He couldn't give Caveman to them. Even if it meant his life.

Luis and Loren also shook their heads, as Eddie said, "No way! They'll have to take you from us."

Scott said to Caveman, "If we were going to give you up, we'd have left you on the island."

Eddie turned and raised his eyebrows at the surfer.

Scott shrugged. "I heard you guys talking. I know they want him. If they're bad guys, they can't have him."

Eddie blew out his breath. "I'm really sorry to get you into this."

Another volley of bullets rained down on them, and they all ducked.

Scott shrugged. "I'm a big boy. You told me the risks."

"They're coming around this side!" Luis shouted.

They all scrambled over the top of the boat, keeping the cabin between them and the gunmen.

Eddie snatched the bigger sniper rifle from Luis, rose, and took a quick shot.

The blue ship continued past and motored a safe distance away before turning and then accelerating back toward them.

Eddie clenched his jaw. "The bastard's playing with us."

Once again, the group scrambled over the top.

Eddie grabbed Luis to help shove him over, but the gun threw off his center of gravity, and his momentum carried him too far. Everyone came to a stop at the edge, and Eddie sailed over, the sniper rifle flying out of his hand and splashing down into the passing waves.

Loren called out and reached for him in vain.

With one arm Eddie caught the pontoon and dragged himself up onto it. He slid down the slick surface to the float itself. It bobbed and jerked in the water, and he braced his feet against the pontoon and held onto the arm in a bear hug. The water raced by, dark and foreboding three feet below him.

A bullet flashed by his head with a whine, followed by the rifle sound.

Eddie shouted, "Get ready to go to the other side!"

Loren yelled, "No, take my hand! You have to come with us! You'll be a sitting duck!"

Eddie shook his head. "There's no time! Go!"

Scott said, "Let go, then. We'll find you after."

Should he do that? Could they ever find him again? Would they be alive to even try?

The blue ship came around, and Eddie met eyes with Loren. "Go!"

She bit her lip, turned, and the group of them helped Luis over to the other side.

Eddie ducked down as far as he could behind the pontoon, hoping to stay out of sight. The boat was nearer now, and he could just see the outline of the three men lying prone on the deck. Shots rang out and sailed over Eddie's head. They must not have seen him yet, but the situation was only moments away from becoming a game of shooting fish in a barrel.

The boat continued around. Eddie's friends returned to his side.

The men on the boat were expecting this now, and several bullets whizzed by.

Caveman cried, "This is crazy. You have to give me to them. There's no point in all of you dying for me."

Scott again surprised Eddie by saying, "We're all dead, anyway. These boys didn't come to talk."

Eddie squeezed his eyes shut and forced the salt water away. They were out of options.

As the group stood to cross sides again, Luis slipped on his own blood. His feet flew out from underneath him, and he crashed to the deck. Caveman grabbed him to keep him from rolling into the water. The others, readying themselves to leap, stopped.

Without a word, they sat back down beside him.

Eddie met Loren's eyes. She opened her mouth to say something. Then the world shook with the sweetest sound Eddie had ever heard.

CHAPTER 60

Frank heard the boom and whipped his head around, looking for the source. In the distance, a Coast Guard cutter steamed toward them, the smoke still curling around the main gun on the deck. "Shit." He threw the throttle forward as far as it could go.

The big ship hunkered down under the force and then slowly rose as the speed increased. He didn't know how fast that cutter could go, but he was going to put them to the test. He'd tap every ounce of power this ship had. His best chance of survival was distance.

Did a Coast Guard cutter like that have a helicopter? He glanced down at the speedometer as it crossed fifty-five knots. "Come on, baby. Fly. Mack, get down here."

He bounded into the cockpit.

Frank said, "Get every weapon, box of ammo, anything we shouldn't have, and pile it all together. If it looks like they can catch us, dump it all in the ocean the minute I say." Mack nodded and started to go, but Frank stopped him. "Everything!"

The blond man nodded and disappeared below.

Frank willed the craft to go faster and looked back over his shoulder, trying to gauge the pursuit. Were they following? He couldn't tell. He flipped on the radar and scrolled until he found their signature. Where the hell had they come from so fast?

Finally, he discovered it and heaved a sigh of relief. The cutter appeared to have stopped to help the sailboat. He scouted every other contact in the area. He wasn't about to be flushed into a trap like a rabbit. The radar screen looked clear, though, so he kept the engines pushed full bore.

He picked up the satellite phone and discovered he'd missed three calls—all from Gemini. He dialed.

His boss immediately answered, "Where have you been? No one was on the island when Tito arrived, and everything was burned to ash."

"I know, sir."

Silence. "You do?"

"I parked offshore and waited to see if they would do anything else unexpected."

Gemini said, "I take it they did?"

"A ship showed up late. It was dark, I didn't know what it was, so I waited and followed them. It turned out to be some sort of damned racing sailboat or some such nonsense. They set fire to everything on the island and shoved off a little after midnight."

"And?" Gemini sounded breathless.

"We waited until daybreak to see what we were dealing with. Once we saw it was a sailboat, we started laying it on them. And we almost had them, too. Then, out of nowhere, the Coast Guard showed up and fired a shot over our bow. So, we got the hell out of Dodge."

Gemini said, "Damn it. Are they pursuing?"

Frank looked back over his shoulder. "Not that I can see."

"Okay. Where are you now?"

"Speeding west southwest as fast as I can."

Gemini was silent for a long time.

Frank kept quiet and waited.

"Go to checkpoint Echo. I will regroup with our people and decide on our next move. Anything else you think I should know?" Gemini sounded angry but was obviously still thinking—still planning.

Did he want to stay with this group? This had all moved into a new area now. Whatever this organization was about, it had migrated from preparation to action. With less-than-stellar results, he had to note. Frank had an intuition that this group was still on the right side, however. Especially if they knew who they were dealing with. "Yes, sir. I don't think this is some agency or other large organization. This is a small, highly skilled, very well-informed group."

Gemini asked, "Really? Why do you say that?"

"Just the way it all played out. Now, I don't know who's feeding them information, and whoever that is, they're very well informed. But you should look for a small, well-trained group."

"Interesting. I'll do that. Gemini out."

CHAPTER 61

With some effort, Eddie worked himself back up onto the pontoon arm and inched forward until Caveman grabbed his hand and hauled him onboard.

Eddie slumped against the side of the boat, his breath coming in deep gasps. He rubbed the saltwater from his eyes. Thank God for the Coast Guard.

Loren took his face in her hands and looked hard at him, her brow furrowed in concern.

Her eyes were the most startling green he'd ever seen.

"Are you all right?" she asked.

"I'm fine."

Loren nodded and kissed him. "I love you. I don't really understand it, but I do."

Eddie smiled weakly. "I know. Me, too. Besides, I couldn't die yet. I still have to kill Craig Black."

She arched one golden eyebrow and smirked. "I'm going to check on Sam."

Caveman started working on Luis' shoulder, and Scott walked back to the cockpit and turned up the radio.

A voice came over the speakers loud and clear. "Coast Guard Cutter *Georgetown* to sailing vessel, do you copy?"

Scott clicked the mic. "This is *Cloud Dancer*. Go ahead, *Georgetown*."

A familiar voice came over the radio. "This is Commander Nathan Williams. Is there an Eddie Mason on board your vessel?"

Eddie looked up. Nathan Williams, where had he heard that name before? Ah! The man who'd asked them to help his friend at the docks a few days ago. Had it really been only a few days? He struggled to his feet and shambled back to Scott. Taking the mic, he said, "This is Eddie Mason."

"Good to hear your voice. Jeff called and said you were in trouble. I guess he was right. Sorry it took so long. We were a long way away when we got the call."

"You guys showed up just in time. You're definitely a sight for sore eyes." How to handle this? His next moves would be critical. As far as he knew, the bad guys still didn't know who he was.

If it became official that Eddie Mason saved Senator Sam Hawthorne, it would blow that one advantage. He had to stay a mystery to them as long as possible. "Commander, we have a U.S. senator on board who was seriously injured in a boating accident. Repeat. U.S. Senator Sam Hawthorne is aboard and injured. He needs to be evacuated. Also, I would consider it a personal favor if you would come over with your men and speak with me face to face."

After a hesitation, Nathan answered, "Roger, *Cloud Dancer*. Please stop your engines and hold steady."

"10-4." Eddie handed the mic back to Scott.

The surfer grinned back, still wearing the cap with the bill blown off, and killed the engine. He had a mischievous look in his eyes, and his face flushed. "I've always been lucky. What a rush."

Eddie clapped him on the shoulder. "Well, I'm glad. We needed all the luck we could get today. I'm sorry we got you into this, but we sure owe you."

Scott nodded and waved off the apology.

Loren returned. "Sam's better than I expected. We put him on the floor and stacked empty scuba tanks and metal footlockers around him. One bullet got between them and grazed his hand. But he's alive." She turned to Caveman. "I need some help with him."

Caveman looked up from finishing Luis' dressing and adjusted his round glasses.

Luis gave him a thumbs-up, and Caveman went below.

Loren shielded her eyes from the sun. "Is the Coast Guard coming over?"

Eddie nodded and slumped into the seat. "Jeff knows the commander, and he called him."

She shook her head and went back below. "Of course he does."

Luis came back and sat heavily on the bench across from Eddie. "Was that the Coast Guard guy we helped?"

Eddie nodded.

Luis smiled weakly. "Well, I'm glad we didn't listen to you and took that job."

Eddie rolled his eyes. "Yeah, yeah. You okay?"

Luis nodded, put his head back, and closed his eyes. "I'll live, but it hurts like a bitch."

The rigging creaked in the breeze, and the sun slid behind a cloud, providing a temporary reprieve from the heat.

Eddie looked around. Two bullet holes in the sail and several others in the hull. He turned to the surfer. "How much was this boat?"

Scott tilted his head to one side. "A couple million."

"Ouch. I'm really sorry, man, but you saved our lives. I'll never be able to thank you enough. We'll get this fixed. You have my word."

Scott frowned and shook his head. "Don't sweat it. I know some wizards who can fix her all up, no worries. It was time for a new color scheme, anyway. Time to evolve. Anything that stays stagnant dies, know what I mean? Besides, you have to get your heart rate up and feel some danger now and then or you ain't living." He sat back, a goofy grin still plastered across his face.

Eddie shook his hand. "If you ever need anything."

Scott nodded. "I know. Jeff is always there when I need him—always has been."

The Coast Guard arrived in a tactical boat, and the men clambered aboard. Nathan, looking tall and imposing in a flawless white uniform, extended his hand out to Eddie with a big grin.

Eddie shook it gratefully. "Thanks again, Commander. You really saved our ass."

Loren took the other Coast Guard men below.

Nathan said, "Glad to return the favor."

Eddie leaned into him slightly. "I need another one."

Nathan's smile faded, and his brow furrowed. "What is it?"

"I need it to be that some Good Samaritans rescued the senator and turned him over to the Coast Guard. If your men can assure me that the boat you chased off is gone, then I need to slip away. I want you all to take Sam and go. Is that okay?" He turned to Scott before Nathan could answer. "Assuming it's okay if we stay with you a little longer?"

Scott shrugged. "Fine with me."

Nathan considered this. "Is this what you really want? Is it important?"

"Yes. It is."

Nathan frowned. "Is the senator going to make a stink?"

Eddie shook his head. "I don't think so. You can ask him, but he owes me one, too."

Nathan said, "It will make the paperwork hell, but I owe you at least that. Are you sure?"

"I am."

"Okay, then. We'll get a chopper to meet us and airlift out the senator. At least let us escort you back to Florida."

Eddie hesitated, not sure how to proceed.

Nathan scowled. "What?"

Eddie cocked his head to one side. "None of us have a passport at the moment. They were—uh, well, let's just say they got lost."

Nathan closed his eyes and shook his head. "Okay, we'll trail you until we get to the other side of the Gulfstream, and then you can find someplace to slip in unofficially."

Eddie nodded. "Perfect. I really appreciate it."

The Coast Guard men carried Sam up the stairs, his body strapped snugly to a wooden stretcher.

Nathan shook Eddie's hand. "Good luck to you, and thanks again for all that you did for Malcolm." He walked over and boarded the tactical boat. The men cast off, and the craft motored back to the cutter.

Scott returned to the wheel. "Eddie, can you and Caveman help me get the mainsail up? Loren, make sure the jib hardware in the front isn't damaged. Let's get this bad boy moving again." He turned to Luis. "Want a beer?"

Luis replied without opening his eyes, "God, yes."

CHAPTER 62

Once all the sails were up, and the boat had settled into a groove, Eddie walked back and sat next to Scott. "The guys who were after us are some pretty bad dudes with access to a lot of resources. I'm going to call in a few favors and get the numbers on this boat changed in the system. Then I'd like you to get it painted and go somewhere far away from Florida for a while. I don't think they'll try to find us through you, but I don't want to take any chances."

Scott frowned and held Eddie's gaze. "My son is in a surfing contest in San Diego next month. I could head that way, check it out."

Eddie clapped him on the shoulder. "That sounds like a good plan. I can't thank you enough."

"No worries." He ran a hand along the boat. "She came through pretty good." He grimaced. "The only terrible news is that they shot the freshwater tanks, so no showers until we get back to a port."

Luis scowled. "Ah, crap. I feel like sandpaper."

Scott shrugged. "A quick dip over the side is all I can offer you."

Eddie grinned and fist bumped Luis. "I'm pretty sure you've showered since I have, but I feel you."

The Coast Guard Cutter cruised past them, but never quite left visual contact ahead on the horizon.

A little over an hour later, Luis waved and pointed forward and to the left.

Eddie shaded his eyes and could just make out a Coast Guard Jayhawk helicopter as it raced up to the cutter and settled onto the landing pad. A moment later, it rose again and raced westward. He relaxed a fraction. Sam was finally on his way to medical help. He turned to Scott. "I need to talk to the group, and I believe the less you know, the better."

He shrugged. "No worries."

Eddie had to decide about Loren right now. Did he think she was in on the game with Sam, or could he trust her to keep Caveman a secret? In some ways, it was moot. She'd seen him, and the cat was out of the bag, so to speak. In his gut, he really didn't believe she knew the senator had planned on drugging him. He thought Loren was as surprised by all of this as he was—so that was that.

He collected them on the bow and said to Caveman, "These are my friends, and I trust them with everything. They can help me find out who put you there. Who you've been waiting for."

Caveman's hazel eyes took in each of them, and then he nodded, his expression once again that of a child, trusting and without guile.

Eddie took in a deep breath and said out of the corner of his mouth to Caveman, "Interrupt me if I get something wrong." Turning to Luis and Loren, Eddie continued, "Sometime, I'm guessing around two years ago, someone dropped Caveman on that island with two crates of equipment. Somehow, these same people pumped a lot of information into Caveman's brain. Like how to build the apartment and do first aid, stuff like that."

Caveman interjected, "Actually, I think I knew first aid from before."

Eddie frowned. Before what? It was the first time he'd heard Caveman refer to the past. "Why do you say that?"

"I don't know, it's just a feeling."

Eddie nodded slowly and then continued, "They also seem to have put in a directive, I guess you'd call it, that no matter what, he was supposed to wait there until someone revealed the next step in his mission."

A crease formed above Loren's nose. "Who?"

Caveman worked his jaw and shrugged. "I don't know."

Luis narrowed his dark eyes. "How long were you supposed to stay there?"

Caveman shrugged weakly. "Until they returned, I guess. Or maybe until they contacted me."

Loren's hair blew around her face as she looked out to sea.

Luis kept his gaze fixed on Caveman.

Eddie waited until he got their attention again. "Whoever shoved all this stuff into Caveman's head also included a bunch of secret CIA stuff. Including details about Loren's and my missions."

Luis slowly shook his head. "Holy crap."

Caveman lifted a shoulder sheepishly and nodded.

Eddie continued, "Now, I don't know what the senator's interest is, but he planned to knock me out once we got to the island and keep me out for a few days. He was coming to get something, and the bad guys who followed him—I assume—wanted the same thing. My bet is, it was Caveman here and the secrets in his head."

Loren bit her lip, shook her head, and said to Caveman, "I don't think you were really waiting there for a mission."

Caveman's pale eyebrows shot up.

She turned back to Eddie. "I think they were hiding him there. Keeping him from falling into the wrong hands."

"It's certainly a possibility. It would explain a few things. And since whoever it was didn't just kill him, it means they cared about him. They wanted to protect him. Otherwise, it would've been a lot simpler to have just bumped him off." He looked from Loren to Luis. "He saved my life, and I promised him I'd help him find that person. Find out who he is, what happened to him, and find the people who put him here to hide him."

Luis rubbed his face. "That's not going to be easy."

Eddie nodded. "And it's going to be dangerous. I took on this mission without asking anyone, so I understand if—"

Luis scowled. "Dude, I'm in. Where you go, I go. I'm just saying it ain't going to be easy."

Loren's attention stayed focused on Caveman as she nodded. "I got you into this mess in the first place, Eddie. I'm in."

Caveman lowered his head. "I feel like I should refuse your help. Keep you out of this trouble, but I have nowhere else to go."

Luis snorted. "We like trouble. Besides, we're already in it, so that ship has sailed." He gestured around himself. "Literally. Don't worry, man. We'll help you."

"Thanks." Caveman turned to Eddie. "I may have saved you, but in the end, I think you guys saved me. I really appreciate it. They would've taken me, I believe it now, but I hate to think what this is going to do to your lives."

Eddie grinned. "We didn't have that much of a life, anyway. Besides, we live in Miami. It's a beautiful place. Have you ever been there?"

Caveman frowned. "Actually, I always thought the beaches in Daytona were prettier." His eyes widened in surprise, and he shook his head. "I've no idea where that came from."

Eddie studied him. "Have you ever been to Miami?"

"Not that I recall."

Loren asked, "Can you picture it?"

Again, Caveman shook his head.

Luis asked, "What about Daytona?"

"I can't picture it, either, but I know somehow, I prefer it. I can't really explain it."

Eddie scratched his chin. If Caveman was just a creation, why would someone put this kind of thought in his brain? It was more like a memory leaking through. Hopefully, that was the case. They needed all the help they could get.

He said to Caveman, "That's good. I take these revelations as progress somehow. I'm glad for them because, unfortunately, I don't know how much we have to start with." He looked around at the others. "What information do we even know?"

Loren said, "If Caveman is right, we now know Selik's first name is Anton, and when he had me captive, he asked about the Mendelson projects."

They looked at Caveman expectantly.

He just shrugged. "There is a project, or I guess list of projects, called Mendelson, on my list of CIA projects, but I don't know any details. It's just a name on the list."

Eddie said, "And in Sam's information, he had a receipt from a company called Apenno, and in the shipping crate on your island, I saw another with that name."

Caveman nodded. "There were more than one."

Luis said, "Not only did you know Selik's name, you knew he wasn't a good guy, meaning whoever gave you that information knew that as well."

Caveman shrugged. "True, I know that, but I don't know what that means, either—just that he's bad, or on a list of bad people. Nothing specific. I'll keep trying to remember."

Loren frowned and added, "The seaplane we stole from Selik. It was registered to a company." She turned to Luis, "Was it Maycock?"

He nodded. "Out of Tampa."

Eddie rubbed his chin. "That's a start. At least we can run those down and see if we get something." He looked over at Caveman. "You have my word. We will figure out what your story is."

Caveman lowered his eyes. "I appreciate it. I really do."

Eddie squeezed his shoulder and then turned to Loren. "You, we have a problem with."

Loren's eyes widened. "We do?"

Eddie frowned. "You're the only one here Selik and his people can identify."

Realization dawned in her eyes, and she nodded slowly.

Eddie took her hand. "I'm sorry, but until we get this all figured out, you can't go back to your horse farm. Warn your people there, but you have to stay with us."

She nodded, absently staring off into space, and then quirked the corner of her mouth. "I think this is just a good excuse to keep me around."

Eddie shrugged. "I didn't say it didn't have its benefits." He pulled her into his arms, kissed her, and turned and shouted back to Scott at the wheel, "Where are we headed?"

The surfer raised a bottle of beer. "I know some people in the Keys. We can slip in unnoticed, and they'll hide my *Cloud Dancer* and fix her up."

Eddie gave him a thumbs-up, turned, and rested his forehead against hers. "I'm exhausted." Her eyes, green like jade, drew him in.

She said, "Sam would be dead if you hadn't agreed to help him. I can never thank you enough."

Eddie nodded and glanced over at Caveman. "I don't know what the deal is with all of this. However, I believe he would've fallen into the hands of terrible men if we didn't stop them. I don't know why that's important, but in my gut, I know it is."

Loren nodded and pushed her hair behind one ear. "I believe it, too."

Caveman lay back on the deck, his eyes closed, and a serene look on his face.

Where the hell had this strange man come from?

CHAPTER 63

Eddie stood at the railing, searching the horizon for the first signs of the Florida coast. Were they ensnared in a cold war or an all-out confrontation? Did enemies lie in wait ahead? He turned to Scott, standing at the wheel.

The surfer shrugged. "Looks good to me. I don't see anything on radar."

Luis, Loren, and Caveman all nodded. Now or never.

At Scott's suggestion, their destination was the Placo Marina in the upper Keys. Owned by a friend of his who he could depend upon for discretion, it boasted a large, enclosed boathouse in which to hide the *Cloud Dancer* during repairs. Out of sight and hopefully out of mind.

Eddie sat next to Scott as darkness settled over the ocean. "How well do you know this guy?"

He frowned. "Ramos? Don't worry. He came from Cuba, so he knows how to keep quiet."

That was a good sign. For someone to survive under Castro, it meant they were careful. He crossed his legs at the ankles. "I want to pay to fix your boat."

Scott waved a hand. "Don't worry about it. I'll probably trade for most of the work, anyway. Besides, it was for a good cause. I'll consider it a charitable contribution. I need to do more of that kind of thing, anyway."

Eddie started to protest.

"Seriously, dude. It was a rush. You get stale without sailing through a storm now and then." He grinned, showing perfect white teeth.

Eddie puffed out his breath. "So you keep saying."

"Besides, I told you. I owe Jeff a lot."

Luis spotted the marina first. A cluster of hazy orange lights ahead to the left. Scott adjusted their heading, and they glided across glassy calm water toward it, the motor's low rumble the only sound.

It felt like coming home after months away, not just a few days. Everyone was exhausted and vulnerable. Their lives were turned upside-down now that they were at odds with a powerful and unknown enemy.

Boats and then individual slips came into view like sleeping horses in a row of stalls.

A slight movement caught Eddie's attention. A man down in a boat's engine well, only his legs and bare feet visible.

As soon as Luis noticed him, Eddie turned to the mangroves on the other side. Just in case it was a diversion. No threats materialized, however, and they sailed on into the marina.

Luis walked back to Eddie, grinning, and pointed ahead at the main building. "Check it out. Jeff is collecting someone. It's rare you get to see the master at work."

Eddie could just make him out, in his bright red Bulls jacket, talking animatedly to someone. He chuckled and shook his head. Unbelievable.

They docked, and Luis leaped nimbly off and tied the craft into place.

Jeff and an older man in faded jeans and a flannel shirt moseyed down to meet them. An unkempt, dull gray beard covered most of the unknown man's face, and his dark watery eyes were in constant motion.

Jeff said, "Man, you all are a sight for sore eyes." He stopped and his mouth dropped open as he got a good look at them.

Eddie glanced down at himself. They'd washed in the ocean as best they could, but his clothes were stiff, ripped and spattered.

Luis' shirt was bloodstained, and a large white bandage was just visible at the edge of his collar.

Loren's yellow sundress was torn and filthy, mostly brown from her hips down. Loose strands of her ponytail waved in the ocean breeze.

Eddie shrugged. "It's been a long trip."

Jeff shook his head. "Apparently."

Loren stepped off and wrapped her arms around Jeff in a fierce hug. "You really saved us."

Jeff turned pink. "Just doing my part. Everyone, this is Ramos."

The older man nodded silently at them.

Luis slapped Jeff on the back and jumped back aboard the boat. "Good to see you, man."

Jeff continued down the pier to Scott. "I can't thank you enough." They hugged.

The surfer grinned. "It was awesome, man. Definitely made the life highlight reel."

Eddie noticed Loren looking back at the boat and turned to see what held her attention.

Caveman stood at the rail, looking down at the dock, his brow furrowed. He seemed unable to take the last step.

"You okay?" Eddie asked.

Caveman looked up and sighed. "Yeah. I'm fine, just working through it."

Jeff ambled over, stuck out his hand, and smiled warmly. "You must be Caveman. I'm Jeff. Pleased to meet you."

Caveman grasped the extended hand, and midway through shaking it stepped off the boat.

Eddie didn't think Caveman even noticed he'd done it.

Jeff continued at a staccato pace. "Eddie told me we needed someplace to put you for now. I bought this place out in the Redlands. It's south of Miami. Lots of farmland and groves—it's perfect." He led Caveman out toward the parking lot. When they came to Ramos, Jeff held up a finger to Caveman. "One second." He turned to the older man. "I'll talk to my friend. I'm sure we can help you out."

Ramos ducked his head and nodded. "Gracias. I really appreciate it."

Jeff shrugged. "It's nothing. I'll call next week." He turned back to Caveman and kept walking. "Eddie tells me you're good at building. This place is a bit of a fixer-upper."

Loren wrapped her arms around Eddie from behind and kissed his shoulder. "Jeff has a new pet."

Eddie chuckled. "I think we all do. He seems to have taken ownership, though, huh?"

Luis stopped beside them. "The magician at work."

Eddie shook his head. "I don't get it."

Loren let him go. "I'm just glad he's on our side."

Luis nodded. "Our secret weapon. Now let's go. If I don't get a shower soon, I'm going to shoot someone."

CHAPTER 64

Loren's life continued its hurricane cycle as Jeff drove them out of the marina in a big SUV, her head resting comfortably on Eddie's shoulder. They rode in silence until they pulled up to the safehouse. The place was set back from the road and seemed perfect to her.

Jeff and Luis volunteered to spend the night there with Caveman and help get him settled, allowing Loren and Eddie to ride back to the house in Coral Gables alone.

After reluctantly sending a text to Sam telling him they were back, she was shy now that it was just the two of them. Why was that? She'd known this man for a long time. The moment of truth was upon them, though. Was this real? And if it was, a real what? "How far away is the house?"

Eddie shrugged. "This time of night, maybe a half hour."

She rested her head on his shoulder again as they drove. "Thank you again, Eddie. I really appreciate it."

"I'm just glad everything worked out." He glanced down at her. "All that's behind us now and we can start fresh."

She sat up, not wanting to begin their first time alone with a fight, but some boundaries and expectations needed to be set. She sighed. "I can't just move in with you, Eddie. I'm not ready for that. We're not ready for that."

He looked over with a smile. "I know. I figured you'd move into one of the apartments in the second building, like Luis and Jeff."

Relief flooded through her. "Thank you."

He shrugged. "I know this is weird. We see each other in these stressful situations, never knowing if we'll ever see each other again. It magnifies and distorts everything. We've never had normal time together, just to get to know each other, with no one chasing us."

He never ceased to surprise her. "That's true."

"So maybe we can go out to dinner."

Her eyebrows shot up. "You mean like on a date?"

He grinned. "We should try it."

Loren didn't think she'd ever been on an actual date. Before Sam, she'd always been on the move with her dad. After Sam, she immediately went into training with the Agency, then her mission, then the horse farm. She had limited romantic experience, and none of it was normal. The idea of a regular date was both thrilling and frightening. "Okay. It's a date."

He parked next to the house, led her into the kitchen, and poured each of them a glass of water, which they both guzzled greedily.

Eddie was a mess. Disheveled hair. Blood splattered shirt with holes in it and dark stubble covering his face. Holy cow. He was some kind of man.

Their eyes met for a drawn-out moment, and then they fell into each other's arms. His face was scratchy and rough on her skin.

Eddie pulled away and looked into her eyes. "I could use a shower."

She smiled. "Yeah, a shower would be good."

Their lips met again, and she eased into him.

She broke away and led him down the hallway to the bathroom, pulling her tattered sundress over her head on the way.

Eddie winced as he removed his shirt.

She leaned forward, kissing the bandage as she helped him.

His eyes traveled down her body, and he shook his head. "You are something else."

She took his face in her hands and brought her mouth to his again, as he turned on the water.

Later, she lay with her head on his shoulder as she ran her fingers through the hair on his chest. "So, I suppose I'm stuck here for a while." She lifted her head. "Not that it's a bad thing. I'm just saying."

He shrugged. "I want you to stay, because I want you to be safe, and also because—well, I want you to. What do you want?"

She laid her head back down. That's one of the main things she thought every woman should expect from her man. Some focus on what she wanted. The problem was, what did she want? "I'm not sure."

"Look, I know you have a life. I'm not asking you to abandon that for me. I'm sorry this happened, and that you got caught up in it like this."

"It's not your fault. Sam and Craig are the ones who dragged me into this. But it has brought some things to my attention. I liked the horses," she sighed, "but looking back, it was kind of lonely. I didn't realize it, but it was. And I think it was beginning to bore me. I never lived in one place before. A home that was all mine. For a while, the novelty of that was enough. But maybe it's not anymore."

He kissed the top of her head. "I know what you mean. It's like now I've seen a hole in my life, and I can't unsee it. And that's just my regular life. Professionally, we're even more complicated. On the one hand, I've known you forever, but I've never spent any time with you."

She looked up at him, grinning. "We haven't even had our first date yet."

Eddie raised his eyebrows. "You don't consider a car chase across Paris a date?"

"For us probably, but not for normal people."

His smile faded as he looked into her eyes. "I know, but I want to see you. I want to try having a relationship with you. If you're okay with that."

A warm sensation spread out over her whole body. She did love this man. "I'm definitely okay with that." She leaned up and kissed him again.

He reached down and pulled her up into his arms and rolled on top of her, kissing her deeply.

Oh, my.

Later, Loren's phone jarred her from a deep and pleasant sleep. They reluctantly separated, and she checked the screen. "It's a message from Sam. He wants to meet, and he's saying he'll make trouble for us if we don't." She yawned. "He can be very impatient and stubborn when he wants to be."

Eddie put his arms behind his head. "We have to meet him eventually. Might as well get it over with. But I'm not going to just walk in there. We have to assume these guys are watching him. Let's call Jeff and Luis and make a plan."

CHAPTER 65

Eddie and his team operated on the assumption that whoever they were up against had at least one person watching the hospital, so they snuck Eddie into the rear of the building using a linens van. He wore a lab coat and carried a hospital badge and driver's license, identifying him as Dr. David Pine. He was sure that the bad guys were there somewhere, and he was determined to stay anonymous for as long as possible.

When Eddie reached his room, Sam was sitting up in bed reading a newspaper. Beige shades covered each window, blocking out the outside world.

Most of the color and vitality had returned to the senator's deeply lined, tan face. He smiled and folded the section. "It's good to see you, Eddie. I wanted to thank you for saving my life." The hint of a smile danced on his lips.

Eddie shrugged. "Just doing my job. I'm glad to see you're okay."

Sam waved a hand at his leg. "Oh, it'll be awhile before I'm running any 5Ks, but I'm going to be all right." He frowned. "Why didn't you come back on the Coast Guard ship with me?"

How to answer that? "The men who were after you never saw my face. Never knew my identity. I thought it was wiser to keep it that way."

Sam nodded thoughtfully. "I see. That's why you required all this secrecy before you'd agree to meet me. I understand." He lifted the small plastic pitcher and poured water into a cup. He took a sip and then his eyes widened a bit. "Oh, yes." He picked up a check from the side table and handed it to Eddie. "I owe you for a job well done. I also included the expense reimbursement for one motorcycle, like you asked." He arched an eyebrow. "I'm not even going to ask what that's about."

Eddie glanced at the check, folded it, and put it into his pocket.

The senator frowned. "Very good job. I don't suppose I could convince you to come work for me full time. I could make it worth your while."

Eddie had expected something like this. "I appreciate the offer, Senator, but I enjoy being my own boss."

"I understand. I do." Sam tapped his chin with one slender finger. "I also understand why you don't entirely trust me, and I can't say as I blame you. But you're going to need my help now."

Eddie raised his eyebrows. "With what?"

He shrugged. "I know you found something on the island, and I know you're smart enough to hide it."

Eddie opened his mouth to protest, but the senator stopped him with a hand. "I also know you're not foolish enough to reveal that so easily. You wouldn't be the right man for the job if you did. But trust me, you're going to need help."

Eddie kept his face expressionless and returned the senator's penetrating gaze.

Sam looked away, sighing. "I see I have no choice here." He turned back. "What I'm about to tell you, I've told no one before. Not a soul. I think you'll see why, afterward, but I need you to understand that I'm putting my life in your hands—again." He shifted in the bed and said half to himself, "I know you already understand the situation. That's why you were so careful about this meeting."

Sam let out a slow breath. "About three years ago, I was walking to a meeting at the Longworth Building in DC. I was carrying some trivial report. I don't even remember what it was. Anyway, a man rushed up to me on the sidewalk. A short man, with a mustache and glasses—sweating like a pig. He thrust a bound stack of papers at me and said, 'I swear on my life it's all true! I'm not crazy, it's all true.'"

Sam licked his lips and swallowed. "Before I could respond, he looked over my shoulder and his eyes got big as saucers. I turned, too, wondering what was having such an effect on him." He shook his head. "I didn't see anything. But something must have been there, because I turned back just in time to see him running away."

Eddie's eyes widened. "Just like that?"

Sam's nodded and his attention turned inward. "Just ran away."

Eddie's skin crawled.

Sam recovered and looked back at Eddie. "I was so surprised, I stumbled and fell backward, dropping the report I was holding as well as the papers the man had given me." Sam took a deep breath. "When I stood and picked up the documents, I must have accidentally switched them." Sam licked his lips again. "I guess I'd have written this guy off as some sort of nut. Hell, he'd dumped this and ran, right? But as I stood, someone rushed by and ripped the document out of my hands. Only I'd swapped them now, and he snatched the trivial report. So, this thief thought he took what the crazy man had handed me and sprinted away into the crowd. But he messed up, or maybe God intervened—something. He left me with the lunatic's papers, and he gave me a good reason to take them seriously."

Sam's unblinking, haunted eyes bore into Eddie. "I'm telling you, it was providence, or fate, or God's plan—it was *meant* to happen."

A knot formed in Eddie's stomach. He desperately wanted to know about this, but he dreaded hearing it. Could Sam fake the haunted look in his eyes? Not likely. "What did the document say?"

Sam held up one finger. "In a minute. You need to hear this first. The man who gave me the manuscript was named Heinrich Stein." Sam took another sip of water. "I'm a very thorough man, Mr. Mason. Always have been. Quickly, in my time in Washington, I learned to never trust a single source for information. I learned that lesson so well that it became a habit, I guess you could say. So I asked the FBI, the CIA, and a private eye I used to use in those days to give me a report on everything there was to know about Heinrich. I also asked this private eye to find him. Which turned out to be easy enough. They murdered him not three blocks from our meeting. Shot in the back of the head, that very same day."

He stared off into space for another beat and then shook his head. "Anyway, the Agency and Bureau reports on Stein were almost identical, but the P.I.'s was different. Very different, indeed. That's when I first learned that these people are everywhere, in everything. I say I *used* to use this private eye because a few days later, he got himself murdered as well."

Eddie swallowed.

Sam repositioned himself again. "That's why I haven't shared this with anyone. Not the CIA, not even Loren. That's also why I was going to drug you. To keep you out of this terrible task I've undertaken. To keep the danger and burden from swallowing you as well."

Eddie shifted from one foot to the other. The knot in his chest tightened. He was approaching the point of no return.

"Unfortunately, I think we're past that now. I never would have wished this on you, Eddie. And I'm terribly sorry you're involved. But if I'm honest, I have to admit that I'm also selfishly relieved that I finally have someone I can at least talk to about this."

Eddie could hear his own heartbeat in his ears. He let out a long slow breath through his nose before asking, "What did the report say?"

Sam looked at the window, the view obscured by the shades. "The Cold War was so horrible, in so many ways. We knew the Russians would do anything, and it scared the hell out of us. So we developed all kinds of military and Agency projects. It surprised me to discover that these didn't really ramp down after the fall of the Soviet Union. For over twenty years, many of these continued in secret." He looked back at Eddie. "Some of these were awful, but the worst was a group of highly classified projects run by a man named Mendelson—Parker Mendelson. I guess you'd call these dark research projects off the books and indescribably crazy, unethical research. Un-American, I'd call them."

Eddie's mouth went dry. Selik had mentioned Mendelson to Loren.

Sam grimaced. "They were so bad that eventually, when the right people found out about them, they shut them down. Every single one of them." He frowned. "The papers my suicidal messenger gave me listed only four by name: Afterimage, Ergot, Midas, and Frolic.

Sam rubbed his forehead. "I've been able to figure out that Afterimage was an attempt to program soldiers' brains with information. To just download facts and skills right into their heads. The procedure was inhuman. Fourteen men died in the attempt, and one went insane. He just lay on the floor, staring blankly ahead, in a sort of catatonic state. It never worked, just killed people, or destroyed them. Awful." Sam shook his head.

Eddie felt lightheaded. Was Caveman part of Afterimage—a failed attempt or reject? Did the process that loaded information into his brain accidentally blow everything else out? Was this what they were looking for?

Sam continued, "And I learned that Project Ergot was a process for poisoning water sources, even lakes, and making them instantly undrinkable. They'd be potable again only if they placed some kind of antidote object in it." A muscle flexed in Sam's jaw. "Think about that. That's not a tool for war or defense, that's a tool for domination. A tool for controlling people. Not American at all, by my way of thinking."

He looked up at Eddie, his eyes bloodshot and sunken. "I haven't been able to find out anything about the other two. I can't even guess what they were. I've also discovered hints that there were projects beyond these four. Can you imagine?"

Eddie met his eyes but didn't move a muscle.

"Anyway, when they shut Mendelson down, he fought the closure and railed against having his research taken away. Until one day he hung himself from an overhead walkway in the Pentagon."

The weight of this information was almost physical. Eddie sat and asked, "All that was in the document this Heinrich gave you?"

"Some of it. Mostly it contained hints, clues that led me to put more together. He loved to leave messages in the margins in cyphers and codes. Some of which I'm still working on. This isn't why Heinrich gave me the document, however. His primary aim was to let me know that certain powerful people didn't want this research to stop." Sam shook his head. "They thought it was necessary to fight the Russians, the Chinese, anyone else, and keep America on top. They formed a secret organization to continue this work. I think it's called Treleous, for whatever reason. I read about them in one of Craig's briefings and I'm convinced they are the same people." He narrowed his eyes. "They believe that a hidden record of the Mendelson projects exists—all the experiments, the data, and the plans. They're trying to find it and continue Mendelson's work in secret."

Sam held Eddie's eyes for a beat. "I believe that record was on that island. So does this Treleous, that's why they followed us there."

The silence slowly filled the room.

Was Caveman the repository? Or were the repository and Caveman separate? If so, was it also on the island? Was Caveman protecting it, or was it possible that he didn't know about it?

"What I've discovered over the years as well, is that Henrich's report on Treleous only scratched the surface of their influence. They're everywhere. So I've been working against them in the shadows. Using my wealth and position to learn what I can and try to stop them. I alone have carried this cross. Until now."

"That's a long time to carry something like this."

Sam frowned as he nodded. "And I didn't believe anyone had a clue. Not Treleous, or the Agency—no one. But I must be getting old or arrogant, or maybe both, because now everyone is on to me." His shoulders slumped. "I'm not sure if Selik works for them or if Treleous just used him to entice me with information. But he got me, damn it. He dangled something he knew I wouldn't be able to resist, and like a fool, I jumped at it. The last piece of information I needed to find the repository on that damned island."

Again, the two men stared at one another. An ambulance siren sounded in the distance.

Sam broke the silence. "I believe you found this container everyone has been searching for, and I think you instinctively understood that it couldn't fall into the wrong hands. You've shown yourself to be an honorable man. So, I ask you to destroy it as soon as you leave here. Don't wait, don't think about it. Just destroy everything you found. End this nightmare for us all."

If Sam had asked for whatever was on the island or offered to protect it for Eddie—even if he just asked to see it—then Eddie would've put him in the same category as Treleous. But the fact that he wanted it destroyed changed everything. It meant he wasn't one of the bad guys. How far he could trust Sam, however, was still in question.

Eddie rubbed his forehead. "The island wasn't what you think it was, but I believe it's connected to Mendelson's work and your mystery. It's much more complicated than you know, though. I can't just destroy it."

Anger and suspicion flashed across Sam's eyes. "Why not?"

Eddie sighed heavily. "Because what was on the island was not a what, but a who."

Sam lay back, wide-eyed, "A who?"

Eddie nodded. "Maybe not what everyone is looking for, but I will tell you this. I believe it's related."

Sam shook his head. "There was a person on the island?"

"For years, as far as I can tell. He doesn't even know his own name, but he knows about secret missions I ran for the Agency."

Sam covered his mouth with one hand and slid it down over his chin. "I don't understand."

Eddie shrugged. "My guess is it has something to do with Afterimage. He survived, or partially survived, one of Mendelson's attempts, and someone hid him away on this island. Trying to keep him and what's in his head out of the wrong hands. But this man saved my life and yours. I will not kill him, and I gave him my word that I would find out where he came from."

"I'm stunned. I didn't expect this."

Eddie continued, "I promise you this, though. I will not allow him to fall into Treleous' hands."

"Then let me help you," Sam implored. "No, let's help each other. With your skills, my resources, and both of our connections, we can help this man, and we can stop them. You just have to trust me."

Eddie believed this story. Believed in its connection to Caveman, and deep down knew he needed the senator's help. "Do you think Craig is part of Treleous?"

Sam shook his head. "In my gut, I don't believe he is, but I don't know for sure. That little doubt is the reason I never shared this information with him, either. I never had a good enough reason to risk it."

Eddie stood. "I'm going to talk to my team and think about this for a while. Decide what I think I can share with you."

Sam's eyebrows shot up. "You have a team?"

He shrugged. "That's how we made it off the island alive."

"Do you trust them?"

"With my life. Besides, they've seen the person on the island, and so they already know. They're involved now."

Sam's forehead creased. "Is Loren part of this team?"

Eddie frowned. "She is now."

He closed his eyes. "Please let her know that I'm not corrupt or anything like that. It's killing me that she might think I am."

Eddie nodded. "I will. And at the very least, I promise I'll help you stop these people. You can count on that."

Sam's shoulders sagged. "That's more than I hoped for. I really appreciate it, Eddie. I won't let you down." He handed him a simple white business card with only a phone number printed in the center. "This is a direct number to me twenty-four-seven."

Eddie put the card in his pocket. "You'll hear from me soon."

"I'm looking forward to it. Anything you need, Eddie. I mean it, anything."

Eddie nodded one last time at Sam. He had a mission again. A purpose. To protect Caveman, find out where he came from and stop the evil people after him. A shiver went down his back. This wasn't the last time they'd run into Treleous. He could feel it in his bones.

Epilogue

Frank stood on the upper floor of a building beside the Nanticoke River and watched the woman board the *Woodland Ferry*. He lowered his binoculars and spoke into his radio. "She's on the boat."

As the ferry lumbered across the water, his men were all over each bank. If someone was following her, this crossing would make it very difficult to keep up without one of his team noticing. He had a man in a chopper overhead, and the low winter cloud cover here in Delaware would give satellites trouble as well. He looked through the binoculars again, and this time, he could see her face. Scared. She should be.

As the craft reached the other side, three black SUVs rolled up, and his men ushered her into the middle one. A moment later, the window lowered, and her cell phone flew out onto the pavement.

Frank nodded, walked downstairs, out of the building, and slid into the front of another SUV.

Mack pulled away from the curb. "Team reports that she's clean. No wires or the like."

Frank nodded and pulled a cigar from his pocket. "Be ready. If anything funny happens, we need to get out of here."

"We're covered."

Armed men were already prowling the woods outside the house when Frank arrived.

He entered and took a seat at the kitchen table.

The woman sat across from him, pale and fidgeting nervously with one fingernail. Streaks of gray lined her thick, dark hair and her brown eyes were bloodshot.

Frank asked, "What've you got for me?"

She pulled out a flash drive and slid it across the table. "That's everything. Her complete file. Everything that Loren Malen ever did for the CIA."

Frank studied the item but didn't pick it up. "Can anyone tell that you took it?"

She shook her head frantically. "No. I invented a plausible reason I needed to see it. So, my accessing this information won't cause any red flags. I promise you, I did everything you asked."

He believed her. Her terror was genuine. He looked over at the door and motioned with his chin.

The man standing there entered and set down a laptop.

Frank pulled up the drive's contents and studied it. It looked complete. He glanced up at her. "And this is all of it?"

"Everything."

Frank said, "Thank you. This is very helpful."

She leaned forward, eyes wide. "Are we even? Does this pay off my debt to them?"

Frank nodded. "I think it does. Yes."

The woman's shoulders slumped, and her eyes filled with tears. "Thank you."

"No. Thank you." Again, he nodded to the man at the door.

He came in and gently grasped her elbow, lifted her, and guided her out to the front door.

When she was gone, Mack entered from the rear.

Frank looked up from the screen. "She needs to have a fatal car accident. Make it convincing. We can't have questions about this."

Mack rubbed a hand over his short Mohawk and nodded. "I'm on it."

Frank looked back at the computer. He'd collected all the information on the entire disaster of a mission at the island and the happenings in the Dominican Republic. It made sense that Loren was Agency, or at least had been. She was well trained and now she was on her own as a freelancer. He was convinced that the other members of her little band were also ex-government types, now on their own as well.

He scrolled down. Their names were in here somewhere. He could feel it in his gut. He knew how it was when people left the government and went out on their own. They worked with or recruited others they knew from their time inside. Just like Frank had with Mack and some of his other men when he left.

This file was the key. Frank could almost smell it. If he carefully worked his way through Loren's CIA career, somewhere in there, he would discover the identities of her little band of troublemakers. He would find them. He would take whatever it was they found on the island away from them. And then he would kill them all.

ABOUT THE AUTHOR

Bret Hurst loves stories of all kinds and reads everything he can get his hands on, regardless of genre. He has always dreamed of being a writer and has been working on novels and screenplays for as long as he can remember. He grew up in Miami, often sailing the waters of the Caribbean, which both inspired parts of this story. He has degrees from Auburn University and Florida International University and is the CIO of a healthcare company. He resides outside Atlanta with his wife and three children.

NOTE FROM BRET HURST

Word-of-mouth is crucial for any author to succeed. If you enjoyed *The Caveman Conspiracy*, please leave a review online—anywhere you are able. Even if it's just a sentence or two. It would make all the difference and would be very much appreciated.

Thanks!
Bret Hurst

Web site: bretbooks.com

Contact me: author@bretbooks.com

We hope you enjoyed reading this title from:

www.blackrosewriting.com

Subscribe to our mailing list – *The Rosevine* – and receive **FREE** books, daily deals, and stay current with news about upcoming releases and our hottest authors.
Scan the QR code below to sign up.

Already a subscriber? Please accept a sincere thank you for being a fan of Black Rose Writing authors.

View other Black Rose Writing titles at
www.blackrosewriting.com/books and use promo code
PRINT to receive a **20% discount** when purchasing.

Printed in the USA
CPSIA information can be obtained
at www.ICGtesting.com
CBHW051140020324
4855CB00001B/1